Battlefields

Thank you, Silvia
& Enjoy!
Van N. [signature]

Battlefields

Vance N. Smith

Copyright © 2015 Vance N. Smith
All rights reserved.

ISBN 10: 1508907889
ISBN 13: 9781508907886
Library of Congress Control Number: 2015904303
CreateSpace Independent Publishing Platform
North Charleston, South Carolina

First and foremost, I would like to take this opportunity to say thanks to all who have encouraged me through this creative process. This project grew out of an ideal of wanting something I didn't have, and an experiment to see if I held the ability to place thoughts to words. I'm still shocked I had anything meaningful to say. With that said, many have assisted me in this journey, achieving a dream I didn't realized I wanted. Family and friends have all help with this new journey and I am forever grateful. I would like to personally thank Dex Graham for his valuable insight and recommendations and for reading my manuscript in its entirety, twice, over a weekend. I thank you. And to my sisters, Shelley and Leslie, who stood strong and pushed me to continue, and provided constructive feedback. A special thanks to GR. Again, thank you all and I hope you enjoy the result of four long hard years of creative work.

Love, Vance

In Loving Memory

We'll always love and miss you, JP

Gone too soon

Prologue

THE MAJORITY OF us lead our lives to the best of our abilities; during our many journeys, we may encounter setbacks threatening to disrupt the very concept of our beings. Often we stumble, searching for the true meaning of our existences, only to rebound fueled by resilience. Through pain, we decipher the important lessons of life with the hope of learning from our mistakes and misfortunes. These lessons might stem from coming to terms with one's own identity. Maybe these lessons reside within a dysfunctional household or failed marriage or from living with an abusive companion or wading the waters of ill-advised financial ventures, creating an impossible burden of hardship with no means of escaping its grip. Choices that affect our lives for years to come, never discerning how a decision so minor would have such a profound impact until it's too late. Immobilized by the repercussions that affect us exclusively or others we have touched. For some, the situation proves to be a short-term complication with minimum consequences, while for others it's catastrophic. If we're lucky, we learn from the pain and move forward.

I am Wilson James, and I've never thought of myself as a victim, even though my life hasn't been easy, when heartbreak seemed to follow at every turn. It wasn't until I entered my late forties that I began to understand the circumstances of my life. An existence powered by crippling odds and a bad deck of cards stacked against me. Having resided in a family of emotional failures and despair—alcoholism, a missing-in-action father, and an emotionally depressed mother. Making choices in the past that marked my life for years to come. I often wondered how any individual could rise above such desolation. As I ask that simple question, I beg of you not to feel pity—this is not a story of sorrow, but a truth on self-redemption, of strength, and of perseverance.

In my early years, life wasn't entirely dismal; as children, my sister and I enjoyed a seemingly blissful childhood. On the surface, my family appeared picture perfect with working parents and two adorable children. My father, a man who enjoyed a successful dental practice, fared equally well financially within his many business ventures. My mother, a woman who projected the image of a loving wife and supportive maternal parent, was an elementary school principal by profession. However, once disorder emerged between my parents and separation was imminent, happier times fled faster than a cascading avalanche! A situation compounded further when my sister and I reached our teen years. Funny how appearances could mean everything, yet mean nothing. A masquerade we protected at all costs with a beautiful, manicured home in the View Park section of Los Angeles County—yet our superficially perfect existence lay crumbled.

My father, Vernon James, may have loved my sister and me. A simple fact I have yet to experience, since the affection and attention I craved never materialized. The father-son relationship every child dreams of—the teachings of a revered paternal parent, the personal, one-on-one interactions, the molding of a young mind—never happened. These were the simplest aspects of life experiences that shape every young boy, valuable lessons gone by the wayside because my father was either unavailable or too drunk to pay attention. Many nights I prayed my father would realize the significance of his only son. And whenever my father would come around, I secretly held the idea of him possibly desiring the opportunity to bond and mentor; sadly, he came and went without an inkling of interest. I guess I should have known when he considered a drink from a bottle far more important than the welfare of his children. And to this day, I cannot remember the last time my father and I actually engaged in a meaningful conversation. He could not have known the nearly perfect report card I received every year since the third grade, or my dreams of becoming a world-renowned architect. Now, anger and hate are all I have left, as well as being plagued with the spitting image of my father. Looking into

Battlefields

a mirror, his lean, slightly muscular frame, caramel complexion, and striking unusual features are reflected back. A handsome man, my father, and I look just like him—thankfully lacking his distasteful demeanor.

A beauty among her peers, my mother, Georgia James, was a whole other matter altogether. A petite, brown-skinned woman with shoulder-length wavy hair, her beauty admired by many, however, disguised the worst kind of parent! She was emotionally unavailable to provide the love her children needed when no one else could, sending mixed messages of support—one day you thought you had the greatest mother on earth, then like the change of weather, a monster blew into town, erasing all pleasantries from view. She would wrap her arms around you for comfort, then with the flip of a switch, she'd give you a backhanded slap across the face for something so minor as not picking up your dirty dishes or cleaning your room.

I recall an instance in elementary school when my third-grade teacher sent home a letter stating I had failed to complete an important history assignment on time. The rage drawn upon my mother's face was terrifying. She yelled and screamed, kicking my ass for what seemed like days on end. My sister, Vivian, pleaded with my mother to stop, but when my mother was through with me, she continued the beating with Vivian for butting in. And to have any opinion other than my mother's always turned into a major altercation. So you learned to keep your mouth shut, pretending your sentiments did not matter. However, the greatest pain inflicted by my mother was when she compared me to a child who had not lived past the age of three. How could any mother compare her son to a child who had not lived long enough to develop an identity? "Your brother wouldn't be a little punk like you," she would say, along with many other negative comparisons. I guess the eldest child of our family, my dead brother, was spared the pain and suffering of living in the James's household. You may say that was a strong statement to make, but at times the truth hurts like a muthafuck!

Through it all, my only saving grace was my sister, Vivian, who is three years younger than me. We survived by sheltering one another from the craziness invading our lives. How we escaped from being committed to a mental institution, I am unsure. I've always considered that Vivian fared far better than I, able to march on with some sense of normalcy, where I have not, feeling trapped in solitary confinement. Then I wondered—had she really?

Yes, the foundation had been set; the minute a seed planted in my mother's womb grew into a new life. Groundwork lay forth, leading to utter confusion and disappointments. All I ever wanted was to feel appreciated, to be considered necessary, and to know my existence was relevant in a time of life when I should have felt free spirited and innocent. I have searched relentlessly, longing for required love, mutual bonding, and consideration, yearning to comprehend the meaning of my life. However, I guess I am destined to live my life in organized chaos, a life on the edge—not quite heaven and not quite hell.

CHAPTER 1

SINCE MY ADOLESCENT years, I have recognized the attraction toward my own sex. I'm not sure how or why or when I became aware; it was something that was embedded in my bones. I just knew, plain and simple. These desires intensified tenfold upon entering my teen years. During this time, a neighborhood friend and I replicated the nightly games of our adult counterparts, hiding behind his parents' garage or in his bedroom, when we thought no one would suspect. At every chance, we would kiss and grind, simulating the act of lovemaking. I fondly remember the satisfaction I received playing that simple game, placating the intimacy I desired. This act of falsified engagement lasted from around the fourth grade until we entered junior high school.

Upon reaching my teen years, I sensed no fear when it came to my own sexual desires. My attractions ultimately moved beyond the neighborhood boys, to fantasizing about my junior high teachers—in particular, my seventh grade math teacher, Mr. Carlson. My naïvety was the only partition standing in the way of approaching an older individual. Unable to recall the exact moment, but I knew I requested the arms of another to sweep me away, erasing the pain I held within.

On a supposed weekend stay with my father the summer my parents divorced in 1975, I met my cousin Nate, some gangsta-ass-looking muthafucka recently released from prison, after serving seven years of confinement. Nate lived with his mother, my cousin Irene, who rented the house my father owned around the corner from his current residence. Cousin Irene and Nate were distant relatives of my dad, and for the life of me, I could not

Vance N. Smith

remember them prior to that day. I could have passed him on the street, fell over him, and would not have known or cared who he was!

On that unsuspecting day, Nate and my dad were in the kitchen talking shit, having a few beers, and catching up on old times prior to Nate's extended stay behind bars. Following our reintroduction, I shook hands with Nate, and upon releasing; Nate slid his index finger down the middle of my palm, igniting a magnetic charge throughout my entire body. After conversing a bit, Nate and my father left for the living room to further their conversation. In passing, Nate brushed against my backside, turned with a quick, smoldering glance then licked his lower lip. Nate's subtle exchange sent chills down my spine. Cracking a faint, inquisitive smile, I remained paralyzed with excitement while my body swooned limp. I was immediately intrigued—well, actually, at that age any man sent my hormones into mad, explosive rage. Standing six feet with a light brown complexion, cousin Nate was a big, thick brutha! I wouldn't say I found him attractive, except that I did, only because he's a man and my hormones indicated as such.

Later that night, as with all my supposed parental visitations, my dad would eventually leave, chasing another bottle of vodka and pussy, not returning till well after midnight. Bored with nothing better to do, I decided to see what Nate was all about. Confidently, I walked to my cousin's house and rang the bell. Nate opened the faded red wooden door.

"What's up?" he greeted excitedly, reaching for my hand.

"Nothing much…bored, so I dropped by to see what you were up to."

"Come on in, have a seat!" he said, gesturing to enter his home. "Yo man, I'm glad you decided to swing by," he said, stepping to the side, clearing my path.

Entering the Spanish-style residence, I noticed the terra-cotta tile roof and the graceful arches, both inside and out, typical of Los Angeles, and the interior was decorated in seventies modern decor and was clean. *Funny how you have family members you knew nothing about. My cousin and her son were one of them. Why I did not recollect them was beyond me.*

"Where's cousin Irene?" I asked while taking a seat.

Battlefields

"She's visiting some of her church friends and should return in about three hours. ...You want something to drink?"

Hesitating slightly before answering, I said, "I'll have a glass of water."

"That's it! Nothing harder, like a beer?" He smiled, flashing a strange look before heading toward the kitchen. Shrugging my shoulders, I switched gears and turned my attention to the dimly lit room. Moments later, Nate returned with a tall glass of water, setting it down on the glass-topped coffee table with hand-carved wooden legs, before he plopped next to me. "You're a big muthafucka! How old are you?"

Big for my age, I nearly reached the same height as Nate. "Thirteen, and you?" I asked.

"Twenty-four," he said, smiling.

"Oh…" I responded.

Nate grinned slightly and leaned in closer. He checked me out from top to bottom then said, "Yeah, you're a big muthafucka. A young, big, pretty fuck!" He scooted marginally closer.

"You have big arms!" I remarked, completely mesmerized.

"You like my arms?" Nate smiled, flexing his large, sculpted biceps. "Do you want to touch them?"

Eagerly, I answered, "Yes!"

Nate raised his left arm, coercing his bicep to dance in place. "Go ahead, you feel it," he whispered sensuously.

Reaching, I stretched my hand wide, attempting to wrap it around his immense muscle. Clearly, in prison, lifting weights was his favorite pastime because his biceps were massive. "Wow!" I remarked.

"You like that?"

Bursting with childlike enthusiasm, I reacted, "Yeah, I do!"

"I like that too! I like how you're rubbing my arm, feels real nice." Nate slid a little closer with his thigh touching mine.

I felt hot all over like a teakettle had blown its whistle. I could feel my manhood blossoming beneath my pants and was overcome with nervous excitement guided by unexplored possibilities. For years, I wanted to relinquish ideas to the consciousness of a man's touch. "I like it!" I announced.

"Do you!" Nate said, sliding his hand up my leg, squeezing my inner thigh. "You like that?"

Barely able to speak, Nate's touch secretly forced my body into a slow quiver. I sighed with a long, slow drag. "Yes."

Staring down, Nate repositioned, clutching a handful of my sacred treasures. Wildly, my back arched by the sensation. "Do you want me to stop?" he asked. "I'll stop if you want me to! No pressure."

"No!" I demanded, clutching the edge of the sofa cushion.

"Do you want me to keep going?"

My mind swam wildly. "Yes!" I pleaded.

Nate pressed harder, causing me to moan like a caged animal in heat. "You like that don't you!"

"Yes," I said, twisting my body in delight with fists rolled tight.

Nate slowly directed his hand under my shirt, caressing my stomach. "I bet your lips taste sweet," he said, removing his hand, placing it to my chin, and gradually turning my face toward his. "Has anyone made you feel this good before?"

I answered, shaking my head no.

"Can I taste your lips?" he asked.

I nodded yes.

Placing his lips next to mine, he gently opened his mouth, forcing his tongue in. Feverously, I darted mine in return.

"Slow your roll, Junior, and let me show you what to do!"

The perception of the moment made my senses explode with each rhythmic exploration. My mouth opened wide, allowing every bit of him inside—with each lunge of his tongue, he held firmer.

"Damn, Junior, what you tryin' to do to me?" He kissed my lips again, his passion intensified. "Let's go to my room! Would you like that?"

I smiled, nodding in agreement.

Nate offered his hand, leading the way. "I want to show you how I can make you feel good!"

Battlefields

Nate's room was filled with memories of his glory years when he was a rising star in high school playing defensive end. Proud photos of days long removed, an instant reminder of a happier period before his lack of judgment turned his world upside down. Choices destroying dreams of his lost and shattered youth.

Nate sat at the foot of his king-size bed, a bed too large for the tiny size of the room. A slight scent of musk lingered in the air with dirty clothes scattered about. Nate reached for me and grabbed the top of my jeans, drawing me into him. Nate observed me intently while unbuttoning my pants and then slid his hands around my ass, pushing my jeans and underwear down around my ankles. Kneeling, Nate kissed just below my navel; my hands rested upon his expansive shoulders. Nate stood, sliding his tongue up my torso until reaching my right nipple. Amid eyes held tight, my body weakened by impressions unimaginable until now. A young boy's innocent body squirmed in delight, left speechless by overwhelming, earthquaking yearnings.

Nate's movements persisted, unrestrained, flowing toward the top of my neck. Nate repositioned against my backside, slowly removing my shirt, all the while nibbling my right earlobe. Releasing his grasp, he slowly moved a few steps back then began to undressed. Reclining upon his bed, I studied the caramel bar looming before me. *Beautiful*, I thought. That was the first time I witnessed a man in all his glory, waiting for me to sacrifice all my inhibitions. I was ready, more than ready! I wanted to experience love, real love—the love I construed, the love I deserved!

Our bodies distorted, entwined, franticly examining every inch of one another. With every movement he made, I followed. I fancied him to understand, determined to prove a thirteen-year-old capable of giving as much as I received. I required him to feel as fantastic as I. An innocent child eager to discover the ways of love, no matter how inappropriate this incestuous encounter had been. I knew what I wanted; I realized exactly what I was doing. And for the first time, Nate taught the pleasures of confident male expression. My mind detonated with new meaning; no way I could turn back now. I was in for the kill. A young child's moan of ecstasy permeated the entire space. I was determined to satisfy him as much as he pleased me. The hunger of the happenstance was indescribable. Sweet aromas of male sweat stimulated the senses, and never could I have envisioned the beauty of this liaison. Forever changed; forever I will remember—thirst at its purest.

Fragile by circumstance, I was a slave to poignant inclusiveness, and my innocence preyed upon by trusted foes, as a naïve participant sworn into darkened territory. There I was, haphazardly sprinted into mature diversions, a choice to cross the line into a world certainly not…Neverland. Bursting through the door without guilt, I was willing to sell my soul to a dirty individual on a search for emotional, expressive independence—with no regrets, no shame, but a fantasied freedom from perceived imprisonment.

The tug-of-war had begun.

CHAPTER 2

CONSUMED BY ADOLESCENT compulsions, I filled my days with idolized notions of grandeur. I pursued a valiant quest for another to rescue me from the walking dead. After Nate's presentation of adult rituals no child should experience, my world became a constant thirst for the affection of others, desires for a child too immature to control. In my subconscious, I knew I was in trouble when the door to promiscuity opened. Forever marked to amble aimlessly down a darken path, I could not return the hands of time and change the past. Patiently I waited, same as a black widow sets her trap, until the opportunity presented itself once again.

It had been three long years since my delicate indiscretion, and without a doubt, I wanted to revisit that day of irresponsible entanglement. Sadly, no other opportunity emerged. Therefore, I spent countless days in the bathroom, reliving my unfortunate experience, and because of Nate, no one my age would do. I now required the expertise of a real man to show the ways of love.

Since my salacious introduction to the adult erotic playground, I quietly became a dependable and honest young man, *except for the deep dark secret I held*. Thinking back, I never had a so-called best friend; all were occasional playmates during the course of the school year, and children in my neighborhood were throwaway acquaintances. In my mind, I could do without them, the only exception being Sedona Jacobs, a fiery young girl with dreams of becoming the next recording superstar. I must admit, Sedona's singing ability was beyond powerful and exceptional. However, she downplayed her talents, though shyness was not a word in her vocabulary. She shined in any environment, whereas I would find a corner and hide. Sedona was my rock, and one was never without the other. My mother felt the friendship was unhealthy, that I should spend my time with the neighborhood boys, except my mother's opinions never mattered. Sedona's strength was the beckon of my admiration; she was always respectful but followed her own rules, rebellious at times and never afraid to speak her mind. Sedona often joked that someday we would marry, have kids, and grow old together. Outside of my sister Vivian, Sedona was the only person in my life I cared for.

Sincerely, I loved Sedona, a beauty born from an African-American father and mixed-race mother of Native American and African-American heritage. Sedona's height was average for a girl her age, but her expressive and bubbly personality projected a far larger sparkling star. Blessed with thick, silky hair hanging halfway down her back, and soft, blemish free skin the color of maple syrup. Soft round face, almond-shaped brown eyes, kissable full lips, and blessed with a figure all the boys and men dreamt to touch—even in her early teens, Sedona was a knockout.

In 1978 I turned sixteen and completed the tenth grade. June marked the end of the school year and the beginning of my first job at a local supermarket. For the first time I would make my own money, become my own man, and finally be on my way to fictionalized independence. On my first day of work I prepared a satisfying breakfast, pressed the clothes I planned to wear, combed my hair, and applied some cheap corner drug store cologne.

Admiring my reflection, I noticed Vivian in the mirror as she entered my room, taking a seat at the foot of my bed.

"Are you excited?" she asked.

"What?" I snapped.

"I *said*...are you excited."

"Yeah, I am!"

"Bring me back some candy!"

"No..." I said, frowning.

Battlefields

"Why?"

"Because you don't need it, and besides, Mom would beat my ass if I brought home candy. You know she's not about to let you have junk food without her permission."

Vivian sighed. "I don't care; I want a chocolate bar!" She rested on her elbows, searching my room before returning her attention to me. "What time are you coming home?"

I stood before the full-length mirror, buttoning my shirt. "I'm not sure…later this afternoon, I guess."

"What is Sedona doing today?" she asked.

"Not hanging out with you," I announced.

"Stop being so mean," she said, twisting her face in a scowl.

"Go play with your own friends and leave us grown folks alone!"

Sticking out her tongue, Vivian ran from my room and screamed, "Big head!"

Completely ignoring her childish tantrum, I rolled my eyes with contempt then continued primping in the mirror.

I arrived at the market around eleven forty in the morning, twenty minutes before the start of my shift. I sat in the employees' break room, waiting patiently across from a row of red metal lockers, eager to receive instructions regarding my new employment. While I waited, a young man entered the room and retrieved an item from one of the lockers. Briefly our eyes met, I smiled flirtatiously—he returned the favor.

"What's your name? You must be new?" the young man asked.

"I'm Wilson and today is my first day!"

"Cool, I'm Isaiah; if you need someone to show you around, don't be afraid to ask."

"Thanks, Isaiah!" I responded.

Isaiah was a skinny, fair-skin black dude with curly hair styled in a close-cut fade, standing about my height, his appearance was average, but handsome in his own way with angular facial features and dimples.

"How long have you worked here?" I asked.

"Since I was seventeen. I started as a bag boy, and now I'm twenty-three and a cashier."

I smiled. "I just turned sixteen…"

"Sixteen!" he remarked, appearing shocked.

"I turned sixteen this past February," I said, grinning. "Why are you so surprised?" *I have no idea why I asked. I was tall for my age, having grown to the height of six foot three, and I started growing facial hair, and my voice had deepened. No one ever believed I was sixteen!*

"Damn, I thought you were at least nineteen, maybe twenty, and you're taller than I am!"

I smiled. "This is my first job, so I'm a little excited."

He chuckled. "That will pass," he said, eying me up and down.

"Nah, this is a big step for my independence!" I declared.

"Dude, you have a long way to go before your independence. Enjoy your youth while you still have it."

Little did he know my youth ended years ago. "How are the other people who work here? You're the only one I've met, so far."

"They're cool, except for a few—stay away from Mrs. Watkins, she's a bitch and lazy as fuck! She'll have you do all sorts of shit; stuff she doesn't want to do!"

Just then Mr. Harris, the store manager, entered, disrupting our conversation. "Mr. James, I'm ready to see you," he said, and then turned to Isaiah. "Mr. Allen, shouldn't you be manning your checkout counter?"

"Yes, Mr. Harris," he responded, turning in my direction with a smile. "See you later."

"Thanks for the tips," I remarked.

"Not a problem" Isaiah said and then winked as he headed for his workstation.

A month had passed since I began working at the supermarket. Settling perfectly into my job, I gained loads of respect from Mr. Harris, who

Battlefields

appreciated my enthusiasm and dedication. Since day one, Isaiah and I became fast friends, the older brother I never had—watching, shielding from the occasional workplace drama and gossip. What I loved about Isaiah was his outgoing and personable nature and straightforward personality. If he didn't like you, he had no problem setting you straight.

One afternoon, I was eating a late lunch at McDonald's, located in the northwest corner of the market's parking lot. Isaiah and a friend sat at an adjacent table, oblivious of my presence, though I could clearly hear their discussion. The two were lost in meaningless gossip, unphased by the world around them, when I overheard his friend speaking of some dude he slept with the night before.

"That nigga had the biggest dick I've ever seen," he said, motioning with his hands, demonstrating just how big before slumping over in laughter. "I couldn't wait to sit on that shit!" he explained, energetically.

"Where did you meet this guy again?" Isaiah asked.

"Gurl…" he said, smacking his lips, "you remember, at Jewel's Room?" He sported a look of exasperation for not remembering.

"I can't remember half the shit you tell me," Isaiah remarked.

Eventually, his friend peered around Isaiah and made some comment, which I assumed was about me. Suddenly, Isaiah examined over his shoulder, finally noticing my presence. The stupid look upon his face said it all. I silently laughed at how quickly his demeanor changed.

"What's up, Wilson?" he said, his voice slightly stammering. "I didn't see you sitting there."

I smiled. "I know—you were too busy hearing about some dude's big dick!"

The expression on his friend's face swiftly conveyed he wasn't at all pleased with my statement. "Who the hell are you?" he demanded, quickly darting his eyes in my direction.

Refusing to give him the slightest bit of my time, I refocused my attention on Isaiah. "What's up with you tonight?"

"Not much, just chillin' with a buddy of mine. You?" Isaiah asked.

"I've been looking for you; I wanted to stop by later, but I see you're busy," I commented.

"He was just leaving," Isaiah answered.

Twisting his neck like some possessed-back-alley-stank-hoe-bitch, his friend then remarked, "Did you just dismiss me?"

"Yeah, I did! I think Wilson and I need to have a chat."

"Bitch," his friend stated, as he rolled his neck.

"Be nice! Anyway, Wilson this is Alex."

I reached to shake Alex's hand, but he stood with no expression, rolled his eyes, and ignored my gesture.

"I'll chat with you later!" he said to Isaiah. Then deliberately, he turned in my direction and said, "It's been a pleasure." He stormed off, disappearing among the cars in the parking lot.

"Pay him no mind, he's just jealous. You're a new face, and he didn't know or have you first." Isaiah placed his arm around my shoulders, as we walked to his car. "I guess you know my secret!"

"No biggie," I said, pausing. "I don't care, but I do have some questions."

"Cool, I've always been honest with you. We can pick up something to drink and talk at my place."

"I'd like that!"

Back at Isaiah's apartment, we sat on the floor of his living room with a bowl of popcorn. My mind raced with the possibility of feeling the touch of a man once again.

"So…are you gay?" I asked.

"Damn boy, you didn't waste any time!"

"I already know the answer, just wanted you to confirm it!"

"Is that so? You just assume that since I was speaking with a dude who appeared to be gay, that makes me one as well."

"Well…doesn't it?" I asked.

Isaiah grinned, shaking his head. "I have a lot to teach you, but if you must know—yes, I am."

"So am I!" I stated proudly.

"I suspected the first day I met you, but wasn't sure."

Battlefields

"What!" I said, totally stunned. *How did he know?* "I didn't say anything to you!"

"You didn't have to; it's the way you looked at me with those I'm-gonna-eat-you-up-eyes!" he said, laughing.

I was not amused. "I did not!" I protested.

"You did too, sent my gaydar straight to red alert!"

"Gaydar?"

"You haven't developed yours yet, but you will." Isaiah leaned back against the sofa. "How do you know you're gay? Have you had any experiences?" he asked, picking at his teeth. "Or just fantasizing—how do you know?"

"I've had sex before."

"You have…with who, some neighborhood boy?" Isaiah questioned.

"Nah, with a cousin of mine," I remarked casually.

The startled look upon Isaiah's face was hilarious. "Your *cousin*—was he the same age?"

"No, he was twenty-four."

He grimaced, "Twenty-four! You're joking, I hope."

"Nope," I remarked, shaking my head.

"Did he rape you?" he stated with concern, slightly raising his voice.

"Nope, I wanted to make love to him."

"Wilson, that was not making love! How old were you?" he asked with alarm.

"Thirteen," I stated matter-of-factly with no shame.

Isaiah choked on his popcorn. "What the fuck!" he said, taking a drink and then placing his can of soda on the floor next to him. "You're shittin' me!" he remarked, leaning forward. "Please say you're shittin' me!"

"I'm not kidding! It was beautiful, and I wanted it to happen. I wanted to feel loved. I needed to feel loved. I never had that before."

Isaiah sat deep in thought; I could tell his mind raced with the idea of me having sex with my cousin. I didn't care what he thought. What we shared was beautiful.

13

"Wilson, that was not lovemaking; you were too young to even know what that meant. An adult cannot make love to a child! He took advantage of you, using your immaturity for his own good!"

I sat sulking like the child that I was, instantly becoming angry because he did not believe me. "He asked if I wanted it, that he would stop if I didn't want to go through with it." *I was the one who was there, he wasn't; he knew nothing about what happened.*

"Please tell me he did not penetrate you?"

"Penetrate, what do you mean by that?"

"See...you don't even know what that means. Did he stick his dick in yo' ass! Now do you understand?" he stated with authority.

Now I grimaced. "No, he did not do that! That's disgusting!" I felt repulsed. *Did men really do that?*

"What's the matter, the thought turned your stomach?" Isaiah asked with a slight grin.

I nodded my head. "The thought..."

"Well, man, if you're as gay as you say you are, you'll be doing a lot of that. You're either giving or receiving, that's what men do; it's all part of being gay. It's what we do, and you'll learn to love it!"

"Do you do that?"

Isaiah couldn't contain his laughter. "Hell yeah, I do! Shit, I can't get enough of it. You have no idea how good that shit feels."

My mind contested the idea. "The thought of doing that—I don't know."

"Man, you will and you'll do it often! Once you get a taste, yo' ass will go stone crazy!" Isaiah reached for his soda. "But promise, you won't do that with any more grown-ass men!" He glared into my eyes with an intensity that scared me to the core. "Did you hear me?"

"I heard you."

"Promise me!" he shouted.

"I promise," I whimpered.

"Have you told anyone about your cousin?" he asked.

Battlefields

Had he lost his mind, I thought, *and ruin any chance of it ever happening again!* "No, you're the first person I've told."

Isaiah glared angrily and said, "Now you have me pissed off!"

I guess nothing was going to happen with Isaiah, I thought, as I continued eating popcorn, attempting to ignore his mental breakdown. *Why was he getting upset? It didn't happen to him, and besides, he is not my father! Even so, my parents couldn't care less what I did. Only I know what's best for me! I know what I want and what I can handle. He is not going to tell me what to do, and if I want to have sex with men, then that's what I'll do, though I would not do the dick thing...yuck!*

CHAPTER 3

A FEW WEEKS had passed since my big brother heart-to-heart conversation with Isaiah. I listened, considering his advice; however, the overwhelming urges within continued to consume and guide me clearly in an entirely different direction. The compulsory need to feel the love of another annihilated every fiber of my body. Though I obsessed over love, no other opportunity had presented itself, so my daily bathroom ritual continued. Whenever I tried to find solitude to release restrained tensions, my sister would conveniently knock on the *damn door*!

"What are you doing in there?" Vivian shouted.

"Leave me alone!"

"Let me in," she demanded.

"Go away!" I yelled, spoiling my concentration with every thud. "Vivian, if you don't stop banging against the door!"

"I'm gonna tell Momma!" she shouted.

My eyes rolled back by the sheer pleasure I placed upon myself, causing my body to collapse limp on the commode. My heartbeat danced in rhythm along with my heavy breathing, and ultimately, I would lean for a towel, removing the juices sprayed from my throbbing muscle. Lurching forward, holding my head in the palms of my hands, I thought, *I couldn't go on like this!* With each release, emptiness engulfed my being. I dreamt of sharing this pleasure with someone who would hold me and confess his or her love. It was all I desired, constantly pining for the affections of another. I had no one to love, to care for me—how long would I have to wait?

Battlefields

"What have you been up to?" Isaiah asked, removing a navy-blue dress shirt from his closet.

"Nothing, really, just working. How come we haven't talked?" I speculated.

"I've been occupied with this dude I met, and he's taking a lot of my time."

"Really, where did you two meet?" I wondered, possessed with questions, unaware of how men would ultimately meet. Isaiah had remained closed-lipped regarding the subject, and whenever I brought it up, he quickly stated *enjoy your youth!* He was too protective, and I did not like it.

"We met at The Study a few Sundays ago," Isaiah answered.

"The Study? What's that, a study hall at your school?"

Isaiah screamed with laughter, holding his stomach, incapable of controlling his laughter.

"What's so funny?" I asked.

"The Study is a bar where we can be ourselves, our safe haven."

"Oh…" I said casually, searching around his room. "Where are you going?"

"I have a date," Isaiah remarked, busy ironing the button-down dress shirt. "So you'll have to leave when he arrives," he said, shifting the shirt's position, continuing with the other sleeve. "Can I ask you a question?"

"Sure."

"Where does your mother think you are, since you've been spending so much time here? Do you have any other friends?"

"My mother doesn't care what I do. All she does is scream and yell at my sister and me. No matter what we do, it's never enough. Therefore, I come here so I don't have to stay home. I have a close friend, Sedona, but she's visiting her grandparents in Oklahoma City for the summer."

"I see—but never make comments that your mom doesn't love you; that's not cool."

"Whatever," I answered, scrunching my face.

"She does! Some people just have a difficult way of showing it." Isaiah appeared surprised by my response, but he dropped the subject anyway. "You have no other friends besides Sedona?"

"I have friends in school, but I don't see them during the summer," I said, sitting at the foot of his bed. I casually answered his question, reaching for a magazine.

"Why is that?" Isaiah asked as he pivoted his body in my direction with a question mark expression.

"I don't know," I remarked, laying my head against the headboard, looking through the magazine. "Just the way it is. You're my friend, that's why I hang out with you."

The doorbell rang.

"Can you get that, please?" Isaiah asked.

I left Isaiah to answer the door and returned with Alex following closed behind.

"Hey, gurl," Alex announced as he sprinted into the bedroom.

"What's up...and stop calling me girl!" Isaiah demanded.

Alex shrugged his shoulders, snapping his fingers. "Bitch, please" he said, fixating his attention in my direction. "So, Wilson, have you found a man yet?"

Isaiah swung around and frowned hard at Alex, infuriated by his inappropriate questioning.

"What! I just asked a question!" Alex responded smugly.

Isaiah sighed. "Leave him alone," he said, looking in my direction. "Wilson, don't answer him. It's none of his business."

Lifting my gaze from the magazine, I remarked, "He can ask anything he wants, doesn't mean I'll answer."

"Is that so?" Alex commented. "How old are you again? Oh, that's right—sixteen! You mean nothing to me."

"That's not what you said last night!" I smirked.

Alex sucked his teeth. "OK—you think you can handle this?"

Isaiah interrupted. "Alex!"

"Fuck him! Every time I see this bitch he has something to say."

Not once would I lift my head, maintaining my focus, ignoring his comments. Besides, Alex was smaller in stature, and I knew without question I could easily kick his ass, if I had to. I continued flipping through the pages, while Alex's glare nearly burned a hole into the page.

Battlefields

Without looking up, I said, "Talk is cheap."

"Alex, you're too old to act like some child. Leave him alone. Why are you always fuckin' with him anyway?" Isaiah remarked before heading toward the bathroom, closing the door.

"He's the one talkin' shit! Say somethin' to him," Alex demanded, pointing his finger in my direction.

Quietly, I laid the magazine down and walked over to Alex, standing so close I could feel his breathe against my skin. "I'm not afraid of you," I remarked, pushing up on Alex. "You got something to say!"

Alex whispered, "Yeah, bitch," standing his ground with heavy breathing.

Stepping closer, my gaze fixed squarely on Alex. "I think you want some of me. That's your problem," I said, egging him further. "You want some of me?" I asked confidently.

Appearing to revel in the confrontation, Alex said, "How about we take this to my place. I do believe I could show you a thing or two." He smiled with a crooked, sinister grin. "I live around the corner, talk yo' shit there. I'll wait for yo' ass outside."

"I'm there, and make sure you can deliver, bitch!" I said, establishing my turf, ready to beat his ass.

"Bring yo' ass on over!" Alex said seductively before yelling to Isaiah. "Hey, Isaiah, I'll check you later, something came up I need to tend to!" Alex walked toward the door; I followed close behind. Once we reached the living room, Alex stopped, providing orders, "Stay here for another fifteen minutes then tell Isaiah you're leaving; you know my car."

Fifteen minutes passed when I informed Isaiah I was heading out.

"Where are you going?" he asked.

"I'm going home."

Isaiah studied my facial expression with a look of concern. "Make sure you do, and stay away from Alex. He's my friend, but he is a hoe, up to no good, and sees you as a challenge. Don't allow that game he's playin' fool you. I mean it!"

"All right, Daddy," I sarcastically stated.

Seventeen minutes later, I found myself standing in Alex's apartment.

"Have a seat," Alex stated, heading for his bedroom.

I sat on the sofa, taking a gander around the average sized living room decorated in earth tones with walls painted a muted dark tan, with contemporary wood side and coffee tables, and with a deep rust-colored fabric sofa and love seat. Clean, comfortable, and fresh.

Shortly thereafter, Alex returned wearing dark blue sweats with a white tank. Alex was a slim-build dude with no ass, a dark brown complexion, and a handsome face, but a little on the feminine side.

"Comfortable? Can I get you something?" he offered, settling beside me.

"Nah, I'm cool." After all that talk, I was actually a bit nervous.

Alex smirked. "You talked all that shit, now you wanna back the hell up."

"Nah, I'm cool…just thinking about Isaiah's comment."

"What that nigga got to say?" Alex questioned.

"To stay away from you, because you're trouble!"

His composure quickly changed. "He said that!" Alex specified, obviously annoyed by the statement.

"He did."

"And you listen to everything that nigga tells you to do?"

"No, I'm a grown man. I do what I want to do!"

"Is that right…and what is it you wanna do?"

Mystified, because I was unsure why I was even there, I said, "I don't know what I want. I'm not sure why you asked me here."

"I thought you wanted a piece of me. So I guess you're wasting my time."

"I want a piece of *you*? I think you meant you want a piece of me. The only thing I had on my mind was kicking your ass!"

Alex laughed. "Nigga, please, the only ass kickin' is gon' be you beatin' this ass with yo' dick!"

I thought for a minute, *so it has come down to this; I have to fuck this bitch! He's not even my type!* "I never fucked a dude before," I confessed.

Battlefields

Alex lit up as bright as a searchlight in the deep dense fog! He had jackpot written all over his face, ecstatic that he'd scored fresh meat. "You've never been with a man before?"

"I have. I've just never fucked or been fucked."

"Well, well, well…have I got a treat for you!" Alex stood, maneuvering, straddling my lap. He leaned forward, gently kissing my lips. We kissed again, but this time longer with urgency I never envisioned. "The kid can kiss!" Alex remarked, coming up for air.

I smiled. My head spun wildly by the intoxicating tongue action causing my joint to grow, as the heated exchange overwhelmed my body.

Alex squirmed with excitement, rotating his midsection against my groin. Hot flashes shot through my torso by the heightened pressure. "Ooh, baby, am I gonna teach you something new tonight!" he said.

Flipping Alex with determination, I mounted him firm with the strength of a pulverizing compactor. I forced the entire weight of my body against his, causing Alex to moan wildly. I sunk in pleasure, as our locked lips reached maximum explosion. Stopping for air, lifting my torso to catch my breath, I panted heatedly. "Do you live alone?" I mumbled.

"Nah, I have a roommate." Alex spoke sensuously, kissing around my neck.

Tilting my head to one side, licking my lower lip, I said, "He's not gonna come home and catch us, is he?" I asked, staring out into space.

"He works till midnight, so we have all the time in the world," he said, biting my left ear lobe.

I grimaced. "You feel so good!"

"So do you!" Alex raised himself, lifting my shirt over my head, placing his mouth around my left nipple, sucking as if attached to a baby's formula bottle.

Closing my eyes, arching my back in delight, I felt the electricity radiate throughout my lanky frame. Instinctively, I began dry humping, causing Alex to shudder with each thrust. Reaching to loosen his sweats then remove his shirt, I ran my hands up his chest and gently grazed his nipples, causing his torso to spike under my touch. Soft and deliberate, I slid my

Vance N. Smith

tongue from his navel to his nipples, paying close attention to each one. Something I learned from Nate. He taught me how to use my mouth, which I could say with confidence, I mastered, judging by Alex's reactions.

Alex draped his arms around my neck, pulling me close, and said, "Let's take this to the bedroom. I have a few things I need to teach you."

I nodded. "Let's go!"

For the next hour, all of our self-consciousness tumbled with a thud; wild abandon unleashed hidden desires. I was weakened by soft, moist warmth surrounding my flesh, drilling deep into his inner sanctum. A seamless, choreographed dance performed with unrehearsed precision. Dueling spirits collided in unison. Dazed, drowned, and drunk with unearthed emotions, I moaned. Rivers of sweat streamed off our bodies, emerging as one. Ferociously, we searched one another, our bodies interwoven and twisted. We were engaged in sensations only two could produce, drenched with excitement unimagined until now.

It was an explosive sexual freedom: finals had been completed and now the procession to graduation had begun. My teachers taught me well; forever I will be the perfect student.

CHAPTER 4

My secret encounters with Alex continued for the remainder of the summer. It was now the second week of the fall semester, along with the beginning of my junior year of high school. To accommodate my classes and school activities, I reduced my hours at the supermarket, managing to work a couple of days a week after school and on weekends. Sedona had since returned from her annual summer visitation with her grandparents a week prior to the new school year. Wanting to profess my newfound affection, I decided to hold those feelings close to my heart. Alone in seclusion, I committed my life stories to a sealed treasure box tucked away from all to see.

My friendship with Isaiah had strengthened over the summer months. He became a trusted confidant, though my dirty secret weighed heavily on my heart. Against his forewarnings, I pledged deep into my inexcusable relationship with Alex, having grown to a depth neither wanted to admit. While in school, my daydreams of love shielded my consciousness from the daily pressures of adolescent pranks. Patiently, I waited until our next proclamation of love, thinking of him often, wondering how his day had been. Believing in his declaration of adoration, I fell hard—swallowed beneath by my own bivouac of love's yearnings. My interactions with Alex had elevated my social development way beyond my years, built upon a foundation laid by Nate. Neither of us exhibited any concern where this association would lead. We were careful, safeguarding our involvement from Isaiah and his roommate, whom I had yet to meet. Honestly, it didn't matter; my only concern was not affecting my commitment with Alex, since our carnal rendezvous had multiplied to several days a week. Never could I believe

Vance N. Smith

entering a man would fulfill my senses tremendously. The once-disgusting idea of a child's mind evolved into notions of romantic lust. Consuming all thoughts, I ached for the heat of Alex's pleasure chest.

On the third Saturday of September, a blistering hot and humid day fell upon the LA basin with temperatures skyrocketing beyond the high nineties. The prior week of school proved to be a stressful, draining parade of assignments and homework. Between juggling my education, work, and the emotional needs of Alex, stress had taken its toll. Sitting in a booth of McDonald's restaurant, with legs stretched to the seat across from me, I rested my weary head against the back of the bench with eyes closed tight. My jumbled mind had finally found peace after my morning duties at the market. Lost in a moment of precipitous, relaxed concentration, I was startled back to reality by an unfamiliar, deep husky voice.

"You can't hang around here all day," a stranger spoke with stern words.

Opening my eyes, I found a menacing, tall figure dressed in all black looming over me. Squinting, attempting to adjust the sunlight blinding my view, I said, "Excuse me?"

The man dressed in black pushed my feet from the bench before taking a seat. "You can't hang out all day and sleep. They have a business to run and don't need you taking up a booth if you're not eating."

Clearly, I was dumbfounded, since I had purchased a meal, finished eating, and was waiting on Sedona to meet me after work. I mumbled, "I'm waiting for a friend to show up." Once my eyes adjusted, I realized it was a police officer ordering me to leave. "Officer, I come here every weekend after work; the manager knows who I am."

"I'm not concerned with your excuses...you're not allowed to loiter all day." His harsh expression verified he was dead serious and certainly not about to budge from his official direction.

Examining the dining area, perplexed by the officer's demands, I asked, "Are you for real?" I struggled to remain composed because the situation did not make sense. "The manager, Mr. Paulson, is a friend of mine," I protested. "He knows I come here every Saturday, in fact, I work at the

Battlefields

supermarket." I attempted to locate the manager, but then I noticed him standing by the counter with arms folded over his chest with that same authoritarian appearance.

"Come on, let's go!" The officer stood, gesturing for me to remove myself from the booth.

I scowled, placing my hands on the table, lifting myself up. "I'm going!" I said, surrendering.

The officer began to snicker when I boosted myself from the table. "Man, sit down. It was a joke. You've been played!"

"What?" I questioned, baffled by his statement. From a distance, a faint laughter jolted my attention. I turned to find Mr. Paulson beyond himself in amusement.

"Sit down, sit down! I noticed you before, so I asked Paulson who you were. He thinks very highly of you and thought it would be funny to clown you!"

"Ha, ha," I said, too tired to be amused, and I didn't even crack a smile. Settling back into my spot, I asked, "Shouldn't you be looking for bad guys or something?" I picked at my leftover food, glaring hard.

"Ah, I see you got jokes, too!" said the officer as he scooted into the booth.

"Did I tell a joke?"

"I believe you did."

I chuckled, relaxing into the bench, taking a thorough examination of the officer. His smooth, dark milk-chocolate skin complemented his dark uniform. The Officer's stature was strong and solid, with chiseled facial features, a short-cropped faded haircut, and a warm crooked smile bearing slightly gapped teeth. "Well, I guess I did," I stated, finally breaking a smile.

"See, I knew I could make you smile. Playing the tuff role doesn't work for you."

Did he insinuate I was frontin'? I ignored his comment. "You still didn't answer my question."

"What was your question?"

"Shouldn't you be chasing bad guys?"

25

Vance N. Smith

"Am I allowed to take a lunch?" he remarked, shaking his head. "I'll be back; I need to fetch something to eat."

"I would like a chocolate milkshake?" I asked, casually.

The police officer made no comment walking toward the counter. I watched his every move when he strolled away; his uniform fitted him well, highlighting his ample, round ass and thick legs. Lately, every man I met I sexualized—a fantasy never to experience. I shook my head, checking my watch for the time. Sedona was late!

A few minutes later, the officer returned with his meal and a milkshake.

"Is that for me?" I asked, grasping for the frosted foamed drink.

The officer removed the drink from my reach. "No!" he said, as he sat and began eating.

"So...you have a Big Mac meal, a large coke, and a milkshake?" I nodded my head snidely. "You're greedy!"

Placing the frosted shake next to my tray of used food holders, the officer said, "Here!" Then, with a smug expression, he picked up his burger, took a bite while glaring hard, and asked, "What's your name?"

"Wilson." I extended my hand for one of his french fries.

"You're a bold fuck," he said, wiping his mouth. "Your dad needs to check that!"

"We're not gonna talk about my dad; he's unimportant to me!" I glared back.

"Wilson...show some respect for your parents," he stated.

"Not all parents deserve respect," I retorted. "And you are?"

"And you are what?"

"Your name," I said smugly, stealing another fry.

"Officer Elijah Busby," he answered, relocating his fries.

"So formal," I kidded.

"You always so bold?"

Unaware of what had come over me, I, too, noticed that my behavior was definitely out of character. "No...never. I'm kinda shocked myself."

Battlefields

"It's cool. I'm impressed, but I want to go back to your parents," he said with concern.

"Do we have to?" The dysfunction in my life was something I didn't care to discuss.

"Yes, we have to." Taking another bite of his burger, he said, "What's the problem?"

"No problem, I don't want to talk about my dad or my mom," I remarked, slowly sipping my milkshake.

"You appear to be a well-educated young man, clean, somewhat well mannered. They couldn't be all bad!"

Was he for real? I thought. "Just because I'm not some delinquent hanging out with gangbangers or some other nonsense doesn't mean my homelife is all cool and shit!" Annoyed, I sunk down into the bench, holding the straw in my mouth, ignoring the officer's rigid stance.

"Do you speak like that to your parents?"

"Speak like what?"

"That foul mouth of yours," he demanded.

I rolled my eyes. "No!"

"Then don't do it with me." Cleaning his hands with one of the table napkins, he said, "What you need is a good ass whoopin'!" Officer Elijah placed the napkin next to his meal, leaning back into the seat.

"You plan on whoopin' my ass? I don't think that's gonna happen!" I stated flatly, grabbing another one of his fries.

"Are you hungry?"

"No."

"Well, stop pilfering my fries," he said, placing a fry in his mouth. "How old are you anyway? Nineteen?"

I mocked him. "Not even close! What are you, forty?"

Officer Busby chuckled, causing his shoulders to jump. "I'm gonna break you, because that hard-ass attitude ain't working." Crossing his arms over his chest, he asked again, "So how old are you?"

I huffed, "Sixteen."

Vance N. Smith

"Sixteen," he said appearing shocked. He shook his head. "If you were my kid, I'd teach you some respect."

"But I'm not your child and…well…my dad didn't. He failed to teach me anything. That's the point; he couldn't care less if I'm even around. All he does is spend money and buy me stuff, like the car I drive, and he thinks that makes everything OK. He means nothing to me, along with his money. I want nothing from him! And as far as my mom is concerned, she doesn't care about my sister or me. All she does is yell, call us names, and feel obligated to take care of us. All I want from either of them is to know they love me, want me!" My eyes welled with tears as rage rushed in with no means of controlling it. Feeling ashamed, attempting to avoid all eye contact, I slumped against the table, shielding my face from Officer Busby. "All I want is to know I'm loved."

I opened my soul to a stranger, disclosing truths and secrets I rarely spoke of. Officer Busby sat without uttering a word, quietly watching me break. He shifted uncomfortably in his seat, finding himself at a loss for words. His demeanor changed, "Wilson—"

"All that I know, I taught myself. I respect others because that's how I want to be treated. Everything I do is because it's what I need to do to survive," I preached, wiping salted tears from my eyes with the back of my hand. "I'm a good kid, but my mom is always telling her friends how fucked up we are! I have never been in trouble, I have never done drugs, I get good grades in school, and it's never enough! I don't know what else I can do," I said, looking around, praying no one heard my tirade.

"Wilson, you'll be OK. I can tell you're a young man with dreams and integrity. You simply need refinement and guidance." He placed his hand on my arm to comfort and said, "I can guide you in the right direction. There's hope left in you." He inhaled deeply, then released. Officer Busby scribbled his number on a napkin, sliding it toward me. "Here's my number, call me anytime you feel the need to talk." I reached for the napkin, placing it in my pocket. "I want you to call me, and if I don't hear from you, I will hunt you down."

"I will," I answered, barely able to speak; my voice trembled in a quiet whisper.

Battlefields

"Call me." Officer Busby searched my eyes. "You understand?"

I forced a smile. "I will."

"Are you going to be OK?"

"I'm fine."

"I'm not leaving until I know you're OK."

With my composure intact, I could feel the rage subsiding by the gentleness he projected, and I felt safe and relieved. Spotting Sedona in my peripheral vision, walking toward the restaurant, I refocused my attention on Officer Busby. "I see my friend, Sedona. I'll be OK," I remarked.

"Are you sure?"

"Yes."

Waving her hand to gain my attention, Sedona yelled, "Will, sorry I'm late." Then not to ignore Officer Busby, she said, "Hello, I'm Sedona!" She greeted him with an immense smile.

"Sedona, this is Officer Busby."

He smiled, standing from the table, and said "Pleased to meet you, Sedona."

"Same here, Officer," Sedona stated with a confused expression.

"Wilson," Officer Busby said, "I need to get back to work—remember what I told you to do."

"I'll remember," I answered, eying Sedona. "And thank you!"

"My pleasure," Officer Busby stated before facing Sedona. "Take good care of my boy."

Sedona lit up and remarked, "I will!" She watched, waiting for my new-found friend to leave, and then asked, "How do you know him?"

"I just met him."

"What?" Sedona asked, with her face forming a scowled expression.

"I just met him when he tried to clown me, then we began talking—I like him!"

"He's cute!" she said, giggling.

I lifted one eyebrow and remarked. "Whatever!"

"How was work?"

"It was all right—busy," I finished what was left of my milkshake. "What did you do today?"

"My mom and I went shopping."

"For what?" I asked.

"Something to wear, of course," she expressed, giving me that around-the-way-girl appearance.

"You have a closet full of stuff already."

"You can never have too many clothes."

"Whatever!" I said, gathering my items and trash. "Let's get out of here, I have things I need to do!"

"I just got here!"

"That's what you get for being late!" Standing from the table, I said, "Now let's go!"

Sedona and I walked through the doors of McDonald's, stumbling upon Isaiah.

"Hey, Isaiah, how are you?" Sedona asked cheerfully.

"Hello, Sedona, you're looking good today."

"Thanks!" she said, blushing.

"What's up, Isaiah?" I remarked.

"Can we talk for a minute in private?"

"Sure. Excuse us, Sedona, I'll be right back." We repositioned about thirty feet away, "What's up?"

"Didn't I tell you to stay away from Alex?" Isaiah said with repressed anger.

"I have stayed away from Alex!" I lied. "What are you getting at?"

"Some friends of mine have been talkin' about some dude Alex's been fuckin' around with...some young kid!"

"Why would you automatically think it's me? I have not even seen Alex." The truth I vehemently denied. *Damn, I'm going to hell!*

Isaiah glared square into my eyes. "You better not be lying to me!"

"What is that supposed to mean?"

Battlefields

Pointing his finger into my chest, he remarked, "You have no idea what you're getting yourself into!"

I know exactly what I'm getting myself into, a whole lot of Alex's ass! That's what I'm getting into! Silently, I laughed. *In fact, I intended to head there later tonight.* "I'm not seeing Alex, so just chill!"

"If I find that you lied to me, I will kick your ass!" In a huff, Isaiah turned to walk away, crossing the parking lot toward the supermarket.

I returned to Sedona. "Let's go!"

"What was that all about?" she asked.

"Nothing that concerns you."

We hopped into my car, pulled out of the parking area, and headed east on Rodeo Drive.

"Damn, baby! You be workin' the hell out my ass! I swear you're gettin' better every time we get together," Alex stated gleefully, falling back onto the bed.

Our bodies were drenched with sweat. Our lovemaking had become more intense with each session, my skills improving to damn near perfection. The student caught on quick, and my teacher taught me well, as the art of passion and affection flowed uninhibited.

"It's my job to make you feel special!" I grinned as I spoke the words.

"Baby, I do! You have no idea," Alex commented, leaning forward, kissing my cheek. "Mmm…you have no idea what I'm feeling right now," he said, reclining against the pillow, wiping the sweat from his forehead. "Even my…" he said, then stopped and turned away.

"What?" I asked, questioning his intentions.

Alex pivoted, facing my direction. "Nothing, I didn't mean anything!"

"You were about to say something." To reassure him, I kissed his right nipple, causing Alex to moan with pleasure. "You don't have to hide anything from me."

"It was nothin'," Alex said, pulling me close. "I want you inside again." Gently he kissed my lips. "I can't get enough of that mojo you're layin' on my ass! I have not taught you all that—that is a natural gift. I check you out, and I see this tall young man, complete with facial hair and all." He smiled. "How tall are you?"

"I'm six foot three."

"At sixteen, see that's what I mean. I think you're lying to me. You have to be much older then you're admitting!"

"I'm sixteen."

"At sixteen I was totally clueless," he commented while sliding his hand across my chest. "Shit, I didn't even have sex until I was nineteen, and no one entered these cakes until I was twenty-one, and here you are, at sixteen, layin' pipe like some grown-ass man!"

"Thanks, I guess." I felt flushed.

"Believe me…it's a compliment!"

"Well, let me lay some more pipe, because my dick is rock hard!" I admitted, sucking his left nipple.

"See…that's what the fuck I'm talkin' about! You even talk like some grown-ass man! Damn, baby…"

"Bring that ass on over here!" I reached around Alex, pulling myself closer and kissing his lips softly, then placed my tongue into his mouth.

Alex whispered, "Baby, I love the way you taste; I get lost in your love whenever you're in my arms. I cannot explain what you do to me. You drive me crazy when I feel you next me."

Alex rolled me onto my back, spreading my legs wide, then he knelt in between, lifted my rock, and slightly licked the tip of the shaft. Instinctively, I grabbed a handful of bedding in excitement. Slowly I felt warmth slide down the length of my swollen manhood—up then down with twirls of his tongue in between. Seizing the moment, Alex readied himself and mounted, placing his hands on my chest. Lifting his body up and down, allowing me to explore the depths of his dark canal. Alex reared his head back, biting his lower lip, enjoying the pleasurable pain creeping throughout his body. His rapid breathing, my thrusting torso, and the frenetic creaking of the bed

Battlefields

filled the room with sounds of wild passion. Declarations of affection and grunts of lust lost in time.

"What the fuck!" a voice yelled out.

Neither of us heard the bedroom door open.

Alex turned, and cried, "Oh shit!" He tried to move.

I pushed Alex off. "Who—" I began to say, but before I could sit up, a figure stood over me.

"What the fuck! I'm gonna kill yo' muthafuckin' ass!" He yanked me so quick, I was unsure which way was up.

"Baby please…" Alex pleaded.

"Muthafucka, you gonna come up in my crib and fuck my bitch?" he stated, punching me square in the jaw.

"Darius, stop—please!" Alex scrambled to remove the man.

Then from left field, before I knew it, another punch hit me in the face. *Damn!*

"Wait, stop!" I begged.

"I'm gonna kill yo' fuckin' ass!" he shrieked, throwing me against the wall, knocking over a lamp from the nightstand. I landed on the floor with his hand around my throat and his knee pinned against my chest. Gasping for air, I kicked, trying to free myself from his grip.

"Darius, stop! You're gonna hurt him," Alex yelled, jumping on his back. "Darius," Alex screamed.

On the floor, I lay naked, while he hammered my ass. What had my life become? Isaiah warned me and that was all I thought about as this mutha pounded down on my ass. Eventually he let go, stood back, taunting me to fight. In a boxer's stance, he solicited me into engagement.

"You wanna fuck my man, now you gotta deal with me. Come on wit yo' punk ass!" He swung, missed, and I planted one punch straight into his jaw. Fighting was not my nature, but it was all I could do to flee the hell I had fallen upon. "Is that all you got, nigga!" He uppercut right into my stomach; I knelt over in pain, grimacing. I coughed. He blocked my path with no escape route.

Think fast! Frantic thoughts flashed in my mind. *Look for your clothes! Get the hell out.*

Vance N. Smith

"Darius, stop! Leave him alone. Deal with me; I'm the one that fucked up. He knew nothin' about you or us! Please...you don't know what you're doin'!" Alex was crying and panting, slipping on some old tattered jeans.

"How could you do this to me again? I love you and this is how you treat me?" The stranger focused his attention on Alex.

I found my chance to escape; I gathered my clothes, which consisted of only my trousers, one shoe, and my socks. Thank God, my car keys were in my pant pocket. I quickly gathered my shit, running as fast as I could toward the bedroom door. I hurried down the hallway, round the corner, sprinting toward the front entrance. The stranger quickly followed suit, detouring through the kitchen. As soon as I reached for the doorknob, a knife flew past, impaling the wall mere inches from my face. In a panic, I bolted naked out of the apartment, scaling down the stairs without looking back. Somehow, I freed myself from an impending disaster. Once outside, hiding behind a row of tall, thick bushes, I dressed. Tears streamed down my cheeks. I shivered in pain, and my face ached with a cut on my lower lip.

The stranger dashed to the front of the apartment complex, coming to a stop when he reached the sidewalk, searching up and down the street with a knife in hand.

I needed the comfort of someone, anyone. Now I was alone, trapped in a game I should not have played. I could not surrender to the arms of my mother, and I had no father to rescue me from the horror I created. There I sat, arms around my knees, crying a torrent of tears. I checked to see whether the stranger had gone back inside, then I noticed him lurching up the sidewalk no less than ten feet away. Holding my breath with a steady eye, I held his location. Forcing the tears within, I deliberately moved farther into the bushes. Quietly I repositioned, not wanting to disclose my whereabouts. Not once would I allow my eye contact to leave his image. I had parked a few buildings away; however, it was too far to make a run for it. Watching him pace back and forth, muttering—emanating rage—I felt a mountain of fear. I waited, cowering in shame.

Fifteen minutes passed before he eventually gave up his search. Once I determined the coast was clear, I fled for my vehicle, wearing no shirt and

Battlefields

missing a shoe. I sped away, uncertain where I was headed; driving to the one person I believed would help. Although I had betrayed our friendship and his trust, I assumed no other choice but to seek solace in his safe haven.

Knocking on Isaiah's door, I silently prayed he was home. There I stood, shaking, my head held in humiliation.

"Who is it?" an unfamiliar voice yelled from the opposite side.

Silently I remained. When the door opened, I did not move.

"Oh, my god," he said and twisted his body to the right. "Isaiah... Isaiah!"

My knees wobbled, and I could hardly stand straight.

"Isaiah, come quick!" he said.

"What is it?" Isaiah said and hurried to the door. "My god, what happened to you," he asked then immediately pulled my lanky body into his apartment. "Wilson—what happened?"

I began crying. I could not stop because of the pain and embarrassment I felt. "I was jumped; I don't know who the dude was. It happened so fast."

"Wilson, where were you? Do you want me to call the police?"

"I'm calling the police right now," Isaiah's friend stated.

"No!" I screamed. "Please don't. I can't let anyone know." I made my way to a chair. "This is my fault. I'm responsible for what happened. I should have listened to you." I held my head in shame.

"What do you mean?" Isaiah stared with concern. "Wilson, what did you do?" He sat on the sofa across from me.

"I...I've been hangin' around Alex."

Isaiah's demeanor swiftly changed. "You what?" he shouted, standing from the sofa. "What the fuck is wrong with your dumb ass! Didn't I tell you to stay away from him! What have you two been doing?" He hovered, chastising me like the child I was. "What the fuck were you two doing? Wait—do not *even* answer that. I know exactly what you were doing. Goddamn it! You're fuckin' sixteen! What were you doing fuckin' around with some grown-ass nigga almost ten years older than you, have you lost your muthafuckin' mind?"

"Isaiah, yelling at him isn't going to help," his friend commented. "Come here, let me help you get cleaned up," he said, escorting me to the bathroom.

"What happened to your clothes?" Isaiah asked.

We reached the bathroom, and Isaiah's friend introduced himself, "I'm Shea, by the way." He wiped the blood from my face, attending to the cut on my right cheek. "Do you want to tell me what happened?"

I could hear Isaiah screaming from the living room. "I can't believe your dumb ass!"

"Don't listen to him. You may have made a mistake, but yelling at you isn't going to help."

"I'm so ashamed. I cannot go home and confront my mom; I'm not in the mood to hear her mouth tonight!" I remarked, resting on the edge of the bathtub.

Isaiah stood in the doorway. "Wilson, you flat out lied to me. I asked what was going on and you said nothing. You flat out lied!"

"Isaiah, go in the other room and calm down. Please…you're not helping. He doesn't need you yelling and screaming at him. Go in the other room."

"I don't believe this shit!" Isaiah said as he stormed out.

"Alex and I were in his bedroom making love when some guy came in and started beating me up!"

"Wilson, it will be OK. You fucked up and learned a valuable lesson. I'll have a talk with Isaiah."

After Shea left the bathroom, I sat thinking about my predicament. Why would Alex place me in such danger? I had no clue Alex was in a relationship. *I am such a fool! Why do I continue trusting people? I trust, and in the end, I'm the one betrayed.* My father, my mother, and now Alex have all used me for their own good.

Twenty minutes passed when I reentered the living room. "I'm sorry," I said to Isaiah, taking a seat on the sofa. However, I would not make eye contact; I sat, fiddling with my hands.

Battlefields

"Wilson, I'm sorry for yelling. I was angry and should have supported you and not yelled, but when I tell you something, just know it's for your own good."

"I know you were looking out for me."

"I told you he was no good. He has a lover, and that's what he does. He finds innocent dudes and fucks around with them until he's caught. It's all a game until one of them finds out—then all hell breaks loose! I don't know how they make it, because they constantly fuck around on each other."

"He told me he loved me and I believed him."

"Wilson, you'll find that's what men do. They tell lies just to get whatever they want from you. It's a game you'll learn to play, and I'm sorry you had to learn this lesson the hard way." Isaiah sat back in his chair, taking a good look at the beaten-up child sitting before him. Then he giggled. "What happened to your clothes?"

"My shirt is still over at Alex's. I grabbed what I could and ran. I thought he was going to kill me!" I rested my elbows on my thighs, picking at my fingers. "He threw a knife at me, just missing my face!"

"What?" Shea screeched.

"Damn…I'm going to kick Alex's ass when I see him. You could have been killed! Darius is a sick bastard. Well, actually, both of them are sick," Isaiah said, shaking his head and wiping his face. "You want to stay here tonight?"

"I can't—my mom would have a fit. I don't need her trippin'."

"Are you OK?" Isaiah asked.

"Yeah, I think I am. I just needed to talk to someone. I was hoping you would be there for me, and I don't blame you for being angry. I deserved it."

I made it home right before ten fifty-five; it was almost an hour past my curfew. I eased the front door open and tiptoed toward my bedroom. Entering the hallway, I found my mom standing in the doorframe of her room, waiting. "Where in the hell have you been?" she said as she stood with folded arms. The monster reared its ugly head. "Didn't I tell you to be home by ten o'clock?"

37

"Yes, Mom, but I was jumped by some dudes, and I hid from them until I was able to get away. I didn't want them to follow me home."

"What kind of trouble have you gotten yourself into? You had better not be out doing drugs, because if you do, I am kickin' your dumb ass out. You can go live with your sorry-ass father. You kids are always causing me grief, just like your damn father!" She turned, went into her room, and slammed the door. I could hear her yelling, calling me every name under the sun. She didn't even notice the cuts and bruises on my face, not even remotely concerned—typical.

CHAPTER 5

The morning after...

"Will, what happened to you?" Sedona asked, as she entered the front passenger seat of my car.

"It's nothing!"

"Will…" Sedona said, placing her tiny hand to my cheek, "don't tell me it's nothing. Look at your face. It's bruised and cut, have you been in a fight?"

Seriously, I did not want to answer Sedona's question, or relive the horror of the night before. My only concern was to get away from that house, away from my mom, and as far away as possible.

After taking an early morning shower and getting dressed, I entered the kitchen, finding my mother consumed with her usual demeanor; she gazed my way with contempt and then returned to cleaning the breakfast dishes, with no questions asked. She had not asked if I wanted to contact the police, what the attack was about, or if I had provoked the individual in any way—nothing, no support whatsoever. I guess I should not have been surprised. Why did I insist on my parents showing even the smallest amount of love when it was evident they did not care. Why did I expect more, when I was well aware it would not happen? So I decided a trip to the mall with Sedona would take my mind off prior events, though I was not prepared for the gazillion questions I knew she would ask.

"I really don't want to talk about it," I said to Sedona.

"You were fine when I left you yesterday afternoon…was it because of the conversation between you and Isaiah?"

"Isaiah was not involved, if you must know. Some dudes jumped me after I dropped you off."

"Why?"

"I don't know why. I stopped by a coworker's apartment in the jungle, when these guys asked me some aimless question…I don't remember what. I answered, then they jumped me." I turned to see if she bought my story. Apparently not, since her expression was, *Pleaseee! You think I'm buying that lame-ass excuse!* I ignored her, altogether.

Once we reached the Fox Hills Mall, Sedona and I shopped for about two hours before stopping by the food court. Sedona ordered some nasty-looking Chinese food; I picked up a hot dog on a stick. We found a table, had a seat, and finished our meal.

"What do you have planned for the rest of the day?" I asked.

"My mom wants to visit one of my cousins later on, so I have to be home around four o'clock. Why?"

"No reason, just asking."

Sedona calmly laid her plastic utensil next to her tray before reclining into her seat, sensing something was wrong. "What's wrong with you? You have been acting strange ever since I returned from my grandparents'."

Clenching my teeth, hoping to avoid her meddling questions, I hesitated before I spoke. "What do you mean?"

"I don't know, but something is different about you."

"Maybe I'm just maturing," I remarked, slumping into the hard plastic bench, picking over the last bite of my corn dog.

Sedona rolled her eyes, as all black girls love to do then said, "I don't believe you."

"You don't have to believe me," I quickly responded, wishing to change the subject.

"Look, I'm just trying to help," Sedona said as she sat back, clearly not pleased. "Fine…I don't care what's wrong with you."

I did not need this now, as if I didn't have enough problems. I missed Alex, even though he hurt me, and I was well aware I would never see him again. I missed making love to him and didn't want another year to pass

Battlefields

before I found love again. I demanded it now greater than I had before. "Don't be mad; I have things on my mind, that's all."

"Like what?"

"Issues with school, work, and I wish I had a girlfriend, that sort of thing," I lied.

"Really...you never talked about wanting a girlfriend before. Do you have someone in mind?"

"No, I just wish I had one, that's all," I mentioned, stopping to gather my thoughts. "There's a lot about me you don't know, Sedona. Stuff I don't want to talk about just yet, so just let it drop."

Sedona shifted in her seat. "You're gonna drop something like that and think I'm gonna let it go, you must think I'm some kind of fool."

"Let it go, Sedona," I said. At that point, I was exhausted with the interrogation, and besides, I had other plans, which didn't include having Detective Sedona grillin' my ass. I had called Officer Busby prior to leaving the house, making plans to meet around two o'clock for a game of tennis. "Finish your food, and let's get out of here."

"I'm not done with my food."

"But I'm done with you," I remarked. *Uh oh,* I cringed. That was a disrespectful slip of the tongue.

Sedona grabbed her meal, stood from the table, and stormed away. She was obviously hurt by my comment, along with the fact that her interrogation went nowhere. She immediately left the food court, so I followed close behind; and though Sedona never looked back, she knew I wasn't too far away.

During the ride back to Sedona's mother's house, neither of us spoke a single word, making for one extremely uncomfortable journey. After dropping her off, I made sure she entered her home safely before driving off.

Arriving at Dorsey High around ten minutes before two, I gathered my gear and headed for the tennis courts. As I approached, I noticed Officer Busby had previously arrived; he was completing his leg stretches when he spotted me. A few feet before I reached the concrete bench, he stood with a greeting and a smile. "Just in time."

"Yeah...I made it," I said, placing my gear on the bench next to his.

His expression changed as soon as he spotted the cuts and bruises covering my face. "What the hell happened to you?" he asked with genuine concern.

Casually, I brushed him off and said, "Nothing...have you been waiting long?"

"No...about fifteen minutes," he commented, reaching for his racket. "You know, I'm not going to let it go until you tell me what happened." Officer Busby's expression was stern, packed with authority. "I'm here because I suspected you needed attention. Help that no one else cared to give; however you must help me help you!" He waited a few minutes to see if I had some sort of reaction, which I did not. "So you stand there, showing no emotion like it doesn't matter? I recognize pain is in your heart, and many have hurt you, but I'm a patient man and I will always be here when you're ready for my help."

Grabbing my racket, I began my warm-up, starting with leg stretches, refusing to utter a word.

"OK, Youngblood...I see you're stubborn, not willing to budge," he said, nodding his head. "All right...then let's do this!"

We played about three sets, and yeah—he kicked my ass. The man could play a mean game of tennis, teaching me a few of his tricks, helping to improve my game. It felt good having someone paying attention, offering knowledge and wisdom. I felt safe, indispensable, and appreciated.

"You played a good game," Officer Busby said, grabbing a towel from his gym bag.

"Yeah...but you kicked my ass!" I remarked, approaching the sideline of the tennis court.

"I did, but you have mad skills; you just need to have them refined. In time you'll improve, then you'll kick my ass!" he remarked, placing a stranglehold around my neck.

Battlefields

"I don't know about all that." After Officer Busby released my neck, I sat along the edge of the bench, holding a towel to my forehead, wiping away the sweat. "How long have you been playing?"

"My dad taught me how to play when I was eleven."

"Your dad taught you how to play?" That idea was so foreign to me; the only thing my father knew how to do was throw money my way to satisfy his guilt, if he had any guilt.

"Yes, why are you surprised?" Officer Busby asked, as he sat straddling the bench, facing my direction.

I hunched my shoulders.

"Don't do that. You know why you asked that question."

"I just asked a question," I said, slightly elevating my voice, removing a bottle of water from my backpack, taking a gulp.

He stared for a second. "Did your father spend time with you?"

I did not want to answer, so I froze, staring off into the distance, wiping invisible lint from my gym shorts. I licked my lips, and after taking another swig from my water bottle, I said, "I can't remember the last time my father spent any quality time with me." I looked beyond the tennis courts; pain flooded my heart while the memories sped to the forefront of my mind. "I honestly don't remember if he ever spent time with my sister or me," I stated, glancing down, kicking a pebble with my foot. "The only memories I have are the arguments between him and my mother. The nights he would come around drunk, causing a scene. My dad provided for us, fulfilling his court-appointed responsibilities, which is the only good thing I can say. There's nothing material I didn't get if I wanted it, but the one thing I would have traded all that for was his love."

I sat withholding painful tears. "I wanted his love so bad, and to this day, I still do! So much so…" I shook my head, leaning forward, resting my elbows on my thighs and placing the palms of my hands to my forehead. "I want his love so much, I think it's slowly killing me inside!" I echoed in a sullen voice. "Life is so unfair…why would God allow such things to happen?" I looked over to my newfound confidant. "Officer Busby, what have I done wrong? Why does God hate me so much?"

Vance N. Smith

The agony I felt affected Officer Busby; I could see it in his appearance. Maintaining a low, steady voice, he spoke with the tenderness and assurance I needed to hear. "Wilson, you did nothing wrong; I beg you to understand that. You cannot allow someone's shortcomings to affect how you live your life. I realize it's easy for me to say; however, you cannot allow his inability to love take over you. It will destroy you if you allow it…and please stop calling me Officer Busby; my name is Elijah or you can call me Eli."

I smiled. "I prefer Elijah."

"See, that's what I want from you; I want you to smile. Forget what he has not given you and accept it. You have your mother and sister who love you."

"My sister loves me. My mother hates me—that I know for sure."

"Don't say that because it's not true."

"It is true," I said, my smile quickly erased, replaced with the pain I lived every day.

"It's not true; I don't believe it!"

"What do you know? You know nothing about my family or me… so easy for you to sit there and place judgment. You had a loving father who taught you how to play tennis, spent time with you! I'm sure your mother was just as supportive, but my parents are not. So don't tell me what my family life is like." I began packing my gear with immediate urgency. "Everyone has an opinion on what my life is, when no one has a clue to the dysfunction I deal with each day!"

"I'm sorry…you're right. I don't know what's going on in your home, or what issues your parents may have, including the dynamics that surround you. Maybe I cannot relate, but I promise I will listen; you'll have to trust me."

I continued packing my backpack, completely ignoring Elijah's false words of encouragement. Just like everyone else, he would betray me in the end.

"Stop," he said, reaching for my arm, "…Wilson, stop."

Yanking my arm back, I stepped away, turning to face him. "Let go of my arm," I said, my expression stern and unsympathetic.

Battlefields

"Don't make a scene."

"Fuck you! You have no idea how much it hurts...so much so, I'm unable to control it! It's like some*thing* is eating me from the inside out!" I held on to the strap of my backpack, falling onto the bench, exhausted. "I can't..."

"Wilson, you have to let that pain go. It's not healthy...I'm worried about you."

Regaining my composure, I said, "I'm cool. I have dealt with it this long...I'll manage."

"That's what has me worried, because you're not handling it. You have no perception of the anger that's slowly consuming and destroying you." Elijah moved closer. "I'm not going to let that happen, so get mad and fight me if you like...I'm cool with that, but I'm stronger, and I will fight you every step of the way."

"I'm not gonna fight you, but trusting, opening up, is another issue altogether. All I've ever known is people gaining my trust then hurting me in the end. I cannot afford to be hurt again. I want to trust you, I do!"

"I will not abuse your trust, and just so you know, I'm not going any-where!" Elijah pulled me into him, laying my head onto his chest, wrapping his right arm around my shoulders, his left around my head. "You can trust me!"

A cool breeze embraced our bodies while his strength, his smell, and his demeanor ignited my senses. Every word he said, I clung to; his warmth covered my body like a well-worn overcoat, offering security unlike anything I'd felt before. I snuggled, finding a new place to call home.

CHAPTER 6

THE HOLIDAYS PASSED, Thanksgiving and Christmas, with the same non-caring family tradition of forced relationships. My mother was unhappy for whatever reason only she seemed aware of, and for the life of me, I did not have a clue as to why. Year after year, as soon as the holidays arrived, the monster that possessed my mother resurfaced like clockwork. When the holidays should bring a family together, they seemed to tear us apart. My sister and I were held hostage to a beast neither proved strong enough to fight, lured by mellifluousness. Once we succumbed to its artificial tendencies, the hidden she-monster appeared, angrier than ever. I would love to take a shotgun and blow its fuckin' brains out just to have our mother back! I am certain inside that vile creature there's a compassionate individual imprisoned by life's nasty games. I knew because there were times when there was enough love to be shared. Yet, the guardian to her encampment only allowed freedom on occasions, otherwise she was trapped, with no means of escaping the shackles placed around her ankles.

An unusual torrential storm blew into town two weeks before my seventeenth birthday, and to my surprise, the she-monster had been nonexistent. The atmosphere around the house was surprisingly pleasant. Alone in my seclusion, I lay motionless, surrounded within uninterrupted concentration. It was a Friday evening, with no plans for the wild, stormy night. In the background, a cassette tape played a mixture of melodic sounds of R&B greats. Lost in solitude, my mind raced to uncharted territory, lulled by the musical messages of life, heartache, and despair. Adrift in thought, I

Battlefields

struggled to comprehend the meaning of my relationships with Elijah, Alex, and Nate, each one battling for my consciousness, while I considered the effects they had on my life today.

Deep in life's translation, a knock at my bedroom door broke my introspection.

"Come in," I said, surrendering.

My mom entered, likely wondering why I was so quiet. "What are you doing?"

"Nothing…just listening to music," I responded.

"Are you OK? Why are you in bed?"

"I'm OK…just didn't feel like doing anything tonight. I felt like listening to some music and thinking about stuff."

"Something must be wrong with you! Why would you want to stay home on a Friday night?"

"No reason…just felt like it."

"Sometimes you are so weird, just like your father!"

OK…here we go, too good to be true! There she stood with that condescending manifestation when she was about to start some of her shit! "Mom, why does it have to be a problem if I want to stay home and do nothing?" I asked, annoyed.

"I just asked a damn question. Every time I ask a question, I'm always the bad guy!"

"What do you mean? I answered your question."

"You're not going out with Sedona?" she asked tensely.

"No, she already had plans," I said, and surprisingly, the she-monster remained in hibernation.

"What do you want for your birthday," she asked, standing in the doorway, searching around my room.

"I don't know, whatever you feel like getting me."

"Why is it every time I ask you a fuckin' question, it's like pulling teeth?" she yelled.

I sat up in bed, giving my mom my full attention. "What are you talking about? Whatever you want to get, I don't care!"

47

Vance N. Smith

"Fuck it! If I'm such a bother, maybe you should take your dumb ass over to your father's house you love so damn much!"

"Mom..."

"I'm always the one putting my foot in my mouth. I know I don't mean anything to you, so why should I keep on living. If I disappeared tomorrow, nobody would even give a damn!" she snapped.

"Why would you say anything like that? No one feels that way!" I lied, knowing that the one thing I would love to do is get the hell out of there, away from the craziness brewing in that house.

"I'm in the kitchen, trying to plan your fuckin' birthday, and you're in here giving me shit! I planned to bake a carrot cake and maybe ask a few of your friends over! And—"

"Mom, I don't even like carrot cake! Why would you make that?"

"See what the fuck I mean, you ungrateful brat! You and your sister are two of the most selfish pieces of shit I know, always giving me goddamn grief. I have no clue what your dumb ass wants. No matter what I do, I'm always the one who's wrong!"

Having enough of the nonsense, I stood from my bed, confronting the she-monster, who had finally shown its true colors. "The problem in this whole scenario is you not caring to know a thing about me, what I want, or what I like! After all these years, you still have no clue what makes me happy!" No longer would I take her tormenting; I held my stance firm, stepping closer, confronting the she-monster head-on. "I don't even know why you had kids; you don't appreciate us. All you do is complain about how bad we are. What we don't do or how we cause you so much pain!"

"I can't believe you said that, you no-good bastard! After all I've done for you, this is how you repay me?"

"I don't owe you anything. I didn't ask to be born, and you did me no favor by bringing me into this world!"

My mom and I were both screaming at each other; it was an upheaval all too common in the James household, and certainly the whole neighborhood could hear the commotion. In the middle of our intense argument, Vivian stormed the room, attempting to defuse the situation.

48

Battlefields

"Momma, stop…he didn't mean it! Will doesn't know what he's saying!" she pleaded, crying uncontrollably.

"Get out of here, this doesn't concern you. You're no better than he is, just like your damn father!"

"Leave her out of it!" I demanded.

"You shut the fuck up! I'm tired of everybody taking their frustrations out on me!"

"Mom, no one is coming down on you. You brought this on yourself. You started this!"

My mother moved closer, but I stood firm, holding my ground; no longer would I be afraid. I could not allow her to bully us any longer.

"You gonna stand there like you some kind of man? You think you're man enough to challenge me in my own goddamn house? Who the fuck do you think you are?"

Vivian pulled my mother's arm. "Momma *please…*" she screamed.

The she-monster turned and pushed Vivian, knocking her into the desk chair, causing her to bump her head against the wall. "Didn't I tell you to get out of here?" she bellowed.

"What are you doing," I screamed. "Move out of my way!"

My mother grabbed my arm with a death grip; even I could not believe she was capable of such force. "Get your ass back over here; I'm not through with you! Besides nothing's wrong with her; she's faking!"

Vivian lay against the wall, curled in a fetal position. "Will," she cried.

Struggling, trying in earnest to free myself from my mother, the devil's incarnate, I yelled, "You're crazy; I hate you!"

"You stupid fuck, you think I give a shit how you feel? If you have an issue living here…get the fuck out! I will call your dumb-ass father myself; go live with him if you think he'll treat you better?" Reluctantly, she released my arm, her breathing heavy and her face consumed by disgust.

In the end, I lost the battle. I was ill equipped to fight the melee raged upon me, left with an impossible situation. I knew I had to get out of that house, but the problem being, I had nowhere to go. My father did not want me, nor did he care that we lived with a crazed maniac. His only concern was that he did not have to deal with the wicked witch invading our home. What happened to cause a woman to despise her children and life as much as she? What pain and heartaches had she endured during the course of her lifetime? I had posed those questions to several family members with no one offering any resolution.

My grandmother was so sweet and thoughtful; she cared about her family and our welfare. So how did my mother end up the bad seed? It appeared that after my grandmother's death, my mom seemed to spiral out of control, followed by the breakup with my father, which certainly sealed the deal. Now, with the pending adulthood of Vivian and I, she appeared to have been pushed over the edge.

To my surprise, Elijah became the buffer I needed, shielding me from the terror reigning upon me. Prior to this unfortunate event, he and I spent just about every weekend together, performing the big brother role I longingly missed and required in my life. I owed him dearly for the valuable knowledge he instilled in my psyche the last couple of months. We spoke often; our conversations ranged from my education, to how my family involvement had transpired, to him offering to step in and pick up the slack left by my father. I ultimately realized that Elijah had a genuine interest in my future, and I was lucky to have found my guardian angel.

Thank God, Elijah had become my savior.

CHAPTER 7

THREE MONTHS HAD passed since my birthday, and it was now May, which proved to be a rather hot month for this time of year. The argument with my mother completely ruined any chance for a joyous occasion. If it were not for Elijah, I would not have had any presents or cake on my birthday.

My days with Elijah had increased since the holidays, and I was eternally grateful for the time he invested in me. My affection for him had grown to unfamiliar territory, and secretly I hoped he would sweep me off my feet, freeing me from the hell I lived. Elijah presented a new meaning for life. He cared for my welfare, he taught the ideas of what a man should be, and he showed me how to treat others the way I would like to be treated. Having Elijah in my life eased the pain I felt from losing Alex; however, not in the way I had hoped.

It was a Saturday afternoon, and I was off from work with a full day of activities planned. Elijah and I would start with our usual sets of tennis, finishing with dinner and a movie. I was ecstatic having Elijah around because he satisfied a need no one else had been able to fulfill.

"When was the last time you've gone camping?" Elijah asked, taking a huge gulp of water after our three sets; streams of sweat glistened down his cheeks, sparkling under the midday sunlight.

"I've never been camping," I responded.

"Your father never took you or your family camping?"

"I've told you he never spent time with me," I said, then I thought for a minute. "Well...that's not entirely true. My father took us on family vacations, but again, it was as though spending money made him a good parent, satisfying his guilt."

"I know, but I thought maybe—"

"Forget it! He's a loser, and I don't waste my time worrying about him anymore."

"Wilson, you have to forgive him. Maybe what he gave was the best he could do."

"That's not good enough," I snapped. "I need him to love me—to know I matter!"

"Who says he doesn't?"

"His actions have. If he loved me, he would have spent time with me and showed me that he loved me!"

"He took care of you," Elijah stated with authority. "He provided for his family; that has to stand for something," he said, leaning forward, sitting his water bottle on the bench. "Give the man a break."

"You don't get it!"

"I do."

"No, you don't...I can't believe you're taking his side!" In a panic, I began packing my gear into my backpack. "Why is it OK to just throw money at your kids and that makes you a good parent?" I stopped packing my bag to confront Elijah. "So is that what you plan on doing with your children? Did your dad do that to you, I don't think so! You spent quality time with your father; he took you to the park, played ball with you and showed you how to be a man. You have a mother who cares for you, who doesn't call you names, call you stupid! Who loves you no matter what!"

"That's not what I was saying!"

Slamming my bag onto the pavement, I cut Elijah off in midthought. "Yes, you did!"

"No, I didn't, I said maybe that is all he could give you. Maybe he doesn't know how to love. Have you thought about that?"

"He knew how to lay down with my mother, knockin' her up with two kids she didn't want. He knew how to do that."

Battlefields

"Life isn't that simple, Wilson. You will learn life can be cruel and unforgiving. Not everyone can cope with the day-to-day madness of it."

"Then he should not have had kids. It's not fair to Vivian or me. He left us with a monster that treats us bad, calls us names, and says we're the worst kids ever. I have never done anything to make her say that. I don't do drugs; I don't hang out with gangs, and I've never been to jail. I'm doing extremely well in school, what more does she want?"

Trying in vain to interrupt, Elijah yelled, "Wilson—"

"Stop taking up for them. They don't deserve it," I shouted.

"I'm not taking up for them, and yes, your dad should have spent more time with you—treated you better!" Elijah said, placing his hand upon my shoulder. "All I'm saying...sometimes you have to love people for who they are, not for what you want them to be. Holding on to all that anger is not healthy; it will destroy you if you continue on the path you're taking."

"What do you know? It's easy for you to make assumptions when you have no clue what it means to have a family like mine!" With my heart rate elevated, I collapsed on the stone bench, wiping at my nose.

"You're a broken young man, and what I'm trying to get you to understand is to learn how to forgive, forget, and move on before it's too late." Elijah repositioned, taking a seat. "Right now, they have the power, and it's eating you alive. Take that power back, show them that you're better than they are, and their hate will not ruin your chance of happiness. Take control of your life, and guide your own destiny!"

"Easy for you to say," I remarked, wiping my face.

Sitting next to me, Elijah placed his muscular arms around my shoulders. "It will be OK, you will make it through this, and I'll make sure that you do," he offered, resting his head against mine. I held on for dear life! For once I felt secured. I sensed hope, trust, and felt loved. A savior had rescued me from the vile dungeon I called home. "Now back to my idea," he said as he released his grip.

I arose from his arms and asked, "You wanna take me camping?"

"Yes, I do, if you would like to go?" Elijah smiled.

"Yes, I would," I said, excited by the prospect of going on an adventure with Elijah, my new, substitute older brother. "When are we going?"

"I was thinking after the end of the school year."

"That's in three weeks; how about next weekend?"

Elijah smiled. "Not so fast, I have to be able to take the time off from work; remember I do have a job!"

"You've been off almost every weekend lately."

"Yes, I have, but my schedule changes, and I think I'm working weekends the next couple of months. I may have to use some vacation."

"I'm excited; I would love to go camping! Where would we go?"

"How about to one of the national parks," Elijah said.

"Yosemite?"

"I don't know if I can get reservations so soon, but we'll see."

"What will we do once we get there?" I asked, feeling like a kid lost in his favorite amusement park, riding all the monstrous rollercoasters.

Elijah smiled. "Well, we'll do some hiking, some fishing, and maybe we could take our bikes and do a little biking, but that depends on where we go. We could visit either Kings Canyon or Sequoia National Parks, maybe travel to the Grand Canyon, or stay somewhere locally in the mountains north of LA."

"I would like that. I've been to Yosemite with my family before, a long time ago, but I don't remember it all that well!"

"I'll have to ask your mother first."

"She's not gonna mind; my mother likes you, which is good because she hasn't been so mean lately." Reflecting on that last statement, I realized that she was rather upbeat since she was introduced to Elijah. The most mind boggling of all was how much my mother liked Elijah, since she could be so judgmental of others. The simple fact he was a police officer and a doting father may have been a major factor in her warm reception. She absolutely loved people with a reasonable amount of status, and Elijah fit the bill on all angles. "How long will we be gone?" I asked.

"Just a few days; three days is good enough."

"That will be cool!"

Battlefields

"Now I know what will make you happy!"

"I always have fun with you. You're the brother I never had."

"Is that right," he said, playfully slapping the side of my head.

"Hey, watch that!" I remarked, punching him in the side of his arm.

Elijah placed his arm around my neck; I sensed his hard, stiff muscles, solid as steel. With my face buried into his chest, his sweet scent of musk infused my nostrils, dancing at the pleasure of his strength and masculinity. My fragile, young intellect swooned at all men that I felt conveyed the idea of ruff-and-tumble figures. Held hostage by my subconscious, I sunk deeper into flashed, vivid images of Elijah naked, standing before me. I became a jumbled mount of flesh as we wrestled about in the evening still air.

"You give in...Huh? Say *uncle* and I'll let you go!" Elijah stated, as we wrestled down to the hard pavement.

"No way am I giving in to you!" I remarked.

"You're not gonna be able to break free!"

Grabbing the back of his tee shirt, I said, "I'm not gonna let you beat me." Secretly, I did not want to let go; the closeness excited my senses, and I needed Elijah next to me. It was all I thought about the last couple of months. This was all I had, and I enjoyed every moment.

Elijah's heavy breath and lips were pressed against my face. "I think you had enough! We need to get going anyway and get cleaned up," he said, releasing his grip, returning to the stone bench, huffing and puffing.

"You're getting old," I playfully remarked.

He smiled. "Nah, man, but it's hot as hell today, plus I kicked your ass again and that takes a lot out of me!"

"Please...I let you beat me. I didn't want you to feel bad." I sat on the hard, hot concrete with my arms and hands extended behind my back, resting on my palms, legs bent at the knees.

"You got jokes," Elijah remarked, reaching with his hand to help me up. "Get up so we can get out of here."

I smiled as he pulled me toward him.

Vance N. Smith

After packing our gear, we left Dorsey High's tennis courts and drove to an unfamiliar home in Hollywood not far from Hollywood Boulevard. We arrived at a quaint forties-era bungalow with two cottages built behind, situated on a corner lot of McCadden Place and De Longpre, north of Santa Monica Boulevard. Pulling onto a side driveway off De Longpre, I examined the neighborhood, confused as to why we were there. Elijah opened his door and exited the vehicle then looked back and said, "We're here."

"Where are we?"

"My home away from home. Come on...get out." He shook his head and chuckled.

I paused for a moment before leaving the car. "What are we doing here?"

Ignoring my question, Elijah removed our bags from the trunk. Still confused, I searched up and down the street surveying the area.

Elijah tilted his head from the trunk, staring in my direction. "You just gonna stand there or do you plan on helping me with the bags?"

After retrieving my backpack and duffel bag, I stood in the living room of one of the back cottages. "Whose place is this?" I asked.

"Mine," he answered pensively, closing the door.

"Yours?"

"Yes, mine!"

"What are we doing here?" I asked, easing further into the room. "I thought you lived near Carthay Circle,"

"I do—with my wife. I have this all to myself when I need to get away." Elijah placed his bags on the floor. "Why the concerned expression?"

"Why do you say that?"

"The look on your face, what's that about?" Elijah stared with concern. "Do we have a problem?"

I knew in my mind I was puzzled but didn't realize it showed. "No, not at all. I'm just trying to figure out why you have this place." After making myself comfortable on one of the oversized side chairs, I gazed around the off-white room, which had a large black leather sofa and chair, hardwood floors, and African art on the walls—all tastefully decorated. I felt at home,

Battlefields

detecting I belonged, like I was meant to be in that space. However, I could not explain why.

"I own this property—the front house and these two cottages. I own a few other residential properties in the Los Angeles area as well. The front house was mine before I married Belinda; this little cottage I kept for myself. When I need space and time from my family, I come here to chill. A buddy of mine lives in the front house now and keeps an eye on the property. I love it because it's secluded and no one knows I'm here if I don't want them to know." He smirked, heading for the bathroom. "Are you satisfied now?"

"Maybe," I smugly remarked.

"You and that mouth of yours, always some smart-ass comment."

I turned to face Elijah, watching him walk into the bathroom. He removed his tee shirt over his head, exposing rich, deep chocolate skin. Instantaneously, impure thoughts rushed my brain as I stared until he entered the bathroom, closing the door slightly behind. Through the opening of the partially closed door, I noticed his reflection in the bathroom mirror, affording me a better view of his muscular, bare chest, producing tightness in my pants as my manhood was called to attention. Adjusting the knot caused by my swollen flesh, I continued watching Elijah strip away his sweats. From where I sat, I had a clear view of his pubic hairs and up. The replication was a remarkable sight; my young mind fantasized about the rest of his body I could not see. In my dazed gaze, I had not noticed he was watching me as well. Quickly, I turned away, perspiring from wrecked nerves. *What he must think,* I wondered. Shortly thereafter, the door slowly closed. Feeling like a fool, I knew he was going to hate me.

After a few minutes, the door of the shower closed with the sound of spraying water. Sinking into the plush oversized chair, I relaxed and continued scanning the room. There were no photos of his family, just African art and other worldly knickknacks. The small bungalow was well kept, ideally fitted for a bachelor, not the married man that I knew. I reached for a photography book of nudes, tasteful images of both male and female that sat on the coffee table. I flipped through several pages of beautiful male models, Black, White, and Hispanic—numerous shots of the most masculine men you could think of. The women were just as nice, but of course, my focus was mainly on the men. The collection of photos was unlike anything I had seen before, and I was mesmerized. It had been months since the last time I felt the warmth of another, and I was long overdue. In fact, I was at the point of explosion if it did not happen soon.

Twenty minutes passed before Elijah emerged from the bathroom. In passing, I noticed he had placed a bath towel around his waist. My insides fluttered with childlike emotions thundering wild as a stampede of deranged buffalos. Calmly, I returned the book to the table before reaching for my duffel bag.

I called out to Elijah. "Are you through in the bathroom?"

"What?" he answered.

"Are you finished with the bathroom," I repeated, standing from the chair.

"I can't hear you; you'll have to come here."

I can hear him just fine. Is he hard of hearing? I thought. I walked leisurely toward the bedroom. The door was ajar, and I knocked.

"Come in," he said.

Pushing the door open, I saw Elijah standing naked with his back facing me, slightly bent over, pulling up is underwear. *Beautiful*, I thought, and instantly became warm all over, speechless. Not a single word slipped through my lips.

Elijah turned in my direction. "What's the matter?"

I remained silent; the sight of him took my breath away, his skin smooth as a silky candy bar, sweet, yet bitter. I wanted a taste; I wanted him to fill me up with his divine decadence.

He smiled. "You should see the look on your face!"

"What?" I responded, quickly regaining composure.

"The look on your face is priceless." He stood before me, wearing fitted briefs, exposing every line, curve, bulge, and ripple.

"Don't make fun of me," I said, annoyed.

"I'm not," he insisted.

"I'm just surprised you're so free with me?" I found my comeback.

Battlefields

"Why wouldn't I?" he countered. "We're both men with the same body parts. I'm not ashamed of my body and neither should you."

"I don't look like that," I remarked, feeling like a five-year-old child all over again.

"You're still young. You can look like this if you want to; all you have to do is work hard for it." Elijah leaned over, gathering his sweats and white tank from the bed, continuing to dress. "You want me to help you build more muscle?"

Moving further into the room, taking a seat on the corner of the bed, I said, "I don't know. It would be nice to be a little more muscular, but I'm not sure if I want to do all the work. I'm not sure I'm up for it!"

"It is hard work, and in the end it all pays off. Both men and women will admire you for the time, effort, and dedication you placed on yourself." Elijah sat alongside me, placing his arm around my shoulder. "I'm here to help you become the man you want to be. I will be the strength, the rock, your father couldn't be."

The more he held me, the more I knew his intentions were sincere. "Thank you, no one has ever said such things to me…I love you."

"I love you too, little bro," he said, sliding his hand across my head. "Come on, no more mushy stuff. You need to take a shower because yo' ass stinks," he commented, laughing aloud.

I hated how emotional he made me feel. "You didn't smell like a rose either!"

"Yeah…sure. I'm gonna fix something to eat. What do you want to see later on?"

"I don't know," I answered.

"Or we could stay in and play a board game."

"That works!"

"Cool…maybe I'll run out and get some junk food. I told your mom I will have you home sometime tomorrow."

"Thanks for allowing me to spend the night," I said excitedly, once again that little child emerged.

"Yeah, surprised?" Elijah gleefully remarked.

59

"Yes, I am, and thank you!"

"OK, I laid out some towels for you in the bathroom on the hamper. Do you like popcorn?"

"I do!"

"I'll pick some up, and I'll return shortly. Make yourself at home; I have water, juice, and sodas in the fridge."

"OK."

About forty-five minutes later, Elijah returned with all sorts of junky treats and Chinese food, placing the items on the dining room table.

"I decided I didn't feel like cooking. I hope you like Chinese?"

"I do!" I said, strolling over toward the table. I removed a chair, taking a seat, ready to dig in.

"Man, I'm hungry!" Elijah pulled out a chair as well. "You have your choice of dishes, plus fried rice and noodles."

"Looks good, I'm not complaining," I said, filling my plate to capacity, making sure I had a little bit of everything.

Elijah smiled. "Nice to see you have an appetite."

"You know I do! You've seen me eat before."

"I have and it always amazes me how much you can eat. You're a big boy, but damn…you can eat!"

"Yeah, right, you're no lightweight either!"

"This is true…but I have to keep my strength up to deal with all those crazy-ass muthafuckas in the world." Elijah shoved a fork full of food into his mouth.

I frowned. "You have a big-ass mouth!"

He stared, his mouth full of food, lips tight as he slowly chewed. Finally he swallowed, gliding his tongue across his lips. "You have a problem with that?"

"Yeah, I do."

"Too bad," he remarked, shoving more food in his mouth, leaving a few noodles hanging down the side.

Battlefields

"You're nasty!" I remarked, shaking my head. "Look," I announced with my mouth wide open, exposing half-chewed food.

"And you call me nasty? That's nasty!"

I laughed. "Now you know how it feels watching you eat like some animal."

"Whatever! Hurry up and finish, so we can start playing a game of cards or something."

After dinner we played two games of Sorry then attempted to watch a movie, but Elijah didn't quite make it. While he slept, I watched his every movement, his breathing, and the funny noises he made, along with his slight snoring. I wanted to reach out and touch his face, choosing not to. I thought it was strange how comfortable he was—his affections and his ability to express his emotions. I did not question it and did not care why. I was just grateful he did. At least someone appreciated my presence, and that was all that mattered. That was all I really cared about.

CHAPTER 8

"Can I go camping with you?" Vivian asked, seated at my desk.

I packed my duffel bag, and with my backside facing Vivian, I said, "No, you can't go. This trip is only for the men." Nothing was going to spoil my trip to Yosemite National Park. For three full days, Elijah and I would hike and bike our way around the park.

"But you're not a man!" she remarked.

"I am too!" I said, facing Vivian, preparing for the forthcoming confrontation I knew would follow.

"No, you're not; you're just a stupid boy," she commented.

"Whatever." It was getting late and no time for games with a child. Returning to the task of packing my duffel bag, I hoped she would simply leave me alone.

"I wanna go!" she pleaded.

"I thought you said I was a stupid boy," I asserted.

"I wanna go!" she begged.

"Stop being a brat," I shouted.

"You're a brat!" she said then quickly stood from the desk chair. "I hate you!" she yelled, running from my room, her cries carried all the way down the hall as she slammed the door to her bedroom. I felt bad; I loved my sister, but I needed time away from this hideous lair. I hated being locked up in that house never knowing when the monster would appear. She was safe; the monster was not after Vivian; I was the one who required shelter from the beast. The monster stalked, tormented, and held us in custody by any means possible!

Battlefields

It was Friday afternoon, and we arrived in Yosemite around two o'clock. Elijah had planned three fantastic days inside the magnificent national treasure. On our way to the campsite, we traveled along Wawona Road, stopping at Tunnel View viewpoint to peer down onto the valley floor below. The view of Yosemite Valley was unlike anything I had seen or remembered: sheer cliffs framed by trees, wondrous waterfalls, and a vast valley filled with dark green speared trees. The scent of pine occupied my nostrils; I deeply inhaled, savoring the fresh smell of nature. This wondrous beauty carved by a slow moving glacier millions of years ago. To our right, in the far distance, Bridalveil Falls fell from its perch with delicate, white silken ribbons and a billowy misty bottom. Tourists stood in admiration by the gift Mother Nature placed upon us.

Turning to Elijah, I smiled and said, "It's beautiful here. The smell in the air...the scent of the trees—I love it!"

"I'm glad to hear that," Elijah said, sporting a broad smile. "I knew you would. This is one of my favorite places; I always feel at peace here. Belinda is not fond of camping, and the children are too little, so I haven't had many chances to visit." He leaned over the railing, soaking in the majestic view.

"Are we gonna go hiking?" I asked.

He smiled. "Anything you want to do." Elijah ran his hand up and down the middle of my back.

"I can't wait. I want to ride our bikes too!"

"We'll do that as well. Everything, whatever you want to do, we'll do it."

"I hope you can keep up," I laughed. "You know your ass is old as hell."

"Don't you worry, I can keep up," Elijah replied, moving away from the edge of the overlook. "Come on, let's get going. We still have a ways to go before we make it to our campsite."

"OK, I'll take one more picture," I said, fiddling around with my first 35 mm camera that I recently purchased from a coworker a month prior to our trip. I had no clue how to use the camera, but it did not stop me. I found a new hobby and a new passion.

Vance N. Smith

"All right, but hurry," Elijah responded.

Our journey continued onto the valley floor, and Elijah was lucky enough to obtain someone else's cancelled reservations for the North Pines Campground, located near Curry Village on the eastern end of the valley. Settling into our slot, he and I set up a large four-man Coleman tent. Having our gear in place, we decided to take a quick stroll around the village, eying the park's offerings. An hour into our stroll, we stopped for a light bite to eat, something about the mountain air made me hungrier than a bear scrounging for food in a locked steel bin. Sandwiches, chips, and sodas were enough for the time being. After our snack, we opted for a short, slow, leisurely hike up John Muir Trail to view Vernal Falls and Nevada Falls.

We returned to camp around six that evening to shower before having dinner in the village. Since we were camping, you would have thought we would cook our own meals, but Elijah did not want to, so the eateries in the park would have to do. I guess you couldn't completely take the city out of the boy.

Elijah and I lingered about the village until around eight in the evening, before returning to our tent, calling it a night. Elijah had arranged a full, rigorous day of hiking from Glacier Point down to the valley floor the following day.

Once inside our tent, we played cards and a few games of Sorry. Still a kid at heart, Elijah loved board games as much as playing cards.

"I beat you again, for the fourth time! Ha, ha," I joked.

"You did! I think you're using loaded dice."

"That's not even possible." I frowned, picking up the game pieces. "Do you want to play another game?"

"No. I'm getting tired, and we need to get up early for our hike." Elijah scooted over to his side of the tent.

"You're no fun." I placed the game pieces into their container.

Elijah turned around. "What do you mean?"

"You heard me, you're no fun. I thought we were on vacation. Who goes to bed early on vacation?"

Battlefields

"It's ten thirty already. I want to be up by six in the morning."

"Six! Are you crazy?" I responded, sticking my head outside the tent. "I love the way the night air smells; I could stay here forever!"

"What did you say?"

"I said…I could stay here forever, were you listening?" I said, raising my voice a little.

"I can't understand you with your head stuck outside the tent," Elijah remarked.

Man, it's dark out, I thought. "Are there bears here?"

"What?" Elijah moved closer; his body leaned against my backside. "What did you say?"

I could smell the clean scent of soap; Elijah always smelled fresh, and even in the woods his slightly sweet masculine fragrance radiated, filling the inside of our tent. My body quickly responded to his warmth next to my flesh; his hot breath penetrated my skin, as I pushed my body against his. "Back up, you're crowding me. You're all in my space," I demanded, though certainly did not mean it

"I'm crowding you," he said, grabbing my waist, pulling and forcing me down inside the tent. He situated himself on top, straddling my waist, holding my arms back over my head. I did not put up of a fight, allowing him to have his way.

"Take it back!" he remarked.

"No, I won't!"

"Take it back!"

Elijah started tickling me (which I hate), and I gave in. "OK, OK! I take it back!"

He rolled off, laughing with his heavy voice. "You're too easy!"

I gave in because my manhood was at full attention. "No, I'm not, but you're heavy!"

"Too easy." Elijah returned to his side of the tent where he undressed, removing his sweats and tee shirt, exposing skin.

I marveled at the sight of how his muscles rippled with the movement of his body. He had a tight V-shaped back, a round rock-solid rear end, and thick ripped thighs, but with the black man's curse of thin calves and ankles—still a remarkable sight. I hastily jumped into my sleeping bag.

"The hike tomorrow will take all day," he stated.

"Is it going to be a difficult hike?"

"No, we'll start at Glacier Point, overlooking the valley, and hike our way down. There'll be some climbs, but nothing you can't handle."

"I never hiked before, so I'm not sure what to expect," I wondered.

"I find it hard to believe you've never been camping or hiking before."

"Never been...this is my first time." I lay on my side, legs slightly bent at the knees, my head rested in the palm of my hand, watching Elijah. "You don't wear pajamas?" I questioned.

"What?" Elijah promptly turned around, surprised by my question.

"You don't wear pajamas?" I repeated.

"No...I don't. I actually prefer to sleep nude, but you're here. That's why I'm wearing my briefs, if you must know," he answered with a slight edge in his voice.

"I just asked a question." *Man, did I feel stupid! Why did I ask that?*

"It's cool...I was caught off guard, that's all. You know you can ask me anything."

"I know." I paused for a second before I continued, "When did you first start to like girls?"

"When I was your age," Elijah answered, slipping into his sleeping bag, turning out the light.

"Who was the first girl you liked?"

"Lucille Mitchell. Man, I haven't thought about her in years." Elijah chuckled from the fond memory. "I first laid eyes on her in junior high school. She had on these tight-fitting jeans and a sky blue top. Everywhere she went I made sure I was not too far away. Nearly a year passed before I had the nerve to ask her out."

"How long did you two date?"

"Not long...you know when you're young it doesn't last long," he said. Shortly thereafter, I could hear Elijah rustling in his sleeping bag. "Do you have a girl you're interested in?" Elijah asked.

Battlefields

"Who me…not really," I lied. I wanted Elijah in a bad way and to have him do all sorts of nasty things to me. "I dated this girl last summer for a couple of months, but it didn't last long."

"Really…I didn't know that. You never said anything about it."

"I know, but it didn't end well."

"What do you mean?" Elijah questioned.

"Well…" I hesitated, wondering if I should go into detail of my affair with Alex. "It was right around the time I met you, when I got into that fight."

"Oh yeah, I remember you gave me attitude when I questioned what happened to your face. So it was over some chick? What happened?"

"Well…she and I were in her bedroom having sex when her boyfriend came home and busted us. I was fuckin' her real good too!"

"What?" Elijah yelled. I could hear him sitting up in his sleeping bag. "Are you fuckin' kidding me?" he laughed.

"Yeah, it was horrible!"

"What was her name?" he asked.

"Alexandria."

"You the man!"

"Yeah, I thought so too, until her real man came in and kicked my ass!"

Elijah laughed aloud. "Was she older than you?"

"Yeah, she was twenty-six and I was sixteen."

"I can count," he swiftly responded. "I realize if you're seventeen now, you were sixteen."

"Whatever…" I said, attempting to ignore his commentary. "I was hitting it almost every day. Man, I had her callin' my name! *Oh Willie, oh Willie, baby, you hittin' my spot!* I was tearin' that shit up, good!"

"Oh damn," Elijah continued, laughing. "I was not expecting that; you started early! Man, the first time I had sex I was eighteen and she was the same age. I can't believe you started at sixteen and with an older woman!"

"Well…she wasn't the first. I ate some pussy when I was thirteen," I added, flipping the script. Dick—pussy—it really didn't matter as long as I got my point across.

"What...now you just makin' shit up!"

"I did and she *was* twenty-seven."

"I don't believe you!" Elijah responded.

"I did!"

"Why should I believe you?" Elijah rebutted.

"You don't have to; I know it's the truth, and I haven't lied to you before."

"I think you're spinning tales."

"Why would I lie about something like that?"

"I don't know! How would you even know about that sort of thing at that age! When I had sex for the first time I had no clue what I was doing, and you're gonna tell me you ate pussy at the age of thirteen? I don't believe it."

"She told me what to do," I said, annoyed because he did not believe me. "You said I could tell you anything or ask. I'm telling you the truth, and you don't believe me."

"Are you mad?" Elijah questioned.

I did not answer.

"Wilson?" Elijah called out.

"I'm going to sleep. I don't want to talk about it anymore," I remarked, turning over in my sleeping bag.

"Wilson, don't do that."

"Do what...you don't believe me. So why should I go on."

"OK, I believe you, but if she did that, it was not right."

"What do you mean?"

"She was much older and you were thirteen, a child."

"I knew what I was doing," I demanded.

"No, you didn't. She took advantage of you."

"I knew exactly what I was doing, and I wanted to do it again, but after that night I never saw her again."

"I understand you may have wanted to, but that doesn't make it right. She was much older than you, and the law clearly states that as fact."

I whispered under my breath. "I love having sex; I wish I could do it all the time. At least I'll know someone loves me."

Battlefields

"I didn't hear you."

"It doesn't matter, besides no one seems to care how I feel." I was upset; Elijah did not understand how I felt. Of all people, I thought he understood.

Suddenly, Elijah unzipped his sleeping bag and shuffled to my side of the tent, lying next to me with his arm around my body. "Wilson, I do understand, but those urges you feel don't mean you need to act on them. You're a young man who's coming of age, and your body is sending you all sorts of mixed signals. Some you have yet to learn how to control. You may think you have a grasp of them, but you don't. At thirteen you had no clue what was right for you. I've been there; everyone has been in your same position."

I was not listening to anything he offered. Elijah was wrong, I knew what I was doing, and it was right for me. I did not care how he felt; I was going to do what I wanted to do. Only I knew what I needed.

"You think you know what to do, but you don't. You can get mad if you want, but I would hope we could talk as adults." Elijah caressed my shoulder, holding me. "I just want you to make the right decision. You're a good kid, and I love you as if you were my brother. I'm here for you, and I never want you to forget that!"

Secretly, my heart liquefied by the sentiments and passion I detected by his genuine declaration. Reaching for his hand, I held it against my chest, after which, Elijah leaned forward, kissing the top of my head. "Thank you" I stated.

"You're welcome. I know you're in pain, and I hope our time together will help erase the hurt." Elijah whispered in my ear, "You have been dealt a heavy blow with two parents who take your love for granted, abusing you at every chance they get. You're searching for appreciation but have yet to find the respect you deserve." My body shuddered as his thoughts and wishes enveloped my soul. "Are you OK?" he asked.

"Yes," I answered. "Thank you for spending so much time with me."

"I'll always be here for you."

"I know."

"Good, now go to sleep." Elijah held me for the rest of the night. Secured in his arms, I fell into a deep coma, drowned by the ideas of a man who sincerely cherished my existence, with no agenda, simply pure affection and a will to supervise my direction in life. How could I have been so lucky he found me that faithful day?

For the next few days we hiked and rode our bikes around the valley floor, weaving in and out between the lush green trees. We experienced the majesty of nature, its creatures, and the beauty of this mighty planet God created. Standing next to the tallest, mightiest trees on earth—the sequoias—I never imagined something so huge in my life. And I listened to the roar of Yosemite Falls plunging strong and powerful down onto the valley floor. We stood at its base; its mist sprayed our bodies, refreshing our spirits.

We continued our nightly games of Sorry, played cards, and talked about every topic that popped into our heads. Elijah exposed me to the best experience ever; I could not thank him enough for the time he had given me the last few days. The bond between us held firm, and with each moment spent together, we sealed it more than ever. As we moved forward, our friendship would evolve to a new chapter, new beginnings, and new adventures.

CHAPTER 9

WHEN ELIJAH PICKED up the receiver, I cried hysterically, barely able to form the words when he asked what was wrong. "I need to get out of here!" I screamed.

The lurking monster hurled from its hideout, unleashing its wrath on everyone in its path. A young child's opinion silenced by an unforgiving soul who stymied any thoughts that were unlike its own. The altercation between the monster and me lasted for nearly an hour, and for the first time, I wanted to lay a hand against my mother, the she-devil!

This had been the most violent outbreak to date: a stern slap across the face, a potted plant thrown, a scuffle resulting in tossed furniture, and phrases no mother or son should ever speak. As much as I wanted to love my mother, she made it difficult with every passing day. I wanted her love, but no matter how I tried, it simply wasn't good enough. What demons could she possibly hold deep in her subconscious, causing her to hate so bitterly? I pleaded on the other end of the phone for Elijah to release me from my perdition. He suggested I wait for him at his Hollywood hideout while he handled the situation.

Lying across the bed, I franticly waited at Elijah's bungalow for over three hours. The pain and hurt etched the guilt I held deep within, obviously unable to remove the events that played out earlier in the day. I wanted to hurt my mother; I wanted her to feel the distress she had driven into us for so many years. Leaning to check the time, I noticed it was half past seven.

A month had passed since Elijah and I returned from our camping trip to Yosemite. It was the middle of July and a typical summer day in Los

Vance N. Smith

Angeles. The downward rush of air from the ceiling fan attempted to cool my body from the brazing heat. I removed my shirt, leaving only red nylon gym shorts. Having left the house in such a hurry, I did not bother changing my clothes, ordering Vivian to wait in my car while I made the call to Elijah. After he and I spoke, I drove to my aunt's house where Vivian would stay until the monster retreated to its lair.

Sadly, our long-held family secret began to boil to the surface. Recently, my mother's tirades had increased. It appeared that whenever my father came around my mother went ballistic, arguing about anything and everything from the money my father gave, to not being there for his family, to leaving her alone to care for the brats they conceived—hateful words that made a lasting impression. Vivian and I felt trapped in the middle, and the reason they fought so bitterly. And until this day, I could not comprehend how they initially got together. They were polar opposites of one another, and to hear my mother tell her story, she was the cat's meow in her youth! Every man wanted and lusted after her, and she could have any man she wanted—yet she chose my dad. The one man she claimed never truly fulfilled her needs. How does one go from wanting and having everything to a supposed life beneath oneself? I wished she would have walked into her closet, found a coat hanger, and ended my life as so many other women did with unwanted pregnancies back in the day. I surmised her life had not lived up to her hopes and dreams, and because of this, she retaliated, taking her pain out on others. So many thoughts filled my mind that I found it difficult to concentrate. And for a split second, I wanted to end my own existence—end it right now, right here—since no one would notice.

I lay with my body stretched lengthwise across Elijah's king-size bed. The sounds of children playing in the yard next door consumed my quiet sanctuary. Finally, Elijah's vehicle pulled into the driveway. A few moments later, the front door opened.

"Wilson!" Elijah yelled.

"I'm in the bedroom."

Battlefields

Elijah walked through the bedroom door with a weary expression. "What the hell happened?"

"I don't know," I said, rising from my reclined position to face Elijah. "My dad came by...I guess to drop off the child support. Vivian was in her room playing or whatever. I was in my room watching TV. Everything was cool; they seemed to be getting along. My father had been over for about an hour, and they appeared to be getting along just fine. But you know... the funny thing...he never came to my room. I said hello when he arrived and that was it."

Elijah moved closer, standing next to the bed.

"After about an hour they began to argue. I'm not sure why, but it quickly escalated. I came out of my room to see what was going on. My mom stood next to my father screaming; he tried to get away, but she would not allow him to leave. The things that came out of her mouth were indescribable. She demeaned my father in any way she could, and he simply took it! When he finally left, she told my sister and me dinner was ready. It was as if nothing happened, life simply continued."

I paused for a moment, catching my breath, before I continued.

"Vivian sat at the dinner table telling some childish story about some girl in school. While standing at the stove, my mother began criticizing Vivian, telling her she was stupid. Kids with their silly notions got on her last nerve," she barked. "Making a vain attempt to protect Vivian, I told my mom it was not a fair statement because Vivian had not agreed with the girl but was simply retelling a story. Suddenly my mom drew back and began yelling and cursing me out. I felt threaten, so I defended myself. We began to argue, and then she got in my face as if she wanted to hit me, and I dared her. Taken aback, my mom knew I was finally standing up to her. She made a fist, drawing her hand, waving as if she wanted to punch me, and before I knew it, she slapped me so hard I thought I was in some crazy cartoon with birds and stars swirling around my head! That's when I picked up a plant and threw it across the room. If I hadn't, I would have hit her! I've never felt that way before, and if I hadn't thrown that plant, I would have knocked her ass out!"

Elijah reached out, placing a hand on one of the bedposts. "You did the right thing. Hitting your mom would have been a big mistake."

"I know, but I wanted to, and I hate myself for even thinking of it," I said, agreeing with Elijah, "and the words from her mouth were so hateful."

"You should not have argued with her. You know your mom is not well; you should have walked away."

"That's easy for you to say! You don't have to deal with all the drama. She's the adult; she should be the one to show restraint. Living in that house, I feel like the life is being strangled out of me, never knowing what's going to happen next. When I tried to leave the kitchen, she followed, yelling and screaming, then she pushed me, and that's when we started to scuffle. I tried to push her off, but she wouldn't let go. Vivian trailed behind, trying to help, but then my mother knocked her into the side table, breaking a lamp."

"I'm sorry you had to experience that, and I've had a long, detailed conversation with your mother. I'm certain she didn't appreciate me coming over, demanding she behave in a more appropriate manner, and if she didn't, I would take the issue further, pressing charges against her," Elijah said as he sat beside me. My left leg was folded under my right, and he placed his hand on my knee. "You will stay here for a few days, until she comes to her senses."

I placed my hand on top of Elijah's. "Thank you...what would I do without you?"

He smiled. "I told you I'm here for you, and I meant that."

"I know," I remarked, caressing the top of his hand.

Elijah gently stroked my knee. "Well...are you hungry?" he asked, as he casually slid his hand down the length of my leg, sending chills straight up my calf and thigh. My body quivered under his touch. Elijah had always been affectionate, but never in this manner; I was confused, though I welcomed the attention. His hand traveled upward, stopping midway along my thigh. He stared, awaiting approval. I closed my eyes suggesting I enjoyed the sentiment. Instead, he retracted his intentions, patting my thigh, and stood from the bed. "What do you want to eat?" he asked.

In a dreamlike state, I answered, "I don't care...I could eat anything!"

Battlefields

Elijah leaned forward kissing my forehead. "I'll grab something quick from one of the fast-food joints, make yourself comfortable."

"I will…I need to take a shower."

"You know where everything is, help yourself." When he turned away, I vaguely suspected he was aroused. *Am I seeing things?* I questioned, watching him leave the room. I heard the front door shut then the start of his engine. I returned to my reclined state, contemplating Elijah's subtle actions. My thoughts made my head dizzy, trying to understand the craziness of this life. Did the man I've known for the last year make a pass at me? A married man with two infant children! What a strange menagerie of sorts he kept— a devoted wife, kids, and a gay teenager.

Jumping into the shower, cleansing off the day's events, I dismissed the idea. After refreshing my body, I returned to the bedroom, flipping through channels. I had hoped to find something worth watching. Resting on top of the sheets, wearing nothing more than boxer shorts, I wanted to test Elijah's true intentions—would he follow through with his subtle advance?

The idea of Elijah and I intimate flooded my manhood with excitement. Immediately, I was ready for some one-on-one, man-to-man adult deeds. Just when I reached down to stroke my swollen flesh, Elijah's vehicle pulled into the driveway. Quickly, I forcibly tucked my manhood between my thighs.

Entering the living room, Elijah called out, "Wilson, I'm back…I bought a pizza. I hope you're cool with that."

"I love pizza…you know that! Give me a minute, and I'll be right out."

"All right, but hurry before it gets cold."

"OK!" I answered, unable to get my erection to settle down, as the thought of Elijah had me so aroused it stood at full attention. Quickly, I entered the bathroom, hoping cold water would do the trick. Ultimately, I joined Elijah, taking a seat at the table. "I called my job, saying I would need a few days off for personal reasons."

"I think that was a good idea; it gives you time to readjust," Elijah said, taking a bite of his pizza.

"I just need some time to gather my thoughts, knowing I will have to return home. Honestly, I wish I didn't have to. I wish I had somewhere else to go."

"I wish you could stay with me, but I know Belinda wouldn't have it. She's fond of you but would not want to take on another mouth to feed. Not right now, Belinda's Mom has been ill, requiring quite a bit of her time in Las Vegas."

"So, that's how you've been able to spend so much time with me. She's been in Vegas!"

Elijah smiled, staring down at his glass of cola. "Something like that," he stated quietly.

"And the simple fact you like having me around."

"What makes you so sure of that?"

"Because I know—I'm smart enough to know what's up." *He's not gonna get off that easy. You make a pass at me, you better be ready to deal with the consequences.*

Elijah sat back in his chair with a quizzed expression. "Is that right?"

"That's right! Never underestimate the kid; I know more than you think I do."

Elijah smirked, clearly amused. "For the first time I think you have me speechless," he said, reaching for his soda.

"Not you," I asserted, picking up another slice of pizza.

Elijah nestled into his chair, wiping sauce from his lips. "You're much older than your years, childlike and manlike all rolled into one."

"I'll take that as a compliment," I said, swallowing a mouthful of food before I spoke. "Can I ask you a question?"

"Sure."

"Why did you get married?"

Elijah immediately choked on his pizza. "What kind of question is that?"

"Just a question, so answer," I insisted.

"I married Belinda because I loved her," Elijah answered but was clearly puzzled.

Battlefields

"Interesting," I remarked.

"What is that supposed to mean?"

"It was just a comment, don't get all crazy."

Elijah leaned forward, staring, and I mean hard, struggling to get into my head, hoping to dissect the thoughts I held. "OK," he remarked, hesitantly.

Gotcha, I thought. *I just fucked him up!* "I'm finished, and you look a bit astonished. I'm going to watch TV," I stated, excusing myself from the table, heading for the bedroom. Elijah remained seated, stunned, not knowing what hit him.

I positioned myself on top of the covers, and again I flipped through channels, hoping to find something worthwhile to watch. Finally, I stumbled on an old Bette Davis flick, *Now, Voyager.*

After about an hour, Elijah entered, taking a seat at the foot of the bed. Glancing over his shoulder, he appeared nervous—I sensed he was consumed with plenty of thoughts swirling through his brain. Returning my focus, I continued watching the movie, propped up with three large pillows cradling my upper torso. Elijah sat silently staring at the television.

The sun began to set with the heat of the day subsiding. The room darkened by the sun fading below the landscape, allowing the light of the television to cast a bright glow against the walls. The ceiling fan whirled, creating a cool downward breeze throughout. Casually, I ran my hand across my chest, slightly caressing my left nipple, completing the motion with an understated movement, not to draw obvious attention. I placed a small pillow upon my lap, shielding my rigid erection.

Elijah appeared flustered then headed for the bathroom where I heard him starting up the shower. After about twenty minutes he reemerged wearing only old sweat pants cut into shorts; the sight of him was simply breathtaking. Elijah coolly strolled around the foot of the bed, not once taking his eyes off mine. I observed his slog, swinging back and forth as he walked. I pretended not to notice, but the visual proved more than I could stand. I wanted him more than ever, and I wanted him now. I needed him to take me away, lifting me to a place I've never experienced. I required feeling loved by him, and after what I endured earlier in the day, the need was greater than it had been before.

Elijah sat along the edge of the mattress, applying lotion to his legs and arms, and the rest he placed upon his face. With his back toward me, I studied his every move, from the way he applied the lotion to the way he stretched his body. Each movement caused his muscles to dance in unison; I stared enthralled by the rippling effect his muscles created.

When I resumed my attention to the movie, Paul Henreid placed two cigarettes in his mouth. One for Bette and one for him—then lit them both, a smoke between friends before they said their final good-byes—a romantic gesture of ill-fated lovers.

Elijah turned in my direction before lying against the headboard. "What are you watching?"

"*Now, Voyager* with Bette Davis," I answered.

"I've seen it before, good flick," he nervously replied. When he spoke, I could smell the fresh mint of toothpaste.

"Yes, it is, so be quiet so I can finish watching the movie," I remarked, glaring back.

"Fine," he said sarcastically. He repositioned, reaching for a book on the nightstand, and flicked on the lamp. We lay still, with the bright light of the television set flickering against the walls of the room. His long limbs stretched laterally next to mine, our bodies mere inches apart. Putting on his glasses, Elijah began reading some nondescript book of fiction. Silently, I laughed because of his intense behavior. His nerves were not in check, and I'm sure he had no clue how obvious he was. I sensed he was planning something, certain the pass he made earlier had something to do with his dubious behavior.

I had gone down that road with Alex, although I had no clue he was involved with someone else. Well, maybe I should have known by the way he sneaked me into his apartment each night I came around, or by the evasive way Alex spoke about his so-called friend. Who was he anyways? How long did he know him? How long had they been roommates? I guess, I

Battlefields

should have known, but at the time, it was all about me getting a nut, nothing more, nothing less!

Now, I was treading new, yet familiar territory, fighting for the love and affection of a married man. A man who would never be totally mine, or possibly he wanted me all along, and his wife was just a roadblock we would have to face at some point.

I watched Bette pine for a man she could never have, as the Hollywood classic played on. In the same predicament, I longed for an individual who had commitments that would be devastating for all involved.

Purposely, I lay in nothing more than boxer shorts, taunting him into making another move. I touched my body seductively, licking my lips, though never in a noticeable way. I played him like a keen game of Chess seducing Elijah the best I knew how, continuing to act the victim of abuse. I gathered that he assumed in my weak moment that I was prepared for the taking. Except, I wanted him to want me. I wanted him to feel that he was the one in control. Little did he know—I was not an ordinary seventeen-year-old boy. My needs were far greater than his, and I had yearned for a man's touch for over a year now.

I stretched my six-foot-three frame with both hands placed at my boxers; my right thumb innocently caught the waistband, pulling it down, exposing the outline of my pubic hairs. My body shook, releasing all the tension built up during the day. Returning the small pillow to my midsection, I placed my right hand across my chest, softly fondling my left nipple. In my peripheral vision, I sensed Elijah squirm, certain he watched my every move.

Paul Henreid replayed the cigarette scene again at their final farewell at Bette's home, when he decided to leave his neglected daughter to her care. A huge gesture of forbidden love the two had for one another. A sign of the times when love and marriage were a sacred bond; you stayed and dealt with your issues no matter what. Unlike the world today, once it became too hard, you said, "Fuck it," and left, forgetting about the children and the vows to love one another until death do us part. Today's world was all about me and not at all about you. Life had become so complicated with all the misguided notions people placed upon themselves.

I guessed I was no better than the rest. Because at that very moment, it was all about what I wanted, and I did not give a fuck how it affected anyone else. My desires far outweighed the opinions of anyone who felt I was being disrespectful. I really didn't care. He made the move, and I was going to make sure he followed through with what he started. I knew my plan worked because he became increasingly anxious as the evening drew on. Growing restless, Elijah placed the book onto the nightstand when the movie end credits appeared.

"Is your movie finally over?"

"Yes, but you could see that," I said as I sat alongside the bed, slipping my feet into a pair of slippers.

"Where are you going?" Elijah asked.

"I'm going to brush my teeth then make up the couch, so I can get some sleep." I headed for the bedroom door.

"Why are you going to bed so early?" he remarked.

"It's eleven o'clock!" I said as I walked to the bathroom.

"I thought maybe we could talk a bit."

"Yeah, sure," I stated, flipping on the bathroom light switch. Then I thoroughly brushed my teeth, leaving my mouth as fresh tasting as possible. When I returned, Elijah had turned off the television, and the radio played smooth urban jazz.

Walking into the room, I asked, "What's this?"

"What do you mean?" he questioned.

"This, the music and all, I thought you wanted to talk?" I said, continuing to play dumb and naïve.

"Oh, that...I just wanted some background music while we talked. Come here and have a seat." Elijah patted a spot on the bed next to him.

I went along, propping myself alongside him. "What do you want to talk about?"

"You...us," Elijah stated.

Wow, that was quick! I thought. "What about us?"

Battlefields

He placed his hand on my thigh, and immediately my body fell limp. His touch radiated throughout my entire frame and flesh. He moved his hand ever so gently down to my knee—my eyes followed, watching his hand maneuver along my skin. "You know I love you?" Elijah remarked.

"And I love you as well," I said, lifting my eyes to his. "What do you want from me?"

"I...I...don't know." Elijah found himself stammering over his words.

"I think you do," I interjected.

He continued caressing my leg, his head lowered, unable to face me directly. "I'm ashamed of the thoughts I have."

"Really...why is that?"

"Why are you making this so hard?" he replied.

"I'm not making anything hard for you." I looked directly into his eyes. "You know what you want."

"I do...but I..."

"But what?" I asked, slithering down, resting my head on the pillow. His hand skimmed up my thigh, slightly raising the bottom of my boxers. "What do you want, Elijah?" I murmured.

"I want you," he remarked, leaning forward.

I placed my hand upon his, directing it around the inside of my thigh. I sighed from the gentleness of his touch that electrified my senses. "Go for it...you know you want to," I whispered.

"I do," he responded in a quivering voice, twisting his torso in my direction.

He paused, positioned his large hand to my cheek, and carefully caressed my lower lip. I reached for his waist, drawing him in, his lips mere inches from mine. When he exhaled, I inhaled the heat of his breath. Elijah leaned closer, our lips touched with the softness of a feather. He trembled when our mouths joined for the first time, still withholding a kiss. I seized him tighter; his stiffened rod pressed against mine; our bodies intertwined. My fingertips followed an invisible line up the middle of his back, causing him to arch and tense, clinching his jaw in pleasure. His eyes closed as indulgence surrounded and consumed him. Elijah's body felt firm, rock solid, yet smooth and comforting, setting my soul in a blaze of fiery passion.

Reaching around his shoulders, I pulled him closer, wanting to taste the lips I longed to kiss. I gave him all I had, all that I knew. We kissed like a powerful hurricane, at its core calm and quiet, with a perimeter of raged emotions uncontrolled by nature. Our tongues tangled, the sensations fueled by lust and desires unleashed with rapid-fired sparks. Our bodies twisted, hands roamed, searching every inch of new, unexplored waters.

Elijah suddenly stopped, lifting himself onto his knees. A warm glow filled the room—as I lay, my breath heavy and beads of sweat formed on my temples. Elijah guided his hand around the contour of my stomach. "You are so handsome," he said, speaking soft and sensual. "I've wanted you since the first day I laid eyes on you," he confessed, reaching for my boxers and carefully pulling them down. I lifted my legs, bending my knees for easy removal. My exposed manhood stood at full attention. It throbbed, pulsating to the point I thought it would explode. Elijah directed his hands down the length of my legs, slowly and methodically, calculating every move with intentions to inflame every sensation within my young flesh. Each touch caused my body to squirm in delight; my back bowed by lightning bolts shot in swift succession.

In Alex, I believed he loved me—a young mind's gallant notion. However, with Elijah, he opened a door, liberating aspirations I did not know existed. Elijah slid his tongue along the inner portion of my thigh, up the right, down the left. Covering my face, my body shook from the unbelievably erotic sensation; unable to fathom that such a simple oral manipulation would send my insides into a tizzy, and wanting to scream in sheer gratification. His exploration moved to my stomach with gentle kisses along the way up my torso until he reached my left nipple, placing his hands to my arms, pinning them against the bed. I did not resist. I wanted Elijah to show me the way to ecstasy. Paying close attention to each nipple, Elijah's tongue licked, circled, and sucked. My mind raced to renewed ideas of happiness I longed for.

Battlefields

The idea of having Elijah in my arms replaced the hungers I dreamt of over the past year. I hungered for a man so long that I had dismissed the concept. Yet, on this night, it was real; it was my reality. It was right, and I made sure I pleased him the best I knew how.

Elijah lifted his head, "Are you OK?" he asked.

"I'm great," I mumbled. "You have no idea how good you're making me feel."

"It's my pleasure," he remarked, searching intently into my eyes, asking for approval.

"You're doing just fine."

Elijah smiled. Then he placed my arm over my head and proceeded to suck and munch my armpit, and to my surprise, it made my eyes bulge with excitement. Another point for him, an area I had no idea would provide such pleasure. My eyes rolled, and I bit my lower lip while his tongue washed my pit clean. After which, he traced down the inner side of my upper arm, sending shockwaves throughout.

"Ooh…" I surrendered and pleaded. "What are you doing to me?"

He smirked, not missing a beat. I was his playground, and Elijah made good use of all the equipment.

Reaching for my stiffened flesh, I began to stroke, but Elijah pulled back my hand.

"No…not yet…let me do all the work," he insisted. "Just lay back and enjoy."

I respired all the demons that haunted me—far too long. My knight rode in, rescuing me from the beast that held me captive. The walls came crashing down when he beat the monster from its lair.

Elijah lay on top of my young body, his weight heavy, though I felt safe. His smooth, dark chocolate skin against mine melted as one. My arms wrapped around him for security; his eyes peered deep, entranced and unforgiving.

As night grew into early morning, our marathon lovemaking lasted well into the wee hours. Endlessly we kissed, his taste sweet and masculine. Our tongues tangled, dueling for dominance. Elijah explored every inch of my body, exposing new erogenous zones I had no clue would drive my ass insane. From sucking my toes to licking my armpits, from the slight sensuous touch of my inner thighs, to the attention paid to my round, firm ass. Never in my wildest dreams had I imagine such sensations in those areas. I emerged changed, renewed, reawakened, and hopelessly in love.

I awakened the next morning sprawled naked across his bed and partially covered by a sheet. Lying flat on my stomach, I remained weakened by the intense erotic sessions I had experienced the night before, drugged by the force of nature. Opening one eye slowly, trying to gather my bearings, I felt exhausted, but then the first and only thing on my mind was, *am I dreaming? Did I actually spend the night enraptured with Elijah?* Glancing over, I found him sprawled against my flesh. Elijah's nude body lay parallel to mine with one arm draped across my waist. His snoring rocked the room, reverberating throughout. I laid my head against the pillow, silently watching Elijah shake the walls with his lion's roar. I smiled, staring at his parted lips, with a trickle of saliva drizzling down in the corner. Elijah flinched when I reached to wipe his mouth, turning his head with a sigh. For a short minute, his heavy breathing stopped, only to return with a thunderous growl. *How did I manage to sleep with that racket?* I wondered. Somehow I managed, because before I knew it, I was fast asleep once again, drowned by memories of the night before.

CHAPTER 10

WITH THE PASSING of summer, and the holidays rapidly approaching, my relationship with Elijah had grown to a level I wasn't prepared to handle. My initial fear presented itself to be true. He was blessed with a life of his own, one that evidently did not include myself. Elijah had his wife and kids to take care of, yet he relegated me as his playmate on the side. My discontent was apparent to me only; I was the one with the problem. Elijah led his life without a care in the world. He had everything, which left me alone to groom my own wishes and aspirations, and as long as my dreams did not interfere with his, we were cool. The problem being, I was a seventeen-year-old senior in high school involved with a man almost twice my age, a man who would never be completely mine. In the end, Elijah had not entirely saved me from one hell but managed to add another.

While my dire existence in View Park marched on, my relationship with the she-devil soured to unfiltered resentment. We hadn't uttered a word to one another unless we absolutely had to; I stayed out of her way, and she stayed out of mine. As difficult as it was, I managed to accept the truth of my life. I was destined, it seemed, to be constantly challenged by the nonexistence of normalcy everyone else took for granted. My choices in life rebuked any resemblance of happiness to date. My mother abandoned me the day of our big blowout, and my dad remained elusive. And what I thought would be bliss with Elijah was simply a continued lack of attention that I had already become accustomed to.

For the remainder of the summer, our affair attested a reserved heaven. Elijah's wife, Belinda, spent quite a bit of time in Las Vegas most weekends, and whenever she was away, he was with me. What made the situation great was that it helped with my problem at home. Every weekend and some weeknights I spent at Elijah's Hollywood hideaway, regardless if he was with me or not. Appreciating the time away from my mom helped me to realize what I needed to do after graduation. There was no doubt I would have to leave the dwelling I called home. With no idea how I would make that happen, the idea of moving out scared the shit out of me, since my earlier choices left a lasting negative impression. Trust was becoming a major issue for me too, since every person I had placed faith in turned their backs on me, left alone to wade in tempestuous waters.

Undoubtedly, I loved Elijah and prayed our relationship would mature into a healthy arrangement. I would have done anything for him, including building my life around his. Yes, the sex was phenomenal, and at every opportunity we practiced the fine art of lovemaking, where our bodies fought for supremacy. In the end, I succumbed to the battle. He had taken my cakes, my sweet treats, and my dignity. I was not complaining, but I had given up the goods with nothing to show for it. And as the summer continued, our encounters became nothing less than sexual, and the honeymoon was over.

Pressing forward, as I always had, I moved on without looking back, and with each battle scar I gained strength, bouncing back stronger than before. At such a young age, I had seen the world through the eyes of someone twice my years. Reduced to a concubine of sorts—not wanting to sound bitter, just well aware of what I had become. Understandably, I was not his equal, and he made sure I resided in my place, but with that said, it was a far better life than I had in View Park.

Another year passed, and I turned eighteen. The winter bowed to spring with a sense of renewal. The conclusion of my senior year was uneventful, except for my lurid affair with a married city police officer. Many would contest it was a simple case of child molestation—in my semimatured opinion, certainly not! It would be impossible to argue my case; you'd just have to take my word for it. I knew what I was getting myself into, with no

Battlefields

intentions of exposing my secret for fear of us being separated, albeit my relationship was an unhealthy union leading to more self-confusion and doubt. Thinking back, my only concern was being freed from the beast that held me captive.

With the class of 1980, I graduated with honors and a member of the top percentile students in my school. Academically I was on my road to success, with my sight set on the prize ahead. I could not allow my mother or Elijah to stand in my way, having been accepted to UCLA to study architecture, slated to start in the fall on a full scholarship. My future was bright, but there was one last piece of the puzzle I still had to figure out. How was I to leave my prison cell in View Park? I had not considered that situation until a new proposition was presented to me. Once again, my sugarcoated white knight rode in saving the day. Seduced by him, I obliged his offer to move into his Hollywood hideout, advancing one step closer to an idea of romance, fleeing the encampment in which I lived for eighteen years.

I felt I had everything...or so I thought.

CHAPTER 11

THE FOLLOWING SUMMER sped along with life reacting in kind. It was the end of August, a typical, hot early afternoon in the City of Angels. Lost in contemplation, I pondered the reality of my existence, sullen by temptations and regrets. Around the time I moved out of my mother's house, I was also promoted to cashier and transferred to a grocery store closer to the Hollywood cottage where I now resided. I was proud of my comfortable life, living rent-free with financial help from Elijah. I saved my money, paid my bills on time, and did not splurge on material things I did not need. These were lessons instilled by Elijah, but nonetheless, he made sure I had everything I ever wanted. Consequently, it came at a price, being that Elijah controlled every aspect of my life.

Two days earlier, I received a call from Sedona saying she wanted to share some amazing news. The information was so great; she did not want to discuss it over the phone. We agreed to meet at Moody Blu Café for lunch. Ecstatic I would spend some much-needed quality time with Sedona. So there I sat, waiting patiently for her arrival. Truthfully, since dating Elijah, I hadn't seen Sedona all that often. Subsequently, after graduation I focused my energy on building a relationship with Elijah and my pending admission to UCLA. However, I missed my childhood friend, and I hoped this would be the start of our reconnection.

A slim-built Caucasian waiter dressed in black jeans, a white button-down shirt, and a food-stained apron wrapped around his waist arrived with an iced tea. Politely, I thanked him, grasping for the drink and settling into my chair while scrutinizing the so-called beautiful people circulating along Sunset Boulevard.

Battlefields

Moody Blu Café was one of my favorite eateries I frequented for breakfast and, on occasion, lunch. It was an eclectic establishment with the earthy smells of homemade breads, pies, and other goodies filling the dining area with intoxicating aromas. I sat alone, street side, next to an expansive floor-to-ceiling picture window, waiting on Sedona for lunch. I had not seen much of her since my move to Hollywood a few months back.

I sat sipping my ice-cold drink, toiling with ideas of grandeur. In my adolescent mind, I sought a dream life, a life fulfilled with the perception of Elijah providing the needs I could only wish for. You see, my move to Hollywood indeed was a blessing, but not without baggage. Elijah ruled with an iron fist, demanding I inform him of my every move and whereabouts. Keeping a close eye on where I spent my time, who called, and who my friends were. Sedona was not an issue, but any male friend was another matter altogether. At first I felt the arrangement was a sign of love and devotion, but it quickly became a burden of freedom lost to another individual. Having escaped a maximum prison cell to a place of lesser confinement, I had to admit the conditions were not what I had in mind. I wanted the freedom to do as I pleased, to be loved unconditionally, and I knew I deserved more. Yet, I still received a lackluster existence.

Watching the room, I noticed lovers holding hands, gazing starry eyed—looking innocent and free from doubt. Lowering my head, I turned toward the window as my emotions raced full force. Holding my head back with eyes closed, pressing all indiscretions from view, I finally opened my eyes to find Sedona bursting through the door of the café, pausing to catch her bearings. I waved my hand to gain her attention. She noticed, smiled, and waved in return.

Once she reached the table, I immediately pulled her into an embrace, wrapping my long arms around her waist. I held tight, not realizing how much I missed her until that moment.

"I missed you so much," I whispered with my face pressed against hers.

"I missed you as well," she said. When she pulled away, I sensed she was a bit taken aback by my reaction. "Are you OK?" she asked with a hesitant grin.

"I'm good, just happy to see you! It's been a while since we last saw one another." Holding her hand, I motioned to the chair across from mine. "Have a seat."

"Thank you," she responded. As I pulled out her chair, she turned, giving a look of a thousand questions. "You look good. How has everything been since you moved from your mother's house?"

"It's been good...everything is good. I've been working in a new store located at Melrose and Vine."

"OK, I know where that is. How long have you been there?" she asked.

"I transferred two weeks after graduation...right after the move." I fiddled with the linen napkin laid across my lap, consumed by scrambled thoughts filling my subconscious.

Sedona's gaze was of concern, complete with the uncertainty of her intuition. "I see...you seem a little tense. How's your mother?"

"I guess she's doing all right." I did not want to speak about my mother. She was the last individual I wanted to place any energy on.

"Have you spoken with her?" she asked.

"Not since I left the house; I've only spoken with Vivian," I remarked, sinking into my chair.

"I'm at a loss; I knew you had issues with your mother, but I had no idea it was that bad." Sedona studied my expression, hoping for answers to her questions. "You were distant the past year, and I must admit, I was concerned but didn't want to push the issue." Sedona scanned the dining room before she continued. "You were so different and distant."

"I know...I've been a loner. I've just been busy."

In reality, I did not want to expose my involvement with Elijah. For some, being gay meant you inadvertently pushed people away for fear of being found out. Not knowing how they would react teaches you to simply distance yourself. It was much easier to deal that way than face the truth. I hated that I was not strong enough to deal with the possibilities of rejection. My personality had so many facets—one minute I was strong and manipulative, then the next, withdrawn and reserved. Many misunderstood and found me hard to figure out. But the past year had been a whirlwind

Battlefields

of emotions, starting with Isaiah slowly drifting from my circle after the disagreement regarding Alex, to my developing affair with Elijah, and then culminating with the dramatic confrontation with my mother. All of this forced me to realize I had to depend on myself. Others would hurt me every chance they got, from my family, right down to the ones that claimed they loved me.

"Trust me, Sedona, I'm doing fine. I just needed time to grow."

"You know you can talk to me about anything. I should have been there for you."

"You had your own life to lead, your projects, church, singing, and traveling to Oklahoma to spend time with your grandparents. I had way too much drama going on, and I had to work that out on my own."

"Have you?" Sedona questioned, as the waiter walked toward our table.

"What do you want to drink?" I asked.

"An iced tea is fine," Sedona said as she unfolded her napkin, placing it over her lap.

"What can I get you to drink?" the waiter asked, standing with his hands clasped together.

"The young lady will have an iced tea. But could you give us a few minutes to decide what we want to eat?"

"Sounds great, I'll return with your drink shortly." The waiter quickly turned, walking toward the lunch counter. My eyes followed until he disappeared behind double swinging doors.

"So...I'm going to ask my question again...have you worked things out?" Sedona asked, staring directly into my eyes.

"I have...I feel as if a massive weight has lifted from my shoulders," I responded, taking a sip of my tea, targeting my eyes away from hers. When I returned my attention, her focus had not been broken.

"I see..." she remarked, placing her hand on mine.

"What are you getting at?" I knew she had something on her mind, she just would not say it. Tightening my jaw, not wanting Sedona to pursue the issue, I changed the subject altogether. "So...what's the exciting news you wanted to tell me?"

Sedona's demeanor changed as if I'd flipped a switch. She leaned forward, suggesting she did not want everyone in the room to hear her big news. "Remember the man from church who said he was a record executive and wanted to meet with me?"

"Vaguely, wasn't that a few months back?"

"Yes, before graduation. Anyway, my father and I have been meeting with him, and he wants to sign me to a recording contract!" Sedona held in a silent scream as she blurted out the news.

"What! He was legit?" I said, in shock

"Yes! Can you believe it?"

"Not really...I mean...I knew you could do it! But to actually know someone who is a recording artist? Yes, I'm a bit taken aback!"

"You don't know how bad I wanted this, singing is all I ever cared about. There's been nothing else I envisioned myself doing," Sedona said, trying not to make a scene.

"I'm excited for you—that is some amazing news! Wow, I'm at a loss for words." I reclined deep into my chair, smiling from ear to ear. Her dream finally came true. Standing from my chair, I said, "Come here, I need to give you a huge bear hug!"

"Thank you!" she said as I hugged her, then we settled back into our chairs.

I automatically reached for one of the menus, even though I ordered the same thing every time I came for lunch. "What do you want to eat?" I asked.

"I think I'll have a salad."

"I'll have my usual—burger and onion rings."

The young waiter approached our table. "Here's your drink and a refill for you. Are you ready to order?"

"Yes, we are. Sedona, you go first."

"OK, let me have...um, I guess I'll have a Cobb salad."

"And you, sir?"

"I'll have a cheeseburger and onion rings, thank you."

"I'll take those from you," he said, and we handed over our menus. "It shouldn't take too long for your food to arrive."

Battlefields

"Thank you." I smiled toward the waiter then turned my attention back to Sedona. "So...when do you go into the studio?"

"I'm not sure, we still haven't finalized the contract, though I'm hoping soon. I want to see my name in lights! On an album cover! I want it all! I want the fame, the fortune—everything. You know I have talked about this since junior high."

"Yes, you have, and I told you then it would happen."

"Yes, you did, didn't you?" She shyly smiled.

I nodded my head yes. "You'll have everything as long as you work hard for it."

Sedona hesitated for a minute and then blushed. "I met a guy!"

"Oh, really?"

"Yes. I really like him," she said coyly, smiling and biting the corner of her lower lip.

"Well, well...where did you meet him?"

"At the offices of Galaxy Records."

"The dude from your church was an executive of Galaxy Records? You left that valuable bit of information out. What the hell, they're big time! Why didn't I think to ask you what record company was courting you?" I reclined into my chair, processing the information. "Now you're going to tell me the boy you met is Jackson Parker," I remarked sarcastically. Sedona neither denied nor confirmed my accusation, meaning I was correct. I raised my voice an octave higher. "You met Jackson Parker, the biggest music producer in town?"

"Lower your voice, have you lost your mind! I don't want the whole world to know."

"Isn't he married?" I asked.

"I don't know," she snapped.

"I think he's married; you better be careful. You don't want to fuck around with a married man," I said, although I should be the last person speaking on the matter.

"What if he is? I'm not the one breaking up his home," she said matter-of-factly.

"I know I didn't raise you that way," I said, completely stunned by her callous behavior.

"All I'm saying is he came after me. I didn't chase him."

"True, but you allowed it." I shook my head, not wanting her going down the same road I already followed—a road that only leads to heartache. "How far has this gone?"

Sedona frowned. "We've been out a few times."

"A few times! Like twice, three times?"

"Four times."

"Have you given up the goods?"

"What! How could you ask me that question?"

"Easily…have you?"

"No, I haven't!" By her reaction, it was evident Sedona was not pleased by my interrogation, though I did not care, I had to protect her. "You better not give up the goods. He's too damn old for you!"

"He's twenty-five!"

"And you just turned eighteen! He's too old." The hypocrisy of my statement offended even me. I had the nerve to tell someone who they should date, when clearly, I had stepped out of bounds, forging a liaison with a married man far older than the one she hungered over. Backing off my insistence a bit, I said, "I just don't want you to get hurt and lose focus on what you're trying to achieve."

"I know you have my best interests at heart; I promise I will not get hurt." Sedona faked a smile, though she was visibly upset. We sat in awkward silence. What should have been a joyous celebration turned bitter with my behavior and contradictions.

The waiter returned with our food, which could not have come at a better time. "I have one cheeseburger and one Cobb salad, enjoy! Is there anything else I can get you?" The waiter stood with his hands clasped behind his back.

"No, I think we're good for now, thank you." I watched the waiter walk away. I picked up my burger and began to eat. Sedona played with her salad, not really eating any of it. I had deflated all the hope she carried when she

Battlefields

entered the café. I felt bad and knew I had to fix the situation. "You're not going to eat?"

"I'm not hungry," she responded.

Consumed with guilt, I placed my burger onto my plate. "Look...I'm sorry. I should not have said those things to you, and I hope you can forgive me!"

"I forgive you."

"Honest?"

She smirked. "Honest...you just make me so mad sometimes, but I love you anyway. I understand you're only looking out for my best interests."

"I know you do, and I love you too...but friends are supposed to keep one another in check," I stated while swatting my napkin toward her face.

Sedona returned a faint smile.

"Anyway...I am happy for you. You have what you want, and I'm working on my dream, too."

"And you can design my first house high above the ocean, somewhere in Malibu, or maybe I'll move to Montecito. As long as I have a view of the ocean, I'm happy!" Sedona's eyes sparkled once again by the possibly of having her dream become a reality. Finally, she picked up her fork and began eating.

I spent the remainder of the day with Sedona, arriving home around eight that evening. Experiencing a fantastic afternoon, I was thankful to still have a true friend in my life.

Pulling into the driveway, I noticed Elijah's parked car and was surprised because I didn't expect him home that evening. I was concerned but happy I would be able to spend some quality time with the man I loved.

Entering the living room, I could hear the sound of the television coming from the bedroom. I placed my keys on a table next to the door as I called out, "Elijah...I'm home." No answer. "Elijah?" I made my way to the bedroom and found him lying across the bed sleeping. I eased further into the room, not wanting to disturb him from his rest. Slowly, I opened the closet door and quietly removed my clothes. When I lifted my tee shirt over my head, I inadvertently bumped my elbow against the closet door, creating a loud thud.

"Where have you been?" Elijah's voice soared throughout the room. His tone proved menacing and injunctive, not of concern.

"I had lunch with Sedona. What do you mean where was I? I didn't know I had to answer all my whereabouts to you," I said, thoroughly annoyed. He was not going to spoil my good time.

"Yes, lunch, and it's now past eight in the evening. I have every right to ask where you were, whenever I feel like asking!" he said, pointing his finger.

"Doesn't mean I'm gonna give you details just because you ask!"

"You know…you have a smart-ass mouth!" he said, sitting up along the edge of the mattress.

"So I've been told many times before, by you and everyone else!" I turned, heading for the bathroom.

Elijah jumped off the bed, grabbing my arm. "Muthafucka, don't turn your ass away from me when I'm talking to you! Who the fuck do you think you are? You just gonna walk out disrespecting me?" We now stood face-to-face, and I must admit, without a doubt, Elijah intimidated me. Uncertain if it was because of the age difference or what, but at times he scared the hell out of me. He was cold and ominous, and his nostrils flared by the rage he held inside.

"Elijah, what are you doing?" I shouted, snatching my arm away.

"Why do you continue to do this?" He held his head down in shame.

"Do what?" I asked, standing my ground, not allowing him to sense I was afraid.

"I love you so much…I don't want to lose you."

I placed my hand to his cheek. "I'm not going anywhere."

My heart sank deep into the pit of my stomach. His defenselessness was apparent as he broke down. "I'm sorry…I didn't mean to do that."

"It's OK, I know you're under a lot of stress," I remarked. I held him closely in my arms, and I could feel him trembling. "It's gonna be OK."

He begged for forgiveness. I gave in. We made love the rest of the night.

CHAPTER 12

Two weeks before the Christmas holidays, I sat alone, watching the penetrating raindrops pound against the living room windows. On that particular day, I was not in the best of dispositions. The feud between my mother and I had not been resolved; ambiguous if I even wanted to reconcile. Harboring so much hate, distrust, resentment, and hurt, I found it difficult to forgive her.

It was Wednesday, and I was home on break from school, with the day off from work. I was depressed, since I knew Elijah would spend the holidays with his family. Sedona also planned to have dinner with hers. Although I was invited to attend, I did not want to impose once again, since I'd spent Thanksgiving with her family. A price I had to pay for being embroiled in this deceptive relationship; every holiday that rolled around, I celebrated alone.

As much as I despised my parents, I prayed and hoped that circumstances would change for the better, and that somehow they would see the light of day and welcome me home with open arms. I did not expect it to ever happen with my father and was cautiously optimistic with my mother. Even with her psychotic behavior, I still loved her. For the life of me, I could not begin to tell you why. I believed my aunt might have played a part in keeping that aspect of hope alive.

My relationship with my Aunt Lorraine, or Aunt Raine as we called her, was everything I wanted with my mother. She cared for Vivian and me the way our mother should have, keeping a positive attitude toward our welfare, and encouraged us to achieve our dreams in life. After the confrontation last summer, Aunt Raine became our benefactor, often refereeing the many disagreements, sheltering us when we needed space. Vivian began to spend a fair amount of time with our aunt, while my mother slipped further into a deep depression, causing distance from everyone in the family, and even reaching the point where she was forced to take a sabbatical from work. Our family secrets were slowly becoming exposed.

I stared aimlessly through the rain-soaked windows, not watching anything in particular, just waterdrops dripping down along the windowpanes. My heart was as dark as the storm clouds in the sky above. A pain threatened to rip straight to the core of my soul, brought on by the prospect of having the holidays pass without my family by my side. Sentiments burned as if hot coals filled my stomach. How did I get to this place? Why would God allow such pain and misery? How could I move forward to a place of happiness? So many questions inundated my mind, as the rain appeared not to cleanse, but to wreak havoc instead. My downheartedness took over, and my confusion flourished to an unimaginable level. Consequently, I laid my head against the back of the sofa; the cold of the room kissed my body, leaving me frozen in thought.

The ringing of the telephone jolted me from my dreamlike state. I reached for the receiver, answering in a dry, sullen tone. "Hello?"

No answer on the other end.

"Hello, who is this?"

"Wilson."

"Momma?"

"Yes, this is your *mother* calling!" Her voice was filled with irritation and contempt.

"What do you want?" I asked, immediately becoming defensive, clearly not in the mood for any of her nonsense.

"Do I need a reason to call my son?"

"Under normal circumstances, no…but for you to actually pick up the phone and make a call, there's something you want." The phone went silent. "Hello?"

"I'm still here," she answered.

"What do you want, Momma?" My voice filled with agitation.

"No matter what I do, I'm always the ass. The one nobody wants to deal with."

Battlefields

"Yeah, you're always the victim. Poor pitiful you," I remarked.

"You know, you can just fuck yourself. I don't give a fuck!" she yelled.

"I don't know why I even expect anything less from you. I had hoped you would be woman enough to say you were sorry, or simply say…you missed me…that you loved me…or possibly even wanted to see me. But no…you call here with that same condescending attitude you always have, as if the world had somehow done you wrong. All anyone has ever tried to do is make you happy!" I paused. "I can't do this anymore; I love you, but this has to end. All I ever wanted was to hear you say 'I love you'.…I know those words will never, ever leave your mouth! The only thing that flows from your lips is hate and harmful expressions, never the statement 'I love you.' You know, it just dawned on me…I've never actually heard you express that before, no form of affection or compassion. When you were pleasant, it was only from a distance."

Any hope of reconciliation was gone by speaking the words of condemnation. Surprisingly, she did not utter a single word. The silence from her end was deafening. I knew I'd hit a nerve, and for once, she did not have a comeback. I must have shocked the shit out of her, for her not to respond. Then suddenly the receiver went dead.

I did not feel comfortable with what I had said, but sometimes the truth must be spoken. Someone had to say it. For far too long, she ordered everyone around, from my father down to Vivian and me. All the beatings we succumbed to, including the half-empty soda bottle she threw at me, barely missing my head. I finally came to the realization that I would not stand for it any longer. Freed from a demonic dictator, I had narrowly escaped the hell I called home.

Aunt Raine invited me to spend Christmas at her home, though I graciously declined, knowing my mother would attend as well. Elijah was nowhere in sight, and he remained absent until well after the holidays.

As I anticipated, Christmas arrived and I was alone. With the New Year's festivities just around the corner, I expected to be alone again as well.

Fate was a muthafucka!

CHAPTER 13

IN THE INFANCY of adulthood, and having recently celebrated my nineteenth birthday, I excelled in school and was hopelessly in love. With that, a hint of sadness consumed my heart. The state of my melancholy was caused by suppressed happiness, and I was ashamed I allowed my relationship with Elijah to continue. Sedona often quizzed me concerning my whereabouts and to pacify her inquires—I simply made excuses or ignored her altogether; eventually she allowed the matter to drop. I was good at keeping secrets, a talent learned within the James household. However, deceit began to break me. How could I continue keeping this secret from my family and my friends, and when everyone found out, what would they think? How long could I keep this charade going? I could not fathom Elijah losing all he had gained in family or career. Since the day we became a silent couple, I knew our relationship would not stand a chance in hell of lasting; but nonetheless, I cherished every moment we were together. Again, I was hopelessly in fuckin' love!

Spring of 1981

I awakened with Elijah's arm fortified around my waist—how I loved the feel of his warmth. Staring at the man I loved so dearly, a subtle ray of light glimmered across his deep chocolate skin; gently, I caressed his cheek. I was hooked—lovesick and completely devoted. Elijah exposed me to another side of life previously unknown. He taught me the fundamentals, the importance of having a secured financial background and independence. However, the knowledge Elijah offered came with several contradictions,

Battlefields

namely his marriage, him loving a younger man, and his controlling personality. Conclusively, I knew I was lying in the arms of a man who would never be completely mine.

During the last several weeks, Elijah's visitations were reduced to only a few days. But then to my surprise, he arranged some much-needed quality time for us, since Belinda was out of town, tending to her ailing mother. Upon hearing the news, I immediately requested a few days away from work, making myself exclusively available to him.

Having placed a tender kiss to his lips, I watched as Elijah slowly raised one eyelid with a slight smile. "What are you doing?" he asked.

"I believe I was watching you sleep."

"No...I think you just kissed my lips."

"Yeah, I did." I smiled, caressing his face.

"You know I love you," he said shyly.

"I do, and I love you too," I remarked, lying my backside against the pillow. "But where does that leave us?" I asked in a sullen voice.

Elijah reared his head back. "What do you mean?" His intense eyes pierced mine, burning a hole through my soul.

"Elijah...I love you so much, but I hate this arrangement," I said then paused for a moment, gathering my thoughts. "I mean...I understand...I don't know..." I felt silly and couldn't quite collect my feelings.

Elijah rose and gazed into my eyes. "Baby, I understand you want me here all the time...but you know that's not possible." He leaned back and shook his head, looking up at the ceiling. I knew he was displeased, trying to hide his reaction. He sighed. "Will, this has to stop. I have no intention of leaving my wife for you. That will never happen. Besides, how would it look if I just upped and left my wife and kids for another man?"

Ouch...that shit stung, like a muthafuck! I withheld my response, refusing to reveal how much his comment had hurt. "Elijah, we had a good time the last few days; I don't want it to end with you angry." When I reached for him, he turned away infuriated, resting at the edge of the bed.

"I need to get ready," he said, his voice sour and stern.

"You leaving so soon?" I asked nervously.

"Yeah, I need to head home before Belinda returns from Vegas."

"Return home?" I said, surprised, since he led me to believe she was not returning until next week. "When did she change her plans?"

"You must be mistaken; I told you she was returning this weekend. See…you never listen…grow the fuck up!" he stated, heading toward the bathroom.

"Muthafucka, don't speak to me like that!" I said with a raised voice. I didn't want to appear like the child I was.

Stopping dead in his tracks, and without turning in my direction, he said, "What the fuck did you say?"

"Nothin'," I remarked cautiously.

"That's what I thought!" He continued into the bathroom, closing the door slightly. "What the fuck is wrong with you? You have a good goddamn thing here. I gave you your own place. You no longer have to take shit from your crazy-ass momma! Yet, you ride my fuckin' ass, giving me grief all the goddamn time!" In between his rambling, I heard the toilet flush. "I might as well be with my fuckin' wife! Hell, I get enough shit from her. I don't need to hear it from you too. And definitely no gay, fag shit!" Elijah shouted, washing his hands.

I sat in silence; my heart sank with each word surging from his mouth. Deep down I knew he didn't mean it; simply his way of dealing with this thing we had. The stress of the affair affected both of us. It's funny how I handled it far better than he. I sought a happy life, to cook for him, to be the one who cared for his every need—the one he came home to every night. Silly ideas of innocent, fragile love, but certainly I was wise enough to know I didn't want to be the other man, his skeleton hiding in the closet. I wanted to be free, sharing my joy.

Elijah walked back into the room with an apologetic look. "Will, I'm sorry. You didn't deserve that, but you must understand it has to be this way."

"I do, but remember that fag shit the next time you're all up in my ass, muthafucka!" I stated with authority, daring him to say something in return.

Battlefields

He stood still for a minute then slowly moved closer. "You know what, you fuck? Yeah, I'll think about that the next time I'm all up in that ass." Elijah placed one knee on the edge of the bed, leaning close and speaking with a slow, smooth voice, sexually draping me with his words. "You know that shit turns me the fuck on. I like it when you talk shit, trying to be tough like you my equal!" He smirked, gliding his hand across his chest. "Yeah, I fuck that ass of yours damn good, knocking that shit out, and you let me know with every thrust." He grinned, knowing at that moment he had me. "Now roll yo' ass over, so I can hit that shit again before I leave!"

I removed the covers, exposing my bare chest, gently caressing between my thighs. "You want more of this, muthafucka?"

"Hell yeah, you know I do, you nasty fuck," he remarked, licking his lips, sending white-hot lightning bolts throughout my entire body.

"Come and take it then." Elijah loved when I gave him orders. "Come take this shit, and when you do, you better work the hell out of it!"

He laughed. "Damn, you're makin' my dick strong as steel, you nasty fuck. You know that shit turns me the fuck on!"

"Yeah…that's what got your ass sprung!"

"You got that shit right. Now roll your ass over!" he demanded.

"You want these cakes, you gotta work for it," I professed. "Come take this shit!"

He pulled the covers back, exposing all my naked truth. "I see you're ready to be plucked." He grabbed my ankles, pulling me to the foot of the bed. "You know you are beautiful," he confessed, sliding his tongue up my inner thigh and down the other. I released a loud, slow moan. When he reached my foot, he licked, sucked, and massaged, and with that—I gave in. What more could I say?

After Elijah left around ten that morning, I lay in bed whipped, exhausted by the intense lovemaking I'd experienced the last hour and a half. An hour later, I still remained in bed, adorned with a smile across my face—never fulfilled, my body cried for more. Remembering our sweet power session, I thought of how I needed his physique entangled with mine more than ever; images I could not remove would linger the remainder of the day.

While I reminisced, I heard the ringing of the telephone, which removed all contemplations. Reaching for the receiver, I answered, "Hello?"

"Will, what are you doing?" Sedona eagerly asked. "How come you're not in class?"

"I'm not in class on Fridays for the twentieth time!"

"Damn! I just asked a question."

"What do you want, girl?"

"Nothing really, I was hoping you would be available tonight."

"What's going on?"

"Monica is having a party, and I wanted you to go with me"

I was not in the mood for another one of her cousin's parties. Monica always had too many ghetto-ass muthafuckas hanging around, and without a doubt, some shit was sure to go down. At her last gathering, some thug-ass muthafucka stepped on my foot then pushed me into a table because I made a remark. I wanted to beat his ass but knew that was going to be a complete waste of time. The dumb fuck looked like he strolled straight out of prison hours before arriving at the house. Sadly, I let it go. Later that night, the police raided the house because of noise complaints.

"I don't know, after what happened the last time, and I do not feel like having my ass kicked tonight."

Sedona laughed. "Get your tired ass out the damn house! You stay locked up in that bitch and do nothing every weekend."

"I'm cool staying in," I specified, hoping Elijah would drop by. I kept myself available like some whipped puppy. I knew it was a sad state of mind, but that's what you do when you're stupid in love.

"Get out and live, you may find some sweet, young thang...maybe you won't be so damn wound up!"

"I don't need no stank," I said. *I gettin' plenty right here*, I thought.

"Come on!" she demanded.

"I'll think about it."

Battlefields

"Don't do that. I want you to come with me. I haven't seen you in two weeks," Sedona pleaded. "Please…"

"Where's April? How come she's not going with you?"

"She's coming. *Pleaseee*—I want you to go!"

Vacillating a bit before I answered, I finally said, "All right, I'll go, but if those muthafuckas start their shit, we're out!"

"OK, pick me up around seven," Sedona stated without hesitation.

"Why so early?"

"She's having one of her card parties," Sedona answered.

"Oh, hell no…you know I don't play cards," I remarked.

"Stop complaining like a little bitch and be at my house by seven!" she ordered.

"All right, talk with you later."

For the remainder of the day, I continued daydreaming of Elijah. I should have been studying, but he was all I had on my mind. After reflecting and napping for almost an hour, I finally decided to use my time wisely and hit the books. I studied for two hours until another phone call interrupted my flow. "Hello?"

"Hey babe, it's me…what are you up to?"

"I'm studying, how's work?"

"Surprisingly quiet, all the crazy fucks must be hiding out. What are you doing tonight?"

"I'm going out with Sedona and April."

There was a notable silence for a few seconds. "Oh yeah…" By his tone, I sensed he was not at all pleased. "Where are you going?" he asked, then before I could answer he said, "Never mind, I don't wanna know."

"You don't want me to go?"

"No, I don't!" He was unmistakably angered.

"I've already promised Sedona…" I did not want to disappoint him, and then I thought, *why should I allow him to hold me hostage in this house all the time?* "Nah, I promised, I'm not backing out."

"You do what you want." His words were filled with sarcasm.

Vance N. Smith

"What is that supposed to mean?" I interjected. Elijah did not utter another word; however, I could hear his breathing becoming elevated. "Elijah." Still no answer, so I called out again, "Elijah!"

"What!" he stated tensely.

Now, I was aggravated. "What was that supposed to mean?"

"I gotta go! You have fun tonight, and you better not even think of bringing some nigga back to my crib! And I mean that." He slammed down the phone—dial tone.

When I checked the time, I didn't realize I had been studying into the late afternoon. Where had the time gone? It didn't leave much time to find something to wear, get dressed, and arrive at Sedona's by seven o'clock. Funny, Sedona was rarely on time yet hated when you kept her waiting. Walking into the closet, I pulled out my favorite pair of jeans and a crisp, white button-down shirt, and laid them on the bed. Then I hopped into the shower, shaved, combed my hair, splashed on a fresh light-scented cologne, dressed, and was out the door by six ten.

I stopped at a gas station on the way, filling my car with a full tank of gas, and then proceeded to travel down Crenshaw Boulevard to Sedona's parents' home. I arrived at about five to seven, but before I could exit the car, I noticed Sedona was already standing in the doorway waiting.

"Damn girl, you in a hurry? You're never on time," I remarked, getting out of the car and walking around the back, heading toward the porch.

"My sister is having another one of her bitchy fits, and I'm trying to get out of dodge!" She shut the door and turned the key. "Come on, let's get out of here!"

"Sedona, get your black-ass back here," her sister yelled.

"Will, hurry! Let's get the fuck out of here!" Sedona grabbed my hand, and we swiftly walked down the walkway toward my vehicle.

"Sedona, stop! I don't want your sister mad at me."

"Shut the fuck up and get in the car!"

Just as we entered the passenger's compartment, Sedona's sister opened the main entrance door, screaming.

Battlefields

Sedona yelled, "Will, if you don't get us the fuck out of here...now!"

"OK, OK..." I said, shifting the gear in drive, and sped away down the street.

Sedona looked over her shoulder, laughing hysterically. "Damn, that was close!"

"What's up with your sister?"

"Who knows? When I returned from the studio, she was in one of her moods. I asked what was wrong; she just stared me down, stating to get the fuck out her face! Then I overheard her and Natasha arguing about something unimportant. Every time my parents are out of town, she thinks she's the shit! I love my sister, but she can surely work a nerve."

"Are you OK?" I asked with concern.

"I'm good, but I'm ready to have some fun and get my party on! You know them niggas will be tearin' that house up! It may start out quiet, but it will not stay that way, and I'm ready, willin', and able...set this shit off!"

"Yeah, I could stand to have a good time and release some tension!"

"Aiight, that's what I wanna hear!" Sedona began swaying, snapping her fingers to the groove blaring out the car stereo. "Turn that shit up, that's my jam," she said, humming along in perfect harmony. That was Sedona's gift, a spectacular singing voice, and one day soon, she'd blast from the radio as well.

"Is April going to be ready by the time we make it to her house?"

"We don't have to pick her up."

"I thought she was going?" I asked.

"She is, but she'll make it later on. Homegirl is still at work."

"Oh, now I know why you wanted me to tag along. You needed someone to drive your silly ass!"

Sedona smiled. "That's not true, I wanted you to come. I haven't seen you that much lately." She shifted her body completely toward me, staring. "What's going on with you?"

"What do you mean?"

"What the fuck is up with you? You're always unavailable. If I didn't know better, I'd swear you're seeing someone." Sedona paused for a moment;

I could feel her glaring, trying to read my mind. "You *are* seeing someone! Who is it? Where did you meet her? Was it at school?" I could barely get a word in; she fired her questions fast and steady. "Who is it? I know you're seeing someone. Don't lie to me!"

"I'm not—"

"Don't lie to me; who the fuck is it?"

"No one, I've just been busy with school. You do remember what that was like?"

Rolling her eyes, as all black girls love to do, "*Pleaseee…there's* something up. Don't think this is over. You're lucky we're here and trust me…we *will* finish this convo later!"

We walked into the foyer of a typical dwelling you would find in the Baldwin Hills area of Los Angeles: a large home with a view north across the city. Monica inherited the home and a sizable sum of money after her parents were both killed in an automobile accident nearly two years ago. Although young, she kept the home immaculate, appearing to handle her newfound freedom, except for her unsavory group of friends.

We walked into the living room where I noticed the same familiar scene as the last time around—the same ghetto-ass peeps! I received an instant contact high from the noticeable stench from the muthafuckas smoking blunts in the family room at the far left of the living room, with the formal dining room and kitchen in between.

To my right was the living room painted an off-white color with hardwood flooring and furnished with a deep-brown leather sectional sofa. A miniature palm sat in the corner next to an entertainment unit holding a stereo system with the volume cranked so loud, I could hardly hear myself think.

On the walls hung framed pictures of various family members, Sedona included. To our left were portable tables with scary-ass-looking mofos slamming down cards, taking swigs from their forties, shouting and screaming profanities. The back wall, enclosed with floor to ceiling glass windows, faced the pool and patio area.

Battlefields

"All right now, it's time to parteh!" Sedona probed around the room, trying to figure out what kind of trouble she could get into. She was in the mood and ready to get her freak on.

Having known Sedona since the third grade, I'm always amazed how well she could mingle in any situation. As for myself, I never quite fit in with the rough crowd. Although, I must admit, the jailbait thugs turned me the fuck on. That cocky confidence they carried, the self-assurance, the "I don't give a fuck" attitude drove my ass crazy! That's what I loved about Elijah; he was cocky, at times arrogant, daring anyone to challenge him. He was not a thug, but he held the same street-smart mentality. He was definitely a man of the streets.

Searching the living room in the direction of the leather sofa, I noticed a slim-built, light-complexion man sitting, holding a drink in his right hand. He was handsome, and I thought maybe tonight would not be so bad after all. At least I had some eye candy to focus on.

As we walked further into the room, Sedona yelled out to another cousin of hers, "Beau!"

"Hey *gurl*, how you doin'?" Beau said.

"I'm good, you remember Wilson?" Sedona gestured in my direction.

Reaching out his hand, he said, "Yeah, I remember you!"

I shook his hand and smiled. "What's up?" Beau was not all that good-looking, but he possessed mad swagger and a muscular physique that had all the women falling all over him. Tall, black, bowlegged...*wait a minute*. I just had a moment! I always felt Beau had a little bit of sugar in his tank—you know, gay traits.

Sedona looked over his shoulder. "Where's Monica?"

"She's in the kitchen," Beau answered.

"Cool, I'll talk with you later. Come on, Will!"

"Nice seeing you again, Beau," I said, but before I could even turn around, Sedona yanked my ass away, pulling me toward the kitchen. Beau stood with a huge smile on his face. I returned the favor.

As soon as Sedona and I walked into the room, Monica screamed, "Hey Cow, what took you so damn long?"

Vance N. Smith

"Bitch, please! I told you I would get here around seven. What's your problem, don't even start!"

"Hello, Monica!" I said.

"Hey, handsome, how have you been?" She moved closer, placing her hand to my chest, leaning forward, kissing my lips.

"Get off my man!" Sedona playfully demanded.

"Will ain't your man! You know this phine red-boned brutha ain't thinking 'bout yo' tired ass!"

"And he don't want yo' tired ass, eitha!" Sedona retorted.

"Ladies, please, you don't have to fight over me," I jested.

"Her skinny ass doesn't stand a chance!" Monica remarked, smiling, wrapping her arm around my waist. I knew Monica held a mad crush on me, always flirting with her hands, touching all over.

I played along with the charade, pulling her close, draping my arms around her waist just to fuck with her head. Monica collapsed into my chest and snuggled. Sedona rolled her eyes. I smiled.

"What have you been up to, Wilson?" Monica asked

"Nothing, just school."

"He's lyin', something's up with him, but he ain't sayin'. I think he's seeing someone," Sedona interrupted.

"Don't start that shit again," I interjected.

"I told you, we're not through with the conversation!"

"Yes, we are," I stated, glaring back at Sedona. Out of the corner of my eye, the door to the outside patio opened, and in walked a man who simply took my breath away.

"Yo, Monica, do you have any more folding chairs?"

Mesmerized, I struggled to refocus, but his sexy baritone voice straight from the hood commanded my attention. Sedona gasped when their eyes met—my sentiments exactly! I stood paralyzed with dirty thoughts quickly invading my mind. A young man's hormones raged wild and uncultivated. I attempted to constrain myself before anyone noticed I had completely lost my mind, *but this muthafucka…damn!* Homeboy was thickly built—stocky, but not fat; a beefy muscular physique some would say. His complexion was

Battlefields

golden brown with a short faded haircut, a thug hood-rat with a pretty-boy face. I lost all composure, licking my lips with the idea of him lying next to me. I completely drifted to another space and time, allowing my arm to fall from Monica's waist. A poke to my rib snapped my ass back to reality. After gathering my thoughts, I noticed Sedona looking confused. I knew she held opinions, and I was certainly in for a thorough grilling later on. *Damn, I'm usually so careful!*

Monica didn't seem to notice as she moved toward the man. "Yeah, I do, I have more in the garage," she said.

Sedona held her stance; her inquisitive expression had not changed.

"You need any help with those chairs?" I quickly offered, my attempt to ignore Sedona.

"Yeah, dude, I could use some help, thanks!" he said, cracking a faint, fake smile.

I turned to Sedona, and the look on her face informed me that I had some explaining to do. "I'll be right back." She nodded with a scowl then sluggishly turned her head, yet her eyes never left sight of mine, as I walked through the door leading to the garage.

When I returned, I entered the living room, hoping to find Sedona among the cast of characters. In social situations, I found myself a lost sheep, feeling uncomfortable in my surroundings. Unable to find Sedona, I decided a drink would help me relax; a Bacardi and Coke would do the trick. Approaching the bar, I spotted another phine-ass dude leaning against the wall. He nodded slightly when our eyes met; I returned the gesture before I began mixing my drink.

The young man dressed in standard baggy jeans and a shirt strolled toward the bar. "What's up with you…how's your evening going?"

"It's all good…and yours?"

"I'm doing aiight, just chillin'. Who are you with?"

I thought, *what's it to you?* But decided not to go there. "I'm here with my friend, Sedona." Before he even asked, I added, "Monica is her cousin. What about yourself?" I turned to get a good look at whom I was speaking with. He appeared to be a dude of mixed heritage; possibly white and black, standing at about my height, maybe six feet even, with thin lips and short-cropped curly hair, tan complexion, and hazel eyes. I would say around my age, too.

"I'm here with Monica's cousin, Beau," he said smiling.

OK, I did not expect that! "Oh, really," I snidely remarked, raising an eyebrow. I finished mixing my cocktail, taking a sip. I turned, positioning myself in his direction.

"You always do that?"

Dumbfounded and a bit annoyed, I said, "Do what?"

"Judge people so quickly."

"I don't, I just said…oh, really." I shrugged my shoulders. *Whatever*, I thought.

"I'm not gonna let you off that easy."

Damn, I was not looking for another altercation. I needed to make a clean break while I still had some dignity. "Man, I'm not trying to start anything with you!" I did mean something by my comment, but I should have kept that to myself. I was surprised he was a friend of Beau's. I did not imagine he was gay, although, I wasn't sure Beau was either. "I'm sorry for any misunderstanding." I turned to walk away.

"I'm Marshall…Marshall Johnson," he said, stretching out his hand. I stopped, eying him for a moment. "You gonna leave me hangin'?" he asked.

I sneered before shaking his hand. "I'm Wilson James, pleased to meet you."

"See…was that so hard," he said smirking. "Why you gotta try to be so tough? What are you trying to prove?"

"Nothing, nothing at all," I remarked, stepping away from the bar, heading back into the living room with drink in hand.

As I walked toward the huge sliding glass door, I turned to see if Marshall was still standing next to the bar. He was, but now Beau had joined him. I noticed they were chatting it up and staring in my direction. Marshall held

Battlefields

his drink high and nodded; I smiled walking onto the large patio and pool area, with a magnificent view of the Hollywood Hills and sign.

Once outside, I inhaled the night air—mild and calm for a spring evening in April. Surveying the backyard area, I had hoped to find Sedona, who was still nowhere in sight. Socializing around the rear yard, I figured there might have been at least twenty people standing around the patio area, smoking, drinking—all having a good time. Claiming one of the lounge chairs facing the pool, I lolled, taking a quick sip of my Bacardi and Coke. In the midst of savoring a few moments of solitude, I heard an unfamiliar voice invade my space.

"You don't mind if I sit here, do you?"

I opened my eyes to find a man with smooth skin, the color of honey, holding a bottle of beer. "Excuse me?"

"You mind if I have a seat?" he repeated.

"Sure, help yourself!" I considered his average appearance; he was not ugly but had a street edge—hard, strong, athletic type—with nice thick lips like I preferred, wide nose, and dark brown eyes. The gentleman sported a Jeri curl and was dressed in baggy Guess attire. I must admit I was intrigued. "I'm Wilson James and you are?"

"Quentin Banks."

"Pleased to meet you, Quentin," I stated, flashing a cool smile.

He grinned. "So...what brings you out?"

"I'm here with a friend, though I've been unable to locate her. I'm sure she's somewhere having a good time, probably all up in some dude's face," I joked.

"And what about yourself," he said smiling.

I choked on my drink, darting my head. "That leaves me here with you."

"Yeah, but you're not all up in my face," he remarked, taking a swig of his beer.

Was I being played? I thought. Someone is trying to get me to spill my truths. "Hmm..." I said, unsure what to make of his comment. "What's that supposed to mean?" The evening had become stranger by the minute. "What are you trying to prove? Better yet, what are you getting at?"

Vance N. Smith

"Ah...trying to be a hard-ass!" Quentin leaned with one arm on the armrest. "I know your type."

"My type...and what might that be?" I frowned.

"You stew on that while I step for another drink." Standing from his chair, Quentin reached with a gentle caress to my chin. "We'll talk again before the night is over."

Watching Quentin walk toward the house, my eyes fell upon a dream among a group of people standing around an open fire pit on the far side of the yard. Instinctively, I sat up straight, to gather a better look. Even from a distance, I knew he was breathtaking, the definitive definition of male sensuality, with apparent Hispanic heritage and possible African-American traits. He had a smooth, dark-tan complexion and thick black hair hanging slightly below his shoulders in neat cornrows. I fixated on his large and shapely full red lips, moist and kissable, his large round ass, and his thickly built, muscular body and broad shoulders. He wore a white tank under an opened flannel shirt, baggy jeans, and construction boots. His thuggish appearance suggested you didn't want to meet him in a dark alley, knowing he would rob your ass blind at the first opportunity. His rugged persona easily matched the other prison element congregated at the party, but his extreme good looks placed him high above all others. My heart rate elevated just looking at him. Lost in my gaze, I immediately had the idea of he and I engaged in aggressive animalistic sex. You know the type that instantaneously conjured up notions of head bangin' steamy lust!

I could not help but gawk, but when he looked my way, I quickly turned in the other direction. Causally, I sipped my drink before sneaking another peek at the phine-ass man across the way. However, this time our eyes met, and he nodded, continuing with his conversation. Holding a longneck bottle of beer with two fingers, taking a long gulp before scouting my way once again. Quickly, I returned my gaze toward the LA skyline. In my peripheral, I found him still watching. Nervously, I began fiddling with the bottom of my pant leg. Shortly thereafter, I lifted my head, deliberating his actions; he had since returned his attention back to the group. This cat and mouse game went on for nearly twenty minutes, after which my nerves got the

Battlefields

best of me, and I eventually decided to remove myself from the equation. Walking toward the house, glancing to steal another peep of my Mystery Man, my eyes locked on his once again; his hard, cold stare followed until I was no longer in sight.

I stepped into the family room and closed the sliding door behind me, and then searched the room for Sedona. In a far corner, I found her conversing with Beau, Marshall, and Monica.

"Where have you been?" Sedona asked.

"Out by the pool, where were you? I've been looking for you for the past hour!"

"You haven't looked hard enough; I was with Monica and April."

"With April...where is she?" I asked.

"She's in the living room."

"Cool."

Snidely, Sedona asked, "Having a good time?"

I noticed Marshall with a smirk on his face. "Yes, I'm having a good time. I was chillin' by the pool," I answered, sneering at Marshall.

"Will, have you met Marshall?" Monica asked.

Before I could get a word in, Marshall answered for me. "Yes, we have!" He smiled, licking his lips.

Embarrassed, trying not to display any reaction, I completely ignored his playful gesture. *What the hell is going on? I have men coming at me from every direction! Do I have a neon sign over my forehead, flashing "gay man in the house?" But this muthafucka is not going to worry my ass tonight!* Quickly, I regained my composure. Out of the corner of my eye, Sedona again gave the black girl glare; I could see her wheels turning fast! *Fuck...that was all I needed, more fuel for her fire, which was not going to make the lie I'd planned to tell any easier. I countered. "Yes...we had the pleasure of meeting earlier."

"Marshall is a good guy. I think you two would make good friends," Monica remarked.

Marshall offered his two cents. "I bet we would!"

Sedona eyed Marshall. "Will is a compassionate man; he could be good friends with anyone he chooses!"

I thought to myself, *this has to be the silliest conversation I've had tonight! I must end this nonsense right now.* Changing directions, I placed my empty glass on the table and said, "I need another drink." I left the meaningless exchange, moving toward the bar.

Mixing another Bacardi and Coke, I noticed Quentin approaching. "I see you're still here. Having fun yet?" I asked.

"I'm enjoying myself, but could have a better time with you."

Stunned because he was so blunt, I smiled nervously. "Are you sure you're barking up the right tree?" I remarked snidely, turning to face him.

Quentin reached for a bottle of gin. "I know what I'm dealing with."

"Is that right?" I said, propping myself against the bar, sipping on my drink.

"That's right. I got what you need," he stated egotistically.

"Are you sure about that?"

"Oh yeah…sure as can be," he remarked, smiling, looking down. "That ass is calling my name!"

I blushed, searching around to see if anyone was listening in on our exchange. "What makes you so sure I'd give that up?"

"Oh baby…anything that big and round deserves to have a taste of me." Quentin moved closer. "Let me hit that tonight," he said, getting straight to the point.

I almost choked on my cocktail. "I'm too young for you!" I stated before swiftly returning to Sedona and the others.

"Who was that you were talking to?" Sedona asked.

I turned toward Quentin, who still watched me from across the room. "I don't know, some dude asking pointless questions." Yet, I was intrigued.

"He's checking you out." Sedona smacked her lips, and then whispered, "You know there's a mixed crowd tonight. Beau invited some of his friends as well,"

Battlefields

"What do you mean?" I responded innocently, wanting Sedona to believe I was naïve.

"Gay and straight—mixed together!" She gave a curious look.

"Oh, that's what you meant." My hunch was correct. "Beau is gay?" I asked, keeping the farce going.

There goes that black girl expression again. "You're kidding, right," she stated animatedly.

"Well...I didn't know!"

"I told you last summer when the entire family found out!" Sedona appeared riled.

"Oh...I don't remember." Maybe I will keep her going a little while longer. I enjoyed seeing her get pissed off.

Rolling her eyes, she finally said, "Whatever," and returned her attention to the rest of the group.

I honestly did not remember her revealing that bit of information; I would have remembered. Though I had suspected but wasn't sure.

Refocusing my attention on Marshall, having enjoyed chatting with him for the past hour, I said, "Maybe we should exchange numbers?"

He smiled. "I would like that! We got off to a bad start, but you're aiight!"

"Cool...I guess you're not so bad after all!" I scribbled my number on a piece of paper handing it to Marshall. "Here, give me a call." Marshall was not my type, but I thought he would make a good friend. Honestly, I preferred older gentlemen.

"I'll give you a call tomorrow. What are your plans?"

"Don't have any."

"Maybe we can hang out, get a bite to eat."

"Sounds good to me," I remarked. While Marshall and I became better acquainted, Sedona, Monica, and Beau left our conversation for the patio. During my exchange with Marshall, I searched the room for my Mystery Man. I had not seen him since I'd left the backyard, and I hoped I would get one last look before he left. As luck would have it, across the family room

Vance N. Smith

I noticed Quentin watching, and when our eyes met, he nodded. I smiled, reverting my attention to Marshall.

"What do you like to do for fun?" Marshall asked.

"I'm open, but have been pretty busy with school, so I haven't had a lot of free time."

"Are you gonna have time for me?" he asked, sounding disappointed.

"I'll make time." But that all depended on Elijah, who pretty much chased away any male friend he felt was a threat. I would have to keep my friendship with Marshall a secret.

"I'd like that." Marshall placed his glass on a side table. "I'll be right back."

"I'll be right here!" I checked my watch, which said twelve forty in the morning. *Damn...where had the time gone!* When I looked up, Mystery Man walked in from the patio, closing the sliding glass door behind him. He strolled in my direction, and our eyes met. Not once did he smile or acknowledge my presence. He passed me, making his way toward the bar, though his eyes never left mine. Breaking our viewpoint, I shifted my position, probing the room. Everyone appeared to be having a suitable time; on the sofa, a man was sound asleep (simply amazing with the noise level), along with a couple holding one another in a passionate embrace.

Reaching down to pick up my napkin, I noticed a tall figure walking toward me.

"Do you know me from somewhere?" the stranger asked.

Standing up again, I found myself facing my Mystery Man, who held a bottle of beer at his side. His thuggish exterior emerged persuasively. "Excuse me?" I asked, nervously.

He asked again, "Do you know me from somewhere?" His slick voice was smothered deep in a smooth, sexual tone; his cold expression did not change, no smile, just a flat look.

I felt weak in the knees and warm inside. "I thought I knew you from somewhere," I lied, trying not to exhibit the uneasiness I felt.

Battlefields

"You look familiar," he said, flipping the beer bottle up, taking a gulp. "How do you know these foo's?" He slid the back of his hand against his lips and leaned beside the wall.

He was taller than me, by about two or three inches, strong and confidant—his clean, flesh scent aroused me—I was intoxicated! "I don't, I'm here with a friend. And yourself?" I caught a glimpse of his chest. Mystery Man had enormous pectoral muscles, large muscular arms, and huge hands with thick, long manicured fingers. *Nice hands were my weakness!* He was blessed with sexy, piercing bedroom eyes the color of cinnamon with flecks of gold, lined with incredibly long, thick lashes giving the appearance of mascara and thick eyebrows. My head spun, he was beautiful in a rugged, outdoorsy kind of way—definitely not a pretty boy!

"I don't know anyone here besides my buddy I came with." He continued this penetrating stare.

"The hostess is the cousin of my friend," I commented, playing nervously with my drink.

"I see," he said, taking another gulp of his beer. "I recently moved here from New York."

"Are you enjoying yourself?" I asked, completely ignoring his last statement.

"I'm cool." He released his gaze, searching around the room. "I'm not much of a social person. I prefer being at home, but decided I should hang out," he said, returning his observation. "You really do look familiar, have you been to New York?"

"No, I haven't." Hypnotized, I wanted to kiss his lips; I required a taste! The more I tried, the more I could not escape his grip, caught in his seductive web. I was hooked! "I'm Wilson James." I reached out my hand.

He placed his hand in mine. "Oscar, but you can call me Oz."

I think I floated ten feet above the floor, as his thick manly fingers wrapped around mine, sending me to the stratosphere. "Do you have a last name, Oz?"

"Escalante."

"I'm pleased to meet you, Mr. Escalante."

He smiled, finally, a broad smile, exposing his beautiful white teeth. "Same...you don't seem like this is your type of crowd."

Uh oh, just when we were doing so well. "Really...what makes you think that?" I questioned.

"I didn't mean anything bad. You appear a little out of place, classier than these other foo's."

Unsure if he complimented me or not, my high was deflated. "Well...I guess you just paid me a compliment. That was a compliment?"

"It was...I'm not *all* about the ghetto shit, but I do feel at home. They're honest people, not all materialistic—down to earth."

Out of the corner of my eye, I spotted Marshall walking in our direction. Damn, not now. Looking at Marshall, I asked, "Where have you been?"

"I had to use the facilities...on my way back someone stopped me." He looked to Oz with gleeful eyes. "I'm Marshall."

"Oscar."

"Pleased to meet you."

"Mutual." Oz's responses were cold as dry ice.

Secretly, I laughed. It was obvious Marshall caught the hint he was interrupting. He quietly excused himself. "I'll speak with you later, Will."

"So Wilson..." Oz began.

"Please, call me Will. My friends call me Will."

"I'll call you Willie...now, back to what I was saying. You seemed a little uncomfortable when I noticed you by the pool. I guess...I see you were holding your own."

"Thanks for your concern, but I've been mingling." I stated with a bit of an edge. "Although, I'm more of a homebody and school keeps me busy."

"What are you studying?"

"Architecture."

"I'm in the construction business," he stated eagerly.

"Really! So, if I designed a house you could build it from scratch?"

"With my bare hands." Oz extended his arms forward displaying his massive hands. "I learned the business from my pa and *tio*. My family owns

Battlefields

a small construction company in New York, and our specialty is remodeling. I also enjoy making furniture," he stated proudly.

Instantly, I perked up, "I'm impressed! What brought you to LA?"

"A change of pace and to get out from under my pa and *tio*. I wanted to pursue my own journey." He paused. "And better weather! I also followed this chick I knew."

I heard him say chick, but my mind wouldn't allow it to register. "Sounds like you have it all planned out. How's it working for you?"

"So far, it's working. I found a job with a construction firm doing remodels, and I have my own little apartment in the jungle." He smiled. "My life is comfortable."

"I'm located in Hollywood—," I said, but before I could finish my thought, some gangsta-ass muthafucka walked up, forcing his way into the conversation.

"I'm ready to roll," he stated, eyeballing me from head to toe. "Finish yo' biz, and I'll meet you at the car." He nodded my way and left.

"I guess he's ready to go," I joked.

Oz watched his friend march toward the door. "Yeah, I guess he is." He smiled, shaking his head. "That's Cedric, a good friend of mine. Pay him no mind."

"I don't…trust me. So, what do you do for fun? What keeps you busy?"

"My life is simple; I love the outdoors, riding my motorcycle up the coast. I try to go camping when I can."

I swooned; I loved a man on a motorcycle. "What kind of bike do you have and how often do you ride?"

Oz's interest level spiked by my question, and his entire demeanor changed. "I just purchased a Yamaha XS 750 Special, and I try to get out as much as I can. You ride?"

"Who me? No, not at all, never been on one. Maybe you should take me out for a ride? So I can get a feel for it."

Oz childishly offered a mesmerizing smile. "Let me think on that."

Maybe that was a bold question to ask, since I didn't receive the response I was seeking. "We should hang out some time." I reached for a napkin from the bar. "Let me give you my number, and maybe I could show you around my city."

Placing his hand to my shoulder, he said, "Hold that thought. I'll be right back."

This muthafucka just blew me off, leaving me hanging. Hastily, I collected my pride and watched him disappear from view.

Unable to make heads or tails of our conversation, since it abruptly ended as quickly as it began, I was surprised we had anything remotely in common. After recovering from my momentary disappointment, I decided to head for the bar; I definitely needed another Bacardi and Coke.

Quentin sauntered over, positioning himself beside me, mixing a cocktail. "Have you thought about what I said?"

"I haven't given it much thought." Well, maybe I had, but Oz removed any consideration of it. "I'll tell you what, maybe you can give me your number and we'll talk some other time." *I needed to get rid of him in case Oz returned. I didn't need him cock blockin'!*

He wrote his number down and handed it to me. "You be sure to do that!"

I placed the scribbled paper in my back pocket. "I need to locate my friends. It was good speaking with you, Quentin."

"Yeah, same here," he said with a smirk. "Play hard to get...I like a challenge!"

"I bet you do. Make sure you can keep up!"

"You seem to be popular this evening, in fact, in high demand," Sedona said sarcastically.

"I've talked with a few peeps," I remarked, looking over my shoulder, "and I may have made some new friends!"

"I don't want anybody taking you away from me!"

"Please, you have your music career taking most of your time. That's what you need to concentrate on."

"You know I love you no matter what, who, or why."

"OK, but why are you so dramatic?"

Battlefields

"I'm not! I want you to be happy, that's all. I would love to see you with someone. Of all my friends, you're the one who deserves it the most."

"What are you two talking about?" Marshall asked, rejoining the group.

"Thanks for saving me! She's being really weird."

Sedona leered. "Whatever!"

Monica walked in like a fly to shit! "Who was that phine-ass Latino brutha you were speaking with?"

I didn't want to answer, and besides it was none of her business. However, it was her house. "He's new in town. He came with a friend; I believe his buddy's name was Cedric." I offered little information. "Sedona, you just about ready to go? I'm getting tired." There was no point in me hanging around, since twenty minutes had passed and Oz had not returned.

"I'm not ready to go!"

"Sedona, it's almost one thirty and I'm tired. Let's go!"

"I'll take her home if she's not ready," Marshall offered.

"I can't let you do that," I countered.

"It's not a problem."

"Go ahead, I'll be fine…go!" Sedona insisted.

"She'll be fine, trust me," Marshall assured me.

I placed a kiss on Sedona's forehead. "I'll give you a call tomorrow."

"Be careful driving home," Sedona stated.

"Thanks for having me, Monica; it was really good seeing you again. Marshall, we'll talk later?"

"Yeah man, let's keep in touch."

I left the house frustrated; I had hoped to speak with Oz again. I arrived at my car and pressed the button on the remote, unlocking the doors. I entered, and before I could relock, the front passenger door opened. "What the fuck!"

"Where are you going? I wasn't finished with our conversation!"

I was startled by the sudden intrusion, but then my panic subsided once I recognized the clothing. "Fuck! You scared the shit out of me! Where did you come from?" I said, my pulse racing.

"I'm sorry…I didn't mean to, but I looked up and you were heading for your car. I called out, but you didn't hear me."

"I thought you left."

"I told you I would be right back," Oz responded, sounding discouraged.

"True, but you were gone for over twenty minutes; I didn't expect you to return, and I'm getting tired."

"I'm hungry…let's find something to eat, then you can take me home." He smiled and I was completely addicted all over again.

CHAPTER 14

"So what's your story?"

"What do you mean, what's my story?" Oz asked with a confused expression.

"Where you from?" I questioned.

"New York...I believe I said that earlier."

"No...I mean, what's your background, your ethnicity? Hispanic I know, but something else, maybe?"

"I'm from the Dominican Republic; we moved to the states when I was six. As for the something else...I guess you're referring to my African ancestry; does that answer your question? What else do you need to know?"

"No, I'm good..." I said, completely changing the subject. "What do you feel like eating?"

Oz stared out into the distance. "A burger."

"All right, I know a pretty good joint not too far from here," I said, turning right onto La Brea, heading north. "You didn't have anything to eat at Monica's?"

"I did...but now I feel like having a burger. You have a problem with that?" Oz smirked.

"Yeah, I have a problem; I never eat this late."

"Right," he stated, shaking his head in disbelief. "You didn't say that fifteen minutes ago, and besides, I'm a big dude with a huge appetite, and it takes quite a bit to fill me up," Oz smiled and added, "in more ways than one." His tone was playful and seductive, as he glanced in my direction.

My body felt flushed by an ensuing sensation. "You are a big fuck." I smiled shyly. "How often do you work out?"

"As much as I can. What about yourself?"

"Not at all," I quickly answered.

"Never!"

"Never...I've been blessed with a natural swimmer's build." I turned to face him.

He smiled, shaking his head. "I feel ya...maybe I can change that."

"If you can get my ass in the gym, you'll be the first...never had any interest. I'm satisfied with how I look, and besides, I never had any complaints."

Oz smirked and said, "So you say."

"Hell yeah, that's right! You feel differently?" I asked.

"Anyway," Oz completely ignored my question, "I'm not saying you have to bulk up, just be more defined. Women love that shit!"

Secretly I frowned, that was not what I wanted to hear. "I've been doing all right, like I said, I haven't had any complaints."

"You'll see it my way." He smiled.

"Oh damn, confident!"

"That I am! I know what the ladies like, want, and need. Feel free to take notes," he said playfully.

OK, this muthafucka is trippin'. I was at a complete loss for words. *What happened to the sexy mofo who was checking my ass out earlier? I was not in the mood to have a conversation about women all night! If that's the case, I'll drop his ass real quick. I knew it was too good to be true.* "So tell me, what happened to the girl you was snooping after; I can't imagine her dumping your ass!"

Right away, I could tell he was annoyed, but he spoke anyway. "She did..." His demeanor changed, and he became solemn and quiet, turning his attention toward the passenger side window. I did not push the issue; the last thing I needed was this big-ass muthafucka going crazy.

With the deafening silence between us, I swiftly downplayed the issue. "You don't have to talk about it, if you don't want to," I stated, turning into the parking lot of some mom and pop burger joint.

"I'm cool...you made me think about the situation I've been trying to forget. Not too many people make me want to open up. Something about

Battlefields

you makes me feel I can trust you." He chuckled to himself. "That's some strange shit!"

"Why you say that?"

"It is, I have the strangest feeling…" he remarked, stepping out of the vehicle, and then continued speaking as we walked toward the take-out window. "Anyway, order me a double cheeseburger with onion rings and order anything you want—I got you." He balled his fist, punching the side of my arm.

I tilted my head down at my arm, then up toward him. "All right, but watch that shit, or I'll have to fuck you up!"

"Yeah, you think so…you think you can take me down? I used to wrestle, and I love to box…so I got something for yo' ass!" He smirked, nodding his head, licking his bottom lip.

Shoving his shoulder, I said, "Shut the fuck up, so I can order our food."

"You think you can handle this?" He surveyed from the top of my head down to my feet with a swaggering stance.

Oz continued trash talking, interrupting while I tried to place our order. "Miss, hold on a minute, please." Directing my attention on Oz, I said, "Will you shut the fuck up," and then turned back to the gray-haired woman whose somber expression had not changed. "I'm sorry about that, now I want…" Oz continued laughing boisterously.

We arrived at his apartment near the intersection of La Brea and Coliseum with food we had no business eating so late at night. Walking into his average-sized one-bedroom apartment, I noticed it was furnished with the usual knickknacks a young bachelor would have, along with a sofa and recliner, some bookcases, and a small dining table. It was nothing special, and rather opposite the hard thug image he portrayed. In fact, everything about Oz proved the polar opposite of his persona. I found him educated, well spoken, at ease, and with a hint of sensitivity.

"Nice place," I remarked.

"Thank you," Oz said, taking a quick scan of his environment, "an easy place to lay my head and call home." He removed his shoes before heading toward the dining area. "You can place the food on the table…feel free to make yourself comfortable, take your shoes off," he remarked, slipping into the kitchen. "What do you want to drink? I have beer, juice, or cola?"

I took off my shoes and removed my jacket, placing it across the back of the recliner. "Water is fine." Searching around the living room, I noticed it revealed personal treasures and photographs, with one photo in particular catching my attention. Warmth swept through my entire body, inside and out. There he stood in all his glory, swimming trunks and all. His muscular frame was beyond spectacular. Evenly muscled, head to toe, with a slightly bulky, yet proportioned torso. He had huge thighs, calves, arms, and chest muscles—I was in absolute heaven. And to top it off, his chest and legs were hairy.

"Water? Is that all you want?" he said from the kitchen.

"That's all I want, thanks." His Kodak moment held me captivated.

Oz returned with a longneck bottle of beer and a glass of water, setting them down on the dining room table. Meanwhile, I pretended not to notice the sexy print. "Excuse me for a second, I need to get out of these clothes," he commented, observing my actions, and then headed down the hallway.

I turned in his direction to respond, "I'm hungry, so I'm not waiting on you to return!"

Oz walked down the hall, disappearing from sight. Shortly thereafter, I heard water running. After about five minutes he returned wearing a tank top and flannel pajama bottoms. His appearance was better than I had imagined, and he was built like a fuckin' god—his body rock solid, his tank top glued to every muscle, his ass nice and round—phenomenal! If I could see him as in the photograph, I would be set for life.

"You started without me…and you're almost finished. What did you do, inhaled it all!" he remarked.

"I love to eat, plus I was hungrier than I thought." I smiled, licking my fingers clean. Hesitating for a moment, I added, "You're a big muthafucka, damn!" My comment was completely out of character. Looking at Oz, he reminded me of my cousin Nate, body wise that is.

Battlefields

He flexed his right bicep. "Jealous?" His muscle danced while he tightened and expanded his upper arm. "You're impressed!" He baited me, grinning.

Teasingly, I dragged my tongue along my lower lip. "Muthafucka, I didn't say all that, and besides, I've seen it already when I peeped your photo in the swimming trunks," I snidely laughed. "You arrogant fuck!" Picking up the last piece of my burger, I took one last bite. "But I'm sure there's plenty out there that do!"

"I'm confident, and confidence is not arrogance, don't get it twisted, son," he said, lifting his burger. "And yeah, plenty do...I'm sure you do, too!" Oz took a bite of his cheeseburger. "Besides, foo'...I saw you checking it out!" I dropped my burger, trying not to spit my food out. He completely caught me off guard. When I looked up, he was smiling. "Jealous, cause yo' ass isn't as big?" he commented, staring hard, dead in my face, eating his meal. The way he chewed his food—like he was seducing me, luring me in.

"Please...you know you're a cocky fuck!" I asserted.

Oz smirked. "I'll show you what a cocky fuck I can be. Keep that shit up!" he stated, licking his fingers one by one, not once did he release eye contact.

"Play ball, muthafucka!" I declared.

"Foo', with one hand I'd pick you up and flatten you on the floor!"

"Bring it!"

He leered. "You got jokes you can't back up."

"Just because you're big as fuck, doesn't mean you can't fall hard."

Oz shook his head. "You're funny," he remarked, taking a bite of an onion ring. "And you can talk some real shit, but you cool, though." Flashing a half-explicit grin, placing his food on the carryout bag, he admitted, "I don't say that about many people."

"Yeah, you aiight I guess," I conceded, stealing his onion ring.

"You guess? Foo', get out my crib!" he stated jokingly.

Looking back at the photograph, I asked, "So, how long ago was that taken?"

Vance N. Smith

Oz looked up. "A few months back. I danced at this girl's twenty-first birthday party." He stood from the table, removing the leftover food and waste, then walked into the kitchen.

"Did you make a lot of money?" I asked smiling, although I was certain he did.

"Of course I did, foo'…what do you expect."

Rolling my eyes, I asked. "How often do you dance?"

Oz returned from the kitchen with another longneck. "Not often, but I enjoy turning women on, getting them hot and bothered. Most usually want all this dick I have, but I only allow a few a chance to taste it." His seductive gaze fixed in my direction, while he moved toward the sofa, taking a seat. "Why you so interested?" Oz settled on the sofa, "You wanna see me dance?" he said, turning up the bottle, allowing the beer to slowly flow down his throat, glaring directly into my eyes.

Staring at him and then easing into the recliner, I said, "What would you do if I said yes?" I smiled, daring him. He wanted to play the flirting game, well then, game on!

He sat for a minute with his head lowered, twirling the longneck in his hand. He chuckled, leaning forward, resting his forearms on his knees, and refocused his eyes on mine. He spoke with a soft, sweet, sensuous tone. "You daring me?"

"Yeah, muthafucka…I dare you." I leaned back seductively into the recliner at an angle with one leg hanging over the armrest. "Now what?"

Oz walked methodically toward the bookcase. Patiently, I waited. He carefully thumbed through a few albums, found what he was looking for, opened the sleeve, and set the LP onto the turntable, playing the Isley Brothers' "Sensuality." Taking a few steps away from the turntable, he gently rocked to the opening notes. Deliberately, he rolled his hips and body in a soft, sensuous motion, while his hands glided up and down his torso. With his head tilted back and his backside facing me, he slowly dipped then spun around, his eyes closed savoring every movement. Oz's sexuality was effortless, inbred, and no one could have taught him that.

Battlefields

His Latin and African influences were evident with every rotation of his hips. His right hand gingerly revealed ripped stomach muscles, manipulating his left, sliding down the waistband of his pajama bottoms, exposing the upper portion of his pubic hairs. Disoriented by the scene, I licked my lips. Oz was lost in the music, swaying in his seductive trance, divulging another facet of his persona.

The music switched to another Isley tune, "Make Me Say It Again Girl," continuing the erotic episode unabated. Never in my life had I observed anything as visually stunning, smoldering, and thrilling as what I witnessed. His movements and sexual overtones were beyond anything I could have imagined; his offering was pure sexual intercourse minus the actual physical contact.

The power of each gyration, the soulful dance, melted me like hot wax. The way he rolled and thrust his midsection, to the tender pinch of his nipple, enthralled me. His freakishly long tongue glided along his lower lip, moist and inviting. All wrapped in a hard, masculine streetwise package. It was all I could do to suppress an involuntary scream of ecstasy.

By the time the second track finished, Oz hovered over me, performing a slow grind and pumping motion set in time with the beat. When the music stopped, Oz was leaning mere inches from my face, and whispered, "I just *fucked* you up, didn't I?" He leered. "You'll know the next time not to dare me, son!" He balled his fist and playfully punched my chest. "Now what yo' smartass got to say?"

Not a damn thing. Nervous as shit; I sat reclined like a whipped rag doll, limp and tortured. I had been sickened with Oz's magic potion. He was highly contagious, and there was no way I was going to beat the virus invading my entire body. In that moment, I knew my life had changed. Silly as it sounds, I knew I'd met my soul mate.

He stood and then seductively backed away, returning to the sofa, leaning for his beer before taking a seat. Holding his drink, Oz eyed my way, nodding his head forward then back, in time with the music. He grinned slyly, gulping another taste of his beer, removing the bottle, and tightened his lips.

Vance N. Smith

Shifting uncomfortably in the recliner, I stared lost in space. My mind raced, baffled by the events that had transpired. Our silent interlude echoed throughout the living room. Neither one attempted to break the fictional truce. I remained motionless for another twenty minutes, with music filling then emptying the deafening silence invading our encounter. I ended the stalemate with a quick good-bye before retreating home.

CHAPTER 15

Two weeks passed and not a word from Oz. Blindly, the love potion outbreak continued, infiltrating my mind, body, and soul, leaving me powerless to shake it no matter how hard I tried. When Elijah and I made love, I imagined Oz's face. Oz was in my every thought, day or night. I would close my eyes and images of his sexual dance flashed vividly in replay. Perplexed by his actions, I was unable to comprehend how a miniscule moment in time could change my life so profoundly, and I was left with a body crying for more. Our secret rendezvous left questions unanswered; Oz sent me to the edge of heaven then left to return alone—a moment past, curtains drawn, stage left, fade to black.

This outbreak consumed my existence in ways I could not imagine. It was written on my face, affecting all my actions. Elijah recognized a change in me, but figured it was nothing in which to place much interest. His sporadic visitations became even more infrequent when his wife remained in LA. Belinda's mother had rebounded and appeared to be out of danger. Honestly, I couldn't have cared less. The outbreak had forced my attention elsewhere. Each night, thoughts of Oz besieged my mind. I needed a fix; I desired him to release the tension built up within me, and with the passing days, the pressure fostered an intense reservoir of despair. Oz left me helpless, drowning without a rescuer in sight.

Two weeks turned into a month and a half before the outbreak plateaued, and Oz became a distant memory. I relied on any distraction I could find to ease a once-sweltering caldron of yearning. Year-end finals displaced sexual necessity, and vigorously, Elijah returned to thwart an unknown adversary.

During the last two months, Marshall and I had become fast friends, spending as much time together as our schedules would allow. I had not confessed my relationships with Elijah or Oz, including my budding attraction to Quentin. My innermost feelings I was unwilling to share. As the days and the weeks conceded, my friendship with Marshall grew to an understanding of mutual trust. A valued allied who stood alongside my friendship with Sedona.

June gloom presented itself on the third Saturday of the month, as I began my day with a simple breakfast and morning cartoons. After finishing my meal, I returned to bed, watching TV and reading the newspaper. Shortly thereafter, the phone rang.

"Will…"

I perceived Sedona's trembling voice. "Sedona? Are you OK?"

"No…I need to see you," she said, instantly beginning to cry.

"Sedona, what's wrong?"

"Can I come over?"

"Sure…tell me what's wrong," I said, as panic swept over me. I'd never heard her this upset before.

"I'll be over shortly," she remarked, hanging up the phone before I could respond.

Franticly, I hopped out of bed, fleeing for the bathroom, showered, and dressed. Thank God Elijah planned on spending time with his family and had not intended on stopping by. Sedona only knew Elijah was my landlord and a good friend who offered help when I needed it. I didn't want to explain why he spent the night. Although, I believed it was time I confessed my involvement with him; however, I had a sinking feeling today was not the day.

Within forty-five minutes my doorbell rang with a constant buzz. Hurriedly, I opened the door, finding Sedona on the other side an absolute mess.

"What the fuck!" I reacted before I thought about the appropriate thing to say. Sedona gave the "don't start" expression, pushing past, and headed

Battlefields

straight for the sofa. I could tell she had been crying. I closed the door and turned in her direction. "What's wrong?"

Sedona held her hand to her mouth, shaking her head, her eyes closed tight as her body heaved from crying uncontrollably. She raised her hand motioning me to stop when I started for the sofa. I obliged, remaining frozen, not knowing what to do or say. Bent over with her hands covering her face, Sedona rocked back and forth with her cries resonating throughout the living room.

I remained silent, though I felt the need to do something, so I decided a cup of tea would provide unobtrusive comfort. Watching from the kitchen, I kept a close eye, knowing it was best to wait until she was ready to talk. I gathered it was significant, so I prepared myself mentally for the news I was about to receive.

Returning to the living room, I placed the hot teas on the coffee table and took a seat, while still providing her space.

Sedona reached for the hot beverage. "Thank you," she commented.

Studying her intently, I calmly asked, "What's wrong, Sedona?"

"Everything is screwed up!" she responded, gripping the stoneware cup with both hands, as steady streams of tears flowed down her cheeks. Wearing no makeup, hair uncombed, and dressed in an old sweatshirt and sweat pants, simple attire Sedona would never be caught dead wearing outside the house.

"What's so screwed up?" I asked.

Lifting the mug to her lips, she said, "My life," and then stared directly into my eyes.

"I'm sure it's nothing that can't be fixed," I commented, trying to lessen the impact of the broadcast I was about to collect.

"I can't believe I allowed this to happen," she stated, taking a sip of her tea. "I don't know what I was thinking. This has to be the worst time in my life for this to happen."

"Sedona, spill it!" I said. I had a sinking feeling about the news I was about to receive, and I was not pleased. Taking a deep breath and then exhaling, I decided I would say it for her. "Don't tell me you're pregnant?"

Sedona leaned forward and continued crying. "I don't know how this happened!"

I slumped deep into the sofa. *Did she really just say that? Did she actually make a statement so obvious to everyone else?* I could hardly contain my composure, and truth be told, I wanted to reach out and shake some sense into her! In this day and age, there was no reason for this to happen. "Have you told Jackson?"

"No...you're the only one."

"Why are you telling me?" *Oh shit! I didn't mean that to come out the way it did.* "I didn't mean that!"

"Well, fuck you too!"

"Sedona, look...I take it back. Truly, I didn't mean to say that. It just slipped out, but how did you make such a stupid mistake?"

"It's not like I was trying to get pregnant!"

"Well, if you weren't trying, you would have made sure you were using some form of protection, like a condom. Hell...birth control pills! You do know what that is?"

"You know what...screw you!" she spat, with tear soaked eyes, quivering bottom lip, and a runny nose.

"You might as well get used to it, because your parents are going to say much worse."

Sedona sat sulking like a jilted child. "I know...but I don't want to hear it from you!"

"Oh...I'm not even finished. What kind of friend would I be if I didn't tell you like it is! I'm not gonna sugarcoat it just because you don't want to hear the truth." Moving closer, placing my arm around her shoulders, I said, "You know I love you and I'm here for you. I will help you through this and support you with any decision you make."

"I hope to God you don't think I'm going to have an abortion! How could you think that?" she said, pushing away with a look of horror.

"I didn't say that!" I remarked, reaching for her hand. Sedona reacted, snatching it away.

"I'm keeping my baby!" A painful manifestation swept over her face.

Battlefields

"And I will be there for you every step of the way. Whatever you need, I'm here." I gently stroked her back. "How long have you known?"

"I found out yesterday."

"How far along are you?"

"About six weeks."

Pulling her close, I felt it was time I exposed my truths. I could not judge her when I was no better in making poor decisions. "I have something to tell you as well."

"Don't tell me you're with child!" she joked.

I laughed aloud. "Funny!" I was not sure how to say it, so I just blurted it out. "I'm gay!"

Her body fell motionless, not saying a word for what seemed like several minutes. Sedona raised herself from my shoulder, placing the palm of her tiny hand to my face. "I know!"

"You know what?"

"I knew already...I was just waiting on you to confess. You think I don't know you?" she said smiling.

"I know you do, but how did you know?"

"I wasn't sure until the night of Monica's party, that's when I knew for sure."

I sat with a baffled appearance. "Why didn't you say anything?"

"I knew it wasn't easy for you." Sedona gently caressed my cheek. "I know you as you know me; there's nothing you can't hide. Plus, I knew you left with that guy from Monica's party."

"What guy?" I quizzed.

"The guy from the islands—what do you mean what guy? The one you swooned over!" She leaned back, grinning. "Oh, honey, please! Marshall and Beau gave up that bit of information as soon as you left. Marshall was jealous and upset he stole you away from him!"

"Please...Marshall didn't stand a chance."

"Why not?"

"He's not my type."

"Marshall is handsome; why wouldn't you be attracted to him?"

"Did you get a good look at Oz?"

"Who's Oz?"

"Take your blond wig off! Who were we just talking about? The Dominican dude."

"Well, I never got a good look at him."

"Well…if you had, you would understand why, besides Marshall is too polished for me. I prefer guys with more of an edge, outdoorsy and athletic."

"Beau did mention he was good looking."

"No…Homeboy is phine!"

"So where did you guys go?" Sedona asked, which I knew she would follow up with a series of additional questions.

"We went to get something to eat, then I took him home."

"And?"

"And…nothing happened. He's straight!"

She frowned. "He's what?"

"He's straight and I have not heard from him since that night."

"Something doesn't make sense," she remarked.

"I believe he just used me to get a ride home, although he did buy the food, and I had a great time with him at his apartment afterward." A quick flashback of that night infiltrated my thoughts.

"Tell me the details?"

"Nothing to tell."

"Liar…when you speak of him, you light up."

"No, I don't!" I insisted.

"Yes, you do."

"Well…it's a moot point. Besides, I'm involved with someone anyway."

Sedona almost choked on her tea. "Excuse me?" she said, coughing with droplets of tea sliding down the side of her mouth.

I smiled. "Yes, I'm seeing someone."

"Who is he? Do I know him? Where did you meet him?"

"Damn, girl, take a breath!"

"Who is he?" she asked excitedly.

"It's Elijah, but that's all I'm going to tell you." That's all I could tell her.

138

Battlefields

"Why are you keeping him a secret?"

"It's complicated!"

"Is he older?"

"Yes."

"Is he much older?"

"Yes." I was a bit ashamed, though unsure why at first, but then I realized it was because I had involved myself with someone unavailable and married with children. "So, who told you I left the party with Oz?" A change of subject was needed.

"Beau! He saw him get into your car."

"You mean to tell me he said that in front of everyone?" I was horrified.

"Yes, those two gave up all your business. Will, you had all them niggas all up in your business!"

"Oh my god…" I said, freaking out. I did not want to be outted that way.

"Get over it, it's no big deal. So, calm the fuck down!" Sedona laughed, "But you should have seen the look on Marshall's face when Beau spilled that tea! Marshall was pissed; he was hoping you would go home with him!" Sedona shook her head. "Men are such whores," she laughed, taking another sip of tea. "Beau mentioned you've been spending quite a bit of time with Marshall."

"It's true, he has become a good friend."

"Does he know you're seeing someone?" she asked.

"Yes, but that's all he knows."

"Why are you so secretive?"

"I'm not—"

"Yes, you are!"

I hesitated. "I don't want to talk about it," I said, standing to return to the kitchen. "But back to that party. That night was crazy as hell!" Stopping at the fridge, I said, "I had Marshall all in my face and this dude, Quentin, was on me all night. He wants to get together, but I don't think it's wise." I pulled a bottle of water from the refrigerator.

"I'll say, you're in a relationship already!"

139

I came back to the living room, taking a seat next to the picture window. "Well…I could do better," I stated, mumbling.

"What did you say?"

"Nothing!"

"Something's up; what's with this guy you're not telling me about?" She thought for a minute. "But before you go on, we need to finish the conversation regarding…what's his name again?"

"Who?"

"The Hispanic guy."

"Oz."

"That's right! Oz…is that short for something?"

"Oscar."

"I should have guessed. Have you called him?" she asked.

"I gave him my number, but I didn't get his."

"That was stupid!"

"Near the end it was a tense moment, and I quickly fled the scene. I left my number on the dining table and didn't think to ask for his. Besides, he didn't offer."

"Do you remember where he lived?"

"Of course I do!"

"Why don't you just go over there and tell him you were in the neighborhood and decided to stop by. What's so hard about that?"

"Have you lost your mind?" Out of the corner of my eye, I noticed Elijah's car pull into the driveway. "Oh shit," I said loudly, giving Sedona more of a reason to be inquisitive about my relationship. "Sedona, you're about to meet my boyfriend!"

"Are you serious?" she stated eagerly.

"Don't get so excited and please behave!"

Elijah placed his key into the lock. Sedona whipped her head around reminiscent of some possessed demon. It would have been almost comical if I were not concerned how Elijah would react. I was so careful not to allow anyone over. Actually, Sedona was the only friend to visit and that was rare. My heart sank when the door slowly opened. Elijah walked in with his head

Battlefields

facing the floor. He had not noticed Sedona sitting on the sofa, and with his back to us, he closed the door behind him. "Hey babe, I'm home," Elijah spoke.

Sedona giggled. "He calls you babe!" she motioned with her lips.

My look informed her I was displeased. I mouthed, "Shut up!"

Elijah spun around so fast, I was certain he was dizzy.

"Elijah, I want you to meet Sedona," I said, forcing a smile.

He stood for a minute, his jaw tight and his feet planted to the floor. If this were a cartoon, steam would have sprouted from his ears. "Pleased to meet you, Sedona. I've heard so much about you."

She smiled, standing from the sofa, reaching to shake his hand. "I wish I could say the same about you." Darting my eyes in her direction, I saw hers turn toward mine, and then she smirked, replaced by a devilish grin. "Well, I guess I better get going." Sedona stopped as she passed Elijah. "Do I know you?"

"I don't believe you do." Elijah stood stone faced.

"I've seen you somewhere before. I just cannot place where, but it will come to me. You have a good evening."

"Likewise," he answered. Elijah slowly turned his attention in my direction, flashing the look of death.

She reached for my hand. "Will, you'll walk me out?"

"Sure, not a problem." My gaze fixed on Elijah. His scowl bore straight through me. He had not moved from his spot, still holding his overnight bag. I looked to Elijah and said, "I'll be right back."

"Yeah, you do that," he responded.

"Come on, Sedona, let me walk you to your car." I opened the door, allowing Sedona to pass.

Sedona stopped in the doorway, flaunting a sly smile toward Elijah. "It's been a pleasure." I pushed her through the door, knowing Elijah was not amused. "He's cute!" She commented. "But I've seen him before."

"No, you haven't!"

"Yes, I have…it'll come to me."

Frustrated, I said, "Why did you have to mess with him like that?"

"Because he was so serious." We walked down the driveway toward the street then to the corner of McCadden and De Longpre where she parked. "And besides, he's old! How old is he?"

"Old enough!"

"OK…" she remarked with sarcasm.

"Listen, I need you to keep this between us."

"I will," she responded.

"Do you hear me?" I stated adamantly.

"Yes," she said, raising her voice angrily.

"Promise!"

"I promise, now let it go!" she shot back.

"Come here," I said, pulling Sedona closer, giving her a hug. "I love you and everything will be all right," I remarked, holding her tight. "You'll make the right decision, and I will support you."

"I know you will, and that was never in question."

CHAPTER 16

AFTER YESTERDAY'S UNCOMFORTABLE assembly, Elijah and I hadn't said much. When I returned to the house, he was in the bedroom lying across the bed, quiet and distant. Watching Elijah from the doorway, he turned in my direction with a swift look upon his face that read, "Get the fuck out!" I wanted to say something—anything—but decided it was in my best interest to leave the matter alone. Besides, I was not in the mood to argue with him anyway. As much as I loved Elijah, I had become fed up with his demands, his childish behavior, and his fear of being "gay" sentiments, when he was a willing participant from the beginning. He chose to involve himself in our relationship, knowing he had other commitments. I concluded that I required a more substantial obligation, since the current arrangement would no longer suffice.

Elijah awakened the following morning, dressed, and then left without saying a word. Remaining in bed, my mind sprinted a mile a minute with unfocused thoughts, unsure of what I wanted. Deep down in my heart I loved Elijah; however, each day, our involvement was dissipating, and confronting how I felt was the reality I had to face to move forward.

"Hello?" Quentin answered on the other end of the receiver.

"What are you doing?" I asked.

"I was thinking of you!"

"Liar!" I responded.

"No…actually I was," Quentin retorted.

"Is that right…what were you thinking about?"

Vance N. Smith

"You and me, and when I would see you again. I haven't seen you since the night we met. Why is that?" he asked.

"You know why."

"You say because you're in a relationship, but it doesn't appear to me that you're happy. Are you?"

"I love him," I professed.

"That's not what I asked. I asked if you were happy?"

I was doubtful how to respond to his question. Well, I guess I did know, but explaining my convoluted arrangement wasn't going to happen. So I held the receiver, refusing to answer.

"Hello, caller?" Quentin tried regaining my attention.

"I'm here."

"That tells me everything I needed to know. I'm not sure how I can compete with that," he remarked.

"With what?"

"Your feelings. You're not ready to move on."

"Who said I wanted to end my relationship? I've never said that."

"Then why are you trying to start something with me?" he asked.

"I never said I did!"

"Don't play games with me; I'm too damn old to play those games. You know exactly why you called, and I've made my intentions clear!" His frustration was evident by his tone. "I'm not at all interested in being your phone buddy, your go-to guy when things aren't going well with your man. If we're only going to be friends, that's what we'll become. If you want something more, you'll have to give me the opportunity to show you who I am."

"That's what I'm trying to do," I stated, instantly becoming defensive. "Why are you making this more than what it really is?"

"You don't even get it," he said.

"I do!" I answered, taking a deep breath, holding it before I exhaled. "I don't know what you want from me!"

"Then why am I trying?" he relented. "I give up!"

"Don't say that. I value your friendship, but you can't place so much pressure on me."

Battlefields

"Pressure? I haven't placed any pressure on you. All I asked was, I would like to spend some time with you, to see you in person! I'm not asking to sleep with you. I understand you have a situation and you're trying to stay true. I admire your dedication, that's what has me attracted to you."

"The night I met you, the only thing you seemed concerned with was getting some ass!"

"That was before I knew you had a man," Quentin said, pausing for a moment. "Is that what concerns you?"

"Yes!"

"I'm sorry if I gave you that impression."

Secretly, I smiled. To be honest, I was fascinated with Quentin, but my feelings for Elijah stood in the way of anything growing between us.

"I'm a good guy and sometimes I come across as an ass, but I assure you, I'm not that guy," Quentin confessed.

"That's good to know." I felt the wall I had built beginning to crumble, wanting to open my heart, but trepidation reared its ugly head. I was afraid of what I might be capable of doing, being that the overwhelming urges to love, and to be loved, consumed every fiber of my being. If I didn't get it here, I would obtain it elsewhere. I sensed I was slipping into an abyss.

"Come over!" Quentin insisted.

I hesitated.

"Enjoy a quiet afternoon with me. We don't have to do anything; we'll just sit and talk. In fact, we don't even have to talk, just come over. I think you need to get away from that house and experience life other than what you have with him."

"I..."

"Don't think about it. Just do it!"

"Quentin, I don't know. I want to, but—"

"But what? What do you have to do that's so important? Come over, I want to see you!" he pleaded.

And with that, I gave in. "Where do you live?"

"I live on Don Tomaso Drive."

145

"I know where that is. Give me about an hour and a half and I'll be there." Before I hung up, I wrote down his complete address. Against my better judgment, I made the decision to spend some time with Quentin. What could it hurt?

Driving down La Brea, passing the intersection of Coliseum, not far from Oz's apartment, my mind immediately wandered, thinking of what he was doing. I wanted to drop by but knew it was an unsound decision. If he wanted to see me, he would have called. I could not maintain playing the fool.

Just as I stated, I arrived at Quentin's apartment within ninety minutes. I parked, secured my vehicle, and then walked toward his building. Butterflies fluttered relentlessly as I approached. Unable to explain the nervousness within, I felt convinced I was disrespecting Elijah and our commitment, which was a senseless thought since he broke his vow to honor his wife by consummating a relationship with me. Yet, I struggled with the concept that I should not position myself in a predicament I could easy avoid.

Walking up the hill toward his building left me cold, straining to persuade myself to turn the fuck around and flee for my car. However, I didn't listen, continuing toward the main entrance of his apartment complex. Approaching the intercom, I found his unit number and buzzed.

"Who is it?"

"It's me, Will, open up!"

"Come on up; I'm on the second floor, make a left once you exit the elevator," he directed.

"Cool...see you in a minute." The door buzzed, signaling it was unlocked. Stepping onto the elevator, I heard the doors close behind me. *Too late to turn back now; I'm here, so make the best of it!* Advancing toward his unit, I noticed my hands became cold and clammy. *This is silly, I need to live my life as I see fit. It was evident Elijah does as he chooses! Why should I care!*

I hit the bell and waited, and from the other side I heard Quentin yell, "Just a minute." I wiped my hands alongside my jeans, removing the excess

Battlefields

sweat. My body became warm by the mind games I committed myself to, and failing to shake the uneasiness I had succumbed to.

Suddenly the door opened and there he stood, his appearance better than I remembered, handsome but in an ordinary way, standing a few inches shorter than myself. Those lips…man, I loved his lips. I smiled.

Quentin extended his hand. "Please come in!" That simple touch filled my body with a blast of instant gratification.

"I'm impressed!" he remarked.

"Why?" I asked, entering his unit.

"You said ninety minutes," he remarked, looking down at his watch, "and damn…ninety minutes it is!"

I smiled. "I like to be on time! I hate keeping people waiting."

He placed his arm around my waist, guiding me into his apartment. A slight citrus scent cleansed my nostril; he smelled good. "Come this way and make yourself comfortable." Quentin offered a seat on a large brown leather sofa, facing a Sony console television set. "Is there anything I could get you? Do you care to have a Bacardi and Coke?"

"You remember what I was drinking?"

"I remember everything. I watched you most of the night, making a mental note."

Major points! "I'm good, I'm not much of a drinker anyway. That night I was a little uncomfortable and needed to relax and have something in my hand."

"Why were you uncomfortable?"

"I have not been to many house parties, so it's still very strange for me." Examining the room, I noticed Quentin owned a sizeable collection of LPs, along with bookcases filled with books. He definitely had a love for houseplants because they were everywhere. The room had simple neutral walls with a few photos scattered here and there.

Quentin returned with a glass of wine and a glass of water. He placed the water down in front of me then sat close enough that I could feel his warmth. "I know we haven't talked much, and I'm not sure why this question hasn't come up, but how old are you?" he asked, lifting his glass of wine to his lips, taking a sip.

Vance N. Smith

I chuckled. "I'm nineteen."

Quickly lowering the glass, he said, "Nineteen?"

"Yes...problem?"

"No...I thought you were young, but of age!"

"I'm of age, just not drinking age. You have a problem with my age?"

He snidely remarked, "Should I?"

"No, you shouldn't...how old are you?"

"Twenty-nine."

Jokingly, I stated, "I told you I was too young for you!"

"Nah, I'm what you need."

"How so?" I quizzed.

"You need a man to teach you the lessons of life and tame your wild ass down!"

I laughed aloud. "You're kidding, right?"

"Dead serious!"

"Many have tried and haven't succeeded as of yet. What makes you think you have what it takes to control someone like myself?"

"Because you haven't dealt with me!"

"Oh, I see," I said, picking up my glass. "I need to wash that foolishness down. You haven't met anyone like me."

"I think I'm up for the challenge, but I like to take things slow. I'm not looking to get you in bed and move on, though I may have made that comment about wanting some ass." Quentin reached for his wine glass again. "I would like to get to know you first. I understand everyone is out doing just that, but that's not me."

"So you say," I smirked.

"Is that all you want?" he quickly asked.

"I get enough at home, thank you."

Quentin leaned forward, placing his glass on the coffee table. "What's so good about this dude you're seeing?"

"He's cool."

"That's it, he's cool?" he appeared mystified.

Battlefields

"What do you want me to say? He's been in my life for a while now, and he gives me all the love and affection I need." I was stretching the facts, when in truth I didn't receive the full emotional support I deserved, but no point beating that dead horse. "We've been dating since I was seventeen."

"How old is he?"

"Why do you need to know all the details of my relationship?"

"I need to know what I'm up against," he stated with a mischievous smile.

I shook my head. "Oh, please..."

"If he's so great, why are you here with me?"

I sat rattled, my fake facade pierced straight through. I remained silent, unable to utter a word, and was completely tongue-tied.

"Say no more, you've said enough." He stood and walked toward his stereo. "What would you like to hear?" he asked.

"I don't care." My mind had drifted somewhere else when the sweet sounds of Phyllis Hyman erased my private thoughts, snapping me back to reality.

"Are you OK?" he asked, returning by my side, his arm extended around the back of my neck. Quentin traced the side of my cheek with the backside of his hand.

I closed my eyes with his tender touch sending chills throughout my body, racing at full throttle.

"I know what you need," he whispered.

"What do you think I need?"

"You need me to take care of you completely, tend to your every need, want, and desire, not just sexually. That's too easy, you need to be swept away."

"How do you know I don't have that now?" I played a man of high morals. How easy it was to camouflage the truth, at least to myself, since I was the only one fooled by the genuineness of my authenticity.

"I think we addressed that fact already," he remarked.

"You think?" I refused to be played by self-seeking games and false intentions, when in the end there was only one thing on his mind.

"I know if he was all that, you wouldn't be here with me."

"Just because I'm here with you, doesn't mean I'm lacking something at home," I remarked.

The expression on his face was, "Who are you kidding?" I could not believe I had made the statement myself. My palms began to sweat, and I shifted anxiously in my seat.

"Nervous?" he asked.

Leaning for my glass, I unexpectedly knocked it over, causing water to spill across the table onto the carpet, and some of it splashed on Quentin's pant leg. I leaped forward hoping to avoid the mishap, to no avail. "I'm sorry!"

"It's cool, its just water, no harm! Hold on, let me get a towel to clean this up." Watching Quentin head for the kitchen to fetch a towel, I thought how stupid I felt allowing my nerves to get the best of me. Quentin returned, removing the excess water from the table. "Give me a second, I don't want this to leave a water stain."

"Let me help," I stated regretfully.

"I'm good, just sit back and relax."

"I think I should go," I said, standing from the sofa.

Quentin stopped abruptly, looking in my direction. "What do you mean?"

"I have to go."

"This was an accident; there's no harm done," he said tensely, his face filled with a pitiful appearance.

"I'm sorry, but I forgot there's some errands I need to do," I said, walking toward the door.

He stood with a confused look. "What's this all about? We were having a good time; you don't have to leave."

I turned, forcing a smile, holding the door open with one hand on the knob. "Thanks for everything."

I quickly walked through the door without looking back.

Battlefields

I left Quentin's apartment in a fog, walking lethargically to my car; my thoughts were a scrambled, jumbled mess numbed by an invisible force pegged for defeat. I tried to think of Elijah, but the only faint appearances were ghostly images of Quentin, along with flashes of Oz, fading quickly in and out like a fast-moving picture out of sync—high paced, incoherent, and garbled.

Dizzily, I made it to my car, unlocking the door, flopping onto the driver's seat, and placed my head against the steering wheel.

I was done, left to fend for myself. Stricken to the core with panic, I knew I was broken, defeated.

CHAPTER 17

WHEN YOUR WORLD has turned upside down, what do you do? Because at that very moment, I knew something profound had occurred. I could not pinpoint the reason or event, but I knew something was coming or had already emerged, and I knew it would not be good.

The events that had ensued the previous day with Quentin sent me into a nose-dive. Unable to explain my actions after the water streamed across the table, I had sensed all the energy within my soul escaping right along with it, leaving me frozen and my chest heavy with guilt. Why was I there? Why had I sought the attention of another? I longed for Elijah, but his absence debilitated me to a point of no return. I was incapacitated by a need to stay true to an idea of committed love. Elijah gave me his promise of affection, with conditions, along with an inability to flourish. But destiny was a mere figment of my youth-inspired imagination. I stepped into the furnace well aware of my imminent doom.

Therefore I sat, curled in a ball of shame—a ticking time bomb ready to explode at any moment—fighting against every ounce of strength I had not to fall victim to the deepening depression that loomed.

The hours passed. I ate no food and remained silent and empty, lost in my solidarity. I hated the simplicity of the situation; I was incapable of escaping the bondage of this relentless chase for a dream. So aimlessly I drifted deeper into a blackened chasm, sucked into a whirlwind of torment.

Saved by the ringing of the telephone, I quickly reached for the receiver, hoping it would be Elijah.

"Hello?" I answered.

Battlefields

"Hey, Will, this is Marshall. What's going on with you today?"

"Nothing," I stated dryly.

"What are you doing?" he gleefully asked.

"Nothing...nothing at all, just sitting here."

"Cool...then you can hang with me today."

"I'm not really in the mood, maybe some other day."

"Nah, I think you need to get out. It's a beautiful Sunday afternoon, and we should take a drive to Griffith Park and see what's up!" His voice spiked with excitement.

"What's going on there?" I asked clearly lacking interest.

"Oh baby, you haven't been to Griffith Park on a Sunday? Hangin' with all the children?"

"What are you talking about?"

"All the gay boys congregate on Sunday afternoons, chillin', socializin', and gettin' their freak on."

A sudden burst of energy overcame my body. "All right, give me about thirty minutes to get dressed...write down my address and I will be ready when you get here."

"I will be there in thirty! See you then."

Thirty-five minutes later, Marshall rang my bell. Grabbing my keys, I rushed for the door. "What's up?" I asked, locking the door behind me.

Marshall wore khaki shorts and an old, worn, white tank. "I'm good, looking to have a good time," he smiled. "Nice place you have." He paused and then said, "How do you afford such a nice place?"

"Oh, I have my ways," I answered, leaving it at that, changing the subject. "This is the first time I've heard anything about Griffith Park besides the zoo."

"Really? It's a huge social gathering. You've never seen so many gay boys together in one place in your life!"

"I'm looking forward to it. Let's go!"

We hopped into Marshall's car, heading east on Sunset, then north on Western Avenue, and within minutes, we reached our destination. The park was abuzz with cars filled with families innocently out for a casual day of fun, along with several other vehicles of individuals with totally different ideas on their minds. We approached "the circle" where all "the children" parked their cars, standing around talking, being catty, and prancing up and down the circular parking area. I was amazed to see so many gay men—black gay men—free with not a care in the world, and completely at peace, enjoying a pleasant Sunday afternoon. I had to admit, I was thrilled and excited. Just being there sparked a renewed interest in having a sense of pride for who I was.

Marshall popped open the trunk of his car, lifting the top from a cooler, and fetched two bottles of beer. "Here, take one."

"No thanks, I'm not much of a beer drinker," I responded.

"I have some bottled water if you like?"

"I'm good for now!" *So many men—beautiful men, ugly men, and everything in between—too many flavors to choose from, so where do I start!* A sizeable smile drew across my face.

"Why are you smiling?"

"Did you really need to ask that question?"

"I guess not," he said, taking a chug of his beer.

"Does this happen every Sunday?"

"Yeah, specifically during the summer months; the warmer the weather, the freakier this place gets!"

"This is all so strange and new!"

"That's because you've been so wrapped up with your man that we know nothing about. Why is that?"

"I don't know what you're talking about," I remarked.

"What's the big secret, is he famous? You never talk about him, and I'm totally surprised you even allowed me to pick you up. I've known you for a couple of months now, but I know little about that part of your life. I know everything about your parents and how they mistreated you, but *this* man of yours...nothing. What's up with that?"

Wow, that was a mouthful, and I wanted to tell him everything, but I didn't feel that level of trust, yet. "He's—"

Battlefields

"Hey, Marshall and Wilson."

I looked up, noticing Beau walking toward us. At least now I was able to change the subject, refocusing the attention away from my personal life. I extended my arms, giving Beau a friendly hug. "It's good seeing you again, Beau."

"What have you been up to?" Beau asked.

"Not much, just working and finishing my first year of college."

"I didn't know you were hanging out today," Marshall quizzed.

"This was last minute! A friend of mine from the Bay Area is visiting."

"Oh yeah, I forgot about that," Marshall responded.

"You know, I'm tired as fuck, I didn't get much sleep last night."

"I know, me too, but I had a bangin' time at the Catch," Marshall commented.

"Where were you last night, Wilson?" Beau asked.

"Home…"

"I'm surprised I never see you at the clubs?"

"Not old enough, plus not much of a partier," I stated.

"I see. So you're fresh meat—virgin ass!" Beau joked.

"I don't think his ass is so virgin anymore," Marshall jumped in.

"Spill the tea, someone has been pounding them cakes?"

I frowned, not at all pleased. "So everyone just stands around doing nothing?"

"Pretty much. We hang out, talk shit, and socialize, while others head for the trails, searching for some fun," Marshall smiled wickedly.

"The trails?" I questioned.

"So young…let me show you the way. Let's go for a walk!" Beau grabbed my hand. "We'll return shortly."

"Don't do anything I wouldn't do!" Marshall took another gulp of his beer and smiled.

After hiking up a few small hills and around some bends of the trail, we found an area with men walking around from bush to bush. Some stood with a look in their eyes, full of lust, while others were shirtless, wearing

Vance N. Smith

shorts and sandals, leaving little to the imagination. A few were a little more reserved but obviously had the same intent. We continued following around a curve; halfway within the bend, a side trail led up toward a small wooded area. Beau stopped. "I'll be right back, wait for me here."

"Where are you going?" I asked nervously, not wanting to be left alone.

"I'll be right back. You'll be OK, just stand there and someone will come up to you."

"I'm scared!" I stated under my breath.

"Nigga please..." Beau said before quickly disappearing into the shrubbery.

Nervous as hell, I felt my knees shaking so hard I could barely stand. There was no way I was going to move from this spot. I sat on a nearby rock, gazing around the dusty, densely wooden area of the park, unaware of what was going on around me, but I had an idea it was not just to talk. I would see men emerge from the bushes, buttoning up their shirts, wiping their hands with a quick glance my way, then slowly flee the scene.

Looking down, brushing a bug from my leg, I faintly heard a strange voice say, "What are you getting into?"

Raising my head, I noticed a thickly built white dude with a slight tummy, wearing faded Levi's jeans and boots. He was shirtless, complete with a hairy chest and stomach, along with his arms. His hair was dirty blond, long, stringy, and greasy; his appearance was average with chiseled facial features, but not terribly ugly. I would have been mildly attracted had he not looked so grungy. I hesitated before I spoke. "I'm waiting on a friend."

He looked around, squinting. "Nice day."

"Yes, it is." I responded.

"What's your name?"

"Wilson."

"What are you looking for, Wilson?"

Not you, I thought. "Nothing, just waiting on my friend." In the distance, I could hear a man moan with pleasure. I knew that sound, and with that, all my questions were answered.

156

Battlefields

"OK, I guess I'll get going." He paused for a second, and then asked, "I couldn't convince you to take a walk with me?"

"No." I politely smiled.

"My loss…oh, well, have fun," he stated, strolling off to find another willing participant.

I watched the man hike around a slight curve and a downward slope before disappearing over a small hill. Afterward, as I was looking in the opposite direction, I spotted a tall, dark-tanned man walking up the trail. Just like the man before, he had a chest full of hair with hairy legs. The sight of him sparked a flood of emotions; my libido immediately sprang alive. He was not what I would consider handsome, but something about him was sensual and attractive, reminding me of those Italian men with dark features, dark olive complexions, and smooth demeanors. Moving closer, he beamed and winked, walking to the edge of the trail, and then stopped. My eyes followed his every move.

In the opposite direction two bruthas appeared, one gangly and tall, the other average height and stocky. They gawked and giggled, continuing down the path.

I resumed my attention to the Italian-looking man who remained in the same spot with his right hand to his left nipple. Nodding to the left, he motioned for me to follow him down the sloping, hidden trail. I sat glued in place, curious, but afraid to welcome his advance, searching the area thoroughly before I returned my focus. He moved a bit further down the embankment, though I was able to see his torso from the shoulders up. He stopped, making sure he had my attention before he departed down the hill.

Leaning forward, I felt a weight in my chest from wanting to follow but being hesitant of what lay ahead. I had stumbled on a segment of gay life previously unknown. Ultimately, my curiosity got the best of me, along with the ever-increasing and uncontrollable need to be in the arms of a man—any man. I walked along the edge of the trail, scouting the brush below, unable to locate the unknown gentleman. I continued surveying the area until I noticed him within a thicket of trees. I hastily looked left then right until I was certain no one was around before I hiked down the well-worn path created by hundreds of thirsty men in search of comfort.

Making it to a small opening between the groves of trees, I stopped and searched over my shoulder one last time, slipping within the secret hideaway among wild vegetation. Once inside the clearing, the stranger stood leaning against the trunk of a tree with a sexually enticing stance. His right hand down the top portion of his shorts while his left played sensuously with his nipple. The gentleman sported a naughty, crooked smile, begging me onward. My heart pounded with anticipation and heightened adrenaline. Easing my way, slowly inching forward, I moved toward the gentleman who stood roughly six feet even, with black, loosely curled hair and a thick and solid physique. Immediately, I felt warm and weak by his rugged exterior and roguish appearance, complete with a five o'clock shadow. I found myself sinking within his seductive lair.

"What took you so long?" he asked.

I shrugged my shoulders.

"Nervous?"

I nodded my head, yes.

"Don't be afraid."

I examined over my shoulders.

"It's just us; I'm not a cop, if that's what concerns you."

"That's not it," I finally spoke.

He continued playing with his nipple. "Come here," he demanded with a whisper, reaching his hand toward mine.

Placing my hand in his, a sudden breeze rattled the leaves of the trees. Gazing up at the canopy above, a childish grin graced my lips. I lowered my head to the right, inspecting my surroundings. He gently pulled me closer, my right hand softly slid up the side of his, cherishing the firmness of his toned arm. A slight soapy scent filtered through my nose. Placing his hand next to my cheek, he stroked tenderly, his touch soothing and comforting.

"I like you," he confessed.

I smiled, as my body quivered.

Battlefields

His voice was lenient and steady, yet deep and commanding. "You're shivering!"

I took a step back.

"Are you OK?" he asked.

"Yes, I've never done this before, so I'm a little nervous."

He smiled. "I'm Niko, if that helps you to relax."

Knowing his name did not quite do it, however, it helped. "I'm Wilson," I stated apprehensively.

"I'll make it worth your while, Wilson, if you just give in to our surroundings, allow your mind to free your inhibitions and relax." His smile pierced straight through my heart, and I melted like molten lava.

He held my arm tight and affectionately pulled me into him. The firmness of his body elevated my soul to heights far from the natural setting surrounding us. Niko placed his lips lightly against the side of my neck. I wilted, snuggling into his chest. Niko nibbled, kissing ever so softly, skills he clearly mastered over the years. My sighs were contained only by my mounting pleasure, which satisfied my body from my toes upward. I held on tight, never wanting the sensation to end.

"You taste sweet," he whispered.

His tongued traced around the nape of my neck, stopping along the way, paying close attention to every inch. He repositioned himself with his chest pressed against my backside, wrapping his arms across my upper torso. He held me firm, and then we gently rocked to an imagined lullaby.

The solid, swollen flesh touching my backside told me he was stimulated, and so was I. Pressing hard against his flesh, I informed him of what I had to offer. He slipped one hand over the top of my shorts, his long, slender fingers outlining the base of my manhood, sending rapid signals of desire and acceptance. Grabbing the back of his head, I held him strongly. My fingers parted his loose, soft, silky curls, skimming across his scalp. Niko's hand pressed deeper into my shorts, and the warmth caused my body to react with a slight jerk, and a half-spoken moan parted my lips. My eyes closed, relishing the intense connection to a stranger unknown before today. Unsettling thoughts flooded my subconscious, and guilt threatened to thwart the insatiable indulgences I was undergoing.

Niko's free hand swiftly unfastened the button to my pants, continuing with the zipper, and removed them along with my underwear, exposing my bare skin. In an instant, he had removed my clothes and spun me around; now we stood face to face. He stepped back, viewing the naked presence before him. He smiled. In all my glory, I stood before him, shorts down around my ankles, shaking, covering my exposed privates. Niko continued to completely disrobe; his eyes never leaving mine. Hastily, I watched him reveal the swollen beauty eagerly awaiting freedom. I reciprocated, removing my tank.

For the first time our bodies joined, and my arms wrapped around his waist. Niko grabbed my buttocks, holding them steady within his hands, slowly grinding to the rustling sounds of the leaves above. Ultimately, his lips met mine, and we kissed sensually, our tongues fished and darted in and out with our mouths wide open. It felt like a bomb going off within the confines of my mind, and the mischievous sensations I felt removed all concepts of culpability.

What appeared to be only a few minutes had been almost an hour of paradise. When I resurfaced from our hidden hideaway, I obtained a renewed sense of sovereignty. I sauntered with a childlike smile down the park's dusty hillside, spellbound in a sentiment of self-worth, pride, and acknowledgement of belonging. As twisted as the perception would be, I could not be convinced otherwise. For that short period of time, I felt coveted, loved, and desired, and that was all I ever wanted.

CHAPTER 18

Where do I go from here? I asked myself. *What lies ahead in my future? Would time heal a broken-down wounded heart?* That was the million-dollar question.

Elijah had been missing in action since the unfortunate run-in with Sedona. Sedona, on the other hand, delved headfirst into her recording career, attempting to finish her album before the arrival of her baby she had decided to keep. I was disappointed with her choice to be careless when it was easy to avoid such life-changing complications, but I supported her decision, concealing my true opinions. Who was I to preach morality when I could not control my own actions?

My discreet indiscretion with Niko plunged my reckless behavior to a new low. In the end, I would treasure that lonely lazy Sunday afternoon memory for the rest of my life. And for the past two weeks, I'd thought of him often and would welcome the opportunity to experience the interlude once again. I fondly remembered the feather-soft touch of his fingertips outlining the small of my back, all the way down to the split of my ass, and how he traced the lines and contours of my body with his tongue, sending sizzling, radiating electric surges of energy throughout. Two weeks later, I was still simmering from the erotic encounter.

And if that wasn't enough, Quentin deployed all forces for an imminent battle for my heart. Forced to seek refuge within my fort, I awaited the doom and gloom that was sure to rage for weeks on end. Finally, his sneak attack emerged, and my weakened defense system proved to be futile. Quentin was persistent with ongoing, day-to-day advances. The hope of a victory counterattack by Elijah was not on the horizon. Raising a white flag appeared to be my only option to thwart an invasion.

"How was work today?" Quentin asked.

Laying my head upon his lap, I de-stressed from the rigors of daily work. Quentin's right hand rested across my chest, while the other carefully caressed my nipple. I lay motionless, bound by stimulating shockwaves shooting throughout my torso. My breathing slightly elevated, and I spoke slow and steady. "It was fine...I'm just glad it's over. We had a lot of produce to move today."

"You appear stressed."

"A little," I said. As I spoke, Quentin removed his hand from my nipple. "Don't stop! That feels so good, you have no idea!"

"You like that?" Quentin asked.

"Yes, I do...having my nipples played with completely sends me to a state I can't explain." Inhaling deeply, I reached to trace the outline of his cheek.

Quentin turned his head to place a kiss on the palm of my hand. "I'm glad you came over today," he attested.

"So am I."

"I wasn't sure you would."

"Why?" I asked nonchalantly.

"You know why...you haven't been the easiest dude to get next to," he said, shifting a bit before caressing the bottom of my chin.

"I'm not that difficult," I protested.

He chuckled. "Get real! The way you stormed out of here, I thought for sure I would never see you again."

Opening my eyes, I stared dead into his. "You think this is simple?" I rose from his lap, hunched with my forearms resting on my thighs, looking down toward the floor. "My life is so complicated, and you know that."

"Don't spoil this," he exclaimed.

I turned to face him, with my blood beginning to boil over. "Don't start with me!"

Battlefields

"Relax," he stated calmly. "Just relax...I'm sorry; my intent was not to upset you, but tell me, how can someone as young as you have such a complicated life? You make your life difficult." Quentin placed his large hands to my shoulders and applied even pressure, expelling the pressure of life from my existence.

I cautiously gave in, forgetting the accusations he expressed, indictments I knew all too well to be true. He judged with the jury still out deliberating on his charges against me. Would they convict me on testimony alone, and if they did, would Quentin forgive and forget?

"Why are you so afraid?" he asked, continuing to massage my tense shoulders. "I'm here and he isn't."

"What do you want from me?" I foolishly asked.

"I'm gonna break you!" he sneered. "You'll see things my way, eventually."

"You think you can wait that long?"

"I'm a patient man with all the time in the world for something I want." He gave me a tender stroke to the neck, a soothing and thoughtful gesture of affection that erased muddled intentions. Quentin played it cool—were his intentions honorable? Or was it a well-thought-out aggressive power play.

As the evening progressed, I sensed my emotions give way to the tactical assault bombarding against my defenses. Unable to fight, uncertain if I even wanted to. Elijah's stronghold had weakened; a once indestructible alliance was now destabilized by lack of support. A new commander appeared on the horizon, and a serious contender was determined, willful and diligent. A new, more experienced soldier wanted my heart, and any innocent bystander in his way was a casualty of war. It required me to be smart, play it cool, and think of different strategies to outmaneuver those who tried to pilfer my valuable goods.

Leaving Quentin's apartment around eleven that night, I had new perspectives surrounding my careful examination of my relationship with Elijah. Sitting in my car with a sly, mischievous grin, I pulled the corner of my shirt close, savoring the scent of Quentin. I could easily imagine a life with him, yet I doubted his sincerity. Could he provide a life better than the one

Vance N. Smith

I lived so far? I had so many questions—how does one decipher the lies from the truths?

On this particular night, I followed a different route home, and instead of heading north on La Brea, I traveled north on Crenshaw. Low on fuel, I turned into a gas station on the northeast corner of Crenshaw and Adams, parked next to the gas pump, stopped my engine, paid the cashier, and returned to my car to begin refilling my gasoline tank. Lost in dreamland, I was romanticizing a fictional life, new and improved. Casually, I bit the lower left corner of my bottom lip with a naughty smirk.

"What's up, Willie? Man, am I glad I ran into you!"

Startled, I nearly dropped the nozzle. I knew that voice, succulent and sweet—an explosion of sex, earthy and profound. I sensed a relapse coming. The potion that once consumed my every thought process was simmering within, boiling and ready to erupt. I closed my eyes in an effort to block it, subconsciously pushing back the toiling detonation of mass sentiments. The strength of his presence pierced the stone barrier I had built, shielding myself from sustained disappointments. All subdued emotions came rushing in, screaming at full intensity. I knew I was condemned without even one look.

I spoke without facing my one desire. "Is that who I think it is?" I said with a steady, smooth voice, not wanting to reveal the excitement I held.

"In the flesh," he responded.

One look and I would be flushed with seething vibrations. I turned slowly, leaning against the side of my car for emotional support. "Where in the hell have you been?" The words blurted from my mouth.

"I've been looking for you!" he said, his attitude strong, confident, and seductive, displaying a wide, infectious, nothing-but-teeth smile with lips to die for. The god of sensuality, possessing the perfect blend of dominant personalities, masked the hardcore muthafucka standing before me.

"You're full of shit."

"So you don't believe me?"

"Not in the least."

Battlefields

"We were having a cool-ass time. The flow was smooth then you bounced."

"Yeah, I did," I remarked.

"What was that about?"

"It was time for me to leave."

He paused for a moment, looking to his side. "You could have left your number."

A bit perplexed, I said, "I left my number!"

"Where, when?" he questioned.

"I told you I'd written it down, leaving it on the table."

"Willie, I don't remember you saying that."

"Well...I did...and for two months I wondered why I hadn't heard from you!"

"And for two months I've been looking for you," he quickly responded. A childish expression fell upon his face—vulnerability I was surprised to witness.

I was not pleased. I thought, *here we go again, another game of cat and mouse!* The insinuation was there, an underlying game of flirtation with nothing said, no overt actions, yet heavy in the air.

With both hands in his front pockets and shoulders hunched, he turned to his right, staring toward a jeep wrangler, where a female passenger sat, shifting impatiently. My composure immediately tightened with disenchantment.

"Who's the young lady?" I asked.

"A friend," he answered nervously.

"Um...just a friend?" I snidely chuckled. "I believe she feels she's more than just a friend," I uttered cynically.

Oz spoke over his shoulder. "You may be right, but I'm not tied-down with anyone. I'm not ready for all that." He returned his attention in my direction.

"Ha, I think you need to tell her that. I bet she feels she has her hooks in you. I mean, really, look what she caught."

"Hmm...that's not good," he said. An awkward silence fell between us. "When are you gonna show me around your city?" he asked, forcing a smile.

Vance N. Smith

"Funny you should ask. I wondered that very same thing two months ago."

His cheerful, boyish grin quickly faded to extinction. Oz's outward appearance morphed to a tough, rigid exterior. I guess he expected a more favorable response. "So you just gonna leave me hangin'?" he said, his surly position proved concise and unyielding.

"What do—," I said, unable to complete my thought before his female companion laid on the horn of his jeep.

Annoyed, Oz turned toward his female friend and yelled, "Hold on... damn!" Positioning closer, removing a pen from his jacket pocket, Oz grabbed my forearm, scribbling his number. "Don't play me!" he stated with authority.

Oz opened the door of his jeep then stopped with a dramatic pause, clinching his jaw. He glanced in my direction with a hard, desperate expression, as he stepped inside with eyes locked on mine. The engine roared then Oz fled into the night.

CHAPTER 19

MY BRIEF REUNION with Oz sparked a fiery storm even the most gifted head shrink could not extinguish. The thought of him had me so wound-up, the slightest touch sent my body into a furious inferno, and once again, I felt my existence turned inside out. Same as he'd walked out of my life, he returned. How could a man I barely knew create such a magnitude of feelings of such tremendous proportions! The love potion I fought against two months prior returned with a vengeance, and what I thought I had conquered had resurfaced, no holds barred!

Cautiously, I gave Oz a call the following day. Curiosity got the best of me, requiring me to know more about the man whose presence permeated my every thought. To date, no one had made such an undeniable mark on me that I could not ignore. To my surprise, Oz's demeanor was one of innocence, excitement, and trepidation.

"I honestly didn't think you were going to give me a call. You seemed like you had some shit on your mind last night. Like maybe you weren't happy to see me."

"Why would you say that when you gave me an ultimatum? And besides, I was happy, but I must admit, I was a little angry."

"Why would you be angry?"

"Why wouldn't I?"

"What did I do...did I do something to you?"

"No...but I had such a good time that night, I assumed you had as well."

"I did..."

"I hear a 'but' coming," I said, bracing myself for the pending bad news.

"It was strange dancing for another dude. I cannot explain why I danced, but I did. I don't regret it, but it fucked me up!"

I held the phone, soaking up his confession. "So, what you're actually telling me is you lied about not having my number. You were too ashamed to give me a call."

Oz gave a heavy sigh. "I did not lie to you, and I never saw your number!" Silence fell between us, crushing any attempt to understand the events of the evening in question. "That evening fucked me up, that's all I can say."

"Oz, I didn't have a problem with you dancing. I don't have those kinds of hang-ups. If you're afraid I might run and tell everyone, I can assure you that will not happen."

"That's not what I'm trying to say."

"Then what are you saying? Help me to understand."

"I don't know what I'm saying, but there's something about you; I don't know what it is or why I feel so connected!"

"I have not been able to explain it either. I'm drawn to you and I don't know why."

"I'm not gay, but this sure feels like some fag shit, and that's what I don't like!"

And with that, I was through with the conversation. "Well, Oz, I have plans today, so I need to get off this phone before I'm late."

"Did I say something wrong?"

"No...you just stated how you felt. It's cool, but I need to go."

"Are you going to give me your number?"

I did not want to continue playing this game of chance. I was already in overtime competing in the Super Bowl with Elijah, and I certainly didn't need another competitive sport. After all, what would I gain? I knew what I wanted. Nonetheless, I gave Oz my number anyway. I had no willpower.

I finished my disappointing conversation with Oz only to receive a call from Quentin.

"Hello?"

Battlefields

"Hey, babe, what are you up to?" Quentin asked.

"Quentin, what are you doing calling me?"

"You gave me your number!"

"Yes, I did, but what if my man was here and answered," I said perturbed, since I gave him specific instructions on when to use it.

"I would've hung up!"

"I gave you the number, but didn't expect you to use it. I stated the conditions."

"I know, but I wanted to hear your voice and see how your day was going."

"I appreciate your kindness, but I'm having a bad day, and I don't need added pressure!"

"Do you want to talk about it?"

"No, I don't want to bore you with my drama, but thank you for your concern."

"So have you thought about what we talked about?"

I thought that was a closed subject, but now here we go again. Is this how it was going to be every chance he got, leaving our nonexistent relationship open for discussion.

"What's there to talk about?"

"You...me...where do we go from here?"

"Right now, I don't see anything more than what we have."

"I see a future between us."

"How do you see that when I'm still involved with someone else? You're a good guy, and if I were single, I could see something developing." How could I get Quentin to see my position?

"I would be good for you. I'd treat you the way you want to be treated."

"There's not a doubt in my mind you would do whatever it took to give me what I wanted, but it's not that simple for me to leave what I have here." I said the words, but did I honestly believe them? *What I have here.* What is it that I have, and if I left now, where would I go? I cannot go back to my mom's, which was clearly out of the question. I had no other place to go.

I held the receiver in silence.

"Hello, are you still there?" Quentin asked.

"I'm here…just thinking."

"Come over, I want to see you."

"I can't!"

"Why not?"

"Today is not a good day," I interjected.

"Come on! You want to see me, you know you do, admit it!"

In a somber tone, I said, "I enjoy my time with you, I do, but today I'm not up for company."

"I can come to you."

"You can't!"

"Let me—"

"I gotta go! I'll call you later," I said, terminating the call.

Before I could return the receiver to its base and barely walk two steps away, the phone rang again. I huffed, reaching down to pick it up, "Hello?"

"I see you're finally available to take my call!"

As if this day had not been exhausting enough. "Elijah, where have you been?" I stated, angrily.

"Where have I been? Where the fuck have you been?" he grumbled.

"I didn't know I was supposed to wait around for you to decide to call!"

"When I call, you make sure your ass is there waiting! And I've told you…you better not be fuckin' some other dude!"

"Is this how the conversation is going to continue, because if it is, I'm not in the mood!"

"What the fuck is wrong with you?" His voiced lifted with each word.

"What do you mean?" I responded cynically. "You leave me alone for the past two or three weeks, and you expect me not to have an attitude?"

Softening his tone, he said, "Baby…you know if I could be there I would, but I have an obligation to my family. I have to keep them happy."

"Well…you have to keep me happy, too, if you want me to remain here waiting on you, plain and simple!"

"So it's like that!"

Battlefields

"Yeah, it's like that!"

"Damn, you turn me the fuck on! You know I love the way you talk shit to me! You got my shit on full steam!"

I broke a smile and swiftly forgot why I was angry. "So when are you coming over?"

"You want to see me?"

"Hell yeah, I want to see you! I want to feel you next to me."

"That's what I want to hear. You got my shit brick hard!"

"That's what I'm talkin' about," I remarked.

"What are you gonna do with it?"

"Anything you want!"

"I'll be over in an hour!"

Within an hour, Elijah bounced through to claim what he felt was his property. I was not complaining, because the man knew how to love, making me drift to another space and time. After about two hours of nonstop lovemaking, I was spent! Whipped, I lay flat on my stomach, drenched in sweat. His naked body wrapped around mine, the rapid thumping from his chest radiated in me, lulling me into sleep.

His deed was done; Elijah was content that his sexual enthusiasm would hold me until the next time he had an inclination to stop by. Little did he or I know, there was an adept adversary waiting in the wings who would not take no for an answer.

CHAPTER 20

A WEEK AFTER what I would have called our farewell conversation, Oz's actions appeared to have intensified. To my surprise, just when I thought I would never see him again, he emerged with barrels blazin', equipped with enough ammunition to fight an onslaught of men. It was evident he was not going to easily give up the fight, and as usual, I remained unable to resist and gave in.

It was an early, sleepy, Sunday morning when my phone rang—it was Oz suggesting we take a drive up Pacific Coast Highway heading north, with no particular destination in mind. We drove along the jagged rock cliffs, following the ocean highway north to Santa Barbara, intermixed with sand dunes in between. The mild weather was pleasant, refreshing, and invigorating.

Oz drove with the soft-top removed from his Jeep Wrangler; his loose shoulder-length hair blew wildly in the hurried wind flowing throughout the vehicle. Sitting with my back partially against the door and the bucket seat reclined, I had my left arm wrapped around the headrest. Contentedly, I watched Oz bob and weave to the beats blasting from the Jeep's speakers. Hypnotic, rhythmic, pulsating music punctuated the crisp summer air.

Miles from the chaotic life of Southern California, the road gave way to secluded beachside mansions and summer getaway houses. I maintained high hopes of having my own designs built within the magical colony of Malibu. Glancing toward Oz, I felt the strange familiar indication of having him in my life, expunging all doubt.

Battlefields

Looking back on that day, the thing I loved the most was the way he erased all disappointments I had endured. With him, I felt capable of conquering the world, which was a sappy cliché, I thought, followed by a smile easing the corners of my mouth. Oz aroused renewed motivations to my once-stifled creative dreams; incentives previous acquaintances had smothered by their own lack of confidence and self-worth.

Oz's invisible virus was taking full control, and for anyone else, his or her time had passed. There was something about him, guiding me toward the right track. He got me; he understood the inner makings of what made me tick. Forget the fact there was instantaneous, explosive energy whenever he graced my company, which I felt, and so did he! He just did not understand the enormity of the vibration, nor was he aware of the impact he forged, but it was apparent to me.

By his side, I knew he was happy, ecstatic even, and although he never stated it, I had changed him. His presence delivered a one-two punch, and resonated persuasively within. I was addicted and there was no turning back. I had come into his life for a reason, and only time would explain why.

Continuing along the coast, we passed through Oxnard then Santa Barbara with silence falling upon us. Having Oz by my side was all I required, and conversation was just a formality when people were unsure of what they had. We were mutual spirits connected as one. With Oz, there was an unspoken alertness that we did not need a meaningless tête-à-tête, as long as our magnetic charge was energized. The calm, casual, and no-nonsense individuality he administered held me, fitting snug like a girdle squeezing the form of a full figured woman. Soaring invincibly, nothing, including God himself, could stand in my way. Oz's persona sheltered me like a well-worn blanket. Finally, someone had saved me from damnation.

Along the way, we stopped at whatever compelled us, including Solvang, San Ynez Mission, and ended with a hike at Lake Cachuma.

"Let's rest for a bit," Oz stated.

We settled on an overlook with a clear view of the lake below and mountains in the distance. Oz was the ultimate outdoorsman who didn't mind getting dirty, appreciating other things this world had to offer. He loved surrounding himself in nature, an attribute that complemented me perfectly.

Standing on the edge of a small bluff overlooking the valley below, I commented, "It's beautiful here."

"It is," Oz said, smiling. "Are you tired?"

"Not at all," I stated, gazing over my shoulder. "I've had such an amazing day. I wish it could go on forever!"

"Me too. I must admit, I've enjoyed your company." He hesitated. "I wasn't sure you would see me. I thought I said something wrong the day you called."

Facing away from Oz, absorbing the rambling vista, "It was nothing," I remarked. Redirecting my focus down away from view, I shielded my angst from Oz. With my hands jammed deep inside my back pockets, I sighed and said, "I've been going through a lot of stuff lately, plus I'm not too trusting of people."

"Are you that way with everyone?"

Hunching my shoulders, I said, "It keeps my heart from getting hurt."

"You've been hurt before?"

"Peoples' intentions are always suspect," I stated, looking over my shoulder. "I've been hurt many times, so I guard my heart."

Oz stood maybe two feet behind. "I would never hurt you," he announced, innocently.

I smiled, returning my gaze across the oak-filled mountains. "I could live here! It's so peaceful."

"Could you?" he asked.

"Yes, I could; I don't need the hustle of the city. The open space is all I would need."

"Me too. My idea of the good life is to own a ranch with horses, open pastures, and lots of acreage. I was born in a country village north of Santo Domingo and raised in the city, but I'm definitely a country boy at heart. It takes me back to the Dominican Republic and the town my *abuelita* lives in."

Battlefields

I turned, taking a few steps back from the edge, finding a huge flat-topped rock to sit on. "Who would have guessed you felt that way?"

"Why are you surprised?" he questioned.

"You strike me as someone who prefers the big city," I said, reaching for a few loose pebbles, tossing them over the edge. "I thought I was the only person who wanted to get away from it all, having space to spread my wings, be free."

Oz smirked. "You think you could live a life as quiet and serene as this?"

"Why would you think I couldn't?"

"I don't know too many bruthas who could!"

I had to laugh. "You may be right, but I'm not like most bruthas!"

"I'm beginning to notice," Oz said, sitting on the rock beside me.

I watched, studying his every move. Oz wore cut-off Levi's, exposing his thick, muscular hairy thighs and equally muscular calves. A warm sensation completely engulfed my body inside and out—I was weak.

"What else have you noticed?" I asked.

"What do you mean?"

Oh shit, I thought. Had I lost my mind? I immediately became flushed with embarrassment.

Oz displayed his infamous toothy smile that simply made me lose control. "I don't know about you? I can't figure you out."

"Why are you trying?" I remarked, tossing another rock into the distance. "Go with the flow."

"Is that what you're doing?" he asked.

"I'm not trying to analyze it," I lied.

Oz sat with his forearms resting on his thighs; his fingers intertwined with an expression of tranquility. "I'm not, but..." he began to say then decided not to finish his thought.

"Don't hold back."

He turned with a million questions written across his face. "It's not that simple."

I chuckled. "What you really mean to say is how you can't explain the connection we have? How mysteriously, two totally different individuals are becoming friends."

"Exactly," Oz replied.

"Neither can I," I smiled.

Oz ran his hand through his hair, pulling it back over his left ear. "It takes me back to the night I met you. I noticed you watching me, and I wondered what the fuck was your problem. Normally, I would have confronted you." He laughed. "Believe me, I have no problem beating a nigga down!"

Surprised by his statement, I said, "Why didn't you? What made me so different?"

"I don't know," he whispered, shaking his head. "When I ran into you later that night, I asked if you knew me. I knew we had never met, but I asked anyway. Once we started talking it felt as if I had known you all my life."

"It was the same with me."

"I was embarrassed," he remarked shyly.

"Why? Why would you be ashamed?"

"I don't know why, that's the point. The whole thing just doesn't make sense!"

"Then take it for what it is. Something greater wanted us to connect, become friends; we should leave it at that. Why make it more than what it is?"

"You're right. It just fucked me up. No one had ever...I don't know what I'm saying. It scared me."

"Do we need to talk about you dancing?" I needed to ask, desiring to know where his head was at, but then again, did I need to know when I was over a hundred miles from home? "You don't have to be afraid to talk to me about anything; I will never judge you."

"See, that's what I mean; I never speak that way with my crew, but with you it's cool."

I detected Oz did not appreciate exposing himself or his vulnerability. And without question, others had never pushed him to reveal his convictions, where I was free to speak the opinions I held. I gathered this was a new concept for him, and because of that, he was unsure what to do with these articulations.

Battlefields

"What makes me different?" I asked.

"Are you trying to get into my head?" He smiled, grabbing the back of my neck, playfully shaking me.

"I'm just trying to understand you?"

"Let me ask you a question."

"Go for it!"

"Who hurt you?"

Wow, I did not see that coming. "My parents," I said, pausing for a moment. "I didn't have the best childhood, and currently, I'm not speaking with either of them, along with others who have hurt me."

Oz's demeanor changed after hearing my declaration. "I can't imagine not speaking to my parents."

"Not everyone comes from a happy household," I interjected.

"I understand and I don't know the circumstances to the problems with your parents. For me, I would find it unimaginable. I love my parents too much. Do you love your parents?"

"At times I did…do. How do I feel now, I'm not sure. There's too much pain for me to move forward," I reflected.

I would like to say the situation didn't affect me, but it did. It took every ounce of strength I had to withhold the tears threatening to flow wild as a mighty river. It hurt so much to know I was without the love of my parents. I would have given anything to have them in my life, and it drove everything I did, affecting me in ways I could not explain. The worst part was, God handed me the burden of living as a gay man, and if that was not enough, I had parents who did not give a fuck about whom or what I would become. Their actions paved a way for heartbreak and disillusion.

"All I want in this life is to be loved." I sighed when the words left my lips.

A momentary lapse into personal thought yielded a revelation for Oz as he stared off into the distance. "That's what we all want. Some never allow those words to be spoken, while others declare it every chance they get. For me, it drives who I am; I can't imagine not having love in my life."

"At least you've had it. You know what that feels like."

Oz reared back and said, "I don't believe you've never had someone to love you. No matter what your parents may have done, I'm sure they love you dearly."

"Easy for you to say," I rebutted, as my voice began to rise. "You have parents who cared for you, loved you unconditionally. I am sick and tired of everyone telling me how I should feel toward my parents. Please understand, I lived it, I experienced it, and I was the one who had to deal with all that nonsense, all my life. I know what the fuck I'm talking about!"

"Hold up! I'm not trying to diminish how you feel. I wanted to provide you a possible brighter side and hope you would open your mind, willing to see beyond your pain."

Not listening, speaking over Oz, I continued to ramble fast and furious. "I'm in a situation now where lies were told just to get next to me, break me, and once they had my trust, they showed their true colors. Ultimately, it was all a game, and an individual preyed upon my weakness and pounced, leading me to believe they loved me, would always be there for me, when no one else would."

"Willie..."

I continued my ranting uninterrupted, completely removing Oz from the equation. My facial expressions burst with hardened anger. It was not until Oz wrapped his arm around my shoulders that I snapped out of my seething affirmation.

"Willie!" he shouted.

I released my rage, beginning to relax, and then I remembered where I was. Never had I felt anger so pronounced, not realizing the extent of my own agony. The raucous outpour shocked me completely. Sinking into Oz's chest, trembling, I felt destroyed by absolute guilt, beaten by clandestine fury. Had I gone over the edge? Would I be able to reinvent myself and be happy? I shut my eyes tight, clinging to Oz's shirt with a death grip. Oz embraced me with one arm around my shoulder and the other arm holding the back of my skull, gently massaging.

Speaking in a calm, temperate voice, he said, "It'll be all right, my friend. I don't know all who have hurt you, but I'm here now, and that's all that matters." Oz rocked me slowly, chasing the despair away.

Battlefields

So many thoughts ran through my mind. *Should I give in? Can I trust another?* I hated revealing this weak emotion, divulging a susceptible side to someone I barely knew.

"You may not understand it now, but we as humans are weak individuals. Some destroy people, preying upon the ones they love the most. While others find pleasure in demeaning people to make themselves feel significant, masking their own disappointments." His unpretentious statements of encouragement spoke volumes. "I'm here now, and I cannot make you trust me. All I can do is hope that someday I will gain your confidence. This is not the time to be afraid, but it is up to you to find peace. No one can give it to you. You must learn at what point you offer your heart to the one who will handle it with care." The soothing strokes against my scalp broke my hindering rage.

Oz continued speaking with conviction, and with each influential testament, I grudgingly surrendered all inhibitions. His sedative character ran through me instantly, inducing a mind-altering narcotic drug. Medicated by his addictive spirit, my veins flowed full, reaching every fiber, as I drifted miles away, safe and secured. Had I not known better, I would have sworn he injected me with some kind of poison, different from the magic potion he slipped on me the very day we met. His strength devoured every notion I had of self-doubt. His toughness became my strength. His virus continued to infiltrate me immensely. In his arms, I lay poised, tethering between hope and despair, profoundly infected. No amount of antivirus would cure me now.

There was nothing more to say.

CHAPTER 21

"WHAT HAVE YOU been up to?"

Visiting Sedona in her newly acquired apartment, I was still riding high on the possibility of having found love at last. "Well…" I answered, struggling to hide my broad smile.

"What's that smile about?" Sedona asked, preparing a quick meal for two.

"I finally heard from Oz, and we spent the entire day together yesterday," I beamed, picking a few grapes from an etched glass bowl filled with assorted fruits.

Sedona turned away from her prep work. "Really…I didn't know the two of you reconnected. When did this happen?"

"A few weeks back. I left Quentin's apartment and ran into him at a gas station on Crenshaw. I'm standing there pumping gas, enthralled by my evening with Quentin, when I heard this voice. My heart sank, I turned around, and there he stood, all six foot five of him, a few feet away with that street-thug stance of his."

"You hadn't heard from him since Monica's party?"

"Not since that night, over two months ago. For a second, I thought I was dreaming. Oz was the last person I expected to run into. At first, I didn't want to turn around, not with all those emotions he conjured up. Just the sound of his voice sent my world into a tailspin."

"Damn boy, sounds like he got your nose wide open!" Sedona stated, holding her stomach laughing. "Now, my only question…what does this mean for…what's his name again?"

"Elijah."

Battlefields

"Yeah, Elijah!" Sedona turned in my direction with a snide countenance. "What's up with him?"

"What do you mean, what's up with him? He's still around," I refuted.

"Don't even! You know exactly what I meant! I've never pressed you about your relationship, but there is a story you're not telling me. Allow me to guess the scenario, either he's married, in the closet, or some other scandalous shit! What's the deal, and don't sit there with that blank-ass stare!" Sedona stopped chopping onions, raising her head with her notorious "nigga please" black girl stare written all over her face.

She was right; any fool would have noticed my empty gaze. I withheld so many secrets that my world swirled wild, ready to explode; maybe it was time to confess my past improprieties.

"Well…fess up!"

While vacillating on how much I should divulge, Sedona's inquiring eyes caused me to squirm uncomfortably. She was dead serious and not about to stand for any more garbage.

Wavering a bit before I answered, I said, "Yes, he's married." And with that, I held my head low, avoiding all eye contact. "And he's a police officer," I quickly exclaimed.

Sedona calmly laid the knife on the cutting board. "That's where I've seen him before! That day at McDonald's, I knew I had seen him somewhere!"

Looking up, confused, I said, "What day?"

"The day I met you at McDonald's, the day I ran late. He was sitting with you in the booth. You should remember because later that night you got your ass kicked."

"Oh, yeah, I forgot about that…yeah, he's the one."

"Oh, my god!" Sedona placed her hand to her mouth. "How long have you been seeing one another?" she asked, pulling up a stool.

"We didn't start off as lovers, but he was aware of my problems with my mom. Elijah became somewhat of a buffer and father figure." My statements meshed together as I spoke and thoughtlessly played with a piece of flatware. "Then…well…it turned into something more…it just happened!"

"It just happened? How does something like that just happen? How old were you when you two started dating, having sex, or whatever you want to call it?" she questioned.

"It wasn't until I was seventeen," I shamefully acknowledged.

"Will, he molested you!"

"No, he didn't!" I shouted back.

"You can say whatever you want, but he did!" There was no doubt how she felt, and her expression of disgust was plain and clear. "You know, I'm pissed! The day I told you about Jackson, you grilled and chastised me, making me feel like shit! When all along you were seeing a married man and have been since you were seventeen! How could you judge me so thick?"

Sedona was right and had every reason to be upset; I looked down on her, knowing I was in a similar situation.

"I'm so angry with you right now, and the thing is…Jackson was never married!" She stood, moving to the other side of the kitchen, leaning against the counter top, both arms folded across her chest. "How old is he?"

"Sedona, please!"

"Will, how old?" Her tone lifted with each question asked. I was trembling, consumed with humiliation, not wanting to admit the truth and face Sedona's displeased perception. I knew the affair was wrong even though I had no regrets. "Tell me!" she ordered. With each insistent question she solicited, my forehead pounded in absolute agony. I began rubbing my fingertips against my temples, hoping to massage the hurt away. She reached over, slapping my hand from for my forehead, causing me to flinch. "Answer me!" she shouted. The look upon her face completely broke my heart. "How old was he when you starting fucking him!"

I clenched my jaw tight before I spoke the words. "He was thirty-two," I confessed, holding my head in shame.

"Oh, Will! Why would you put yourself in that situation?"

"He loved me, I loved him, and I wanted to prove my love. I desired his attention, and it felt right. He offered hope, a chance for a happier life. You don't understand, I was so lost, drowning in a bottomless pit, starving for

Battlefields

affection!" I inhaled deeply then exhaled before I continued. "I was dying a slow death, a prisoner, when I should have been celebrating my youth. You cannot imagine how that feels! Everyone around me with their perfect lives and loving parents, and I...I was tormented every fuckin' day! You explain to me how I was supposed to survive that. I survived the best way I knew how, and Elijah became my savior!" Lifting my head, I could see that Sedona was visibly shaken, standing with her small, delicate hands covering her mouth. Her tear-filled eyes symbolized the compassion that swept her face, noticeably disturbed by the revealing horrors of a childhood no child should have experienced.

"Will, I'm so sorry. I took my happiness for granted and assumed you were as well. I'm ashamed I didn't realize what you were going through."

"It's not a big deal," I stated solemnly.

"It is a big deal! I should have never discounted what you were going through. I guess I figured you were exaggerating how bad it really was."

"Why would I lie about something like that? I wanted my parents to love me. I wanted my father to realize I was alive, and I needed him, but he never cared."

"Will, you were never alone. I may not have shown how much I cared, but you meant the world to me, and you should have been more open. There's nothing I wouldn't do for you!"

"I know you care for me, but it's a different kind of love I seek. I desire the love and affection, the connection you should have with blood relatives, the bond that cannot be broken no matter what. The kind of love that designs and weaves a fabric leaving you coveted, secured, and without doubt. What you would die for! I crave that so much so, it hurts," I said, wiping at my runny nose, "and without it, I'm lost!" Speaking the words brought back all the pain and rejection I tried in vain to forget. Fighting back tears and shaking my head in defeat, I said, "You have no idea how broken I feel. Like, why should I even care when no one else does? Then Elijah stepped in offering a promise no one else proposed. There was no way I would reject such an offer. My only concern was to stop the suffering and be happy. I deserved to be happy just like anyone else."

Vance N. Smith

Sedona offered a sentimental hug. The sweet aroma of her perfume ignited my senses. Limp and drained of any emotion, I felt numbed by the craziness occupying my life. Elijah had not fulfilled his promise; Quentin made demands I could not comply with. Now, Oz returned with a toxin that jostled my current sensibilities and realities. I could not comprehend what was happening with Oz creating fervor deep within me, which overwhelmed and distorted my survival plan.

"I'm so confused! In one respect, everything is cool—I love school, I'm working toward my dreams—but my personal life is in shambles. And as much as I love Elijah, I know in my heart I need to walk away. With him I understand I have no real future. He is never going to leave his wife and will never truly commit to a relationship with a man, let alone someone as young as me. Deep down I knew that to be true, but I could not turn away. Again, I'm held captive to an existence I cannot escape—first my mother, now Elijah. Funny how I ran to the very thing I was trying to get away from!"

"It's not so strange, so don't beat yourself up! You ran to what was familiar."

"But why...why did I do that?" The scene was too dramatic, so I pushed away from Sedona, sitting back into my chair. "Enough of this! I cannot keep doing this. This emotional shit is dragging me down," I said, taking a breath, gently pushing Sedona away.

Sedona reached for a towel, dabbing her eyes. "Will, I'm so sorry, and it pains me to see you like this. It's breaking my heart." Leaning against the counter top, she screamed, "Fuck!" Returning to complete her prep work, she finally said, "On a lighter note, how was your date with Oz?" she asked, forcing a smile.

I sighed. "It wasn't a date, and besides, I don't believe he's gay."

"You don't?"

"No...I mean..." I said, thinking for a minute, "some of his actions are suspect, but I don't believe he is. There's definitely a connection, but I don't believe he's gay."

"How can you be so sure?"

Battlefields

"I know my experiences have been limited, but someone like him couldn't be gay."

"Like him? That's a silly statement; just look at Elijah, I would never have suspected!"

"True, but you know the macho-street type. The thugs you know from the hood, that's all about getting the pussy!"

Sedona frowned. "Will!"

"Oh, I'm sorry. The ones that are all about their manhood."

"I get it!"

"There *are* things I question."

"Like what?"

"It's his actions; he's sometimes too free with me. Expressive—"

The sound of the doorbell rang through the house.

"Hold that thought. I forgot Monica was coming over."

In the other room, I overheard several voices. Two I recognized as Monica's and Beau's, but there was another male voice I could not identify.

Sedona returned with Monica following closely behind.

"Hey, Will, how you been?" Monica asked.

"I've been good!"

"You're looking handsome as ever!"

"Thank you! I thought I heard Beau?"

"He's coming," she answered.

"Will and I were just talking and making dinner. Can I offer you any?" Sedona asked.

"No, girl, we just ate! This is a quick visit to pick up the dress."

"It's hanging on the doorknob of the closet in the hallway, and you better not get anything on it!"

"Where are you off to?" I asked.

"It's not for tonight; I'm going to a beach party next weekend," Monica remarked.

"And you're wearing a dress?" I questioned.

"It's a sundress!"

"Oh," I said, raising my head in gesture, lifting my eyebrows.

"Beau told me he ran into you a few weeks back," Monica stated smugly, hinting she had dirt to disclose.

Great, I thought. I had not seen Beau since Griffith Park; I can only imagine what info he provided. "Yeah, I was hangin' with Marshall."

"How is Marshall?" Sedona wondered.

"He's good!" Both Monica and I answered at the same time.

"OK, that was strange, are you reading my mind?" I asked.

Monica smiled. "I think you read mine!"

"What's yawl up to?" Beau remarked, entering the kitchen. "Well, well...look who we have here!"

"What's up, Beau?" I stated, dryly.

"I can't complain. I haven't seen you in the park since the last time."

"I haven't been back."

"Is that right...I expected you to run back after what happened!"

I gave a disapproving stare.

"Maybe I've said too much," Beau snidely remarked.

"What are you talking about?" Sedona asked.

"Nothing," I quickly replied. "He's not talking about anything."

"I guess I'm not," Beau scoffed.

"Beau, who's your friend?" I asked. "With your rude ass!"

"Whateva, nigga, this is Trent," he said, gesturing in my direction. "Trent, this is Wilson."

"Pleased to meet you, Trent!" I smiled. Trent stood a few inches shorter than me. He was stocky but built nice—solid—with a deep brown complexion, short hair sporting a Jeri curl cut into a shag, and wearing a tee shirt with some sort of cartoon character and blue jeans, Jordache's, I believed. He sported a warm smile with perfectly straight teeth, leaving me to assume he had worn braces at some point since they were too perfect, and his face was average but handsome still, with dimples.

"Nice meeting you, Wilson!" Trent responded.

"Have a seat," I gestured toward the chair next to mine.

"Thank you."

Battlefields

I smiled, returning my attention to the rest of the group.

"What's for dinner?" Beau asked, looking over Sedona's shoulder.

"This isn't for you. This is for Will and me. Monica said you guys ate already."

"We did, but there's nothing like a home-cooked meal!"

"Then I guess you need to consult with Monica and have her cook something for you," Sedona retorted.

"Don't look my way, cause it ain't happenin'," Monica joked.

"I guess you're shit out of luck!" Trent remarked.

"Nah, I'll just go over to your crib and have you fix my dinner," Beau responded.

"How about you go to your own place and cook dinner. How about that," I said, stating my opinion as well, fed up with his bullshit.

"Anyway, girl, I need to head on out. Thanks for the dress, and I'll return it as soon as I'm done with it." Monica started for the door, motioning toward Beau. "Get yo' triflin' ass up!"

"It was nice meeting you, Trent, and hopefully I'll see you again," I said, reaching to shake his hand.

"Same here," he responded.

I left Sedona's about two hours after Monica and her crew departed, returning home sometime after eight that evening. Pulling into the driveway, I found Elijah's parked car and was surprised since I had not heard from him. However, lately he was showing up unannounced. As soon as I walked through the door he started with his shit!

"Where in the hell have you been?" He sat on the living room sofa with a glass of wine and a menacing appearance.

Rolling my eyes, I was not about to engage him with any nonsense. I simply walked past, ignoring his silly ass, heading for the bedroom without uttering a word.

"Did this muthafucka just walked past me?" he mumbled, speaking to himself. Shortly thereafter, he shuffled toward the bedroom, appearing at the door, where he stood for a moment sulking.

"What is it, Elijah? I'm not in the mood to argue with you tonight!" I paused, providing my attention.

"What…you don't have time for me?"

"I'm not doing this with you; it's late and I'm tired!"

"Tired! You gonna blow me off like that?"

"Like what?" I asked, removing my clothes. "You think I'm gonna continue to wait around hoping you spare a few minutes of your time!"

Elijah moved further into the room.

Stopping to face him, I said, "Don't walk up on me like that!"

"What the fuck is wrong with you?"

"You, muthafucka!"

"Oh, I see. You want me all to yourself!"

"It doesn't even matter anymore!" I remarked, placing my bikini briefs and clothes into the dirty garment hamper.

Elijah approached, placing his arms around my waist. Instinctively, I pushed him away. "That's not gonna work this time. If you want the goods, you're gonna have to do better than what you've been doing. You can't have your cake and eat it too!"

"So it's like that?"

"Yes, it's like that!"

It turned out I was all talk with no action. The night ended with our usual intense lovemaking. I barked a good game, but as always, I gave in.

CHAPTER 22

IMPRISONMENT, BATTLEFIELDS, AND toxins left my body ravaged, beaten down to its core. How was I to recover from such a deadly assault? Scarred and mutilated by deceit, my war wounds certainly would take years to heal. My mind clouded by this devastation, however, when the dust settled, optimism miraculously appeared.

In the distance, a mysterious figure appeared with a hand extended, offering hope. Reaching to place mine in his, I tenderly spoke, "Is it you I've been waiting for?"

The faceless figure replied, "Take my hand."

Eagerly, I obeyed. "Rescue me!" I pleaded.

"I'm here to offer protection," he stated, soft and tender.

"Where will you take me?" I asked, bowing at his feet.

"To a safer, faraway place."

"Who are you?" I asked, staring at the faceless creature standing before me.

Observing to his left, searching the vast open space surrounding us, he slowly stepped back. "Hurry...we must go."

Lowering my head in gratitude, I said, "I've waited so long for someone to rescue me!"

The mysterious figure inched forward then remarked, "I'm here now... come...come with me; we haven't much time! Take my hand."

Stretching, unable to grasp his hand, I pleaded, "Help me."

"Come with me...I'll show you the way to safety."

Suddenly, the fog lifted and a faint image slowly appeared. "It's you!"

A smile broadened across the face of the dark figure.

"I know who you are! You're—"

Awakened by the sound of my alarm clock, I sat up as my heart raced, shaken from my reverie. *Damn...dreams can be a muthafuck,* I thought, wiping my eyes, leaning forward to check the time.

Fall of 1981

For the past few weeks, Elijah made frequent rounds to the house, slithering in and doing his deed, before selfishly escaping. Once absent, there was now an onslaught of daily phone calls, and the constant creeping in and out whenever he found space to slip away from Mrs. Busby. I suspected he detected my wavering allegiance; so dutifully, Elijah covered his tracks with a presumptuous offensive assault to regain trust and honor. Unknowingly his feeble, preemptive defense was far too late; he couldn't fix the damage that had been done, with my heart fleeing to a more adept opponent. Deeply hurt by false promises, ulterior motives, and ambushed by childish dreams of fairy-tale romances, I offered my soul to a deserving ally. Throughout recorded history, treaties had been shattered, and it was time this strained agreement was dissolved.

Just as Elijah attempted his push, affirming his higher position, secretly, a silent antagonist had him dethroned. While the impending battle raged, I carried on as I had before, scouting possible advantages that may appear. Until then I laid low, hunkered down in the trenches until better living arrangements arose. Besides, I still received valuable benefits, which cooled smoldering desires I had yet to receive from the other side.

Lying flat on my back, lifeless, I stared at the ceiling above. Restless, fighting the plight crossing my path, I thought, *what should I do now?* Sorrow became a constant companion I could not escape. Refusing to be beaten, and too young to succumb to a foe that placed no true value on my existence, I stumbled through the trenches, wearily and trounced, knowing I was far better than that.

Battlefields

My interactions with Oz unexpectedly intensified since our excursion to Santa Barbara and Lake Cachuma. Cautiously, I requested if he would be interested in meeting, spending the evening with my Aunt Lorraine, who planned a family dinner with Vivian and me. Oz easily accepted my invitation without hesitation.

During our interactions, it became clear Oz would do anything I asked of him. Thinking back, the loyalty Oz displayed was endearing, but at the time I would not believe he was truthful. You see, Oz was a strange animal: frightfully scary, not taking shit from anyone. Since our friendship blossomed, I'd witnessed two heated altercations with unknown individuals. Each incident resulted in face-to-face confrontation, and not once would he relent and walk away. Standing his ground, Oz intimidated all those foolish enough to challenge him. To make matters worse, Oz was a skilled boxer, possessing a fearless eagerness to fight anyone at the drop of a dime.

His reckless behavior could be unsettling; thankfully, his loose-cannon temperament never reared in my direction. No matter what I would say, he received it, never raising his voice. I must admit, I found it arousing seeing a man who left no prisoners quickly transform into a gentle beast when it came to me. He treated me with respect, never disclosing any hostility.

We arrived at Aunt Lorraine's mad-ass hungry, looking forward to a pleasant family gathering. Aunt Raine, as I called her, reluctantly announced she had invited my mother, but thankfully, knowing I would attend, she declined the invitation. There was no way she would allow herself in the same room with her ungrateful son. At odds for years, however, my mother and aunt remained cordial, with Aunt Raine maintaining the highroad, including my mother in most family gatherings.

Charismatic, carefree, and unselfish, Aunt Raine's personality was the polar opposite of my mother. Whereas my mother straddled the fence of beastly demeanor and enduring personality, like a mixed bag of nuts, never knowing which would fall into your hands, my Aunt Raine was always the same, never changing, and you knew exactly what you were getting. Supporting all you attempted to accomplish, even when you were wrong,

Vance N. Smith

Aunt Raine presented a way of correcting and comforting all at the same time. Knowing how my aunt felt, I never questioned her intentions. Lately she became our mediator when Mom flew the coup and the beast reappeared.

I must state, the situation between my mother and I did not sit well with my aunt, though she remained neutral, supporting my efforts as a silent partner. That way she was able to keep the peace, easily stepping in when times went awry.

Aunt Raine was a woman of means, having married Charles Michaels, a well-liked gynecologist. She never worked, living a comfortable life of a black socialite. Her home, a massive colonial-style brick residence, was located within the Hancock Park section of Los Angeles. A regal five-bedroom home with a guesthouse above the rear detached three-car garage. My mother held a long-standing resentment toward my aunt, feeling the life she held should have been hers. Unclear of the details, I only knew that my mother dated Uncle Charles first. I'd asked my aunt about the details on several occasions after loose lips exposed the long-held family secret. However, Aunt Raine would not reveal any information, simply stating, "Mind your own business, boy!" I loved my aunt and knew when I crossed the line. Whatever happened between my mother and Aunt Raine, I knew to drop the subject.

The formal dining room of my aunt's home featured an elegant Waterford chandelier, and beneath it was a large walnut dining table with six sets of fine Italian bone china dinnerware. The room had muted beige walls and hardwood flooring covered by an antique Persian rug, and a matching credenza centered across from the expansive bay window.

Aunt Raine sat at one end of the table, and I was to her right with Oz on my opposite side. Vivian positioned herself across the table with a family friend, Margret Channing, to her left. Uncle Charles commanded the head of the table.

Prime rib, mashed potatoes and gravy, assorted roasted vegetables, dinner rolls, and all the fixings made for a fanciful and soulful feast. Aunt Raine knew how to throw a party, whether it was an intimate setting or a large extravaganza, and this small family gathering was no exception.

Battlefields

"Oz…it is Oz, right?" Aunt Raine asked.

"Yes, ma'am," he remarked, displaying his mesmerizing smile.

"What is that short for?"

"Oscar, ma'am. Oscar Escalante."

Leaning forward, she said, "Enough of the ma'am. I give you permission to call me Aunt Lorraine." She flashed a quick smile. "How did you meet my nephew?" she asked, reaching for her glass of wine with eyes fixed upon Oz, sizing him up. Investigative reporting at its best!

"Aunt Raine!" I retorted.

"Am I embarrassing you?" she asked.

Oz placed his hand to my shoulder. "It's OK, Willie," he said, returning his attention to my aunt. "We met at a party back in April."

"What do you do…are you in school?" she quizzed.

"I work for a construction company."

Aunt Raine nodded with approval, lifting her glass. "Do I detect a New York accent?"

Oz smiled. "Yes, I'm from the Corona neighborhood of Queens."

She smiled back at him. "You're a handsome young man!" Then she paused, picking up her linen napkin, and gently wiped at her mouth. "Girlfriend?" she asked, her question undoubtedly directed at Oz, but her eyes fixed on mine.

I hunched deep into my chair, exasperated. "Please forgive my aunt," I said, signaling a disapproving gaze.

"It's OK, I don't mind. She has every right to ask any question she wants. She's only interested in getting to know me better," Oz remarked. "I'm not seeing anyone in particular."

I noticed Vivian seated motionless, captivated by Oz, her dreamy-eyed state proved evident to everyone in the room. I gave Vivian a swift kick to her shin, causing her to promptly straighten up and reach for her dinner fork.

"Lorraine, leave the boy alone, and stop with your cross-examination!" Uncle Charles snapped.

"Thank you, Uncle Charles," I stated, picking up my fork, placing a piece of prime rib into my mouth. Returning my gaze, I saw Aunt Raine's probing stance, her left elbow resting upon the table with hand extended upward—fingers twisting among one another. Something was on her mind; I could see the wheels turning fast and steady. Ignoring her quiet inquisition, I asked Oz, "How's your food?"

"Good as hell," he stated softly.

I smiled, playfully punching his thigh. Oz took a mouthful of food and grinned.

"My darling, Will, where are you living again?"

"I'm in Hollywood on De Longpre; I thought I told you that?"

"You may have, but I don't remember. You live alone?" she asked, presenting a cavalcade of questions.

"*Yes*, Aunt Raine! Why are you grillin' me so hard tonight?"

"How are you able to afford such a place? Is it an apartment?"

"It's a bungalow." Oz, for whatever reason, answered for me.

Darting an unhappy scowl in Oz's direction, I said, "I'm doing OK. I make do."

"How can you afford a bungalow?" Aunt Raine continued the inquisition.

"If you must know, I'm renting from a close friend, so I pay very little."

"Oscar, do you know this friend?" My aunt redirected the pressure.

Oz shifted uncomfortably in his chair. "No, ma'am, I don't."

Rearing into the high-back chair, I said, "No, Auntie, Oz doesn't know the individual I rent from!"

"Why is that, and who is he? How do you know him?" She sampled a nibble of the feast before her. "Your mother mentioned some cop had come around threatening her...is he the one? Your mother hinted she was a bit concerned."

"Aunt Raine, please drop it!" Tiny beads of sweat began to form along my temples and forehead, and franticly, I darted my eyes toward Oz.

"Enough...this conversation is not appropriate in front of mixed company."

Thank God for Uncle Charles! I knew I needed to have a heart to heart with my aunt, but damn, I was not about to explain my life story to an entire

Battlefields

congregation. Aunt Raine remained removed from the conflict between my mother and me, I had thought, but apparently my mother had filled her ears with God knows what! I did not want my aunt thinking I somehow disrespected my mom. As of late, it was no secret to my aunt that dysfunction reeked from the James household and for the most part remained muted. In fact, Vivian mainly lived with my aunt after I left the house last summer. Most certainly, my mother was spreading her vicious lies, playing the victim.

Just when I thought the cross-examination was over, there was one more sucker-punch statement.

"Will, you can relax; I approve of your new *friend*," she remarked, filled to the brim with innuendos.

Vivian sat with a huge question mark expression upon her face, Oz completely zoned out, and Uncle Charles loudly cleared his throat. I, myself, nearly fell out of my chair in embarrassment. *OK, just kill me right here on the spot. Did she just try to out me in front of my family and Oz?* Quickly regaining my composure, I said, "I wasn't worried," but still fumbled over my words.

Aunt Raine just smiled. I thought she was finished, but *no*—she was not quite done with her line of questioning. "Where do you live, Oscar?"

Still recovering from the former question, Oz nervously took a gulp of his soda before answering. "I live near the intersection of Coliseum and La Brea."

"I realize I may not show it, but I'm fond of you," my aunt informed him, glancing in my direction.

"Was I under inspection?" Oz asked.

"Of course you were," she said, mischievously smiling and picking up her wine glass—appreciating the moment.

"Good to know I passed the test," Oz joked.

"Don't pay her any mind," I said frowning, facing my aunt.

My aunt smirked, sipping her wine, nodding her head ever so slightly.

"Aunt Raine, the meal was fantastic," I remarked.

"Yes, it was; I haven't had a home-cooked meal since I left New York!" Oz proclaimed.

"I'm glad you two enjoyed your supper!"

"Vivian, why are you so quiet?" I asked.

Seated silently for most of the evening, Vivian hunched her shoulders, picking at her food. I was sad knowing she hated when I left her alone to fend for herself. It worried me to see her so distant and detached—it was unlike her to be so removed.

After dinner we continued our visit until around half past nine. Twisting my wrist to check the time, I said, "Aunt Raine, thank you for a wonderful evening, but we need to head on out." I motioned to Oz, who was talking with Uncle Charles; each held a bottle of beer. I could tell my uncle was excited he found a friend to discuss the latest of the baseball season.

Oz gestured, wrapping up his conversation, shaking Uncle Charles's hand before turning to walk away.

"He's a good kid, a little rough around the edges, but I like him," my Aunt remarked. "How long have you been dating?"

I absolutely froze! *Where in the hell did that come from? In my gut I knew she held opinions, but I never suspected she would actually voice them.* Luckily, I faced away from my aunt, because my reaction of horror would have confirmed her suspicions. With my feet planted firm, I could not move. Standing my ground, I quickly recovered and calmly responded, "What kind of question was that? What are you insinuating?"

She smirked. "I see right through you."

"You see nothing and you're way off base!"

"Am I?"

"Yes, you are!" I angrily answered.

"My loving nephew, you keep telling yourself that. You can't fool me." When Oz approached, Aunt Raine held out her arms. "Give me a hug, handsome; you take good care of my nephew."

He smiled. "I will, but I don't believe he needs me to do that."

Battlefields

With Oz in her arms, she glanced my way. "He does, he just doesn't know it and neither do you," she said, gently placing a kiss to his forehead.

"Thank you for everything," I stated.

Humiliated, I walked toward the door.

"Wilson, where are you going? You better get over here, right now, and give me a hug before you leave!"

The drive back to my place seemed like hours, without a word spoken. Resting with my seat reclined, I closed my eyes. Oz reached to pat my left thigh, which I flinched under his gentle touch.

"Are you OK?" he asked.

"I'm good!" I remarked, sharply.

He knew I was upset though decided to leave the situation alone.

Once we arrived at my home, I proceeded to exit the vehicle. "Good night and thanks for accompanying me tonight; I'll call you."

Oz opened the driver's side door. "Wait!"

I continued walking for the front door.

"Willie, what's going on with you?" Oz grabbed at my shoulder. "What's gotten into you?"

"Nothing, I'm just tired," I remarked, coercing a smile.

"Did I do something wrong?"

"Not at all, it's me. It's been a long day!"

Clearly not convinced, Oz stood with quizzical eyes, searching mine. "OK..." He clinched his jaw. "I'll let it go this time." Searching over his shoulder, he returned his attention to me and said, "Give me a hug."

I obeyed without hesitation.

Locked in his arms, he said, "You're my boy, and I don't want to see you upset."

"I'm cool and you have a good night; we'll talk later."

And that was that.

CHAPTER 23

THE WAR RAGING for control of my affections continued unabated. Two unsuspecting foes fought in silent, blind combat; neither knew the other existed. It was clear to Elijah someone had arisen when his back was turned, but who that might have been, he was unsure. Unable to lure the enemy to the surface, he prepared a full-on assault, making his presence known, attempting to lure the enemy from the shadows.

Holding my ground, like an elusive spy lodged away from danger, I would never slip and disclose the position of his rival. I held this closely guarded secret safe in my heart, remaining careful; I knew to play it safe.

The counterattack strategy of Elijah's challenger remained shrouded in mystery. What were his intentions? Were they simply a joint force to push back an unworthy commander in chief? On the other hand, were his intentions purely self-motivated? Oz distinctly played his position cool.

Sweet memories played continuously in my subconscious. Summer turned to fall, and Oz and I continued our games of masquerading flirtations. With each passing day, my feelings grew substantially. In return, I never questioned how Oz felt, having sustained more love from this man than any other individual. Up until now, all others had given pause to question their intentions. In Oz, the only query that remained unclear was his mixed messages of affection—was he a man of closeted emotions or simply an openhearted individual who loved freely? Unfortunately, whenever I thought I had the answer, Oz would throw a wrench into the balance, left lingering, obscured in secrecy. However, I cherished every

Battlefields

thought-provoking conversation, every awe-inspired moment spent watching the sun paint the sky in magnificent colors of pinks, reds, and oranges before vanishing beneath the sea. Whenever time permitted, we often found ourselves perched on the rocky cliffs of the Southern California coast far from the city, mesmerized by the spiritual light show created before us.

On a rather warm November day, the sun had not disappointed with a spectacular show of wondrous colors. The heavenly sky above splashed with an impressive array of warmth and brilliant hues.

Sitting with my back against Oz's jeep, I felt my face kissed by the radiance emanated from the setting sun. Oz wore cut-off Levi's and was shirtless, positioned at an angle to my right. I watched him intently, gazing at the cascading sunset before us. His loosely curled hair danced in the breeze, racing around his face.

Breaking his observation to turn in my direction, Oz asked, "What are you staring at?"

"You," I casually remarked.

Shyly he beamed. "I gathered that."

"You bothered by it?"

"No." Oz sparked a slight smile, staring toward the Pacific Ocean. "Should I?"

Turning to face the open body of water, I answered with a grin, "No, you shouldn't. You seemed so at peace, lost in thought; I wondered what you were thinking?"

"Life—that's what I was thinking about," he paused, clinging on the thought poised upon the tip of his tongue, "and about you and me, our friendship, how free I am to speak with you regarding anything and everything." Staring off into open space, he held his head high, allowing the swift breeze to caress his face. "You're good for me!" he confessed.

"How so?"

"You make me want to do right."

"You don't need me for that. You can do that on your own."

Oz paused. "I see what you're trying to accomplish with school, work… nothing stands in your way, and you haven't allowed the tragedies of your childhood to block your dreams, and for that you're much stronger than you give yourself credit."

I turned toward Oz with a curious expression. "You see all that in me? I know I'm a strong individual, but sometimes I feel hurt stands in the way of what I need to do."

"Willie, you have to realize the great man you are! I have known you now, for what…seven months, and never have I met anyone like you before. You bring out the best in me. The way we speak to one another, I would never talk like that with my other boys. The only other man I have ever looked up to was my father, but with you, there's something special I can't explain."

"No one has ever said such kind things before."

"You probably think I'm some punk." Oz held his head low.

"Don't say that," I stated firmly. "Just because you speak your feelings don't make you a punk!"

"My boys would say I'm weak."

"Who gives a shit what your boys think; they're not here, I am. It's just you and me and no one else."

"That's what I love about you. You don't fall for my shit, and you make a brutha wanna walk right." Oz leaned against a large boulder with his hands clasped around the back of his neck. "Where do you want to be ten years from now?"

"In love," I answered easily, looking straight ahead, catching the breeze against my face.

Oz rose, fixing his gaze in my direction. "I didn't expect that answer! Is that all you want?"

"Why not? Isn't love something you want in your life?"

"Of course I do!"

"Then why would you think that's such a strange answer?"

"Because, I expected you to say something regarding your career. All this time I have known you, you never made a comment regarding the affections of another."

Battlefields

"That doesn't mean I don't have them."

"No, it doesn't. I speak of babes I may be interested in, but you have never led on to your desire to be in love."

"Oz! Be real! The only women you speak of are the ones you want to fuck, or have fucked then tossed aside. That is not love; it's simply stickin' your dick in a hole and moving on. I'm speaking of a much deeper connection. A deeper love that causes daydreams of possibilities, the kind of love that makes your stomach queasy every time you're in their presence, never wanting to live another day without them in your life. That's the kind of passion I'm speaking of."

"Is that what you think of me?"

I smirked. "Well…" I said, turning toward him.

"Is that how you really feel?" Oz asked.

"Prove me wrong!"

Oz sat motionless with hurt written all over his face, and when he opened his mouth to speak, his voice was barely audible. "Who are you to say I'm not in love already?" Oz reached for support, and then stood to walk around the other side of his jeep, leaning forward, grabbing another beer from the cooler. He placed the bottle next to his lips, taking a quick chug before wiping his mouth with the back of his hand. "You know, we all want the same thing."

"Yeah, you coulda fooled me."

Oz returned, stopping dead in front of me. "Stop fuckin' with my head!"

"I'm not. I'm just speaking on what I've seen."

"I've shown you love."

"Yes, you have, but you and I are not fuckin', so that doesn't count."

"You're just fuckin' with my head," Oz stated with hurtful eyes.

"I'm not playing games with you, Oz," I said, as I stood, brushing dirt from my jeans. "It's getting late; we should leave."

Placing both hands against the jeep, beer bottle still in hand, Oz blocked my path. His jaw clinched tight, staring hard and tense with controlled, heavy breathing.

"What," I asked, stepping closer. Oz's stance held steady and firm. "Something you want to say?" His eyes rolled down then up, sizing me up. I pushed him away. "I didn't think so!" I stated, opening the passenger side door, stepping in.

I was not in the mood to play games.

CHAPTER 24

SEVERAL DAYS PASSED with neither Oz nor I attempting to contact the other. Our last rendezvous had not ended on a good note. In fact, during the return home from our sunset excursion, neither of us uttered a word—uncomfortable to say the least! As far as I was concerned, I had said nothing wrong, just the facts to my observations—he had no commitment and a different girl every week. On another note, who was I to blame him if women allowed that sort of treatment. Oz knew he could have any woman he coveted; his good looks and personality made for a desirable man, and yes, I ached for him just as much as everyone else.

Silly me, I thought, *love can be a muthafuck!*

Listening to the swollen raindrops tapping against the windowpane, I watched Elijah sleep unfazed by the melodic sounds of a crying sky. The cloud-filled horizon was dark and dreary, casting a murky, muted floodlight into our bedroom—a day made for sensuous lovemaking. Once again, Belinda flew to Vegas to visit her ailing mother, presenting Elijah and I the opportunity to spend a peaceful weekend together, after so many nights of not being able to.

Elijah tossed restlessly before slowly opening his eyes, greeting me with a smile. "Good morning."

I placed a tender kiss against his forehead, and then asked, "How did you sleep?"

"I slept well." Overextending his long torso with a grunt, he said, "I'm hungry as hell, what's for breakfast?"

"What do you feel like having?"

"Pancakes."

"Pancakes! And what do I get in return for fixin' a hearty breakfast?"

"A whole lot of me! I need all the strength I can get."

"Well, let me get up right now and get to cookin'!"

As soon as I stood from our bed, someone laid against the doorbell. *Who could that be?* I thought, gazing at the clock. It was six minutes past nine in the morning.

"Who in the fuck is ringing my bell so early in the Goddamn morning?" Elijah grumbled. "Were you expecting someone?" he snapped.

Wearing only briefs, I reached for a bathrobe to cover up. "No, sit tight and I'll see who it is," I remarked.

"Tell them we don't want any!"

I made my way through the living room; approaching the door, I yelled, "Who is it?"

"Open the door, Willie!"

Oh shit. My heart sank. *This cannot be, not today,* I thought, pausing a minute before I opened the door. Of all days he decided to stop by unannounced! There was no one else to blame but myself, since I had allowed him access to the possibility of stopping by.

"Willie, hurry up, it's cold and wet out here!"

Quickly scanning over my shoulder, checking to see if Elijah remained in the bedroom, I cautiously opened the door. "What are you doing here?" I stated, stepping onto the porch, leaving the door slightly ajar.

"We need to talk."

"About what?"

"About the other day."

"Oz, this is not the best time. Let me call you later and we'll talk," I said, peering around the corner of the door, checking to see if Elijah remained in bed. "Please, I'll call you later, I promise." A worried expression consumed my face.

Battlefields

"What's wrong with you? Do you have someone with you?" Oz asked, with jealousy plastered clear across his face.

"Can we talk another time…cuz right now is not the best time?"

Elijah bellowed from the bedroom, "Who's at the door?"

Wincing, holding the door open just enough to poke my head inside, I answered, "It's nobody!" I said the words and knew—I *knew* they pierced the core of his soul. I closed my eyes and cringed.

"Oh, so I'm nobody? What's up with that?" He tried peering over my shoulder. "Who was that?" Oz asked.

"He's…" I simply could not state that the voice on the other side was that of the man I shared my bed with the last two years. Instead, I shook my head in defiance.

"Who was that?" he demanded.

"You have no right asking that, and besides, you should have called first," I said, deflecting the tension back on Oz.

"What's going on, Willie?"

"Oz, please…I'm begging you!"

"Willie!" Oz exclaimed.

"Oz, please!"

"I'm not leaving until you tell me what the hell is going on!" Oz moved for the door. I raised my arm, placing it against the frame, blocking Oz's path. Oz shoved my arm out of the way. "Move, Willie!"

"Oz, what the fuck are you doing?"

Oz stopped. "Willie, tell me what's going on!"

Placing my hand to Oz's left shoulder, struggling to hold him back, I said, "You can't be here right now, I'll explain later. I don't want any trouble!" I knew Oz had an explosive temper, as did Elijah—with the two of them meeting like this it would not end well.

Before I could move Oz from the porch, the door swung open with Elijah on the other side, glaring down. "Who the fuck are you?" Elijah snarled, surging with venom.

"Man, I'm not here to start no shit with you! I'm here to see Willie, so mind your own business!" Oz turned his attention in my direction. "Willie!

Vance N. Smith

Who's this muthafucka?" Oz remarked, without breaking our eye contact, pointing his finger at Elijah.

The showdown was ready to commence; two adversaries unknowingly about to enter battle. The conflict, which had been brewing since this past June, was ready to erupt into an all-out war!

"Elijah, go inside and let me handle this!" I interjected.

"Oh, hell nah…this muthafucka gonna come up in my crib!" Elijah stepped onto the porch, wearing nothing more than pajama bottoms with bare feet. "Get the fuck out of here before I throw your ass out!"

"I'll leave…but I'm not leaving until I speak with Willie." Oz's stance held firm. "Are you fuckin' this dude?" he asked me, his expression filled with hurt and disappointment. "What the fuck is going on here?" he shouted.

"Oz, I don't know what to say!"

"I'm gonna tell you one more time, get the fuck out of here!" Elijah directed his anger by shoving me to the side. "I told you before, you better not be fuckin' some other dude! And this mutha gonna come around my crib unannounced! Uh huh, yeah, I knew you were fuckin' behind my back!"

"Elijah, we're not fuckin'! He's just a friend!" I pleaded.

"You don't have to explain our relationship to him! Besides, how old is this dude anyway? What the fuck is this shit!" Oz bellowed from the top of his lungs.

As the minutes passed, tensions grew, and with each word spoken, the heat of battle forged ahead, escalating to heights where someone was sure to get hurt. Armed forces geared up for warfare, as the words sliced, causing damage beyond repair. Hand gestures, finger pointing, as each antagonist determined to gain the upper hand.

During the melee, I stood holding Oz in a vain attempt to separate and defuse hostilities before someone caused bodily harm. With the fury of his aggression—the bulging veins, the small particles of spit as his lips moved—he blurted vile statements of contempt.

Elijah held his ground, but not once would he leave the safety of his fortress. Returning with rapid exchange, Elijah fired hate in fluid

Battlefields

succession. "Yeah, muthafucka…I got something for your ass! Keep that shit up!"

Mocking Elijah, Oz said, "Come on, bitch, I got something for your ass too!"

"Oz, he's a cop…don't do it!" I stated.

"I don't give a fuck who he is! Bring your punk-ass out here, nigga!" Oz demanded.

While the ensuing altercation marched on, I managed to maneuver Oz toward the front of the property. With the commotion heating up, a few neighbors stepped outside to investigate.

"Oz, you guys are causing a scene. Look, the neighbors are starting to come out. Don't do this! You have nothing to prove. I know you can kick his ass, but he's a police officer, and you don't need the trouble he'll cause." Staring into his eyes, pleading, I said, "For me…do this for me, I'm begging you! He's not worth it."

In the meantime, Elijah had retrieved his forty-five caliber handgun, holding it down at his side, and said, "If you don't leave my property, I will blow your fuckin' head off!"

Oz calmly marched around my side with arms extended, walking right up on Elijah. "Shoot, muthafucka! You think that scares me? I've dealt with worse punk-ass bitches than you…so go ahead and shoot, but you had better make sure you kill my ass, because I will wipe your ass up and down this fuckin' street!" Oz moved in closer, stopping just a few inches short. His head cocked to the side, he eyeballed Elijah up and down with a smirk.

I stood petrified, while one of the neighbors screamed, "Call the police!"

I yelled, "Oz, you crazy fuck! What are you doing?"

With clenched fists, Oz roguishly grinned. "Yeah, bitch…I thought so!" With a scowl, Oz stepped back, turning effortlessly to walk away, heading in my direction. When he approached, he stopped and demanded, "You owe me an explanation!" then pushed past me and walked to his jeep and sped off.

Once Oz left the premises, I stood next to the curb, watching him flee the scene. I turned toward Elijah who paraded back and forth alongside the

Vance N. Smith

walkway, mumbling indecipherably. Returning toward the house, I stopped once I met Elijah at the base of the stairs. "What the fuck was that? Now the police are on their way! What were you thinking?" I shook my head before stepping inside. Elijah remained with a blank appearance.

I sat on the living room sofa, wet, cold—angry as hell! The steady light rain tumbling from the darkened sky above soaked my robe. Within five minutes of Oz leaving, the police showed up—Elijah waited outside and quickly dealt with the matter. To his advantage, one of the officers, a friend of his, was able to defuse the problem. It was unclear what lie he told, but whatever was said, it worked, since the police did not stay long. Elijah returned inside without acknowledging my existence. He entered the bathroom, slamming the door, where he remained for about an hour.

Once he emerged, he was ready to talk, although by that time I had nothing left to say. The issue was pointless, since the damage was done.

"I can't do this anymore," I said.

"What the fuck is that supposed to mean?"

"Are you deaf?" I huffed. "I'm done!"

"*You're* done? You have one of your pieces come to my house and you're done? Nah, muthafucka, you're done when I say you're done!"

"You're sick," I said, rising from the sofa, heading for the bedroom.

"Where the fuck are you going?"

I stopped, looking over my shoulder. "I'm packing my shit…and getting the fuck out of here!"

"You're running to that muthafucka?" Elijah stated.

"You don't get it, do you?" I snidely chuckled. "No…it's because of you! You left me here alone, stopping by when you only wanted some ass, and it has taken me all this time to realize what we had was nothing meaningful, only physical. You had it all…a wife, children, a home, and a young piece of ass on the side, who would do anything to make you happy."

"I gave you everything!" he shouted.

"What have you given me?" I screamed.

"I gave you freedom and a roof over your muthafuckin' head when you had no other place to go!"

Battlefields

"Elijah, I give you that. You gave me a place to stay, but it came with conditions. There was no freedom…you controlled everything, including who could come around, who I could speak with, and what friends I could have. You were no better than the situation I had with my mother."

"Funny, you didn't complain before!"

"You're right, I didn't complain. Confusion is what I was used to, and you provided plenty of it, but it ends today, and that's why I'm leaving your dumb ass!"

When I moved out of my mother's house, I brought only my clothes and a few personal items, so I did not have much to pack. I had no idea where I was going, but I knew I had to get away from here.

While packing my bags, Elijah tried in vain to convince me to stay. He pleaded, "Baby, don't go!"

"It's over, Elijah!"

"I need you!"

"Oh, that's convenient…now you need me!" I laughed to myself. "You'll get over it."

With his last, best effort, he turned on the waterworks, sobbing, begging me not to leave.

I finished packing my shit, hopped into my car, and did not look back.

CHAPTER 25

As I LEFT Elijah's house, I had no idea what my next game plan would be. Gratefully, Marshall offered the opportunity to stay with him for as long as I liked. The next dreaded business I had to take care of was finally divulging my life to Aunt Raine, which would be an extremely difficult conversation. Delicately, I danced around the sorted details of my past living arrangements. Thankful, as I suspected, she was supportive, offering the use of her guesthouse until I was financially capable to stand on my own. I could not believe the windfall. I guess someone high above held my best interests after all, knowing I could not return to my mother's house.

Once I settled in, I knew that explaining my relationship with Elijah to Oz was my main priority, and Oz required my forgiveness, too. Hesitantly, I cautiously dialed. Waiting for Oz to pick up, I felt sick to my stomach. My insides were a churning mess, complete with extreme somersaults.

"Who is this?" Oz answered after about five rings.

"Oz, it's me, Wilson…how are you?"

"I'm good," he answered, followed with dead silence.

I waited a few moments before speaking up. "Oz!"

"I'm here."

"Don't make this hard for me."

"I'm listening," he responded.

"What are you doing?" I asked.

"Nothing…"

"I'm coming over."

"I'll be here."

Battlefields

The phone went dead.

Arriving at Oz's about an hour after our conversation, I pressed the front gate intercom button.

"Hello?" he answered.

"It's me, open up!"

Before I could extend my arm to knock, the door opened. Oz stood stoned faced with a tensed posture, undoubtedly still fuming from the event that had transpired a week prior. Carefully I entered the room, offering him a bottle of Belvedere vodka, and quickly made my way for the recliner positioned at an angle to the sofa. His demeanor changed a bit by my peace offering, his favorite alcohol of choice.

"Thanks for the juice!" he commented.

"You're welcome," I said nervously, avoiding all eye contact, but my left leg bobbed at a record pace.

Placing the bottle on the dining table, Oz preceded toward the sofa, taking a seat, his legs spread wide with forearms resting on his lap, hands clasped together. With a tightly clinched jaw and his eyes fixed on mine, not once would Oz remove his gaze. Together, we sat in silence.

Shifting awkwardly within the recliner, I broke out in an uncomfortable sweat, overwhelmed with remorse and guilt, not comprehending why. *Why should I feel I've done something wrong? No one told him to come around unannounced, demanding he speak with me. I'm not the one who pulled out a gun.*

In the background, music filled the empty space left by our lack of communication. Finally, someone had to break the ice. "What took you so long to call me?" Oz hesitated. "I called you, but that muthafucka answered the phone! Where have you been?" Oz fired from all angles; no way was I dodging that bullet.

"I moved."

"I gathered that…where?" Oz asked, biting down, chewing at the corner of his lower lip. "Why didn't you ask for my help?"

"It was unexpected," I regrettably answered.

Vance N. Smith

"Again…why didn't you ask for my help?"

"Oz, I didn't know I was moving until the commotion settled. It wasn't until that moment I realized I had to leave." Leaning forward, resting on my elbows, and looking straight ahead, I said, "Besides, having you present would not have been a good idea. Someone would have ended up hurt."

"I could easily handle that mofo," he said, his head gently nodded back and forth. "Why haven't you been honest with me? I thought we were above that!"

Again, more questions, I could barely keep up. "I have!"

"Have you?" he questioned.

"Yes, I have!" I remarked, defensively.

"I think there were aspects of your life you left out!"

"Like what?"

"Oh, so you're gonna play games with me!" Oz bobbed his head, continuing to bite his lower lip. "OK, I guess I'll have to spell it out. You and him…what did you think I meant?"

"You think it's easy to confide something like that? You think it's that easy?"

"You knew you could talk to me about anything! Why wouldn't you be able to tell me something that important?"

"It's easy for you to pass judgment! Like…how I should be able to open up, confessing everything there is to know. If you recall, I have not had a simple life. Must I remind you, I had to leave my childhood home; I have no relationship with my parents. Everyone I've trusted has turned his or her back on me. Oz, you mean everything to me; we have good times together, and I wanted you in my life, but I was afraid I would lose you. When we first met, we were cool, we chilled…then you disappeared. I suspected you were no different from anyone else. I now know you're different, but I had to be sure. I would never tell all my secrets right off the bat! Eventually, I would have told you, but the time had not presented itself. Then again, you haven't told me about your love life, so why should I?"

"Don't make this about me! I've told you everything there is to tell!"

Battlefields

"So you say!"

Oz reared deep into the sofa, his face frowning with a questioning expression.

"What...you have nothing to say?" I remarked.

"What are you getting at?" Oz asked.

"It was just a statement, an observation."

"I have nothing to hide."

"No? OK...I'll take your word for it, and I'll leave it at that!" I gave him the opportunity to confess, to acknowledge this hidden game of mutual attraction. As I suspected, he blew me off, continuing with the charade. Standing from the recliner, I said, "I need to use your bathroom."

"You know where it is," Oz stated with sarcasm.

When I returned, Oz stood at his makeshift bar mixing a drink. "Here," he said, extending his hand holding a tall glass of rum and Coke.

"I don't want any."

"Take it. I have more questions I need to ask."

"Like what?"

"How long have you known you were gay?"

"I've always known."

"How could you know something like that?"

"Easy, the same way you knew you was straight. Instead of me wanting girls, I lusted after men, plain and simple!"

"You weren't molested or influenced by someone?"

Perplexed by his question, I asked, "Oz, you actually believe I would choose this...to be different from everyone else, living my life in secret, wondering who might find out, and if they did, would they accept me? It's not that simple. I didn't choose this, and I did not wake up one day deciding to be gay. This is who I am, what God wanted me to be, if you believe in that sort of thing. Do you know how simple and easy my life would be to pretend I wasn't, but that is not who I am. I am a gay man, and to make matters worse, a gay black man! Not only do I have the stigma of being black, I have the title 'gay' attached!"

Oz sat with a sullen expression. "I don't know, Willie; I never met any-one gay before. People think it's something you choose. That's what I was taught."

"I'm sorry, I didn't mean to come down so hard. It just infuriates me that people honestly believe we choose this, living our lives hidden behind closed doors, unable to express how we feel, or walk down the street holding the hand of the one you love. Why do you think so many have committed suicide? You have to be a strong individual to deal with the shit we endure."

"I guess, I never thought of it in that way."

"You can ask anything you want, and I'll be truthful. I will not hide any secrets from you, I promise." A truth I already breached, since I was not coming clean about how I truly felt.

"Who's this mofo you were dickin' around with?"

Sitting along the edge of the recliner, I thought, *Yeah...I guess I will have that drink,* and reached for the glass, placing it next to my lips. *Damn, that burned.* I contorted my face as the fiery fluid traveled down my throat.

Oz smirked. "Too strong?"

I nodded yes, wincing, with one eye partially closed,

Oz leaned in, taking the glass. "Lightweight!" He walked toward the bar reaching for a bottle of Coke. "So, who is he?"

"Why do you need to know, is it that important?"

"To me, yes!"

"He's someone I believed loved me, but it turned out I was only a toy to him."

"How long have you known him?" Oz placed the glass of rum beside me, returning to the sofa.

Lifting the tall glass, stealing a quick sip before I spoke, I answered, "I've known him since I was sixteen."

Oz raised an eyebrow after hearing that bit of information. "You've been fuckin' ole boy since you were sixteen?"

"No...I *met* him when I was sixteen," I stated with sarcasm. "We didn't become involved until I was seventeen."

"What's the difference?"

Battlefields

"And your point?" I snapped.

"My point is…he was too damn old!"

I scoffed. "You think because I was seventeen I didn't know what I was doing?"

"I'm sure you thought you did, doesn't mean it was right!"

"This is pointless because I bet you were the same age or younger when you started."

"That may be true, but they were all around my age, not twenty years older!"

"Are you mad it wasn't you? Is that why you're so upset?" *There…I said it!*

Oz's manifestation was as if someone had blindly knocked the wind out of him. Dumbstruck, stumbling for support, he announced, "Let's get this straight—I'm not gay, never have been, never will be!"

"Thanks for setting my ass straight!" I said, gulping my drink. I raised my glass toward Oz. "Cheers to you!"

"You don't get it, but it's cool!" Oz remarked.

"Oh, I get it…got it…and had all I could take! He served it up splendidly! That's the only thing I'll miss!" Oz's demeanor quickly changed—the sheer expression on his face was not of disgust but of, dare I say, jealousy.

Oz slammed his empty glass on the coffee table, stood from the sofa, and headed for the bathroom. Watching him walk away, I raised my glass, saluted once again, and took another gulp.

Our friendly battle lasted for the remainder of the evening. Oz continued firing questions from all angles, and before I could answer, he'd shoot another from a different direction. Refusing to allow him to frustrate me, I fired back with ammunition decidedly more powerful. At half past nine, Oz finally relented, calling a truce. "It doesn't matter what your lifestyle is. I love you for who you are, and I don't care that you're gay, that was never my issue. In the future, I would prefer if you were honest with me. If I do something you don't like, tell me! I want you to know you can tell me anything; I'll never judge you."

"Oz, I appreciate that, and I promise I will as long as you are the same with me."

"I will…you know you mean the world to me."

"Come here," I ordered, smiling at him.

He smiled with his usual toothy grin. "What do you want?"

"Come here!" I repeated.

Oz hesitated before seductively strolling forward and remarking, "I'm here…now what's this all about?" That wide smile, his wet, moist lips, the sight of him licking the left corner of his bottom lip made my legs weak!

I grabbed a portion of his shirt, pulling him into me. Oz stiffened as he fell into my chest. Wrapping my arms around his waist, I whispered, "Thank you." Oz recovered, giving me the warmest bear hug, sinking his solid physique firmly against mine—placing a tender kiss delicately alongside my neck.

And once again, he displayed that contradictory behavior.

CHAPTER 26

PREPARING SEDONA A mug of hot tea, I asked, "How's the pregnancy?"

"So far, so good! The baby is healthy and everything is normal."

"How far along are you?"

"I'm five months."

"I'm excited, are you excited?"

Sedona smiled broadly. "Yes, I am extremely excited and happy! I was worried at first, but now…" Sedona smiled, "I love this baby so much!"

"You're going to make a perfect mother, and I wish you the best."

Since moving into the guesthouse, Sedona and I spent nearly every Sunday afternoon together, whenever I wasn't working. Coming out to Sedona was a blessing, helping to strengthen our friendship, as with Oz.

It was the second week of December, and the winter season proved to be a rather wet one, as another storm blew in, dumping more than an inch of rain.

The guesthouse featured a medium-sized living room off the entry stairwell with a fireplace covered in reclaimed red brick and a protected balcony above the carport below. It had a manageable sized kitchen and dining area and a decent amount of bedroom and bathroom space. My new digs were decorated with a few pieces of furniture donated by my aunt and a few items picked up along the way, making it a comfortable place to call home. All mine, with no strings attached. I could come and go as I pleased and have over whomever I wanted. I was finally happy!

"How are the recordings coming?"

"So far, I'm pleased. Jackson is working with me, pushing me to write a few songs of my own. Will, I didn't know I had the talent to write. The one track I love the most, I wrote all the lyrics myself!"

"What type of song is it, a ballad or dance track?" I asked.

Taking a sip of her hot tea, she smiled and said, "It's a ballad about really loving someone for the first time."

"I take it you're speaking of Jackson?" I remarked, smiling mischievously.

"Maybe!" Sedona stated coyly, holding the hot beverage to her mouth. I smiled. "Are you in love?"

"I like to think I am!"

"Does he feel the same way?"

Sedona nodded her head yes.

"Well, as long as you're happy, I'm happy."

"I am!" Sedona lifted her mug, holding it to her mouth, and picked a banana from a bowl on the table. "How's Vivian doing?"

"She's doing well; we spent last weekend together."

"That's good to hear, and Oz?"

I smiled before standing to prepare another kettle of boiling water. Reaching for a tea bag, I said, "He's good; we've been spending quite a bit of time together."

Peeling back the skin of the banana, she asked, "Oh! Are you two together?"

"Not even!"

"As much time as the two of you are together, you might as well be!"

"I know! It's so confusing. I'm certain he's hiding what he feels, refusing to say it! I've hinted on several occasions, but he completely ignores me."

"Why don't you just ask and stop with the bullshit."

With a horrified expression, I said, "Are you crazy? I'm not going to do that and possibly destroy what we have. What if my intuition is wrong?"

"You'll never know unless you ask, and besides, what if he is waiting on you to make the first move?"

Battlefields

"I don't think so; Oz is not the shy type. If he wants something, he goes for it. The boy is definitely a player; he has more women chasing after him than you could shake a stick at."

"Where does he find the time when he's always with you?" Sedona commented.

"Good question, I believe they mostly come around late at night."

"So, he's just fuckin' them?" Sedona questioned, shaking her head in disbelief.

"Pretty much, and I stated that fact, which he didn't like one bit! Recently, we had a disagreement over that very subject."

Sedona laughed. "Only you would involve yourself in such a complicated situation!"

Turning toward Sedona, I frowned and said, "I know, right!"

"Have you heard from Elijah?"

"No, I haven't, and he doesn't know where to find me. I just packed my shit and left! For me, that chapter is finally over, no looking back."

"Good…he was scandalous!"

"Maybe, but I must place some of the blame on myself."

"I understand, but he took advantage of you, don't forget that. You may have known what you were doing, but what makes it all the more wrong was that he had a wife and kids, and you were underage; let's not forget that fact!"

"I hear ya, and you're right. But when you're in love, your judgment is clouded, and you make silly mistakes. I was so involved that I could not see my way through. I simply cannot allow that to happen again."

"I hope so," Sedona remarked, placing her mug down. "What are you going to do about Oz? Where is that relationship going?"

"What do you mean? We're just friends."

"So you say, but I know you, and you're in love with him! I see it written all over your face whenever you speak of him, and I see it in him as well…both of you are fools! Do you want me to have a talk with him?"

"Hell no! You stay out of it," I said, retaking my seat at the table. "There may be some truth to what you are saying, but he claims he's straight, and there's nothing I can do with that. However, I do enjoy having him around. He makes me laugh, he comforts me when I have a lousy day, and he always knows what I'm thinking, which was more than I could say about Elijah. But what is so confusing is that he's affectionate with me, not afraid to hug or kiss me!"

Sedona sat staring with her left eyebrow raised, giving me that black girl smirk. "I've never heard of any straight man doing that!"

"It's new to me too!"

"Well…I don't know what to make of that, but you know him best. Sounds like another convoluted situation you've gotten yourself into—be careful!"

CHAPTER 27

February, winter of 1983

It'd been a little over a year since my breakup with Elijah, and it wasn't until I packed my shit and walked away that I realized how much strength I possessed. Leaving Elijah was one of the best decisions I'd made; disrobing that drama lifted a huge weight from my shoulders. Same as the day I walked away from my mother. Conclusively, I felt the sense of freedom I long desired, providing the opportunity to concentrate on school without the distractions incurred by Elijah. I was scheduled to graduate on time, and I excelled at the top of my class with one more year of undergraduate to complete before I would start working on an internship.

Within the past year or so, my friendship with Oz had blossomed beyond anything I could have imagined. Needless to say, it came with blurred lines. I knew we were friends, although incidentally, it became much more than that. We spent every waking moment together, it you saw one, the other was never too far behind. Our bond proved stronger than most relationships or marriages I knew. Our unlikely union confused all of our acquaintances; my friends often questioned the depth of our friendship. His ghetto thug-ass crew had no clue what the hell was going on, and I often found acrimony pledged against me. In addition, their puzzlement led to animosity, which Oz dealt with by ignoring it, taking my side, never giving in to their demands. Unfortunately, a riff formed with a few of them; however, he knew where he belonged.

We never spoke about our friendship, though silently he and I understood how we felt. Oz's affections continued to flourish, emotions he frequently displayed with the progressing year. Knowing I had his love, I became a stronger individual, and his support was undeniable. Never had I felt such love and devotion, but with his love came bewilderment.

The complexity of our friendship teetered the fine line of forbidden love. In a sense, we *were* lovers—confidants. We simply lacked the physical aspect. During the last year, I'd grown weary of my numerous sexual encounters to satisfy the urges I held within, hoping to connect the missing dots of unfulfilled concepts. On the one hand, it pained my heart each time Oz left my side to engage in a tryst with some unnamed female. Nonetheless, I retained my thoughts to myself in an effort not to show how I sincerely felt, and like clockwork, the next day he returned the devoted friend. Unwittingly to me, these unspoken truths harbored festering anger.

Remembering the weekend of my twenty-first birthday, it was a cold Friday night in February—outside the wind and rain blew vigorously. I sat on my living room sofa wrapped with a throw around my legs. Oz snuggled, nestling his head on my lap, before sliding his left hand under my thigh. I held my breath when he maneuvered, placing our friendship in uncharted territory. My heart fluttered and nausea filled a once-calm stomach, causing an invisible smile to display hidden romanticisms. Wondering how much more of this torment I could take, and within that anguish, I accepted all that he innocently gave. Maybe it was a calculated move, or an unconscious passage to gain my love, subtle and subdued, all the while sweet and enduring. I followed suit with a gentle placement of my arm across his chest. Within minutes, I heard a snore rattle from his lips.

Thinking he was sound asleep, I carefully caressed the side of his cheek. Oz repositioned himself before unsuspectingly running his hand up and down his arm. Unsure if he awakened, I returned my hand to his chest.

"Don't stop," he stated methodically.

"I'm sorry…I shouldn't have done that."

"No…I'm cool, it felt nice."

"I thought you were asleep."

Battlefields

"I was…I'm a little cold…that's what woke me up. Rubbing my cheek helped me sleep." Oz tilted his head up with his left eye slightly opened. "I'm OK, you don't have to stop." He replaced my hand against his cheek. "Is the movie almost over?"

"Almost," I answered.

"What do you want to do for your birthday," Oz asked.

"I believe Sedona is planning something."

"Really…" Oz grunted. "I guess I should have spoken with you first. I had hoped we could spend the evening together."

I smiled. "I would have liked that!"

"Then that's what we'll do!"

"As much as I would like to, I can't. I think she's planning something with my aunt."

"Like what?"

"I'm not sure, maybe a surprise party. I overheard them whispering the other day."

Annoyed, Oz responded, "They didn't ask for my help!" Reaching for my hand, holding it firm within his, he said, "I want to do something with you, just the two of us!"

"I'd like that," I remarked.

My mind spun with excitement; Oz never ceased to amaze and surprise me, but with elation came uncertainty. I simply could not overlook the mixed messages he sent and that worried me.

The happy reflections I held came crashing down once I blindly stepped upon the battlefield. A decisive war threatened beyond the horizon, and there was no way to avoid the turmoil that waited on the other side. Again, I was doomed. Failure seemed to follow me at every turn. No matter how I tried to resist, I knew I was heading dead onto a collision course.

Damn!

CHAPTER 28

EARLY SATURDAY MORNING, the ringing of the telephone awakened me from a deep sleep. Fumbling for the receiver, I answered, "Hello?"

"Willie, get up!"

"Oz, what's going on?" I answered groggy and unfocused.

"Get up and get dressed. I'm coming to pick you up in about thirty minutes."

"Where are we going?" I asked, rubbing my eyes, attempting to adjust to the light.

"It's a surprise. Now get up!"

Immediately, I launched out of bed, heading straight for the shower then shaved. Whether it was stated or not, I knew my appearance was paramount. In my heart, I appreciated where we stood, and in time, Oz would come around. At least, that is what I kept telling myself—what a fool! Affairs of the heart played dirty tricks on the mind, but with this one game, I needed to come out on top. It required that I remained patient and determined.

Oz arrived by ten with a day full of activities, starting with a hearty breakfast at Moody Blu's with easy breezy conversation. After breakfast, we headed for Fox Hills Mall, shopping for anything I wanted. Once completing my shopping spree, we ended the afternoon with a Hollywood flick. Simple by most people's standards, but for me, it was the right antidote providing happiness. And that is what I loved about Oz; he understood how to make me feel justified. In all my twenty years, no one knew me the way he did.

Later in the day, Oz dropped me off to change for dinner, having made reservations for two at Lawry's Prime Rib on La Cienega. I quickly freshened

Battlefields

up, dressed in black wool slacks and a red plaid dress shirt with black leather loafers. Style was a natural gift, and whenever I stepped out for the evening, I made sure I was dressed to impress, and tonight was no exception. It was a given I would turn heads, walking in with a man as handsome as Oz, garnering jealous attention from all. A silly young man's attitude, but I did not care; Oz brought out the best in me.

By seven on the dot, Oz arrived with one last surprise gift. When he entered, a slight scent of earthy citrus cologne aroused my nostrils. Oz leaned in, placing a tender kiss against my neck; the compassionate gesture lifted my spirit tenfold.

Pulling away, I remarked, "You smell good."

"Thank you," he said, flashing his brilliant, ice-melting smile. "You look nice!"

Closing the door, I moved toward the center of the entrance hall. "So do you," I responded. Just as dapper, Oz dressed in black slacks, a white printed button-down dress shirt and black tie, sporting a leather jacket. "What's that behind your back?"

"A little something extra," he said, handing over a small giftwrapped box. "Happy birthday," Oz announced.

"*Wow*! Oz, this is too much; you've done enough already!"

"You deserve it! This is my way of expressing how much I care. You've been more than a friend, you've been my rock, and I wonder if you understand you mean the world to me! This is my way of expressing my feelings. In addition, I love you for what you give me each day, whether you know it or not."

Instantaneously, I grabbed Oz by the lapel of his jacket, causing him to fall into my arms like a weak, helpless puppy. Our embrace was soulful and intimate. Holding him tight, burying my face deep into his chest, I inhaled his romantic scent, which infused my senses, knowing I never wanted to be released from the shelter of his grip.

In our embrace, Oz whispered, "We better get going before we miss our reservations."

"Can I open my gift?" I asked.

"Sure…I hope you like it!"

"I'm sure I will!" Enthusiastically, I opened the box revealing a handsome gold watch. "*Oz*…this is…" I choked on the words I tried to express.

"You don't have to say it, I already know. Let me help you with that?" Oz removed the elegant gold timepiece from the box, placing it around my wrist.

Running my fingertips along the smooth surface, I said, "I love it! Thank you."

"It looks good on you." Oz smiled, placing the empty box on a table.

"Dinner was amazing!" I stated, settling into the booth, feeling stuffed.

"That was one of the best prime ribs I've ever had!" Oz commented.

Lifting my glass of iced tea for a sip, I said, "Today has been unforgettable, and I owe it all to you!"

"I'm glad I made you happy."

"You have…you have no idea."

A childish grin graced Oz's face.

"What's that?" I asked leaning forward.

"What?" Oz sheepishly turned his head.

I was always surprised when Oz revealed his susceptible side, something he seldom allowed himself to expose. I knew then I had his heart. "Never mind, it doesn't matter," I responded with a smile.

Embarrassed, Oz quickly regained his tough composure. "Have you heard from Sedona?"

"I have. We talked briefly this morning, and I promised I would return her call later tonight. Why you ask?"

"Just wondering, it's your birthday and you hadn't mentioned her at all."

"Well, I do believe you kept me pretty busy today."

"Are you complaining?" Oz playfully snapped.

I swiftly kicked his calf. "Funny!"

Battlefields

"Ouch…that hurt," he said, reaching down to rub his calf, "So tomorrow you become legal, twenty-one…drinking age!"

"Whoop, whoop!" I cheered. "Although, I rarely drink, and I'm not much for hanging out at clubs or bars. I've never been big on the party scene!"

"Why not?" he questioned.

"I've always felt uncomfortable, never knowing what to say to others. I'm more of a one-on-one type of guy," I said, leaning forward, resting on my elbows and forearms. "Today was perfect. That's how I like to spend my time."

There was hesitation within Oz. I sensed he wanted to ask a question, though choosing not to. Nervously he began to fiddle with his dinner fork, thoroughly scanning the room.

"Something on your mind?" I asked.

"What?" Oz jumped, startled out of his concentration.

"You heard me…don't make me repeat it," I smirked.

Small beads of sweat formed against his temples. "I'm just thinking, nothing important."

"Then what's the apprehension?" I reached for his hand, which he quickly moved away.

"Don't do that," he snapped.

"I'm sorry…" I said, shamefully turning away to examine our surroundings. "I didn't mean…I…" I stammered. "I only meant to comfort you."

"I know…I'm an ass. I didn't mean to snap."

"It's OK…I should not have done that. I forgot where—"

"How come you don't have a man?" Oz quickly announced.

"What?" Stunned and unsure how I should respond, I said, "Why would you ask me that?"

"I don't know why I ask." Oz turned, placing his attention on the waiter approaching our table.

"Would you gentlemen care to review our dessert menu?" the thinly built waiter asked, standing with his hands clasped behind his back.

"What would you like?" Oz questioned.

"I don't want anything," I responded.

"It's your birthday, you need something…"

"Today is your birthday?" the waiter asked.

"Yes, well…officially it's tomorrow; I turn twenty-one."

"Let me take care of it; I have something special for you!" the waiter acknowledged.

Oz's wide, toothy smile gleamed bright and prominent. "That sounds perfect!"

"Oz, I can't eat another bite!" I proclaimed.

"Sure you can!"

I grinned. "OK…so, who's the lucky lady tonight?"

"What do you mean?" Oz answered defensively.

"Oh, come on, it's Saturday night! You're never alone on the weekend, and I know you're not spending your night with me," I stated, extending for my glass.

Oz hunched his shoulders like a defeated pupil. "Tonight is not about me," he murmured.

I sat straight in my chair. "I see."

"You need a man," Oz stated, returning to the former line of questioning.

Again, I was completely caught off guard. "What?"

Oz grabbed his glass of merlot and gulped, motioning the busboy over. "Can you tell the waiter I'll take another?"

I sat with disapproving eyes. "I think you had enough."

The waiter returned singing happy birthday with a few others, carrying a small candlelit chocolate fudge cake. The waiter sat the cake on the table; I leaned in with closed eyes, wishing upon a wish, and then opened my eyes, placing my gaze upon Oz. I blew out the candles and prayed my wish would come true.

"Happy birthday, Willie," Oz proclaimed.

If only my wish would come true.

CHAPTER 29

THE MORNING OF my twenty-first birthday, I awakened to an abundance of celebratory calls, welcoming me into complete adulthood. Vivian, the first of many, who now attended Howard University in DC, unfortunately could not attend my birthday celebration. By the end of the morning, I received calls from all my closest friends. Life, as I now understood it, painted a clear picture to the possibility of gratifying adventures ahead. Cautiously, I stepped off the battlefield with feet planted firmly on solid ground, the vision of an impending battle now only a presumed mirage. I thanked God for the good fortunes he placed upon me since my breakup with Elijah.

I stepped out of the shower, preparing for an intimate dinner that Aunt Raine organized for my birthday. During my preparation, I thoughtfully recalled the magical events of the preceding day with Oz. A day I would forever treasure and would not allow the mixed signals I received to ruin the time I spent with him.

After receiving a call from my aunt stating she was awaiting my arrival, I dressed, making my way for the main house. Entering through the back door, I called out, "Aunt Raine, I'm here!" I proceeded through the kitchen, calling out once again, "Where are you?" I stopped to examine the spread of goodies lying upon the countertop, grabbing a crab cake from a silver-serving platter before advancing toward the dining area. "Uncle Charles?" I shouted.

I hesitated before venturing further, since the house appeared eerily silent, when out of nowhere a thunderous chorus of cheers ignited the room. Taking a step back, frightened, I yelled, "What the fuck!" My heart raced a mile a minute.

Vance N. Smith

"Happy birthday, Wilson," cheered the hidden crowd of friends and family members. Regaining composure, I watched as guests revealed their presence one by one: Sedona, Marshall, Beau, Monica, and of all people, my parents. *What the hell are they doing here?*

My mother placed her hands to my shoulders, cracking a hesitant smile. "Happy birthday, baby," she stated, leaning in and placing a tender kiss to the side of my cheek.

My gaze firmly planted on Aunt Raine, who smiled and nodded. "Thank you, Mother, it's nice seeing you." Then reaching for my father, who I had not seen since I graduated from high school, I forced a grin. "Hello, Dad."

"You look good," my mother stated.

"I'm well...life is good," I remarked. Looking over her shoulder, I observed Oz leaning against the archway separating the dining room and foyer. Our eyes met, I smiled; he nodded.

"Happy birthday, Will!" Sedona placed her slender arms around my waist.

Overwhelmed by congratulatory thanks coming from every direction, I did not know where to start. Handshakes, kisses, slaps across my back, I was unable to keep up. Among the people and their niceties, I searched the room for Oz. He was perched against the archway, where he remained in silence, oblivious to the busy bees swarming around him, pollinating their love and devotion.

Amid the gaiety, someone tugged at my arm. "Happy birthday, Will."

I turned toward the individual and to my surprise—Isaiah. I gasped, "Isaiah, what a nice surprise!" We hugged. "Man, it's good to see you again!"

"Yes, it is...long time...how have you been?"

"I'm good, man! Are you still working at the Baldwin Hills store?"

"Yes, I'm still there. How's school?" he asked.

"School is great; I'm expecting to graduate next year." I took a step back, examining Isaiah from head to toe. "Man, you look good. Life has been treating you well."

"It has...but a new man in my life can work wonders."

Battlefields

"Well, I wouldn't know about that," I jested, and then added, "What happened to Shea?"

A pained expression formed before Isaiah spoke. "He's gone, I'm sad to say."

"What do you mean?" I asked.

"We'll discuss it later," he stated solemnly.

"OK." I searched his eyes, looking for answers.

"No one special in your life?" he asked.

"Yes, but he doesn't know it," I eluded.

"You mean the one leaning against the wall, examining the crowd and scrutinizing your every move."

Without even looking, I remarked, "That's him!"

Isaiah smirked. "He's a classic closet case! He wants you in a bad way, but will never admit it. Be careful, he'll break your heart!"

"I know, but I love him so much." I paused, changing the subject. "Man, it's really good seeing you!" I repeated.

Isaiah smiled. "Enjoy your party, make your rounds, and we'll talk later."

"It really is good seeing you again after so long."

Isaiah hugged and kissed my forehead. "Same here!"

Making my way around the room, my eyes were on Oz where he maintained his position, watching and observing. As I headed in Oz's direction, he beamed with excitement. Unfortunately, before I could reach him, Beau redirected my actions.

"Will, I want you to meet a good friend of mine," Beau remarked.

"Hey, Beau, glad you could make it." A quick hug was good enough. Afterward, I made a hasty glance to Beau's right. "Hey, Monica."

"Happy birthday, Will, you look handsome this evening! How does it feel to finally turn twenty-one?"

"The same as it did yesterday," I joked.

"Will, this is Skylar...Skylar this is Will!" Beau gestured to a young man standing to his left.

Vance N. Smith

Reaching to shake Skylar's hand, I thought the one good thing I could say about Beau was he knew how to pick 'em! This dude was handsome. Golden brown complexion with chiseled features and full, perfectly shaped lips...*there was something about kissable, thick lips!* He had smoldering hazel eyes and, as black folks like to say, had good hair. Tightly curled locks, the grade many tried to achieve with a Jeri curl, cut into a fade with about five inches of hair on the crown of his head. Skylar stood nearly five foot eleven with a slightly muscular frame. "Pleased to meet you, Skylar, and welcome to the festivities!"

With his hand in mine, he said, "My pleasure, but please call me Skyy."

"Skylar is an unusual name for a black dude," I commented.

Skyy smiled. "I guess you can say that."

"Where did your parents come up with your name?" Speaking with Skyy, I noticed Oz glaring hard; his expression filled with a hint of jealousy, which I ignored, continuing to focus on my current conversation. The clever host I knew to be, I smiled, listening intently to his every word. When he spoke, he leaned close, so close I could feel his hot breath against my skin. My insides swooned by the spell he casted. And for a moment, I forgot all about Oz, because whatever incantation Skyy summoned caused me to have a wildly imaginative visual. Skyy did not exude sex as in the manner of Oz, but something about his demeanor beckoned an effect of the sensual language of passion. I must admit, I was actually engaged, but as luck would have it, inevitably he was another one of Beau's pieces. Nonetheless, I was clearly smitten.

Skyy and I talked for a good fifteen minutes before moving on to my other guests. Releasing my mental grip, I searched the room for Oz, who was nowhere in sight. A hurried sense of loss swept through my entire body. I felt consumed with guilt, duplicity; I had noticed another man in his presence. I could not shake the sensation of disloyalty. My mind went numb, engaging a sudden perception of an out-of-body experience erasing all space and time.

"Will...Will!"

I overheard my name called.

"Will...where in the fuck is your mind?"

Battlefields

I felt a tug on my shoulder and lifted my head to find Sedona standing, front and center, sporting her notorious ghetto black girl scowl. "Where in the fuck is your mind?" Her posture was unsympathetic and filled with edginess, while one hand perched firmly against her hip.

"I'm sorry! I wandered off."

Sedona's lips were tight and tense. "Uh huh! I bet." A quick turn of her head to the right as she eyed Skyy from head to toe. "What's on your mind?" she smirked.

"Nothing…have you seen Oz?" I remarked.

"He's somewhere around here. Last I saw of him; he was having a conversation with your Uncle Charles." Sedona silently laughed. "You're a trip!"

"How's my little goddaughter?" I asked, completely ignoring her last comment.

"Sahara is doing fine, getting just as big and feisty!" Sedona glowed whenever she spoke of her baby girl. "You haven't been over in a while; I'm a little upset with you!"

"I know…I've been so busy!"

"I don't think Oz is a good enough reason not to come around. You seem to spend all your time and energy on him. You meet these men and forget all about your friends!"

Ouch, that hurt. "I haven't spent all my time with Oz," I lied.

"Please! What's going on with you two anyway?"

"Nothing," I opened my mouth to finish my thought when Marshall approached.

"What are you two talking about?" Marshall probed.

"I'm trying to get the scoop on Will and his man, but the only response I get…is nothing!"

"What man?"

"Oz, of course," Sedona quipped

"Oh…I should have known!"

"It's true, we spend quite a bit of time together and that's all it is, which I have stated to you on numerous occasions. Besides, I've been busy with school," I said, downplaying my involvement.

233

"OK, where were you all day yesterday?" Sedona remarked. "You were supposed to call me and you didn't!"

I hesitated to answer.

"Exactly, you don't even need to answer, but I'm not mad at you. You do your thang," Sedona retorted. "I need a drink."

"She clocked you bruh!" Marshall laughed. "But I don't blame you either, cuz he's the one!"

I blushed. "That he is, but nothing is going on. There's nothing more to it, we're just good friends."

"You need to find a good man to settle down with," Sedona commented.

I nodded my head yes.

"What are you doing the rest of the night?" Marshall asked.

"I don't know, why?" I wondered.

"I want to take you out for a drink."

"Let me see...I'll think about it!"

"Nah, nigga! You're not playin' me tonight!" Marshall reached for Sedona's hand. "Let's get a drink." He returned his attention and said, "Be ready, cuz we heading out to Papa Bears!"

I grimaced; I certainly was not in the mood to hang out. I had school in the morning and work later in the afternoon. I followed Marshall and Sedona, but before I reached the bar, Oz pulled me to the side.

"Are you ignoring me?"

"What? I've been looking for you!"

"I bet! I saw you checking out that foo' with your boy, Beau. Who is he?" Oz tried jokingly playing it off, but his body language told a different story.

"Jealous?"

"Why would I be jealous?"

"Why would you ask who he was?"

"It was a joke!"

"If you say so!"

Oz changed the direction he was taking. "Just looking out for you," he said, checking over his shoulder. "I don't think he's right for you."

Battlefields

"Now, how would you know that?"

"I just know," he said, looking around the room. "None of these foo's are good enough!"

Puzzled by his actions, I asked, "Then who would be?"

"I don't know, but none of these foo's!"

With a snide, side eye, I excused myself, making a quick exit. After about ten steps, I stopped, resuming my gaze upon Oz. Not moving an inch, his eyes remained fixed on mine, locked. With an uncompromising expression, Oz raised his longneck bottle of beer; I shot a faint smile and strolled off. Walking a few more feet, I stopped; I felt a haunting presence swirling around. My body quivered before continuing on my way.

The rest of the night would undoubtedly become a fond, memorable evening. Having my parents present to celebrate my birthday, even if we did not spend any quality time repairing our indifferences, meant the world to me. Maybe this would be the start of a new beginning.

We partied until maybe ten that night, until my aunt politely, unknowing to all, led everyone toward the door. She had that way about her; she would have you surrender without being conscious to what happened.

Ultimately, we stood loitering in the front yard saying our good-byes, attempting to decide our next plan of action.

"Good-bye, Sedona, thanks for coming!" I extended my arms. "Come here and give me a hug, girl!"

Sedona returned with a comforting hug. "I'm happy to celebrate it with you!" Releasing her grasp, she asked, laughing, "Did your aunt just kick us out?"

"She did!" I answered smiling. "That's my Aunt Raine!"

"I guess she had enough." She still held me in her embrace. "I'll speak with you later."

Beau yelled walking away from his vehicle, "Will, what are your plans for the rest of the evening?" Monica and Skyy tagged along close behind.

"I'm not sure...Marshall wanted to take me to some place called Papa Bears!" I answered, with my arms remained wrapped around Sedona's waist.

235

"Cool…we'll go along with you!" Skyy remarked.

"Yeah, that sounds like fun; I haven't been out on a Sunday night in a while, but I need to drop off the ball and chain first," Beau said, pointing toward Monica.

Monica huffed, "Nigga, please!"

"Gurl…you don't want to hang with them nasty-ass hoes," Sedona joked.

"Good night, Will; here's my new number, please give me a call when you have a chance." Isaiah grabbed my hand, placing the torn piece of paper in it.

"Thanks for coming! I'll be sure to stay in touch."

"You can thank me!" Sedona remarked. "I was the one who told Isaiah about your party."

I placed a kiss against her cheek. "Thank you."

"You're welcome."

Isaiah smiled and kissed Sedona as well. "Keep in touch."

"I will," Sedona replied.

In the distance, I noticed Oz sitting on his motorcycle, arms folded across his chest, his posture firm and defensive. "Hold on, I'll be right back."

Sedona looked over her shoulder. "Uh oh, someone is in trouble."

Isaiah commented, "Homeboy is straight-up in love!"

"Who…Oz?" Sedona asked.

"Yeah him, we had a conversation earlier and all he could talk about was Will."

Sedona laughed. "Will claims he's straight!"

I swiftly stepped in to say, "Let it go! I'll be right back."

"Yeah, take care of your man," Sedona quipped.

"Why are you waiting here all alone?" I asked, approaching Oz.

"No reason," he remarked.

"Were you waiting on me to say good-bye to you?"

Oz tightened his jaw. "I planned to stay until I learned you were going to hang with that dude I don't like."

Battlefields

"What dude?" I quizzed.

"Ole boy who used to come around when you lived with the old man!"

"You mean Marshall?"

"Yeah him, he's trouble."

"Nah, he's harmless"

"He's trouble, watch your back!" Oz sucked his teeth, holding a toothpick steady between his lips, scrutinizing my group of friends who were obviously watching and commenting. He slowly returned his attention. "I guess I'll jump off out of here…" He glanced back at the others, scowling at them. "We'll talk tomorrow."

I was expecting our usual embrace, except Oz kick-started his bike.

"Be careful," he spoke, without looking my way.

"Good night!" I said, however before I could get the words out, Oz revved his engine.

He turned in my direction, nodding tight-lipped, placed his bike in gear, and sped off. I stood uncommunicative, sad, and befuddled. Searching over my shoulder, Marshall waved for me to come on. Briefly, I remained motionless. It was true I wanted to devote as much of my time as I could with Oz, though it was clearly futile to continue, since our relationship lingered shrouded in mystery.

A night at Papa Bears…

We stepped inside the dimly lit bar with about twenty patrons scattered around the somewhat empty establishment. We paused just past the doorway, scanning the club.

"I'm scared," I whispered.

"You're such a little bitch!" Marshall stated.

"Fuck you!"

"Why are you scared, no one is going to harm you!"

"I don't know, I just am. I've never been in a bar before, let alone a gay one!"

"Nigga, *please…*"

"Do you come here often?" I asked.

"Pretty much every Friday night," Marshall stated. "On Fridays it's so packed, you can barely make your way around. All kinds of fine-ass niggas crowd into this joint!"

"You need to chill, besides everyone is nervous their first time," Beau remarked. "I need a drink, come on Skyy." The two made their way for the bar.

"Stay close to me, big-ass baby," Marshall insisted.

"Whatever," I remarked, examining the slightly empty dance floor, checking out the men populating the room.

"What do you want to drink?" Marshall asked.

"Bacardi and Coke," I remarked.

Making our way around the small dance floor, we passed a group of young men who surveyed our every move: one stood about five foot nine and pudgy, and the other about an inch taller with a slender frame and a greasy-ass Jeri curl, puffing on a cigarette. The taller man smiled when I strolled past; I nervously returned the gesture. He tried to speak, but I swiftly redirected my attention elsewhere, shutting him down.

Music blasted, filling the air with the current dance grooves. Wallflowers stood bobbing, while others engaged in robust conversations. A few pranced on the dance floor rockin' to the jams, their bodies twisting and bouncing to the tunes blaring from the jukebox. My eyes fixed wide in amazement, as I had no idea this type of place existed.

Standing behind Marshall while he ordered our drinks, I nervously probed the room, checking out the variety of men that loitered. Seated at the far side of the bar was a man in his forties, dressed in a suit with one elbow placed against the bar, holding a cigarette in one hand and a drink in the other. He caught my gaze and nodded, taking a puff of his smokes. I blushingly smiled, turning my attention to the other characters in the bar.

Marshall nudged then handed over my drink. "OK...who are you checking out?" he asked.

"No one!"

"Liar," Marshall laughed, taking a swig of his drink.

Battlefields

"Hey...Skyy and I are going outside for a minute," Beau remarked.

"Where are you two going?" Marshall asked.

"Outside to smoke a joint." Beau looked my way. "You want a hit?"

"Nah, I'm good," I responded.

"Are you gonna be OK?" Marshall asked.

"Yeah, I'm cool."

"We'll be right back; I wanna get a hit off that bud!"

"I'll be right here, holding up the bar."

"Whateva'," he said, "Mingle...you might get lucky!"

"Sure." Taking a sip of my Bacardi, I leaned against the bar facing the dance floor. Watching the carefree individuals romp, swaying to the rhythms, I noticed an extremely feminine dude with hands cocked and limp; he twirled, kicked his heels, and dipped, not missing a beat, undoubtedly in his own world.

"Where are your friends?"

Startled, I swiftly turned my head. "They went outside for a minute."

"Do you come here often?" the stranger asked.

"Nope...my first time. What about yourself?"

"I come on occasion." The stranger stood invading my personal space, and his cologne was overwhelming.

Eying the gentleman from head to toe, I thought he was handsome, sporting a long Jeri curl, dressed in slacks and a dress shirt, clean shaven and neat, with skin the color of rich dark honey, and a perfect set of teeth. Blessed with dark brown eyes, wide nose, and shapely lips, not too full but not too thin, his speech echoed with authority.

"What brings you out tonight?" I asked.

"I'm here with a friend." He smiled, licking his lips.

I held my drink close to my mouth, refraining from taking a sip, studying the stranger who stood before me. "I see."

He smirked. "So what brings you out tonight?"

"Friends, and it's my birthday!"

"Happy birthday." He clinked his glass against mine.

"Thanks!"

"I'm Jessie, and you are?" he remarked.

"Wilson…pleased to meet you!"

"So, Wilson, can I buy you another drink?"

"Sure…Bacardi and Coke."

Jessie motioned for the bartender. "I'll have another gin and tonic; my friend here wants a Bacardi and Coke." Jessie paused for a moment before asking his next question. "So, Wilson, what year are you celebrating?"

"Twenty-one," I smiled.

"Ah…first time out?" he asked.

"Yes…"

"I can tell…you seem a little nervous."

"I'm cool, just something to get used to."

"How did you spend your birthday?"

"My aunt threw a surprise party with a small gathering of family and friends. Now, I'm here because a buddy wanted to take me out for a drink." Studying Jessie for a moment, I asked, "Where's your friend?"

"He's around somewhere." Jessie ran his finger down my arm. "So, what are you getting into tonight?"

"Nothing, why you ask?" I said, moving my arm away.

"I thought maybe we could split and hang out at your place."

"That was quick!" I responded.

"You know you want to!" Jessie turned his head when a young man approached. "Where you been, nigga," Jessie asked.

"None of your fuckin' business." He reached to shake my hand. "I'm Bryce."

"Wilson!"

"Pleased to meet you, Wilson."

"Likewise," I smiled.

"I'll be right back; I need to take a piss!" Jessie announced.

I frowned.

"He can be a crude fuck, ignore him!" Bryce remarked.

As soon as Jessie left our side, he quickly began socializing with other eager individuals, obviously keeping his options open until someone bit his

Battlefields

bait. Whereas, Bryce and I engaged in a seemingly stimulating discussion, hitting it off right from the start. Discovering we enjoyed the same interests, the same type of music, and although I found him attractive, there was no obvious love connection. Instead, it felt as if I had been speaking with a lifelong friend. During our dialogue, Bryce revealed he was from Oakland, born and raised, visiting Jessie for the weekend.

Bryce was about my complexion, golden brown and four inches shorter, but stockier with a thick, muscular frame. He was dressed similarly to Jessie with his shirt unbuttoned, exposing his muscled chest, and had a raspy voice, speaking with loads of confidence that disclosed he was educated and smart.

Jessie returned after working the room, spoiling the mood. Shortly thereafter, Skyy entered the main entrance.

"So, Wilson, how can a nigga get in touch with you?" Jessie asked.

"Maybe you should ask Bryce, since I gave him my number while you were patrolling the joint!"

Bryce could barely contain himself from laughing hysterically.

Jessie snarled and stormed off.

I had to laugh. *Now that was funny!*

"No you *didn't*. Man, you just played my boy!"

"I did, didn't I?" I chuckled.

"Nigga, you ain't right!"

"I know..." I said, reaching into my pant pocket, pulling out a ballpoint pen. "Give me your hand!" I scribbled my number. "Call me!"

Bryce smirked. "Maybe I will!"

"You will!" I stated confidently.

Skyy approached, broadcasting he was ready to leave. "Are you ready?"

"Yes, I'm ready. Where's Marshall?"

"He and Beau left!"

"What!" I placed my drink down with a thud, startling the bartender.

"They went to purchase more weed. I'm not into that, so I told them I would take you home."

I was highly pissed because I had only come out because Marshall had wanted me to, and now he left me here alone. "All right, cool," I responded.

Vance N. Smith

"Are you leaving now? I can take you home, if you aren't ready to leave," Bryce remarked.

"I guess I am! I enjoyed our talk, but it's best I leave with Skyy. When are you coming down again?"

"In a few weeks, I'll call you!"

"I'm looking forward to it!" I turned to Skyy, "I'm ready."

On the drive to my apartment, Skyy and I rekindled our conversation, picking up where we left off earlier in the evening. Again sparks flared ever so slightly with sexual tension bubbling carefully to the surface. Skyy stopped his vehicle, parking in front of my aunt's house.

"Thanks for driving me home," I stated, reaching for Skyy's hand, holding it tight.

"My pleasure." Skyy gazed down at our joined hands; with his thumb, he softly caressed the top of mine. "Can I walk you to your door?"

"I'd like that."

Skyy smiled and stepped outside, maneuvering around the tail end of his vehicle. "Let me get that," he remarked.

"You don't have to hold the door for me."

"I know, but I want to." Skyy held the door and smiled.

"Thank you, Skyy…that was kind of you."

"It's my southern ways, I can't help it," he remarked.

"Nice," I beamed.

"How long have you lived with your aunt?"

"I don't, I live in the apartment around back, above the garage. I've been here a little over a year now."

"Cool…"

We slowly walked the long concrete driveway approaching the wrought iron gate, the entrance to the rear yard. I reached deep into my pocket gathering my keys.

"Your aunt has a nice home."

"Yes, she does. She's been a godsend, allowing me to stay rent-free! She helped me when I was in a delicate situation," I remarked, opening the gate

Battlefields

before we continued toward my apartment. "This is it!" I said, pausing at the entrance. "Thank you for walking me to my door."

"You're welcome!" Skyy stood with nervous poise, while a faint grin surfaced.

Skyy rested against the plastered wall, where I placed my hand next to his chest. In the heat of passion, I felt his heart thump with excitement. The shadows of night beckoned his readiness to surrender all, egging me toward him. I placed the palm of my hands against the cold damp wall, surrounding him. His eyes searched mine; his breathing became heavy and steady.

"What are you feeling?" I asked.

"You!"

"Yeah," I whispered, leaning close enough that our lips scarcely touched, passion expanding within the confines of my pants. "I have to get up early in the morning."

"So do I." When he spoke, his lips grazed mine.

I moved my face in a sensuous circular motion. "I need to go to bed so I can get up in the morning."

"Me too. I should get going." He spoke in a slow, deliberate tone with lips slightly parted, his head cocked to one side.

The heat of his breath fluttered around my face; however, I did not want to give in to the heat of the moment. "It's one in the morning."

"I know..." He reached around the back of my jeans, cupping my ass, pulling me closer.

With hands planted firmly against the wall, I restrained myself from giving in. I pushed away, "It's getting hot out here!"

"It could get hotter!"

I stepped back. "Maybe we're moving too fast."

"But it feels right."

Yes, it did feel right. I wanted him in a bad way! All I wanted was to feel warm, hot flesh. Yet the man I wanted was not standing before me.

CHAPTER 30

The morning after my twenty-first birthday, I awakened refreshed, welcoming the dawn of another year of life. Gently I stretched, yawning, and adjusted my vision to the light before raising my torso with one arm. "What time is it?" I asked, scratching the crown of my head.

"It's a little after six," Skyy answered, tying the laces of his oxfords

I smiled. "I need to get up. I have class at eight."

"I have to be at work myself, but I'm glad I had the opportunity to spend some time with you." Skyy stood at the foot of the bed, buttoning his shirt.

"I enjoyed last night. You're wild as hell under them sheets," I jested.

Skyy chuckled. "You brought out the beast in me!"

"Oh…so you're gonna blame that on me!" Running my hand over the crown of my head, I said, "I don't believe I had to teach you a thing!"

Skyy smiled, reaching for his jacket from a chair located in the corner of my room. "What time do you normally return home?"

"I have classes in the morning until noon then I work at the supermarket. I should return home around nine this evening."

"Can I call you later?"

"I would like that!" I lifted a pen off the nightstand, scribbling my number on a piece of notepaper. "I hope to hear from you!"

"You will, I'll give you a call tonight. Hopefully I can get another taste."

"Just say when and I'll serve it up some more!"

I returned home that evening around nine twenty, exhausted. The lack of sleep the night before had taken its toll. Hungry as hell and fatigued, I

Battlefields

had only one thing on my mind—a relaxing hot shower then bed. I laid my keys on the table at the top of the stairs, stopping long enough to kick off my shoes, and then laid my backpack on the floor. I flipped on a light casting a warm glow about the room. With mail in hand, I checked to see if I had anything important, but most of it appeared to be junk and fliers. Afterward, I laid the mail down on the dining table and proceeded to the bathroom.

I removed my clothing and turned on the hot water, adjusting the temperature before stepping into the revitalizing massaging spray. Stooping under the shower nozzle, with hands resting against the tiled wall, I swayed from side to side, allowing the water to escape down around my body. After thirty minutes of intense scrubbing, I emerged renewed and relaxed.

Following my shower, the only thing on my mind was the comfort of my bed. Lying propped against the headboard with a bowl of cereal, I was flipping through the television channels when the phone rang. Before answering, I knew exactly who would be on the other end. "Hello?"

"Hey! I wanted to hear your voice before I headed off to bed," Oz stated. "How was your day?"

Our late-night phone calls had become our daily ritual. "My day wasn't so bad, busy as usual." Whenever I spoke with Oz, it provided me with a sense of comfort and security.

"Did you enjoy your party last night?"

"I did! It was good having everyone around, specifically seeing Isaiah again after such a long time."

"How did you feel having your parents there?" Oz wondered, harboring a bit of concern.

"It was nice, but there's still animosity deep in my heart. I tried having a conversation with my mom, but she completely blew me off! I wish they had come to support me; however, I'm sure Aunt Raine arranged to have them present. My dad was more open to chatting, although I could tell he was not at all interested in what I had to say. Not once did he inquire about my life." I sighed, "Some things never change!" Fading memories forced me to stare off into space, glaring blankly at the television set. The pain of my childhood treaded lightly to the surface.

Oz exhaled. "I now understand what you have been saying all this time. I had a few words with your father, and the only thing I could decipher was that he felt you had not been the perfect son. I found him to be disrespectful, and it was all I could do to keep from beating his ass!" Oz tried to conceal a laugh. "I may have said a few choice words before I bounced. For fear of what I might say or do, I stayed clear of that mofo the rest of the night!"

I smiled, knowing Oz was my protector, never allowing *anyone* to insult or belittle me. "What did you say?"

"That's not important," Oz quickly answered.

"Did you speak with my mother?"

"I introduced myself, and her response was to sit and stare smugly, offering nothing much of value. Willie, I don't get your parents! You are such an amazing individual; how are they not aware of the man you have become? You know…forget them and continue being who you are!"

"Thank you! You always know what I need to hear."

"Anything for you." Oz chuckled. "What are you doing?"

"I don't think you want to know," I remarked, gliding my hand across my chest, slightly pinching my right nipple.

"Oh, tell me!" Oz insisted.

"I just had a shower and now I'm lying in bed butt-naked!" I waited patiently for his reply.

"Sounds like you're waiting for one of your boys to come over."

"Nah, that was last night! I already had a good piece of ass, so I'm good. Unless you plan on coming over," I stated matter-of-factly.

Oz remained silent…nothing but dead air! I waited. I wanted him to break the ice. Even if we continued without uttering a word, let it be.

After what seem like several minutes, Oz finally spoke. "Where did ole boy end up taking you?"

As I suspected, Oz completely ignored my insinuation. "We went to a bar called Papa Bears."

"Who else went with you?" he asked without much of an expression.

"Beau and Skyy met us there."

"What's up with your boys? I don't trust any of them!"

Battlefields

Remaining calm, even though I was becoming highly annoyed, I said, "Why do you feel that way? What have they done to you?"

"I don't feel they have your best interest!" Oz appeared agitated.

"What's up with you? Why are you upset?"

"I'm not upset!"

Taking a deep breath before I spoke, I said, "OK, fine, I need to get off this phone and get ready for bed. Call me tomorrow."

"Fine...I'll talk with you later," Oz replied, sounding like a sad little boy.

I hung up the phone and rolled onto my side with my elbow bent, resting my head on the palm of my hand, and continued flipping through channels, scowling, since I didn't get my way.

Within fifteen minutes of my call with Oz, the phone rang again.

"Hello?" I answered.

"Hello, may I speak to Wilson?"

"This is Wilson."

"Wilson, this is Skyy! How are you?"

"Skyy...good to hear your voice! I was hoping I would speak with you before I went to bed."

"Is that right? I've been trying all evening. First, the phone just rang and rang, and when I tried about forty-five minutes ago, I kept getting a busy signal. I see you're a popular guy," Skyy joked.

"Popular...not me! I didn't return home till about nine thirty," I replied, and then readjusted my position.

"When are we gonna hook up again?" Skyy asked.

"Soon, I hope! I would love to have another repeat of last night!"

I think I may like this dude! I thought. Only time would tell.

CHAPTER 31

TWO SATURDAYS AFTER my twenty-first birthday, I was still fuming over the events that ensued the night of my party. My introduction to LA nightlife had not been a pleasant experience after Marshall left me high and dry at Papa Bears. Already not much of a nightlife type of guy, the Papa Bears experience did not help! However, two good things did arise; I met Bryce, and I had the chance to spend a heated night with Skyy.

Since my birthday, I spent at least seven seductive nights with Skyy and had several telephone conversations with Bryce. My involvement with Skyy hovered on the verge of becoming more than simply friends. Skyy obviously wanted our association to evolve from friends-with-benefits to a more emotional connection; however, my unspoken allegiance to Oz held me from committing to anything more than a few nights of shameless gratification.

As expected, Oz maintained his usual schedule of daily phones calls and mostly daily visitations, before running off to some sordid rendezvous with a member of his growing harem. Nevertheless, with respect to me, he kept his indiscretions to himself, even though it was clear where he sauntered off to once he left my side. Well aware of each other's foray into the adult world of thirst and hedonism, not once did we acknowledge how we felt about it. Each night we slipped away to our respective partners; Oz's demeanor became increasingly sullen, distant, and mute.

With Bryce, our friendship flourished to one of gratitude and respect, purely platonic—partners in crime! In just two short weeks of multiple calls, I knew I had a friend I could count on. Nothing on the level I had with Oz, but a trusted associate of mutual admiration nonetheless.

Battlefields

A month after our introduction, Bryce made plans to return to Los Angeles for a quick weekend turnaround for a few nights of clubbing at Catch One disco, the one and only place to be on a Saturday night within the black gay community. Since I had not considered myself a night-clubbing individual, I had yet to walk through the doors of the infamous nightclub. Anxious and not knowing what to expect, Bryce assured me that he would show me a good time.

I completed my last few minutes of prepping, while Bryce leaned against the bathroom doorframe. "I'm surprised you haven't been to the Catch," Bryce stated with arms folded across his chest, one leg slightly bent.

Staring at my reflection one last time before heading out, I said, "I've heard the stories but was not at all interested in going, besides, after Papa Bears, I wasn't exactly thrilled with the idea of hanging-out with Marshall again," I confessed.

"What about that dude?" Bryce asked.

"What dude?"

"You remember the one that pulled you away, saying he was ready to go." Bryce smirked.

"You mean Skyy?" I laughed. "Nah, I don't want to go out with him either. I like him, but he's trying to sink his grip too deep!"

"You don't want to be tied down? Nigga, you know yo' ass is praying for a husband!" Bryce remarked.

"I didn't say that!" I said, leaning close to the mirror, inspecting a pimple on my right cheek, and then switched my attention to Bryce. "Don't get me wrong, I do like him—"

"Well, what's the problem? He seemed real cool, handsome and all."

"Not sure I want a relationship with him. He is handsome, however...I don't know...I mean...the sex is good—"

"What!" Bryce shouted with a roaring laugh. "You got busy, already?"

I glanced at Bryce, not amused. "I did! I wasn't trying to, but there was something about him I couldn't resist." With a comb in hand and a bottle of Jeri curl juice, I inspected my reflection, making sure every curl was in place. "He offered to drive me home since Marshall left without me."

"OK, I remember him saying that," Bryce remarked, shifting his position within the doorframe. "Then you invited him in?"

"No...he offered to walk me to my door."

"And..."

I innocently glanced at Bryce before continuing to recall the events with Skyy. "And...we stopped at my door to say good-night—"

"OK..." Bryce interrupted.

"Let me finish!" I interjected.

"Nigga, you're taking too long—tell the damn story!"

"Whatever! The next thing I knew, we were rollin' around, butt-ass naked!"

"Slut," Bryce said with a laugh, in his deep, raspy, commanding voice.

I smiled. "Well...maybe a little. I was good for the picking and ready to explode! So I just took it."

"You got into his ass?"

"*Boy*...did I, and then some!" I stated smugly. "I worked it out," I said, rolling my midsection, simulating the gyrating motions of intimate relations.

"Oh damn!"

"He laid it on me!" I placed the comb down on the counter top, massaging lotion on my face and taking one last look. Then I turned to Bryce.

"So what's the problem? What's wrong with this dude?"

"Nothing's wrong...we've spent some time together; I just don't want to settle down." *At least not with him*, I thought. "Anyway, why are you grilling me on my involvement with Skyy? He's not what's important tonight. I'm ready to see what the Catch is all about!"

Strolling into the bedroom with Bryce following closely behind, I stopped in front of a full-length mirror for one final inspection before heading out the door. I sported black wool slacks with black leather loafers, no socks, and a charcoal-gray wool crew neck sweater. I felt good, ready to turn as many heads as I could.

Battlefields

Bryce was similarly dressed, except he wore a tight-fitting white-and-black-printed shirt with over half the buttons undone, revealing a chest full of chiseled muscles. I must admit, Bryce had an amazing chest and killer abs!

"I think you're not telling me the entire story," Bryce continued with his cross-examination, heading for his suitcase situated in the corner of the room.

"There's nothing more to tell," I eluded, hoping he would drop the subject.

Bryce rummaged through his suitcase, searching for some undisclosed item with his backside facing my direction. "It sounds to me you like him, but something is holding you back...someone else, maybe?"

"There is no one else, so let it go!" I unconvincingly stated.

"There is, I knew it...who is he?" Bryce stood wearing a huge smile.

"Are you ready?" I asked, gathering my keys, heading for the front door.

Making our way down the driveway, passing through the wrought iron gate, I made an abrupt stop, with Bryce nearly crashing into my backside.

"What's the matter?" Bryce asked.

"Hold on a minute!" I quickly turned around. "I'll be right back...wait here," I said, heading toward the rear of the house, entering through the back door that lead into the kitchen. I called out, "Where's everybody?" Then, hearing voices, I paused, because one in particular caught my attention.

"Will, we're in the family room," I faintly heard my aunt reply. Maneuvering around the center island of the kitchen, I entered the family room, where I found Aunt Raine watching television with Uncle Charles and Oz seated at a game table playing dominoes.

"I thought you were going out?" my aunt asked.

"I am...I was on my way when I noticed Oz's motorcycle parked outside." I veered toward Oz, though he refused to lift his head or acknowledge me. He remained focused on his game, making some snide remark about taking too long to make a play. Moving further into the room, I stood a few feet from the table. "What are you doing here?" I asked, attempting to mask my anger.

I was a little perturbed that Oz still had not looked up, even after I addressed him. Earlier, when I asked him to meet Bryce, he explained he could not because he had work to do. But now he was not too busy to spend time with my aunt.

"He came over to see me for a change," my aunt politely announced, which was her way of saying *mind your own business!* "Where's your friend?" she asked.

"Outside…I told him I would be right back." I returned my attention to Oz with a curious expression. "You still didn't answer me?" The tone of my voice was firm and straight to the point.

"Leave the man alone! You're sounding like some jealous female!" Uncle Charles stated. I lifted my head, turning toward my uncle in shock and a bit humiliated. "Go on…tend to your company and leave us alone!"

Oz finally elevated his head quickly enough to give a hurt, wounded stare then continued with his game of bones.

Aunt Raine enjoyed having Oz around, obviously enamored by his charm. He gloated over her at every chance he got. She, in turn, became his West Coast mom, his maternal sounding board. Secretly, I knew Aunt Raine hoped we would become more than friends. Oz loved Aunt Raine as much as I knew he loved me, and I admired him for that. Just another example of how he wove his life into mine. He cared for anyone who was special in my life, and catered to his or her needs as he would with me. Oz often visited with my aunt and uncle, however, never outside of a visitation including myself. And for him to stop by without me knowing was bizarre to say the least! I stood in disbelief with my mouth open to form words that could not find a way out. It's comical how life played out! Here I am, mixed up in a situation where it could end either with a happy conclusion or a tragedy. How was I going to satisfy my needs and accommodate all the desires of the people around me, namely Oz?

I must admit my disappointment with Oz's actions chewed at my heart, but to completely blow me off and totally ignore me just because he did not

Battlefields

get his way was another matter. I could not keep guessing his intentions. Oz needed to speak up and state the obvious. Then again, I was no better, since I remained silent, unwilling to disclose my true feelings. I was just as guilty.

Since I was getting nowhere with Oz, I simply recused, tucked my tail between my legs, and retreated. But before removing myself from the situation, I glanced back at Oz to see what, if any, reaction he had, which was none. Facing my aunt, I said, "I'll speak with you later, Auntie," and headed for the door.

"Where are you two going?" my aunt asked.

"Out to a club!" I yelled, leaving the family room.

"What was that all about?" Bryce asked once I returned.

Swiftly walking past him, I said, "Let it go," without confessing, barely grazing him as I passed.

Bryce grabbed my arm, stopping me in my tracks. "What's wrong with you?"

"It's nothing, it'll pass. Just let me be mad, and I'll be OK…I'll be OK, I promise!"

Bryce stepped back, nodding. "Aiight!"

"Thank you, now let's go!"

We arrived at Catch One around a quarter to eleven. A line to enter hadn't yet formed, which was good, since neither of us wanted to stand in the chilly night air. We entered the main doors off Pico Boulevard, leading to a flight of stairs forming an L-shape, turning to the right about three-quarters of the way up. The ticket window was positioned to the right at the top of the landing. While Bryce graciously paid the young woman, I peered through the doors leading to the main lobby, where partygoers were in a festive mood, sashaying back and forth with drinks in hand. I knew then this was going to be a night to remember!

Walking through the doors, we stopped to gather our bearings. To our right, about thirty feet away, several men stood or leaned alongside a lengthy wooden bar, holding drinks and conversing.

Bryce signaled for the bartender, and speaking over his shoulder he asked, "You want something to drink?"

"My usual Bacardi and Coke would be good, thanks!" Waiting behind Bryce, I searched the room, taking notice of the available men. Some were handsome, while others were average, along with the usual scary types and visually challenged. Slowly, I rocked to the pulsating beats blaring through the dance hall. I dipped and bounced in time with the sounds, igniting the soul. Instantly drawn to the vibe radiating all around. I bopped with eyes closed, allowing the sensory overload to take over.

"I see someone is enjoying himself!" Opening my eyes, I saw a tall specimen of a man standing before me. His smile was warm and inviting with large, even teeth. At first glance, I would have said he was not at all attractive, but something about him drew me into his grasp. Immediately I was captivated. His complexion was a deep brown color with clean features, and he sported a full beard and mustache. His hair was the long, greasy Jeri curl that every dude at the time rocked, including me, except mine was not at all greasy. He had on leather pants, a form-fitting muscle shirt, and matching leather boots.

I smiled. "I am!"

"Been here long?"

"Just walked in."

"I'm Vince and you are?"

"Wilson."

"Pleased to meet you, Wilson! You here alone?"

"Nah, I'm with a friend."

"Boyfriend?"

"Not at all!" I remarked, giving him the once over.

"Like what you see?" he boldly asked.

"Maybe!" I cracked a faint smile, seductively licking my bottom lip, eying him up and down, bouncing to the grooves.

"Can I buy you a drink?"

"Maybe, later." I glanced toward Bryce who was watching our every move. I turned back to Vince. "My buddy is taking care of my drink. You should have stepped up sooner!" I stated cockily.

Battlefields

He laughed. "If I noticed you sooner I would have, but I'm here now!"

"And?"

"So it's like that? You gonna give my ass a hard time!"

"Yeah, something like that." I again closed my eyes, feeling the grooves take control. "Can't let you in so easy!"

Bryce nudged my arm to gain my attention. "Here!"

"Thanks!" I reached for the straw, taking a sip.

"Who's your friend?" Bryce asked.

"I'm Vince," he answered before I could formally introduce them.

"Bryce," he said, reaching to shake Vince's hand. "So, what brings you out?"

"I'm out with friends," Vince offered.

"Where are they now?" Bryce asked.

"On the floor where I should be with yo' boy, Wilson!"

"Don't let me stand in the way! Nigga, go do your thang, I'll be right here!" Bryce reached for my drink, removing it from my hand.

I gave Bryce that look—you know, the side-eye you give when someone makes a decision you're not at all happy with. "Well, why not." I respectfully gave in. "Save my spot!"

Vince and I headed for the dance floor. Rufus's "Ain't Nobody" began to spin, and as soon as the first note ripped, the crowd roared with excitement. Vince took my hand, leading toward the middle of the floor, and pulled me close. The intoxicating aroma of his cologne fanned the flames of lust. In sync, we rocked and dipped, working up a sweat only the heat of heat could produce. Completely mesmerized and removed from all space and time, each beat reduced all my inhibitions. Vince's movements were intentionally sexual, brushing against my body. Instantly aroused, my mind spun willy-nilly, drowning in his emotions.

"Yeah, baby, I like that!" Vince whispered in my ear, his lips traced my earlobe then went in for the kill and sensuously bit. My body shivered.

Pulling away, I spun around, facing him with arms up, waving; rhythmically, I stepped closer into him. My eyes were fixed, holding him in my trance.

Vince shook his head back and forth. "Ah shit!" he exclaimed.

"You like that?" I asked.

"Hell yeah, you know I do!" He rocked back, taking in the full view of my moves.

After we danced through five full songs, I announced, "I need a break!"

"Cool, I need one too. I'm gonna run to the restroom, and I'll see you in a minute."

Sweaty and hot, I excused myself, walking off the floor drenched. Instantly, I was hooked; the allure of Catch One had taken hold, apprehending me within its grip, and Vince as well! I weaved my way through the crowd, wiping beads of sweat from my brow. Reentering the lobby, I spotted Bryce propped against the bar, speaking with some tall, slender dude.

"Have you been dancing all this time?" Bryce asked, acknowledging my presence.

I reached for my cocktail, taking a sip. "Yes."

"Damn, nigga! I'm sure yo' drink is watered down by now!" Bryce remarked.

"That's cool; I need a glass of water more than I need alcohol!" I pulled the top of my sweater, fanning cool air down my chest.

"Will, this is Arthur," Bryce said, grabbing the top of my forearm and pulled me closer. "Arthur, this is Will."

"Pleased to meet you, Arthur," I remarked.

"My pleasure!" Arthur smiled, showing a mouthful of crooked teeth. I thought, *oh my!*

"Where's the dude you were dancing with?" Bryce asked.

"He went to the restroom. He'll be right back, at least that's what he said."

Bryce looked around, glancing hard. "Who cares if he returns or not, you have all this candy in the store to choose from!"

Battlefields

"I don't need all the sweets, that's how you get cavities. One potent flavor is all I need!"

"Since we're mentioning flavors, yours is walking toward us as we speak." Bryce motioned in the direction of Vince.

Immediately I turned, repositioning in his path. When he approached, I greeted him with a wide smile.

"You happy to see me?" he commented.

I shrugged my shoulder, broadcasting a slight smile. Vince had a solid, stocky build with broad shoulders, big hands, big feet, and a slick, velvety voice. Although he was definitely shorter than I, by at least two inches, he commanded an in-charge, cool confidence.

Vince ran the back of his hand next to my cheek. "So, what's up?" he stated, with eyes on mine, while reclining against the wooden bar. Turning his gaze away, Vince motioned for the bartender. After ordering his drink, he asked what I wanted.

"Bacardi and Coke, then I want you," I said in a playful commentary, as I moved in closer.

Vince leaned away with a surprised expression. "Is that right...I'm not sure how I should take that!"

For whatever reason Oz popped into my head, and I thought, *He's out having fun, why shouldn't I?* I leaned in closer and said, "Take it any way you want. Open your mind to interpretation."

"Damn...you always so forward?"

I smirked. "Wouldn't you like to know?" I grabbed Bryce's hand and said, "Let's dance!"

"Can't you see I'm busy?" Bryce responded.

"This is my jam, and you haven't danced with me all night!" I turned toward Vince and said, "We'll be right back!" Fleeing for the dance floor, I quickly pulled Bryce away.

"What is your problem?"

"Nothing, I wanted to dance," I retorted.

"I was having a conversation and you were too!"

"Vince will still be there when I return."

"Are you sure about that?" Bryce asked.

"I *guarantee*...he will!"

"*Nigga*...you're a trip!"

"Many have taught me well, and I'm letting him marinate for a minute!"

We danced for another three tracks, and when we returned, I found Vince waiting patiently.

CHAPTER 32

I WAS SWEPT away by the energetic pulse flowing freely within LA's gay nightlife, and I received an instant high whenever I entered that notorious club on Pico Boulevard. Whether it was boys' night out on Wednesdays or the regular Friday and Saturday outings, I was drawn in—set on autopilot. Like clockwork, I was there twirlin', dippin', and swayin' to the music of the city...my city.

In the disguise of night, my adult exercises continued full force. Between juggling the interests of Oz and maintaining the cravings of Vince and Skyy, I kept my dance card jam-packed. Along with my nightly explorations, I sought comfort with any willing participant.

My frustrations with Oz opened a door to unquenched thirsts incapable of appeasing. Oz stirred hidden passions within me, set them on fire, and then fled, leaving me smoldering hot. With each precious moment we spent together, it sent me to the edge, dangling precariously close to the hopes of splendor, and then subsequently he released his command. False hopefulness and reneged faith wreaked havoc on a soul burned and bruised countless times before.

Round and round, I spun, circling wildly with no way of stepping off this dizzying merry-go-round; I held on tight to this dangerous ride. Yet, I kept spinning; I was tangled, disoriented, and dazed by the relentless shadowboxing game we played. Neither Oz nor I stated the obvious, ignoring our unspoken truths. Within his concealed sentiments, the veracity of subtle invitations followed by contradicting behavior, which removed all outward advances of affection. Playful kisses upon the forehead, a lingering embrace among friends; lonely eyes searching the inner depths. Nevertheless, with the call of night, those fleeing romanticisms vanished to the waiting arms of another.

Along with the nightly games, the summer of 1984 beckoned. With the end of the school year already two weeks passed, the ritual of weekend activities pledged on. My involvement with Vince had reached a plateau; evidently the magnetism was simply aberrant hunger for affection, reduced to convenient fucks when the other had no one to satisfy the urges of life. Once fulfilled, we slipped away to our respective domiciles within the City of Angels. I admitted, I wanted more, but it was well defined that Vince was only interested in a casual acquaintance.

One typical Sunday morning during the latter part of June, a perpetual barking dog in a neighboring yard awakened me. Opening one eye, I squinted slowly, allowing my vision to focus. Searching my surroundings, I replayed the events of the night before that led to this unfamiliar room. I was still slightly intoxicated by one too many Bacardi's that held my head hostage to the mind-numbing juice.

A rumbling, bellowing noise blared, so I rolled over to witness a woolly mammoth sprawled beside me—an all too familiar escapade of meaningless romps with anonymous individuals this past year. The stage was set for a downward spiral to the pits of damnation. My weekly adventures of implied romantic encounters had unknowingly hardened me, a once promised heart of fortified peace. The constant cravings of desire and love lured an already broken young man to deepened mistrust and icy revelations.

The woolly mammoth lay like dead meat, and for the life of me, I could not remember his name. A dense, hazy fog clouded my mind, revealing little details of the night before. Maybe it was John something—I was uncertain—but really, did it matter? I got mine and I was satisfied, and that was the only important thing, at least for the moment. Rolling back onto my side, I placed my hand to the top of my forehead, gently massaging. I could have easily spent the evening with Vince or Skyy, but as usual, I chose an unknown instead.

Battlefields

Concentrating on the pain of life and my persistent poor judgment, I thought about the demons I held. Amid the incessant backlash of others and the false pretenses of people who alleged their love then threw me away, I wondered how I would escape the clutches of an ominous outlook that plagued me?

Finally, the woolly mammoth awakened, reaching and stretching, welcoming the dawn of a new morning. Observing over my shoulder, greeting the hugely bearish man I had spent the night with, I thought, *was I that drunk?* I forced a smile.

He placed his hand around my chin, leaning for a kiss. The stench of his breath fried the sensors within my nostrils. I instinctively turned away, lifting myself into a seated position.

"I have to get going," I stated, my backside facing him, hiding a repulsed expression.

He slid his hand down the center of my back. "Don't go…lay with me."

Turning to my left, barely gazing over my shoulder, I said, "Nah, I have to get going! I totally forgot about a lunch date I have this afternoon." I forced another smile, "I'm sorry I have to leave." I reached for my underwear lying on the floor next to the bed.

"I had a good time last night," he remarked.

"You did? That's good to know!" Speaking as I stood, pulling my underwear over my ass, I realized I could be a cold-hearted bitch when I wanted to.

"When can I see you again?" he asked.

"Why don't you write down your name and number, and I'll give you a call when I have time. But I'm warning you, I've been busy with school and work," I said, picking my slacks off the floor.

"What are you doing later tonight?" he asked, grabbing a pen and paper from the nightstand, jotting down his number.

Searching the room, I asked, "Have you seen my shirt?"

The woolly mammoth sat up, placing his back against the headboard, exposing a chest and stomach full of tightly woven hair; it was then that I understood what had attracted me to him. He was the hairiest black man

I'd ever met! I held an extreme affection to men with lots of body hair; it was a major turn on!

"It may be in the living room," he remarked.

I fastened the clasp, buttoned, and zipped my slacks; and with the palm of my hand, I brushed away lint picked up from the dirty carpet. "Thanks," I answered.

"Here's my number, call me," he said, handing over a folded piece of blue notepaper.

"Thank you." I opened the scribbled note, which had the name John Reeves written along with his telephone number. *I was close!* "I'll be sure to give you a call when I have some free time." I did not intend to call this dude, but I lied so he would feel good, or was it so I felt better about myself? Checking my pockets, making sure I had all my valuables and keys, I stepped away from the bed. "Are you gonna walk me out?" I asked, inching closer toward the bedroom door.

When I began to walk away, he swiftly leapt to his feet, pinning me against the door. Nude with his male anatomy slightly aroused, his tongue extended, and his mouth opened wide, he forcefully tried to kiss me. A tussled ensued; I scrambled, managing to push him off.

"What the fuck is wrong with you?" I shouted.

He stood, stroking his swelling manhood with a crazed look. "I'm not gonna let you go that easy!" he smirked.

My heart began to pound. "You come near me again, I will kick your ass!" I said, as I slowly backed my way out of the bedroom.

He remained in the bedroom stroking his stuff, leaning back, which made his actions more pronounced. Upon entering the living room, not once would I turn my back, switching my eyesight between him and the pathway out. I picked up my shirt from the back of an easy chair, and from the bedroom I could hear him speaking. "I'm gonna get me some more of that! Get yo' ass back here!"

As soon as I had a clear path, I fled for the door.

Twenty minutes later I was walking up the driveway toward my garage apartment, when I came to a halt before entering the rear yard. Aunt Raine

Battlefields

and Oz sat at one of the patio tables; both had their backs facing my direction, neither aware of my presence. Remaining silent, I watched with regret and was unhappy with my behavior, having placed myself in danger with some crazed maniac. Easing back from eyesight, I eavesdropped on their conversation.

Five minutes passed before I made my attendance known. Oz twisted in his seat toward my direction and Aunt Raine looked up, rotating with a disapproving stance. My all-nighters were not a secret, but she remained quiet, keeping her thoughts to herself; however, her appearance said it all.

Oz readjusted his position, whispering something to my aunt, then proceeded to stand, leaning forward, kissing her forehead. "We'll talk later regarding the bookcases," he said, touching her shoulder.

My aunt grabbed his hand, tilting her head, holding it close to her cheek. She smiled and said, "I liked your ideas! I'll be around if you want to discuss the details further."

"We can do that." He turned his head to his right, his stare seared cold.

Ignoring Oz, I said, "Good morning, Aunt Raine!" With keys in hand, I continued walking toward the door of my apartment.

"Will…" she responded, taking a sip of her coffee.

Oz followed without saying a word, although I sensed he had plenty he wanted to say. He basically withheld his tongue until we were out of earshot of my aunt. Walking into the living room, I laid my keys on the table at the top of the stairs, kicked off my shoes, and entered the kitchen.

I pulled out a carton of orange juice from the fridge and then removed a glass from the cabinet. "You want something to drink?"

Oz leaned against the counter. "No…nothing for me. I had breakfast with Aunt Lorraine this morning. I've been waiting since quarter to nine, hoping to surprise you, but I guess…I was the one surprised, finding you had not returned home. Where have you been?" Oz's tone was peppered with sarcasm.

Quietly, I sat the glass and carton of OJ on the counter top. I did not know if I should be angry, flattered, or if he even had the right to question my whereabouts. "I've been out," I answered.

Vance N. Smith

"I gathered that," he responded cynically.

"I never ask where you go, so why are you asking me. Why now?"

"Who is he?" Oz asked.

"I don't believe you have a right to ask me that?"

With both hands placed along the edge of the counter top, Oz focused his attention outside the window to the yard next door. He paused, inhaling deeply, before speaking. "Since when has it been a problem asking you a question?"

"Since when have you been so concerned with whom I've spent my nights? I never asked you about all the women you seem to be with every night!" Speaking those words caused my heart to feel heavy with resentment. "What is it you want from me?"

"What do you mean?" he said with pain overwhelming him. "Willie, I care about you!"

"I know you do but..."

"But what!" he snapped.

"What are we doing here?" I waited patiently for an answer.

Oz stood in silence, tight-lipped, refusing to gaze my way.

"I don't know what you want from me!" I chuckled sarcastically, shaking my head. "You're a trip!" Picking up the glass of juice, I gulped it down, wiping my mouth with the back of my hand.

"And you're a whore!" he blurted out

"What the fuck did you just say? What did you just call me?" I shouted. *I could not believe he fixed his lips to make such a statement!* "As *if*...you have a lot of nerve! What a fuckin' hypocrite!"

"It's not about me!"

"And you're making this all about me? This is about us, you and me!"

"I'm not the one who has to worry about dying, contracting some disease from some stranger!" he stated, just short of yelling.

My heart sank. I heard the comment, but did not want to believe the words he uttered. Yes, there were rumblings of something evil lurking in the call of night, killing innocent men one by one. I was well aware of the menace hiding in the shadows. A new enemy raged a full-on assault, taking

Battlefields

no prisoners, discarding bodies left and right. A smart and determined foe that slid in without you knowing, enforcing his deed on all whom unsuspectingly welcomed the masked intruder.

Angrily, I placed the glass down and walked off. "Fuck you," I shouted.

"Willie, get back here!"

"I'm not listening to any of this!" I yelled.

"I'm scared for you!" Oz ran after me reaching for my arm.

"What the fuck are you doing; let go of my arm," I said, snatching it away. "Don't grab me like that! Who the fuck do you think you are?" I ranted.

"I refuse to argue with you!" His grip was firm and forceful, as I struggled to free myself, being that Oz fought back each time I tried to resist.

"Let go of me!" I demanded.

"Stop it!" he stated firmly, wrapping his arms around me with a death grip. My backside pinned against his chest, and his cheek rooted squarely next to mine, "Don't fight me, you're not going to win," he maintained with authority. Oz wrestled, restraining me next to the wall. "I can't lose you!"

Holding my head low in shame, I gave up the fight, knowing I would not win. "Oz, you have no idea the pain I'm in!"

"I do!"

"No, you don't, cuz if you did, you wouldn't treat me the way you do!"

"Then help me understand!" Each time I tried freeing myself, the stronger he held.

"Oz, I can't breathe."

"I'm not letting you go until you cooperate!"

I tried to twist myself loose, but it wasn't working.

"Relax, don't fight me!" he insisted. "Relax!"

"I'm cool…let me go."

"No." With his body constrained beside mine, I felt his heart jump inside his chest.

"Oz, I need to take a shower. I'm not going anywhere."

Another five minutes or so passed before Oz released his clutch. Exhausted, I wearily moved toward the bathroom where I immediately hopped into the shower. Forty minutes later with a bath towel around my waist, I found Oz sitting on the floor next to the bathroom door, eyes closed, his right leg bent at the knee with the other extended straight. I stopped before proceeding. "Are you OK?" I asked.

"Yes," he responded.

I reached out my hand for his. "Oz..."

He slowly opened his eyes. "What?"

"Take my hand..."

I led Oz into the bedroom where he sat at the foot of the bed. Facing away, I removed the towel, picked up some old, gray cotton sweats and dressed. In the mirror, I noticed Oz with his head hung low, hands clasped together.

"I'm sorry."

"So am I," he responded.

"I don't want to hurt you."

His posture remained the same. "I don't want to hurt you either."

Propping up a few pillows, I positioned myself above the covers, resting my head. "Come here," I said, stretching my hand toward him.

Oz solemnly turned in my direction, hesitating before complying. He repositioned, laying his face against my chest. "I don't want to fight," he whispered.

I ran my fingers through his hair, relaxing my chin against the crown of his head. "I won't fight you," I said, cradling him in my arms. "I need you here by my side."

Oz lifted himself and stared into my eyes, resting upon his forearms. Our lips only a split-hair apart, he held his gaze carefully. I held him close, my breathing elevated. Our deadlock lasted several minutes until Oz abruptly rose from his position, sitting at the edge of the bed.

"I gotta go!" He stood and not once did he return his attention to me, announcing, "I'm sorry!"

"Where are you going?" I remarked, pivoting, resting on my left elbow.

Oz stopped in the doorway, his backside still facing me. "We'll talk later," he announced then continued on his way.

CHAPTER 33

"HAVE YOU SPOKEN with Oz?" Aunt Raine asked, holding a glass of orange juice.

Sitting at the breakfast bar of my aunt's kitchen, I said conclusively, "No, I haven't."

Aunt Raine hesitated before continuing with her interrogation, concerned. "What's going on with you two? What happened?"

"We had a minor disagreement, that's all. It will pass," I stated with confidence, though knowing in my heart I was worried. A little over a month had passed without a word from Oz, with several calls left to no avail. He couldn't be that upset over what happened or what was stated; I believed we were beyond that.

Aunt Raine placed a tall glass of orange juice beside my plate. "He's been by but will not speak of what happened."

Shocked, I sat back to face my aunt, dropping my toast on the stoneware plate. "He what! Oz has been by?"

"Yes, while you're at work. He's been working on bookcases for the den. His carpentry skills are quite good, exquisite I might add!"

"I know, Aunt Raine, I've seen his work before," I said, taking a sip of my juice. "I can't believe he's this upset!" I mumbled.

Aunt Raine's expression was of dissatisfaction and concern. Pulling a stool beside mine and sitting with her legs crossed and one hand resting upon her lap, she said, "I'm not going to ask what was said, but I know he's hurting something awful."

"Are you blaming me?" I asked, feeling betrayed.

"No, I'm not blaming you, alone. I think both of you are at fault. I know he loves you dearly, but I sense he's unable to except the love he feels for you."

"And you know this how? He said that to you?"

"No, he has not," Aunt Raine stated, reaching for a napkin.

"Then how do you know?"

She shook her head, exasperated. "Why are you so afraid to admit the truth? You are in love, refusing to allow him the opportunity to love you in return!" She sighed. "How long are you going to play this game with him?"

"It's not me, it's him! He's the one who refuses to give in!" I said, defending myself wholeheartedly. "Why am I the one who is always wrong? Why do I have to cower down to everyone's needs? When will someone else provide what I want for a change? It's unfair that I'm the one who continues being stomped on, and I'm sick and tired of it!" Gritting my teeth, I shook my head in contempt.

"Will, stop feeling sorry for yourself. Yes, you have been hurt, but you have someone who loves you, who would do anything for you! He secretly seeks guidance, quietly begging for your help. Forget what others have done, whoever it may be!" Aunt Raine reached for my hand. "Holding on to pain and disappointment will destroy you. Will, honey…life is not fair, you simply learn to move on, building strength from it. He's no better and has to learn as well."

I left my aunt's home angry as hell, beaten and blamed for the standoff between Oz and me. Retreating to my apartment, I lay in bed for the next hour wallowing in a self-induced depression. Refusing to allow Oz's defenses to dictate my actions, I knew it was time for him to standup, be a man, face his demons, and come to terms to whatever he was hiding. No longer would I afford others the opportunity to take advantage of my kindness, my love. It was time someone else stepped to the plate!

CHAPTER 34

ANOTHER MONTH PASSED with no word from Oz, and I began losing all expectations of ever seeing him again. Finally, I gave up calling, since it was clear he did not intend on returning my calls. In Oz's absence, my relationship with Skyy prospered, having grown comfortable with him, and he fulfilled an empty void.

"What do you want for dinner?" I asked Skyy, as he sat watching a repeat of *I Love Lucy*, while I stood alongside the edge of the sofa.

"Something simple is cool with me," Skyy responded.

"Simple like what?"

"I don't know. What do you have?"

"I could bake some chicken; how does that sound?"

"That works!"

I turned to walk away then stopped. "I forgot to tell you Sedona is on her way over."

"Cool, I like her. We had fun the last time she was around!"

"It makes me happy that you're fond of her," I remarked, cheerfully ambling into the kitchen. "It's important to me that you two get along."

"I do, and she's been good to me." A knock at the door caused Skyy to look over his shoulder. "You want me to get that?"

"Please."

Opening the fridge and pulling out several pieces of chicken wrapped in storage paper, I laid them on the counter then proceeded to season the pieces one by one. Luckily, I purchased them earlier in the morning and had yet to place them in the freezer. I had not planned on Skyy's company and was a bit thrown having to think of something to prepare.

Vance N. Smith

"Sedona, is that you?" I called from the kitchen.

"Yes, it's me. What's for dinner?" she stated, laying her bag down on the dining room table.

Washing my hands, I spoke over my shoulder. "Where have you been?"

"I have something to show you," she said with hands hidden behind her back. Her eyes gleamed. "Close your eyes and hold out your hands!"

"What's this?" I said, sensing a flat object placed upon my palms. "Is this what I think it is?"

"OK, you can look!"

I opened my eyes finding a 45 record in my hands. "Sedona, you didn't tell me you were through! It's your first single! We have to play it right now!"

Sedona squealed. "I can't wait until you hear it!"

"You didn't tell me you were recording music?" Skyy remarked.

With a mystified glance, she specified, "Was I supposed to? It's not something I went around telling everyone I met!"

"And she made me promise not to say anything to anyone!" I stated, placing the single on the turntable.

The recording started with a slow, melodic beat, which quickly flipped to a hard dance groove, complete with an infectious, rippling drum section. Immediately, it made you want to get on the floor and shake your money-maker! The poignant background harmonies, along with her bone-chilling vocals, beckoned us into her spell. I was hooked the moment I heard the first chord. Sedona's vocal gymnastics were simply amazing, leaving me unable to fathom that the girl I'd known since the age of nine could produce a sound that spoke so hauntingly.

"What's the name of it?" Skyy asked.

"Take Me in Your Arms, One Last Time," Sedona answered.

"I like it!" he remarked, excitedly.

"I love it! Damn girl, you put your soul into it!" Rockin' to the beat, I said, "When does it hit the airwaves?"

"Any day now!"

"I knew you had skills, but damn! You were holding back!"

"You think I have a hit?"

Battlefields

Before I could answer, Skyy jumped in. "Hell, yes! All the children will rock to this shit!"

"I think you do!" I commented. "You're on your way to stardom, and with Jackson guiding you, there's no doubt you have a winner!"

"Jackson—Jackson Parker produced this?" Skyy stated almost jumping out of his skin.

"Yes, and composed it as well," Sedona smiled.

"Oh, you *are* going to be famous."

"Thanks, but I can only hope."

"You will," I assured her. "If you don't I'll be surprised because that has hit written all over it."

"That's what Jackson and my record label tell me. I'm going on the road in a few weeks to promote the single. I'm scared; everything is starting to move so fast! Plus, I have to leave my daughter." Sedona's voice suddenly became somber.

"Think of the kind of life you'll be able to provide for her. You will have the means to give her everything. This is about your dream—think of how long you have wanted this to happen. Now it's within your reach."

"I know!"

"Will your mom keep Sahara?"

"Yes, until I'm able to have her with me. My sisters and my cousin Keisha are going on the road as well. They're going to back me up."

"Really! You know they can blow. The four of you singing together, *wow*!"

We must have replayed the song a hundred times over the remainder of the evening. The more I heard it, the more I knew a star was born. We danced, be-bopped, and sang until we could do no more. But hearing and understanding the lyrics forced the thought of the one person I was trying to forget. If I had known he was going to vanish, I would not have allowed him to leave so freely; I certainly would have put up a fight.

Long after the last note played, Skyy and I retreated to my bedroom. Quietly we lay in the light of a full moon illuminating the darkened space.

Bleeding hearts melded together after a session of romantic exchange, expressions of obligatory love. Expecting to relieve myself to the servitudes of another's captive spirit, I once again played with fire. I was powerless to beat it, unwilling to expel it; and in the back of my mind resided an unreachable corner where Oz's virus surreptitiously recoiled.

So there I lay with my arms holding a man I felt sympathy for but did not love. Warmheartedly, my affections grew for him over the passing year. Skyy's demeanor was resilient enough to shelter me from the edge of obscurity. On the surface, all seemed copacetic, since I hid my feelings well. However, underneath, I dwelled upon a life evading me at every turn. A life that cheated, promised courage, and then pocketed it away, laughing as it bolted.

"What are you thinking about?"

"You."

"What about me?" Skyy snuggled deeper into my arms.

Leaning my head against his, I said, "I wondered what you felt about me, if you truly cared."

Skyy shifted, kissing my chest. "You know I do!"

"Do I?"

Skyy ran his fingertips alongside my right nipple. "Why do you ask me this?"

"Just wondered."

"I could stay here with you forever."

"That's sweet," I commented.

"You don't feel the same?"

Skyy *would* ask such a complicated question. How was I to answer such a difficult subject? I held my breath, not wanting to blurt out some minuscule reply.

Apparently, I took too long to respond, because Skyy raised himself from my arms. "You don't feel the same?"

"It's not that simple for me."

"You have been leading me on for a year now. When are you going to admit what you're feeling?"

Battlefields

I thought, *do you really want to know what I am feeling?* I falsely reassured him with the better choice. "Relax, I'm not going anywhere."

"You came into my life for a reason. You may not be able to see it, but you will." He kissed down the left side of my torso until he reached just beyond my navel.

"I like that; it feels so good!"

"What else do you like?" he spoke, not missing a beat, kissing and pleasing all in the same breath. One thing I could say, Skyy had mad skills and knew what I liked. Making an all-out effort to keep me satisfied.

"Oh damn! Keep that up, and we'll be sweatin' up the sheets all over again!"

"That's the point!" Skyy's mouth nestled firmly in the wild, hairy bush at the base of my manhood.

I quivered when his moist, warm mouth surrounded my stiffened flesh. I licked my lips with eyes closed, placing my hand behind my head. "Ooh, baby…" I groaned. "Damn that feels so good!"

We made love for the next hour.

CHAPTER 35

Extending my long torso, I said, "You're up early?"

"I'm surprised you're not," Skyy responded.

"What is that supposed to mean?" I remarked, yawning.

"You didn't hear all that noise coming from down below? There were some men unloading furniture. Good thing I had to get up early!"

"No, I didn't, I must have been knocked out," I said, scratching my head. "Where are you going?"

Skyy sat at the foot of my bed, lacing his sneakers. "I have to go to work, remember today is Monday."

"Oh yeah, I forgot." Sitting upright, I wiped my eyes, squinting. "What time is it?"

"It's six twenty-one, and I'm running late. I have to be at work by eight thirty. My manager is not kind to people who are tardy."

"But wasn't I worth it?" I joked.

"I'm not even going to answer that!" Skyy stood up, straightening his shirt. "Come walk me out."

"OK, give me a second," I said, stretching my long frame, removing myself from bed. "Did you sleep well?" I asked, reaching for my bathrobe.

"You know I did; you seem to have that effect on me. I absolutely love sleeping next to you."

I smiled, grabbing Skyy's hand, approaching the front door. "Call me later?"

"I will, what do you have planned today?" Skyy wondered.

"Nothing, really, I need to clean my apartment. Plus, I have ideas for some floor plans I would like to work on."

Battlefields

Skyy and I remained at the door in a warm embrace.

"Really...you never discussed working on your plans before?"

I reared back completely confused because Skyy was well aware I was on an internship at an architectural firm. I answered perplexed, "OK, I guess this is something you just learned about me. I have an entire book of ideas I've been sketching since junior high."

"You need to brush your teeth!" Skyy jokingly stated, withholding a huge laugh.

Playfully, I pushed him away. "Get the fuck out! Have you smelled yours?"

Skyy cupped his hand to his mouth and exhaled. "Smells fine to me!"

"Whatever," I remarked.

We walked hand in hand, dreamy eyed, unaware of anyone that early in the morning. Skyy and I were no more than ten feet away from my apartment when Aunt Raine and Oz emerged from the shadows of the carport, directly into our path. Startled, I hastily released Skyy's hand and stood deer-eyed frozen. Out of respect, I'd never shown any affection toward another man in the presence of my aunt, keeping that part of my life hidden, even though she was well aware of my sexual preference. And to make the situation more problematic, Oz was present. My heart sank with a thud.

The four of us stopped cold, with tensions hung high by the weight of fifty concrete blocks. Skyy swiftly turned to face me. Impulsively, I became sick to my stomach. Oz immediately halted, shifting his attention in an entirely different direction, his demeanor wrought with concealed sentiments. And if I could have read Aunt Raine's expression, I would have gotten an earful. So, I pretended to ignore the unpleasantness of the encounter and said my good mornings before continuing on my merry way. Skyy forced an innocent smile as we hurriedly passed. Aunt Raine nodded with pursed lips, her gaze followed; Oz simply did not acknowledge.

"What's the matter, Will?" Skyy asked, as I rushed him to his vehicle.

"Nothing," I stated, nervously.

"Stop! Who was that?" he said, grasping my arm, keeping me from avoiding his questions. "And don't tell me nobody! Who was he?"

I sighed and conceded, "A family friend."

"I thought your aunt knew about you?"

"She does."

"Then what was that all about? Are you ashamed?"

Turning to the right, searching down the street, I said, "I'll call you later," ignoring his questions altogether.

Skyy stood pissed, eyes darting back and forth, searching for answers. I declined to face him, not wanting him to see the anguish swelling within. Skyy reached out to place his hand upon my shoulder, but I evaded his touch, politely moving a half step away.

"OK, it's like that?" he snapped.

Playing it off, I smiled wearily. "Like what?"

"All right, since you gonna play games, yeah, we'll talk!" Skyy turned and stormed toward his car.

I reached out, grabbing for his arm, but Skyy immediately snatched it away without looking back. "Skyy," I called out.

"Fuck off!" he replied.

I stood with a tense, rigid stature, with both hands deep inside the side pockets of my bathrobe. As Skyy sped off down the street, my eyes followed until he was far into the distance. A few more minutes passed before I reluctantly proceeded up the driveway. Upon entering the rear yard, I found Oz and Aunt Raine positioned in the garage, inspecting a set of beautifully constructed bookcases. Aunt Raine stood scrutinizing, making comments I could barely comprehend, though through her mannerisms, I suspected she was pleased. The radiant smile gracing her face said it all. I must admit I was impressed with his craftsmanship. Oz's woodworking talent was magnificent, and these beauties were by far his best work. I'm sure my aunt's persistence summoned his best.

Oz stood with the confidence of a royal king admiring his treasures with hand to chin, his usual wide-open smile baring nothing but white, perfect teeth. Aunt Raine stepped back, wrapping her arm around his waist, pulling him close.

Battlefields

"I just love them," she said, placing hand to cheek, giving the bookcases a thorough once over. "They're everything I asked for. What a wonderful job!" Aunt Raine laid her head against his shoulder, admiring the gorgeously crafted woodwork.

Oz returned the gesture. "I'm glad you're satisfied. I was worried you wouldn't like the finished product."

"They're exactly what I wanted. You need to do more."

"That's what I plan to do, design and create my own custom-built furniture. I love working with my hands; it's my passion!"

Eavesdropping on the conversation, I advanced toward the garage with neither aware of my presence. It wasn't until I was approximately fifteen feet away that I ultimately spoke. "You know you have mad skills."

Oz turned in my direction. "Thank you," he stated softly.

"You're extremely talented, you should be proud. I have always respected your ability to work so well with your hands. I'm looking forward to the day you'll complete my designs with your custom furniture." I smiled.

"Now, that idea I like!" my Aunt remarked.

Oz refocused on his work, nodding yes, however his smile faded.

"Can I fix you breakfast before you leave for work?" Aunt Raine asked.

"I wish you could, but I have to get going. I'll take a rain check, my lovely one," he responded.

"OK, but you two need to talk," she politely announced. "This standoff is ridiculous!" Aunt Raine turned to walk away then halted. "Talk!"

I gave a disapproving stare.

Aunt Raine flashed the same stance in return. "Don't look at me with that tone, have you lost your mind?" she stated, slightly raising her voice.

I did not respond.

"Did you hear me?" she said, her voice stern and forceful.

"Yes, Aunt Raine, I'm sorry."

"That's better. You two have an agreeable morning and talk, stop this nonsense!" She frowned before walking through the rear door of her home.

With both hands clasped together on top of my head, I huffed, unconvinced of what was needed to resolve this unfortunate impasse. Should I give in, be the first to speak? I didn't feel I should, so I held my ground stubbornly and purposely bit my tongue, declining to give in—not this time! Oz's contemplation fixed far into the distance, slicing through me like a razor. True enough, we were at a stalemate, and neither wanted to call a truce.

I noticed Oz's jaw flinching, his lips anxious and his words wanting to form but repudiated. His eyes scurried in my direction with a painful, uneasy expression. His slight, fresh, soapy scent cleansed and aroused me, chipping away at my defenses. There he stood, dressed in a white, tight-fitting, Fruit of the Loom tank with cream-colored, beat-up carpenter's pants, complementing his naturally dark-tanned skin. I knew I was destined to cave whenever I was in his company. I wanted to run to him and beg forgiveness; however, my pride forbade me from doing so.

Our deadlock lasted several minutes before he hesitantly began to step away. When he moved, I held my position firm, allowing my head to follow. With my backside facing him, I detected his footsteps had stopped.

"I'm sorry." He spoke just above a whisper.

"What did you say?"

"I'm sorry," he reluctantly repeated. "I'm sorry," Oz stated, trailing to a whisper.

Repositioning in his direction, I said, "You know I love you."

"I know." Oz remained distant and removed. "I'll be over later."

"I'm looking forward it."

With his head marginally turned to the right, not quite looking over his shoulder, Oz paused; his mouth poised to forms words he found hard to speak. "I'll return around six."

"I'll have dinner ready, your favorite dish."

"I'd like that." He broke a faint smile. "I better get going, and I love you too."

Hearing those simple words of adoration made my heart sprint with jubilation. I watched him march down the driveway out of sight. The agony I endured the last few months had been a nightmare.

Battlefields

The remainder of the day, I cleaned, preparing for Oz's arrival. I mopped the kitchen, swept the hardwood floors of the living room, and dusted the tables. I was excited to have Oz around once again, and everything had to be perfect.

Oz loved to eat, and I knew he could not get enough of my fried chicken and baked tomatoes. I fried that chicken to damn near perfection, I also prepared rice, salad, and my tomato dish I learned from my mom. I had cold beer chilled in the fridge and a homemade apple pie.

After cooking and cleaning for most of the day, I obtain just a few hours of relaxation before Oz's arrival. Finally, around five thirty I hopped in the shower, shaved, placed lotion on my body, splashed a slight scent of Polo cologne, and dressed in navy jogging pants and a gray muscle tank.

Once I finished dressing, I headed for the kitchen, checking dinner one final time, making sure all was ready. With minutes to spare, the doorbell rang. Like clockwork, Oz was on time; it was six on the dot. I took one last scan of the room before answering the door. The doorbell rang once again. "I'm coming," I called out.

I reached the door. "Who is it?"

"Guess!" Oz answered.

I opened the door cheesing. "Come in!"

"How are you?" he asked, entering the entrance hall.

"Are those for me?"

Oz smiled. "Just a little something, I know how you love roses," he said, offering a bouquet of salmon colored roses.

"I love them! No one has ever given me flowers before."

We headed up the stairs, entering the living room.

"Have a seat, dinner is almost ready." I walked into the kitchen, fetching a vase. "How was your day?"

"Good, but I need to take a shower," Oz stated.

"You know where everything is, besides you don't have to ask."

Oz smiled. "I'm working on a house not too far from here and didn't want to go all the way home first."

"Really? You excited to see me?"

Oz did not answer, lingering in the living room with a silly childlike grin.

I smirked, shaking my head. "Where's the house?"

"It's a rebuild on June Street." Oz walked into the bedroom, laying his duffel bag down upon the bed.

Several minutes later I entered the room. Oz had already undressed down to his underwear and was bent over removing his socks. Oz had the nicest ass, big and round, with massive thighs and thick, proportioned calves. My stomach immediately churned with excitement. I felt weak. The thoughts speeding through my mind were sinful. The things I would do to him were nasty to say the least.

"I see you have your hair cornrowed again, I like!"

"Yeah, this girl I know from the jungle braided it." He laid his socks on the bed next to the rest of his clothes.

"You want me to throw those in the washer?"

"You don't have to do that."

"I don't mind," I said, moving further into the room, standing next to the bed and picking up the dirty clothes.

"Here, take these as well." Oz slid his boxer briefs over his ass, dropping them to the floor.

I stood, hypnotized. *Goddamn!* I thought, nervously reaching to pick them up. Awkwardly, we both reached at the same time.

"Oh, I'm sorry!" I remarked.

Oz smiled. "No problem…here," he said, handing over the boxers.

I shivered. He had a medium amount of silky, course hair on his chest with a trail leading down his stomach to his hairy pubs, along with his ample plump ass and legs. His physique was a deliciously sculpted masterpiece, and I desired a taste from head to toe. The dirty thoughts I held were only magnified by the solid mass of flesh standing before me.

"I'm gonna place these in the washer. You'll find towels in the hallway linen closet."

"Cool, I'm hungry as a mutha!"

"Then I suggest you hurry up," I stated, walking out of the bedroom.

Battlefields

After dinner, we relaxed on the sofa, watching the Los Angeles Summer Olympics. Oz sat stretched along the sofa with his feet resting upon my lap, his favorite position whenever we watched TV. The past Saturday I had attended one of the track and field events at the Coliseum with Skyy, thrilled I had the opportunity to witness history in the making.

That night we never discussed our disagreement; we simply resumed as if nothing had transpired. I was happy to have him back, at whatever cost. In addition, although we had not spoken to one another in over two months, being with him that night made our fight no longer relevant.

CHAPTER 36

Where do I go from here?

It was a simple question in theory, but a complex enquiry into the state of mind, which was the dilemma of my complicated lost soul. Six months had passed since my delicate reunion with Oz, and the winter of 1985 was drawing to a close. My relationship with Skyy had yet to surrender to a bona fide commitment, and so we simply glided on a level path. I wished I could state Skyy was pleased with the arrangement, but sadly he was not, and for me, I preferred status quo. As luck would have it, life was not that simple. Tensions were mounting; Skyy insisted Oz spent too much time with me than he should, which left little room to advance our relationship. Oz, on the other hand, couldn't have cared less—he was where he desired to be, and since I wouldn't state the obvious, clearly Oz had no intentions of changing. This is where I placed blame on myself.

Knowing how either felt, I never attempted to rein in the fermenting dysfunction. As long as it simmered and didn't discharge into drama, I thought it best to ignore the obvious. To pacify Skyy, I convinced him that Oz's actions were purely innocent, and he was making it a bigger production than he should. It worked for a while, except Skyy was not stupid, knowing I withheld pertinent information. It was evident to everyone but me, and in vain, I kept the charade afloat. I needed Skyy to complete the package left unfulfilled by Oz. By having the two men around, I obtained everything I required. Oz satisfied all my emotional and mental yearnings, whereas Skyy provided all my physical demands. A perfect match, if only I could roll them into one perfect person. Except one player had become uncooperative.

Battlefields

I spent an energetic Saturday afternoon with Skyy, bicycling from my apartment in Hancock Park to Venice Beach, and then back again. Both of us were drop-dead tired, wanting nothing more than a hot shower and a relaxing evening.

"Have you heard from Sedona?" Skyy asked.

"Yeah, she's in New York promoting her album."

"She's getting a lot of radio play; I'm hearing her single all the time. How's the album doing?"

"It's doing quite well I believe it's number two on the R&B charts, and number twelve on the pop charts. She crossed over!"

Late Sunday morning, cuddled in bed with Skyy semi-asleep, the phone rang. Holding him in my arms, I gently twisted, reaching for the receiver in a failed attempt not to disturb him.

Skyy softly spoke, "Let it ring."

Stopping in mid-movement, I halted my action.

"You know who it is, for once can I have you all to myself? Doesn't he have a girlfriend to occupy his time?" he questioned.

Ignoring his comment, and after having such a fantastic weekend, I refused to spoil it with another argument, specifically one that centered on Oz.

Skyy raised his head, waiting for a response.

"What?" I remarked with eyes averted, reacting in jest, "What are you talking about? We're together all the time," I relented.

"You know exactly what I meant, the other man in your life who never seems to stay in his own home. The one you claim is just a friend!"

"Please tell me we're not going down that road again."

"As a matter of fact, we are!" Skyy jumped up, turning to confront me. "Every time he gets wind I'm here, he's either calling, just happened to be in the neighborhood and decided to drop by, or some other lame-ass excuse, and frankly, I'm getting sick of it! Are you in a relationship with

Vance N. Smith

him or me?" Skyy expressed, animated with several hand gestures, not all of which were masculine. One of the many understated feminine mannerisms of Skyy's that irked the hell out of me. "You have kept me hangin' on for two years! What am I to you, are we just fuck-buddies? I've told you from day one, I wanted more than that!"

Damn, has it been two years of this bullshit, I thought. "And you're still here," I stated coldly. As soon as the words left my mouth, I knew I had made a major blunder, having set him off. I needed to think fast and defuse the situation quickly. This mofo had the look of death with anything in his path suited for destruction. "Please, I didn't mean it to come out the way it did. What I meant was, you're still here, I'm still here, and that should count for something!"

"Do you think I'm some kind of fool? Something is up between you two, why can't you admit it."

"Because there's nothing to admit! *Yes,* he and I are extremely close, and I'm sorry you can't comprehend the bond we have. He is the brother I always wanted. Oz listens and never judges, remains in my corner without a doubt, and would back me no matter what, no questions asked, and would never allow anyone to hurt me. And I mean no one!"

"And I wouldn't do that for you?"

"I have no clue, would you?" I questioned.

Skyy gasped, as if gut-busted, forcing all air from his lungs. "You low-down muthafucka!"

The phone rang again.

Skyy reached around and crudely answered, "He's not here," slamming the receiver down on its base.

"Are you fuckin' crazy?" I yelled, pushing him off. "You don't know who the fuck that was. What if that was my aunt! What if someone I loved had been in trouble and that call was an emergency?"

"Go ahead and run to him. You know you want to!" Skyy hurled from the bed. "I'm sick of this shit!"

"Where are you going?" I asked.

"Where do you think I'm going? I'm getting the fuck out of here!"

Battlefields

"Come back to bed and calm down," I pleaded, shifting gears. "You don't have to do this!"

"I can't keep doing this!" Skyy sat at the foot of the bed.

"I know, I'm sorry!"

Feeling bad, I understood his plight, but declined to face the truth staring me dead in the eye. In my subconscious, I knew it was wrong placing him in suspended animation, unaware of our status and future. I was torn by the situation; however, I was not ready to give him up. I needed Skyy to complete me.

After Skyy appeared to have settled down, it afforded me time to reflect on the day eight months prior when Oz insinuated I was a whore and that the road I traveled frightened him. I found that ironic since he was the reason for my moral decay. At least that is how I justified my actions. Through a tangled web of lost humanities, I searched with high hopes of discovering a simpler place of existence, creating an ambivalent man. And although I found Skyy to be a solid individual, the idea of settling down with him was not on the foreseen horizon. Skyy did not satisfy me wholeheartedly because something within him was amiss.

The day Oz eyed Skyy and me walking hand in hand, something within him clicked, I surmised. He was faced with the danger of losing me, recognizing he had stiff competition staring him dead in the face. Refusing to confront his foe, he knew a decisive plan of attack would prove a better tactical assault. From the time he and I swept our disagreement under the rug, Oz became more attentive, ready for war, fighting a cause he knew he could easily conquer. Oz's contradicting behavior was still apparent, except his revolving door of female donors had decreased.

My prior, indiscriminate sexual conduct had been on the rise until Skyy stepped up his advances, slowing down that runaway freight train, and the disaster diverted. For the time being, Skyy quenched the rumblings of unsatisfied thirst plaguing my every thought. Oz's return unleashed undeniable feelings I knew Skyy would never be capable of satisfying. No matter how hard he tried, he proved no match to Oz, and the only thing in his favor was that he provided the outlet to placate my sexual necessities—the only weapon Skyy owned to thwart a looming battle. Obviously, Skyy misunderstood the power of that weapon—had he known, he would have been more at ease, unwilling to throw in the towel.

A cunning general, Oz held all the power, delivering the edge, knowing when to lay low, withholding his position, and confusing his enemy into disclosing their location. Acting as a dual intelligent agent, I connived, providing valuable information benefiting either party. War was a dirty affair, but the forces of life lead to unscrupulous decisions, a pivotal game of survival in a cold-blooded world.

However, I lay beside a man uncertain whether I could love him the way he needed. The ambiguity I held sent my world spiraling out of control. I reached to place my arm around him to console and appease, in an otiose attempt to win him over once again. I required him to release me from my self-induced encampment.

"Are we cool?" I asked.

Skyy remain seated at the foot of the bed, threating to leave, although he had yet to make a move. His deafening silence hung loud and clear. When I reached for him, he jerked away.

"Talk to me!" I pleaded.

I ran the palm of my hand along the crown of my head, feeling troubled with a hint of fear creeping in. Again, the phone rang.

"I think you should get that; he's the one you want to run to," Skyy finally spoke, his head turned to the left, barely looking over his shoulder. "I can't compete." He returned his gaze forward, shaking his head in defeat. "I no longer have the strength to fight for you."

Turning toward the phone, I was frozen, unable to lift the receiver. After several more rings, it fell silent. That was the third time the phone rang since Skyy rudely answered, then hung up.

"I think I should be going," Skyy stated, standing, searching for his clothes.

"You don't have to go."

Skyy snidely chuckled. "You're kidding, right?" He pulled his jeans over his ass, fastening the top button. "I give in. He wins."

Battlefields

"Skyy, don't do this!"

The phone rang once again. In a huff, Skyy marched toward the phone before I could intercept, picked up the receiver, and answered.

"Hello?" Glaring hard, Skyy listened momentarily then replaced the receiver.

"Who was it?" Unsure why I asked, I knew exactly who it was. His expression read Oz all over his face.

Skyy grabbed the rest of his belongings, bolting for the door. I called out, following close behind.

"Skyy stop, what the fuck!"

"It's over," he cried, sprinting through the door.

The ringing of the phone once again caused me to abruptly halt at the top of the stairs. "Fuck," I mumbled. Reaching for the receiver, I said, "Hello?" I heard voices in the background, sounds of a busy office, and I could barely make out the many muffled conversations. It appeared Oz was speaking with someone else. "Hello, who is this?" I questioned once again.

"Hold on, Officer, I have someone on the other end," I overheard Oz say.

"Oz!" I stated in a panic.

"Willie!"

"I'm here. Oz, where are you?" I asked.

"Willie, I need you to pick me up from the police station!"

"What?"

"I'm in jail, come get me!"

"What happened?" I questioned.

"I don't have time to answer all your questions, just come get me!"

"All right, I'm on my way. What station?

"Hollywood, located at Wilcox and De Longpre Avenue."

"I know where it is. I'll be there as soon as I can!"

Thirty minutes passed before I arrived at LAPD's Hollywood Station. After completing all the necessary paperwork needed to have Oz released, I waited in a small, cold room with all sorts of thoughts filtering my mind on what might have landed him in jail. Released two hours later, Oz finally entered the waiting room.

When he walked into the waiting area, his appearance was disheveled, and he had a bruise and cut above his right cheek; his shirt was torn, bloodied, and dirty.

"What the hell happened to you?" I asked, when he approached.

Oz wrapped his large arms around my torso, hugging me tightly, visibly shaken. "Man, am I glad to see you," he whispered.

"Are you OK?"

"Yeah, I'm OK." He still held me tight. "It was a huge mistake."

"What did you do?"

"Let's talk about it later. I need to retrieve my jeep from the impound." Oz grabbed me by the neck, leading me out the station.

Once we reclaimed his Jeep, I followed Oz to his apartment, where he provided the details of the night before. Oz sat on the floor with his back against the sofa, holding a bottle of beer in his left hand, resting on his thigh. His right leg folded under his left. I lay across the sofa, resting my head on a set of propped-up pillows.

"So, how did all this go down? What happened to your boy Cedric?

"Cedric is still locked up, turned out he had a warrant on his ass!" Oz took a quick swig of his beer.

"What's the warrant for?"

"I don't know, parking tickets I think; some stupid shit he didn't take care of." Oz paused for a minute before continuing with the events of the previous night. "I should have let that foo' go about his business, because after all the shit went down, she still took his side and defended his dumb ass!"

"Who did?"

"The reason I ended up in jail! I was chillin', having a few drinks with Cedric, when this foo' and his girl got into an altercation over some other dude in the joint. The argument became heated when he started shovin' ole girl around. At first, I wasn't going to get involved. I felt it was none of my

Battlefields

business, but the dude started to get violent. Therefore, I told mofo to back the fuck off, and that's when he came at me, so we exchanged words. Ole boy got up in my face, telling me to mind my fuckin' business, and I told him to fuck off and leave the girl alone!"

"What did the girl say or do?"

"She stated everything was OK, that he wasn't going to hit her. I asked if she wanted me to do anything, and she said no. The bartender told them to leave, and then ole boy started mouthing off with the bartender, getting loud and causing a scene! I backed off, but ole boy came at me again." Oz lifted the bottle of beer, gulping a few chugs. "I told the foo' to back the fuck off! He stepped closer, getting all up in my face. I tried to remain calm, but you know how I hate that shit!" Oz looked in my direction, making the statement, stressing the fact. "Cedric said to let it go then grabbed my arm, pulling me away. Ole boy reared back to throw a punch, and something in me just clicked, and I lost it! I began pounding on ole boy, beating his ass silly! Cedric tried to step in and break us up, but he couldn't. Then she became hysterical, crying for her man! Next thing I knew the cops were pulling us apart, handcuffing and hauling my ass outside. There was so much commotion that nobody knew what was going on. In the end, the police transported all of us to the station. It wasn't until this morning that everything was sorted out."

"Oz, you know I've told you about your temper!" I stated, gently grazing my fingers through his hair, massaging and comforting. Oz tilted his head to the side, welcoming the gesture. "So what happens now?"

"I believe I'll have to go to court since mofo pressed charges against me! The police informed me that I shouldn't worry because they felt he didn't have a case, and I acted in self-defense."

"And what did the girl do?"

"She stood up for his dumb ass, saying she was sorry, and it was all her fault!"

"That's some crazy shit," I remarked, continuing to massage Oz's scalp, making him feel like putty; and I knew if I asked, I could have anything I wanted. "Everything will be all right."

"I know, but it's a pain in the ass when you try to help someone and this is what you get for it." Oz took another gulp of his beer. "What was up with your boy, and why didn't you answer the phone?"

"Man, I had my own drama going on," I sighed.

"What was up with him?"

"You!"

"How do I figure into the equation," Oz questioned.

"Everything! You, our friendship, you name it. Point being, he's jealous of how close we are, that's all."

"He thinks we're fuckin'?"

Choosing to ignore the subject, I wanted to leave that delicate territory unanswered. When I did not answer, Oz turned to face me. "I'll take that as a yes." Oz turned back around, facing straight ahead. "Fuck 'em," he said, taking another swig of his beer. "If he's that insecure, leave his dumb ass alone. I didn't care for him anyway."

"Well, I think we broke up." I relaxed my hand

"Don't stop. You know how I love it when you do that." Oz held his head back with his eyes closed. "He's a fool, forget his dumb ass!"

If it was only that easy, I thought to myself.

CHAPTER 37

By the summer of 1986, my studies in architecture were complete. I finished at the top of my class, which helped land me a position with a leading architectural firm in downtown Los Angeles. All that I wanted appeared to have fallen into place. At the firm, I made great strides and was beginning to stand on my own two feet. My career was on a solid path, but nevertheless, despite how good my professional life appeared, my personal life was unraveling.

Skyy was long gone after our last altercation, the day I picked Oz up from jail. Unable to find love, I slipped back into the decay of late-night conquests. Prowling the debauched streets, I searched for individuals to nourish a deepening depression. My relationship with Oz returned to its usual playing field of imaginary lovers, with me feeling I was the only one that mattered. That was until Oz became involved with some fake-ass girl named Jasmine. Mind you, I had nothing against her—well, hell yeah, I did! She was taking my one true thing I loved. It's ironic how life found ways to throw a curve ball. At one time, Oz had maintained a parade of women. Now, I was the one who opened the floodgates at a time when it was the most dangerous to engage in anonymous sexual liaisons. True enough, I practiced safe sex, but the need to feel loved overpowered any idea of laying low until Mr. Right came along. The urgency directed my desires down a darkened road of destruction. Whatever the cost, I remained determined to find the solace I desperately longed for. If Oz wasn't for me, then someone else was.

Vance N. Smith

One lonely Friday night, I sat alone, sipping my usual Bacardi and Coke. Even though Jewel's Room was abuzz with the weekly happy hour crowd, I felt incased in a bubble removed from all festivities fluttering around. Funny how a hundred people surrounded me, yet I felt isolated from all the gaiety.

By drink number five, I became numb to all the lessons endured over the years. With each drink I summarized my life, including the lack of a relationship with my parents, the heartbreak sustained by Elijah, and the most damaging of all—my never-ending rollercoaster ride with Oz.

Holding the liquid concoction close to my lips, I paused before I savored another sip. With closed eyes, the silky liquor flowed, warming my throat, taking me further to a faraway place.

"Looks like someone had a bad day!" A haunted voice pulled my disappointments from the brink of destruction.

Scrutinizing over my shoulder, I answered, "If you only knew!"

"Couldn't have been that bad?"

"Try me!"

"Boyfriend troubles?"

I shook my head no, taking another gulp of my firewater.

The stranger dwelled for a moment. "Drinking isn't going to suppress your troubles."

Holding my gaze straight ahead, I sarcastically answered, "Nope, but it's a good place to start!"

"Do you mind if I have a seat?"

Lifting my glass, downing the last of my liquor, I said, "Only if you buy me another!"

"I think you had enough for tonight," the stranger remarked.

Waving to obtain the bartender's attention, he approached, throwing a wet, white towel over his shoulder. "What can I get you?"

"Another Bacardi and Coke, and whatever the gentleman wants."

The stranger cracked a faint smile before taking a seat. "I'll have a scotch on the rocks." Turning, repositioning in my direction, he said, "Thanks for the drink."

Battlefields

Reaching for my wallet, I threw a twenty and waited with my elbows resting on the bar, leaning forward; my head cocked low, and eyes fixed on several bottles of alcohol lining the back wall. I refrained from taking a good look at the man who rudely intruded my pity-party.

The stranger sat with his body facing mine, leaning against the edge of the bar, with his right foot rested at the base of my stool. "I'm Aaron Whitfield," he said with hand extended.

"Wilson James," I coldly returned.

"You just gonna leave me hangin'?" he remarked.

Without giving him my full attention, I reached to shake his hand. Moments later the bartender handed over our drinks.

"Are you always this guarded?"

I gave the stranger the once-over. "What do you really want?" I said, lifting my glass for a sip.

"Just because someone speaks to you, doesn't mean they want something." Aaron brought his glass to his lips. "Being tuff and shit doesn't become you!"

"What do you know?" I stated cynically.

"Enough to know this was pointless." Aaron tilted his head back and with one gulp finished his drink. Calmly, he sat the glass down. "Thanks for the cocktail," he said and then stood. "I hope you find what you're looking for."

My eyes followed, watching him ambled away. Shrugging my shoulders, I continued to fill my insides with the mind-altering fluid, and then I thought, *what am I doing?* Holding my glass to my lips, I watched him disappear amid the crowd of happy hour revelers. Rearing back into my stool, I searched the room until I observed him standing at the opposite end of the club. I hesitated before deciding I should start the conversation over. I had allowed my past to dictate my future, and if I were to continue down that path, I would never be happy. Therefore, I sluggishly rose from my seat, beginning my walk of shame. Once the crowd parted, revealing my presence, Aaron's demeanor transformed as I advanced. His expression was consumed with crushed hurt and dissatisfaction. Moving forward, I playfully bit my lower lip in a silent plea for forgiveness. He responded with a slight nod of his head, no. I forced a smile nodding yes, slowing my stride to a creep. Nearing his position, I outstretched my hand and mouthed, "please?"

Aaron turned his attention toward the people packed on the dance floor. His head bobbed to the beat of Gwen Guthrie's "Ain't Nothin' Goin' on but the Rent." Taking matters into my own hands, I hooked my finger through the belt loop of his slacks, forcing him onto the dance floor.

"What do you think you're doing?" he protested.

"What does it look like I'm doing?"

Moving in close, allowing him to feel the heat, I rocked in time to the pulsating rhythm blaring throughout the room. Aaron held his rigid stance, though he grudgingly loosened up, bouncing to the groove.

"That's it, give in to me!" I raised my arms up in the air alongside his body, fingers snapping. "Come on, you know you want to!"

As Aaron rocked, I scanned the stocky-framed man dancing before me. I hadn't realized how handsome he actually was. His long, naturally loose curls transitioned to a close-cut fade and a dark-tanned complexion with my absolute weakness, thick full lips, beautifully shaped. He was my equal in height, but thicker build; a strong, round face with deep-set dimples and sneaky dark bedroom eyes, which reminded me of Oz, minus the overt sex appeal. He radiated a clean, fresh smell and was dressed to impress in his business suit with his tie loosely undone and the top button of his dress shirt unfastened, relaxed. However, I was certain trouble loomed, because dudes with eyes like that preyed upon the weak, casting their spell, sucking you into their seductive lair.

His initial apprehension softened as the musical selections continued to play. Aaron wrapped his arms around my waist, penetrating his eyes into mine. One song turned to six in a row; we danced fanatically into the evening. Sweat streamed down the sides of his strong-featured face.

"I need to take a break!" Aaron finally announced.

I nodded OK.

We made our way through the packed dance floor, heading for the bar. Reaching for a napkin, I wiped away the moisture around my neck and forehead.

Battlefields

"Do you want something to drink?"

I handed Aaron a napkin before I answered, "Yes, I'll have a Bacardi and Coke."

"Thanks," he stated, reaching for the paper napkin.

"I'm going to the restroom. I'll be right back."

Aaron smiled. "OK."

A few minutes later, I returned, finding him standing against the slightly curved staircase directly across from the bar, waiting patiently.

"Did you miss me?" I playfully asked.

"Not at all!"

"So you say," I smirked.

He handed over my drink and smiled.

"Do you come here often?" I asked.

"Nope."

"I see."

An awkward silence fell upon us.

Aaron clumsily broke the peace. "I rarely make it out to the bars or clubs," he said, taking a sip of his drink. "Not my thang."

"I see, so are you having a good time?"

Completely ignoring my question, he said, "What made you change your mind?"

"Excuse me?"

"What, you didn't hear me the first time?"

"I changed my mind. So what!"

He smirked, taking another sip of his cocktail. "I knew you would!"

I frowned. "Is that so?"

"I know your type. I know what you really want."

I was not at all amused. "Typical," I mumbled under my breath, setting down my drink. "You have a good evening!" I stated then walked away.

I left the bar angry as hell; I did not need some judgmental asshole analyzing me. Walking east on Pico Boulevard, I crossed Norton Avenue when I heard a voice from the distance call my name. I turned to find Aaron with a slight jog chasing after me.

"Wilson, wait a minute!" he yelled.

I stepped off the curb, proceeding to cross Pico near Sixth Avenue.

"Hold on, talk to me!"

"Fuck you!" I yelled in return from across the street without breaking my stride.

I turned the corner along a row of storefront businesses. Aaron would have caught up had he not been held back by traffic on Pico. I stopped next to a dark passageway, which was out of sight behind the rear of the closed stores, and I waited for Aaron to catch up.

"Why did you leave like that?" Aaron asked.

Sizing him up, I asked, "So you think you know my type?"

"I was joking!"

Looking both ways up and down the street, I stepped closer. "Do you want to know what I'm all about?"

Puzzled, Aaron answered yes.

With both hands, I pushed Aaron into the dark, secluded area.

"What are you doing?" he quickly asked with concern.

Seductively, I began removing my shirt with only the light of the full moon illuminating the night sky, casting a silvery glow against my body.

"You think you know so much about me. Is this what you expected?" I unfastened my belt, leaning in close, allowing my lips to graze his cheek. "I bet you weren't expecting this."

Aaron's breathing became heavy and rapid. "I don't know what you think you're doing, but I'm out of here!"

I smiled, taking a step back with arms extended from my side. "You're free to go. I knew you would punk out!" I withheld a devious laugh. "You talked shit, but when it came down to actions, you punked out. Just like I knew you would!" I smirked.

"You're crazy as fuck!"

"Then leave muthafucka!" A lubricious smile graced my face.

Aaron slowly backed away then stopped, scanning over his shoulder. He hesitated for a minute before proceeding. He took three more steps when he halted, leaning against the side of the building; his expression was a

Battlefields

confused mix of excitement and fear. Nervously he scanned back and forth, surveying our dark, secluded surroundings.

"I've never done anything like this before!" Aaron stated with excited, cautious concern.

Approaching Aaron with circumspect, I placed my hands to his chest, carefully unbuttoning his shirt. "Give in to the moment!"

"Can I trust you?"

I leaned in close, my lips mere millimeters from his. "Without a doubt," I contended sweetly. Under my touch, his trembling body heightened the salacious encounter between opposing generals. "You have nothing to be afraid of."

"Easy for you to say; I've never done anything like this before," he confessed.

"You never had sex with a man?"

"I've had sex with men, but never out in the open. I'm not that adventurous! I'm extremely conservative when it comes to my emotions and actions."

Placing my hand on his crotch, I said, "Well, that's not what your dick is saying." I slid my fingers around, outlining his tool. "You want it, don't you?" With his shirt completely unbuttoned and necktie loosely knotted, I slid my hands down, revealing a beautifully sculpted, rock-solid chest. "Take your jacket off!" I commanded.

Aaron obediently removed his suit jacket, allowing it to slide down his back. With his arms and hands restrained within the sleeves, I seized the moment and kissed him deeply. Aaron let out a moan that reverberated from him into me. I countered, pinning him into the cold brick wall. My hands held his arms firmly, holding him captive to my advances. His lips tasted sweet and salty yet soft and safe. Our tongues tangled feverously in a state of enthusiastic relinquishment.

I released my grip for a hint of air. "Yeah boy, I knew what you wanted all the time," I whispered, standing back, and playfully punched him in the chest.

His breathing heavy, he asked, "What else you got?" while continuing to undress, removing his jacket and shirt, leaving his silk tie around his neck.

Vance N. Smith

I dropped my cream-colored linen shirt to the ground. "Everything you need is right here!" Aggressively, I pushed Aaron back into the cold redbrick wall, holding his hands and arms over his head, pressing my body into his.

"I see you like to play ruff," Aaron stated with motivated authority.

"Why play dull? I like to freak within reason."

"I do too!" he remarked.

"That's not what you said a minute ago. You were ready to run off like some scared schoolgirl."

"I said I never had sex outdoors or with some stranger I barely knew!"

"I'm not some stranger."

"Then what are you?"

"I'm your daddy for the night!"

I meticulously kissed and nibbled, tracing my tongue around the contours of his right ear. With each bite, Aaron's sighs intensified, as I tasted his bittersweet skin. Paying close attention to his ear, I continued down the side of his neck, with a kiss here, a kiss there, gliding my tongue around and under his chin to the left side of his face. His body quivered with each methodical motion I made. Down toward his perfectly shape pectoral muscle, I licked, stopping to attend to his left nipple. My mouth fully engulf around the dark-brown-flesh pacifier. Aaron placed his hand around the back of my head, holding it in place while the warm, moist sensation enthralled him from the inside out. Aaron muttered, "That's right, baby, you know exactly what I like!"

I washed Aaron thoroughly with my tongue, making my way to his right nipple. The scent of his cologne intoxicated my mind while I kissed and licked, savoring every inch of him completely. A wet trail marked my journey down the middle of his stomach where hairs slowly emerged, revealing thick, silky strands overlapping the edge of his boxer briefs. Hypnotized, I buried my face into his forest, inhaling the beguiled scent of male sweat.

Innocence gave way to innate male sexual freedom, and Aaron slurred incoherently, caused by my oral activities wooing him into an incarcerated frenzy. His swollen manhood signaled its release from the confines

Battlefields

of the cotton jail holding it prisoner. Like a warden who retained the key, I unbound the throbbing inmate from its darkened solitary confinement, jumping with excitement. A devilish smirk cracked my lips as I gazed upon Aaron. Rolling my tongue over the top portion of my lower lip, I was eager to savor the meal placed before me.

Aaron grabbed me, pulling me toward him, kissing my lips softly and sweetly with the intensity of a man locked away, far from the touch of another human. Not one to give up my position, I regained control, continuing my quest to the uninhibited. Holding him against the wall with one hand, I prepared Aaron's piston's journey down my hungry throat. Gingerly, I divided the split of his throbbing muscle, savoring the sticky substance secreted onto my lips. Aaron pivoted his midsection, forcing himself fully. Not allowing him complete power, I regulated the assault he pledged against me. In a counterattack, I pushed the prisoner back. The skirmish once again in my jurisdiction, I continued my ambush, weakening his defenses, finishing my conquest.

It was his goodie bag I sought, just a few inches away, where the real treasure lay. The hot box, that deep, dark love canal I had to explore. To obtain the hidden fortune, I played it cool, preserving my game plan to capitulate the prisoner of war to my terms, maintaining the upper hand. My skills of pleasure forged an unrelenting confrontation; the heat of battle surrounded his piston, in and out, deeper and deeper he plunged. With each stroke, he lost the advantage. When I sensed the explosion, I retreated, moving my forces closer to the buried treasure. A concealed trail led past twin hanging woolen sacks, giving way to a dark passage; I tasted the salty treats along the way. Drowned by an inebriating scent, a rich bounty awaited, and I planned to pillage the sacred treasure. Cries of a fallen foe pierced the night sky.

"Be quiet! Do you want someone to hear us?" I spoke, placing my hand over his mouth.

"It feels so damn good!" he moaned.

"I know, but shut yo' ass up!" On bended knees, I leaned back. "Now turn your big ass around!" With one look, I knew I'd hit the mother lode.

Vance N. Smith

"Damn, baby!" I carefully ran my hand down the center of his cheeks. Aaron arched forward by my touch. "That's right, you know you want it!"

"You like that?"

"Hell yeah, you know I do! I can't wait till I get a taste!"

"*Hell* yeah, baby. Eat that ass!"

"You ain't said nothing but a word!"

I pulled Aaron's slacks down to his ankles, sliding my hands over his plump ass. The moonlight cast a soft glow, highlighting the firm roundness of his trunk. Eagerly, but slowly, I proceeded, exploring the indulgence placed before me. Gently I kissed, laying my face next to his warm, rock solid, and coated with a silky layer of hair, ass cheek. Parting the hairy crevasse with nothing but nose and mouth, I inhaled, relishing the soap-laced musty scent. A fog clouded my every thought process, delving into his deep abyss. Several minutes passed as Aaron bucked and weaved while I tongue whipped, devouring his smoldering hot box.

A good twenty minutes passed before I came up for air. When I stood, I laid a hard slap across his right cheek—*POW*! "Damn, baby, you tasted good." Weak at the knees, I removed my slacks then reared up on Aaron's firm ass. "Open up!"

"Nah, man, I can't do that here," Aaron responded.

"Don't tease me!"

I laid my shaft, parting his dark passage, shifting my midsection up and down, grooming, enticing. Aaron responded, arching his back, lifting his ass for easy access. My motions grew pronounced, grinding harder, allowing the head of my stiffened flesh to pierce the glory hole I searched for, and gently pushed forward.

"No—stop!" Aaron groaned.

"Come on, let me slide it in. I'll go slowly."

"Not without a condom!" he contended.

"Man, I don't have one, but it's OK, I'm clean," I reassured him.

"Hell nah, hold on a minute, I have one."

"All right, but hurry up…you feel so damn good, and I'm ready to slide it in"

Battlefields

"Just wait!"

"Come on, don't do that!"

"Damn, you feel so good!" he responded.

I pushed a little more, I was right at the door. The heat surrounding my flesh was beyond anything I could imagine. I knew I was playing with my life, but at that moment, nothing else mattered. I wanted to feel love, I needed to be loved; I required his warmth around my flesh. I pulled Aaron's mouth toward mine and kissed him forcefully. My right hand held his lips to mine, while my left fondled his nipple. As our kisses deepened, I plunged deeper into the cavern of desire. Aaron sighed with each advance. Slowly, I drilled, inching my way in. Steady motions led to complete entry to the heart of his hidden treasure. Resting my head on the center of his back, I pumped and plowed, and with each stroke, Aaron's body convulsed, shuddering in pleasure. Aaron rode my pony, steering to the realm of forbidden territory.

Slap—pop—smack—the sounds of hard flesh beating against one another.

In heated and bated breath, I said, "Your ass feels so good!" Goodpussy had me so wound-up, I could barely speak the words, plunging, alternating between long, slow strokes and quick, rapid ones. The intimate sounds of raw man-sex permeated throughout the back alley of the closed stores.

A quick change of positions, I pulled out and repositioned myself along the hard, cold concrete. Aaron straddled my body, easing down, burying my manhood within. Rocking back and forth, sliding in and out, I began to feel the building eruption looming.

"Rock that shit faster!" I grunted.

"...You cumin'?"

"Hell yeah! Don't stop!"

With that, I blasted my load. Aaron quickly followed. I jerked and twitched by waves of concentrated gratification. I fell limp, relaxed. However, shame immediately swept over me, removing all satisfaction. Again, I was a victim to my own degrading self-worth, and at what cost was I to endure fulfilling an idea of what I felt was missing in my life? Had I allowed the hurt, the pain, and the suffering sustained over the years to rule my every thought? Who was I to blame for my own behavior?

I just wanted to know love, was that too much to ask? I wondered what my life had become.

CHAPTER 38

ONCE WE REDRESSED, Aaron walked me to my car in awkward silence; we did not utter a single word along our long walk to my vehicle. Before driving off, Aaron reached into his coat pocket, pulling out a business card. Knowing I had no intentions on calling, I thanked him, placing the embossed card into my wallet.

After my reprehensible encounter with Aaron, I realized I had succumbed to an all-time low. No amount of repentance would remove the stigma of that night. Maybe this was the moment to reevaluate, taking a step back, removing myself from all temptations. To my defense, I considered Aaron often, but couldn't bring myself to appeal forgiveness and take our happenstance to the next level.

A month later, I reminisced how soft and warm he felt. Yes, the sex with Goodpussy was phenomenal! But my heart just wasn't in it. I used him, fulfilling a necessity I required at the time. Like all others, he temporarily filled a void—I got what I needed and bounced, and I hoped he did as well.

Oz and I spent the day strolling the Venice Beach promenade, talking about whatever came to mind—politics, sports, and music, including Sedona's success. Afterward, Oz and I rummaged through several small merchant stalls, completing the day with a quick lunch at one of the many ocean-facing cafés. Later that evening, we caught a movie, ending the day at his apartment. Oz popped a bag of popcorn into the microwave, while I showered, cleansing the grime of the city from my body. Once refreshed, I retreated to his bedroom, watching an episode of *Saturday Night Live.* Oz entered the bathroom where he remained for nearly forty-five minutes until finally emerging with cut-off sweats and shirtless. Securing a spot at the foot of the bed, Oz applied moisturizing lotion, covering his entire body, as I surveyed his every move. Observing his taut muscles undulating with each movement awakened a sleeping beast within me. Sensing the intensity of my gaze, Oz rotated, facing me to ask, "What are you looking at?"

I answered seductively, "You," and then deliberately placed a kernel of popcorn into my mouth. Oz dashed a scintillating smile, and then slithered under the covers.

As usual, Oz lasted only thirty minutes before he slipped sound asleep. Strange as it seemed, we often shared the same bed, whether it was my place or his. It gave me the simplest edge of hope, sustaining me from releasing my heart to any other individual. Because of that muddled possibility, optimism held me captive to my nightly rendezvous. Sedona could not comprehend the concept, and Bryce chose not to even try. Generally fond of Oz, Sedona frequently remarked how much of a fool I was placing so much interest in a man who couldn't decide where his true feelings lay. We never listen to the ones we know we should.

Early Sunday morning, a flickering ray of light streaming through Oz's bedroom window awakened me. Rolling onto my side, I found Oz's side of the bed was empty. Frantic, I called his name with no reply in return. Grasping for the alarm clock, I noticed I had slept much longer than anticipated; the time read forty-two minutes past ten. Closing my eyes tightly, I overextended my long frame with a groan, shaking off the intense laziness that crept over me. Reaching for the TV remote, I flipped through channels. In a lethargic haze, I lay sprawled and lost in thought, stretched across Oz's bed, dressed in basketball shorts and nothing more. A slight case of guilt invaded me, as my mind raced between my nights of salacious interludes, to the men in my life, namely Oz, and of all people, Elijah. In those moments of solitude, I felt most vulnerable to the demons intruding my darkest, innermost feelings.

Because of Oz's increasing fling with Jasmine, our platonic sleepovers were becoming a rare occasion. This particular weekend Jasmine was out of

Battlefields

town, having flown to New York for a modeling gig and a hurried visit with her parents. Recently, by way of a Freudian slip, he revealed that Jasmine was the nameless girl he followed to LA. Yes, the one and only he refused to speak of the night we first met. Understandably, I wasn't thrilled with the idea of having to contend with real competition. All the other women were distractions I didn't concern myself with, nothing more than fly-by-night throwaways that proved inadequate opponents. Now, how he reconnected with Jasmine was beyond me, but I suspected they never really lost contact. However, he was with me, and I was the one in his bed. Maybe not in the way I wanted, but at least by my side, even though our relationship remained swathed in mystery.

A whining creak from the main door to his apartment snapped me from my voluntary misery. Heavy footsteps marched across the living room, fading toward the kitchen. "Oz," I called out, "is that you?"

Oz's muffled voice returned, "You finally awake?"

A smile crept across my face; I sat alongside the edge of the mattress, stretching my arms high above my head. Lunging myself forward, retrieving my gym socks that lay beside the bed, I slipped each one on before I stood. Just as I was about to stand, Oz entered carrying his duffel bag, wearing a dark gray jogging suit. His long, curly locks pulled into a tail, covered by a red bandana. Face unshaven and scruffy, he radiated male sexuality like no other. Oz was the kind of man that, no matter how unkept or polished, triggered your mind to automatically think of sex. He was the walking definition of male sensuality. It was in his walk, his talk, and his eyes—how easily they pierced straight through you. It was in that wide toothy smile that melted butter in two seconds flat, along with those lips, those kissable, red, plump lips—what more could I say! In all his beauty, even his mixed signals of latent, confused sexuality, there wasn't a hint of femininity. Whenever he was around, his kindness and gentleness covered me like a well-worn overcoat. The toughness everyone else knew, the willingness to fight at the drop of a hat, never existed when it came to me. Through all the pain we shared, all the arguments, I knew his love for me was never in question.

305

Vance N. Smith

Oz sat his duffel bag near the foot of the bed and removed the bandana that shackled and bound his locks, permitting them to cascade freely around his face. He proceeded for the closet where he undressed, leaving only his boxer briefs, and then neatly folded his jogging pant. Oz looked over his shoulder, flashing a seductive smile. An instant flutter surrounded my body as the concussion of warmth blasted through me—I became weak with no means to resist. Though we spoke no words, we communicated intuitively.

"Are you hungry?" Oz asked.

"You have no idea," I said, smiling. "I'm famished!"

"Famished," Oz cried out with huge laughter. "You getting high society on me?"

"Nope," I remarked childishly.

Oz headed for the door. "I had a good workout this morning. Boxed a few rounds to release some tension, and I knew yo' ass would be greedy as a mug when I returned. I'll prepare breakfast after my shower."

"I may not be able to hold out that long!"

"Then I suggest you begin breakfast and have it ready when I'm finished!"

"I'd rather wait and have you fix it."

Oz changed his direction and instead leaned in close. "You need a man to take care of your ass…big-ass baby!"

"You know someone?"

Oz did not answer, but stared for few second, stood, and stepped back, giving a seductive smirk and then walked off.

After breakfast, we returned to bed where we remained the rest of the afternoon. Oz watched whatever sports event he could find, while I sketched floor plans I envisioned. I must enjoy this while it lasted…since his fake-ass girlfriend would return in a few days.

Little did I know a storm was brewing!

CHAPTER 39

Fall of 1986

"What are you doing?" Bryce asked.

"Nothing really, waiting on Oz to finish washing my car and his jeep."

"Must be nice! Isaiah and I were on our way over if it's cool with you and your man," Bryce stated with reserved cynicism.

I kept my opinions to myself, since it was no secret I had been spending the majority of my time with Oz. Thankfully, Jasmine returned to Europe, walking the fashion runways of Paris, Milan, and Rome, and posing for several high-profile photo shoots, leaving Oz all to myself once again. Jasmine and I had not had the opportunity to actually meet face-to-face, but on several occasions we spoke over the phone. I gathered my presence didn't excite her, since I conveniently occupied all of Oz's time.

During the few conversations we'd had, her attitude appeared to have grown cold and distasteful. Mind you, she was always respectful; however, the uneasiness in her voice specified otherwise. Although Oz never stated it, I concluded that he'd mentioned I was gay. It was something in the way she reacted toward me that indicated there was aversion. Since I never gave her reason to dislike me, that was the only conclusion I could ascertain. Besides, it was obvious that Oz made a conscience effort in keeping us apart. During my last dialogue with Jasmine, I struggled through the conversation, while an unsettling pause filtered the air. When she ultimately spoke, her tone proved dry as a parched desert lakebed, eventually posing the question as to why we never met. Unable to answer and certainly not interested in having anything to do with her, I realized there was something about this chick that just rubbed me the wrong way. Therefore, I casually brushed her off, stating I'd been extremely busy with work. *Why are women so damn nosy, always asking a million questions? Sedona has a knack for that, which bugged the hell out of me!* Again, Jasmine's slight pause stated everything. Silently, I relished every minute knowing I had the upper hand.

Bryce and Isaiah assumed a different opinion altogether. Both agreed I was locked in some sort of lover's triangle with Jasmine unknowingly fighting for her man's affection, and possibly losing the battle. Whereas I held his full attention, yet lacked one major component, the physical intimacy. There may have been some truth to their summation, but I walked with blinders, refusing to see past the truth. So the farce I participated in with Oz marched on, and because Jasmine was away, you would not see one of us without the other.

Because of a job transfer, Bryce relocated to Los Angeles some months back. Around the same time, Isaiah and I began to strengthen our damaged friendship. Neither Bryce nor Isaiah were pleased being thrust aside like two recycled toys I pulled out on occasion whenever Oz was unavailable. Both voiced their viewpoints loudly and often. Thankfully, Sedona was in the midst of completing a successful world tour as the opening act for an up-and-coming artist named Bulldawg. With Sedona away for most of the past year, I had the luxury of not hearing her rants, though on rare occasions she voiced her concerns as well.

Returning my full attention to my telephone conversation, I said, "We're here, but give me an idea how long before you guys arrive?"

"Do you have somewhere to go?" Bryce asked.

"No, I'm just trying to get an idea how long."

"Oh, one more thing, I'm bringing someone I want you to meet."

"Who's that?"

"This dude I met, Rafael. We hooked up a few weeks back; he's real cool, and I think you'll like him."

"Is this some new trade of yours?"

Bryce chuckled. "I may have hit it a few times!"

Shaking my head, I said, "All right, I'll see you when you get here."

Battlefields

"Tell Oz I said hello," Bryce remarked.

"I'll do that."

Leaning over, replacing the receiver back to its base, I had planned on a quiet Saturday afternoon and was not in the mood for additional company, especially with someone I didn't know. Standing from the bed, I scratched my scalp then lazily trotted toward the bathroom to take a shower. With Oz working just about every weekend on a huge construction job in Beverly Hills, I expected to have him all to myself the entire weekend.

Passing the bedroom window, I noticed Oz had finished washing our vehicles. I tapped the windowpane attempting to gain his attention. Barefoot and shirtless, he stopped and stood, turning in my direction, and with his right hand he pulled his long, loose curls behind his ear, nodding with a flirtatious smile. I returned a grin then headed off to freshen up.

Later that afternoon...

I stretched my body lazily along the sofa with my head planted against the armrest. Resting my feet upon Oz's lap, he massaged them, kneading and releasing the achiness locked inside, placing me in a comatose state. The gentleness of his touch lulled me into a state of flaccid tranquility.

Those tender moments infused the chaotic sentiments continuing to occupy my intellect. I lay with eyes closed, my right hand draped along my forehead, drifting afar. Each stroke, soft and slow, caressed with enough pressure to transport me to subtle convulsions. Every once in a while, his hand would saunter up around my calf before returning his attentiveness to my foot.

By six o'clock, Bryce and the rest of my crew had not arrived, along with my growing impatience.

With the palm of his massive hand gently massaging the top portion of my left foot, Oz broke the silence. "How long before your boys get here?"

Vance N. Smith

"They should have been here hours ago. It was before noon when I spoke with Bryce." I opened my eyes, finding Oz's gaze fixed upon mine. "You don't have to hang around if you don't want to."

"Are you trying to get rid of me?"

"No, not at all. I thought maybe you had something else to do."

Oz returned to his task. "I'm cool, I don't mind having Bryce around, although, Isaiah can be a real bitch sometimes. Besides, I thought we had plans this evening," Oz stated with disenchantment.

"I thought so too, but I haven't spent much time with them lately, and they have aggressively expressed their dissatisfaction with me. They've been on my ass since I haven't spent any time with them!"

"Why? Do they have a problem with me?"

"It's not you," I hesitated before continuing, "well, maybe they feel you're taking me away from them."

"Am I?" Oz quizzed, stopping mid-motion.

"Are you?" I quickly returned.

Oz didn't answer, lowering his head and slowly sliding his hand down the center of my foot, retracing his actions before starting over. Again, we tipped the subject, shirking the issue at the nick of time. After all these years, we still had yet to disclose the true meaning of our involvement. What were we? What was I to him? Truthfully, what was he to me? I was uncertain how much more of this charade with Oz I could withstand. However, my foolish pride held me captive to an idea of love and all its many possibilities.

Scrutinizing Oz, I plainly saw what our future could be and the undying devotion he held within his heart. I knew instantly from day one where I wanted to be. That day he infiltrated my mind, body, and soul with a virus I'd been unable to shake. Of all the men I had succumbed to—for this one thing, I didn't possess the ability to fend off such a powerful concoction. Still, his love potion continued to intrude every fiber, every cell, and every tissue within my body.

"Oz—" I opened my mouth to speak.

Knock.

Knock.

Battlefields

Knock—knock.

I turned toward the sound of the door. Oz innocently interrupted as if he knew my next statement. "I think you should get that," he remarked without looking up or missing a beat.

Remaining still, I held my breath with closed eyes, trying not to show my exasperation. Another knock at the door, then the individual laid on the doorbell.

"Are you going to get that?" he questioned.

I centered my gaze on Oz. "Come in," I yelled. "Are you happy now?" I stated with sarcasm, slowly rotating my gaze toward the stairs.

Oz swiftly pushed my feet from his lap. "I'm not doing this with you!" he remarked in a firm but smooth, even manner.

I was not sure if I was pissed or hurt. Oz had my emotions so chaotic that frankly, I couldn't tell anymore where I stood on the matter. I mean—I knew—but I couldn't straightforwardly specify what I felt. Honestly, I loved the man more than I loved any other, and it pained me so. Looking over my shoulder, I raised my limp body. "Where have you guys been," I asked, when Isaiah reached the top of the stairs.

"Shopping at Fox Hills Mall," Isaiah stated, annoyingly. "We've been there for over three hours then we stopped by Bryce's crib."

"For what? And where's Bryce and his friend? And why are you so dressed up?"

"They're coming. Rafael is having some issue with his outfit. Therefore, I left them at the car. We spent all that time walking around aimlessly because homeboy didn't know what he was looking for, or wanted. I was ready to kick his ass!"

"And Bryce thinks I'm going to have something in common with this dude?"

"Just go with the flow. He's cool, but a little on the girly side and man hungry. Every man we passed, he assumed wanted him. Oh, but I forgot, you haven't had the pleasure," Isaiah stated snidely. "Hello, Oz, nice seeing you again...what have you been up to?"

Without cracking a smile, Oz replied, "What's up, Isaiah?"

"The two of you look cozy. What's going on here?" Isaiah inquired.

Oz quickly gave that look, and I hastily changed the subject. "You didn't answer my question. Why are you so dressed?"

"Hoping to get you out this damn house for a change. Oz, are you coming along with us? You need to spend some time with Will's crew."

Before Oz could answer, I answered for him. "I don't think Oz is in the mood to hang with you tonight, and besides, I can't up and leave. You guys should have asked first!"

"You speak for Oz as well?" Isaiah quipped.

I turned to investigate Oz's expression. His appearance was stoic and taut.

"No, he doesn't speak for me." Oz stood from the couch. "I'll hang out, let me freshen up and put on some clothes."

"Do that! We would love to get to know you better. No point Will keeping you all to himself." Isaiah sauntered toward the sofa, hovering. His eyes followed Oz until he left the room. As soon as he was out of earshot, Isaiah voiced his opinions. "You've got to stop doing whatever you're doing with this guy!"

"Mind your own business, Isaiah!" I said angrily, sitting up. "You have no clue what's going on here!"

"I know this, whatever you want to call it, isn't going anywhere. How long has it been? You've known him since you were what, nineteen? You have to know by now he is playing you for the fool. He keeps you close, just enough to get what he wants, whatever that is! I understand you're in love, but you need to get a grip and take a long, hard look at what's really going on!"

"What have I missed?" Bryce stated, approaching the top of the stairs.

"Me, schoolin' this fool," Isaiah said, returning his attention. "You never listen to me! I tried to warn you about Alex, and you chose to do what you wanted! I don't even know why I'm tryin'." In a huff, Isaiah sat at the opposite end of the sofa.

I sat, tongue-tied. There were no words left to say; everything he stated was the truth. I was a fool for placing so much energy in Oz when our future was so ambiguous.

Battlefields

"So are we going to dinner or not? And by the way, this is Rafael."

Vaguely, I flashed a smile and said, "Pleased to meet you, Rafael, I'm Will."

"Same here, I've heard so much about you!" Rafael stated with a wide, overemphasized smile and a slight, limp wrist. He was not outright girly, but he had ways about him that wreaked female, which was just Bryce's type.

"So are you two dating? What's the story here?" I questioned.

"Nothing to tell," Bryce quickly retorted, "we're just friends."

The guise on Rafael's face insinuated he assumed there was more to the story, and to think they wanted to come into my home, giving me grief. When they had shit sprinkled all over their own damn house!

"Let me get dressed so we can get up out of here," I announced, walking toward the bedroom.

"Yeah, you do that, and tell your man to hurry up!" Isaiah remarked.

CHAPTER 40

DESPITE THE ROCKY start of the earlier part of the evening, the mood was surprisingly pleasant. Isaiah appeared to have chilled with his opinions; Oz on the other hand remained quiet, yet entertained. His calm at-ease disposition stunned even me.

The five of us sat at a large, dark corner table, with our stomachs stuffed and our mind-altering drinks flowing unrestrained. Even with the heavy consumption of alcohol, we still had the ability to maintain all our faculties. Excluding Rafael, whose mannerisms became more animated as the night progressed, which was comical and annoying all at once. Hands waved loose, limp in the wind, telling seemingly endless suspect stories of his many male companions. Keeping a close eye on Oz, I studied his every move, preparing myself for the moment when he felt he had enough. Thankfully, to my surprise, that time never came.

Bryce ultimately chimed in, informing Rafael no one wanted to hear his fables of loves past, causing Rafael to slump deep into the high-back wooden chair with a sullen expression. A low, slow chuckle crept from Oz, along with the rest of us, who tried in vain not to show our relief that someone finally stepped in, closing the floodgates—enough with that raw sewage flowing unconstrained from his lips.

Oz lifted his bottle of imported beer, taking a slow swig, savoring the bitter juice before placing his massive hand to my thigh, followed with a gentle squeeze. I struggled to suppress a faint, innocent smile, cocking my head low toward Oz. When I returned my attention to the rest of the group, Isaiah's gaze was one of withheld perplexity. On my part was a failed effort to evade his scrutiny, since Isaiah held his stance steady until I acknowledged

Battlefields

him. To my dismay, he was not the only individual who captured the subtle exchange.

Bryce, oblivious to Oz's affection, continued his rant chastising Rafael who appeared to have lost interest. Ignoring Bryce, Rafael leaned forward, resting his elbows along the edge of the table. "You two make such a handsome couple," he stated, rudely interrupting.

My entire body cringed. *Oh, hell no! That was all I needed was some silly-ass queen opening a can of worms that didn't need exposing.*

Bryce broke composure, rearing back into his chair with a look of utter aggravation. Oz's body tensed by the words spilled from Rafael's mouth. If Oz could have shoved the observation back into that hole it came from, without a doubt he would have. Instead, he coolly removed his white linen napkin from his lap, excused himself, and then sauntered off for the restroom. It amazed me how freely he appeared to express his feelings, but as soon as someone confronted him, his reaction was of complete avoidance.

"Did I say something wrong?" Rafael remarked in a quizzical statement.

"We're just friends, and besides he's straight," I retorted.

"Straight," Rafael shrieked with laughter.

"Please! He's so into you, with his confused ass," Isaiah rebuked. "I wish you two would fuck and get it over with!"

"I don't want to talk about it, and besides, didn't you just tell me I would never have a relationship with Oz. Now, you're stating how he's so into me. What the fuck!" I remarked, glaring back at Isaiah.

"Whatever! And don't give me that look; you know I'm telling the truth!"

"Change the subject, please!"

"I don't get it, why haven't you talked about the tension between you two?"

"Have you expressed your feelings toward him?" Bryce stated, reaching for his glass of wine.

I turned in the direction of the restaurant's facilities. "He's affectionate, and that's all it is—nothing more, nothing less," I stated, pragmatically.

315

"Please," Rafael chuckled with amusement, "I've never met a straight man showing affection to another man in that way! It's the way he looks at you, his demeanor—"

"It's everything!" Isaiah expressed, throwing up his hands in annoyance. "What about you? Is that all it is for you, nothing more, nothing less!" Isaiah leaned forward, twisting his body toward mine. "Have you learned anything over the years? You dwell over one man who shows you a little attention, pulls you in just enough to hook you, and then walks away. Yet, you turn away anyone else who comes your way. When are you going to allow yourself to be happy? Don't you think you deserve that?"

"I do, I know I do. I want to know what it is to feel loved; I need it more than you can imagine, and it's all I ever wanted! But I don't want to talk about it now, not here," I pleaded.

Isaiah sat back into his chair, squinting at Bryce with that I-don't-know-what-I'm-gonna-do-with-this-fool expression.

"What is he afraid of?" Bryce asked.

Holding my head low, I confessed, "We've never talked about it."

"So you continue playing a game where no one has chosen a side," Bryce questioned.

"Why is it you never speak of this? You're so quick to tell everyone how good he treats you, but in actuality this whole situation is a fucked-up mess!" Isaiah exclaimed. "And you know I'm a little perturbed by the whole thing. I like Oz, but I'm not on board with—*ouch*!" Isaiah reached down for his ankle. "Bitch, did you just kick me? What the fuck is your problem?"

"Shut the fuck up, Oz is heading this way," Bryce responded.

"What did I miss?" Oz asked, taking a seat.

"Same ole shit," Isaiah sarcastically remarked. "You know how we are."

"Well, actually I don't. I mean Willie speaks of you guys all the time. This must have been a gay thing?"

"A gay thing! Why would you assume that?" Isaiah asked in a huff.

"It was just an observation; the look on everyone's faces…like some shit was going down!" Oz offered.

Battlefields

"How did we get on this subject?" Bryce asked a bit confused.

Motioning toward Bryce, Isaiah said, "Let me get this!"

I turned toward Oz and noticed how the onslaught of anger slowly changed his game face. "Let it go, Isaiah!" I snapped.

"You stay out of this, Will. He brought it up!"

Oz slid forward, resting on the edge of his chair, rotating to confront Isaiah. "Let him speak, Willie," Oz snarled.

Seething with pleasure, Isaiah accepted the challenge. "If you must know, we were talking about your ass!" Isaiah remarked with a deviant smile.

"As I suspected, though you shouldn't concern yourself on anything regarding me."

"It concerns me when it affects my boy," Isaiah answered.

"What Willie and I do is none of your business! If I remember correctly, you weren't even speaking for a period of time, so I do believe your opinion is a moot commentary."

Placing my hand to Oz's thigh, I whispered, "Please let this go!"

"Are you going to allow him to speak to me in that tone?" Isaiah asked, infuriated.

"Isaiah, you started it; maybe next time you'll keep your mouth shut and stay out of other people's business," I remarked.

"I'm just trying to have a good time and experience how you guys have fun. I am not looking to pick a fight with any of you," Oz stated.

"I see. So, are you willing to experience what we gay boys do for fun? You want to see how we release some tension?" Bryce offered.

"What are you proposing?" Oz asked, not at all amused.

"How about hanging with us tonight? Bryce and I are heading to a house party in the Hollywood Hills; thought maybe the two of you would attend as well. My boy here needs to get out and release some pent-up anxiety. I had hoped to pry him away from you for the night, but I see that's not going to happen. Although, it might do you some good as well—you seem a little tense," Isaiah smirked.

"Oz, you don't have to do this; I don't need to hang out," I interjected, offering my opinion.

Vance N. Smith

Isaiah shifted his attention in my direction. "Will, let the man speak for himself," he stated with a disapproving glance before returning his inquisition on Oz. "What's it gonna be?"

"Why are you all in my shit tonight?" Oz's composure turned cold and calculating. "I'm getting tired of your bullshit!"

"Is that a threat?" Isaiah shifted in his seat. "Did you just threaten me?" he asked, raising his voice.

"Oh shit!" Bryce whispered, throwing his dinner napkin onto the table.

I knew all too well Isaiah, in any situation, would not back down easily. His temper matched Oz's equally, minus the willingness to fight on the spot.

"Oz, you don't need to do this," I stated, placing my hand to his shoulder.

Oz sternly looked down at my hand and then at Isaiah. "If you want to take it as a threat, then that's what it is, but if you're asking if I wanted to spend the night partying with you and I misunderstood, then please accept my apologies."

Once all parties calmed down, the five of us headed for the social gathering in the hills above Hollywood, with a city view southeast toward downtown Los Angeles. We arrived around eleven twenty, and one by one, my crew and I filed into the foyer of the large home perched at the top of the mountain. Standing just beyond the main door, we stopped to gather our bearings. The usual parade of characters marched back and forth within the huge living room overlooking the back patio. Just beyond the living room to the right, past an archway, was the section of the home where the kitchen and family room joined. With all the furniture removed from the family room, it opened into a large area, permitting the party freaks room to dance.

The early autumn night was still balmy with a hint of summer past, allowing the boys to prance around in as little clothing as possible. Skintight biking shorts left little to the imagination, along with tight muscle tanks. That's what I loved about LA; if you wanted to see the finest black men, all you had to do was walk the streets of the city, and tonight was no exception. A literal candy store overflowed with goodie treats for all to indulge.

Battlefields

Immediately upon entering, we headed toward the bar for another round of mind-altering concoctions. Bryce ordered our drinks, beginning with my usual Bacardi and Coke and screwdrivers for Isaiah and Rafael. Oz ordered a Belvedere and orange—I guess he required something stronger to get him through the night. I was still surprised he even agreed to tag along.

Once we received our cocktails, we huddled betrothed in mindless chatter. It was the kind of malicious gossip all gay boys loved to involve themselves in, along with the casual ogling of men who made our temperatures rise. Oz remained quiet, engaged, but offered very little by way of conversation, standing close behind with his back against the custom-built mahogany bar.

With a drink in his right hand held high, Rafael bobbed and weaved to the beats, his eyes closed, lost in his own surreal world; shortly thereafter he sashayed toward the dance floor. Isaiah held court dishing the dirt on all the fallen souls and scandalous tales that followed them.

Turning to check on Oz, I mouthed, "Are you cool?" He flashed a warm, reassuring smile, shaking his head yes. Seductively, I ran my right index finger down the middle of his rock-solid chest. Oz's gaze followed my every move, lifting his glass to his lips, sneaking a sip. A trace of electricity bolted throughout my body. Afterward, I returned my attention to the hefty dish of chatter Isaiah offered.

We remained in that state for a good twenty minutes until the DJ played Janet Jackson's "Nasty."

"Oh shit! That's my jam! Will, we gotta burn this mutha up!" Before I could answer no, Bryce grabbed my arm, dragging my ass for the dance floor. With a swift move, I handed my cocktail to Oz.

Bryce and I danced for a better part of thirty minutes before I could break myself free. Parading toward us, Rafael dipped and twirled in his best supermodel walk, replacing me as Bryce's dance partner—affording the chance to make my clean getaway. I left the dance floor soaked with sweat, my summer-best linen shirt clung limp from my shoulders. I made my way through the wide opening leading into the area where Oz remained with his back against the long wooden bar. The houseflies swarmed around

Oz, hungering for fresh meat—an unfamiliar face had stumbled onto dangerous territory. The flies always knew when unsuspecting prey had fallen into their trap.

Slowing my gait, I watched Oz's interaction with Isaiah, his head angled downward, listening intently to whatever news Isaiah fed. Suddenly Oz lifted his head, spotting me from across the room, followed by a quick nod acknowledging my presence.

Maneuvering through the crowded room, a familiar voice echoed loud and clear, forcing me to halt dead in my tracks. "Hey muthafucka, it's been a long-ass time; good thing I didn't hold my breath waiting on you to call my ass!" Before I could respond, a hand reached for my arm, yanking me from my path. Turning to face my aggressor, I realized my worst nightmare. Goodpussy stood with a scowl, which read like a front-page headline in full block letters. "Do you remember me?" he prodded with his hand planted firmly against my chest. "You're not going to get off that easy! Why haven't you called me?"

"I—I intended to," I said, making a desperate attempt to explain, but Goodpussy fired his statements fast, leaving little room to gather my thoughts quickly.

"Don't procrastinate, be a man about it!"

"Hey man…"

"You don't even remember my name!" he stated.

Somehow I managed to take a step back, regaining composure. "You can remove your hand," I said, pushing him away. "Yeah, I remember you. We met a few months back at Jewel's Room." I smirked, sizing him up and down. "Nice seeing you again, Aaron," I stated, steering my way around.

"Muthafucka," I heard him reply.

A hint of fear formed a cloud of suspicion; I knew my past would one day reappear to haunt me, but why tonight. The last thing I needed was drama following me, and when I caught Oz's gaze in the distance, his expression framed a facade of concern. What I did not need was Oz flying off the chain over someone who didn't matter. Besides, it was only a shameless fuck

Battlefields

several months back. I forced a smile with the hope of steering him away from any notion he needed to control the situation.

"Come dance with me!" I pleaded, grasping Oz's hand. At first, I received resistance before he relaxed and gave in.

"What was that all about?" Oz remarked.

I held firm. "Dance with me," I said, completely disregarding his question. "I want you to dance with me," I repeated.

"Tell me what that was about, first!" Oz pulled me into him, wrapping his free arm around my waist. "Answer me, if you want me to dance with you."

I hesitated, weakened by the suggestion he needed to defend my honor.

"Tell me what that was about!" His grip slowly intensified. "Who was that?" he slowly commanded.

"Nobody, just someone I met a while back." Sick as it may seem, this indication of jealousy fanned a fire, long simmering from the day I first laid eyes upon him, holding me captive all these years. "Damn, you're making me hot!" I joked in a soft, playful undertone.

Freed from his command, Oz stated. "You want to dance, then let's go!"

Stepping onto the dance floor, we heard the opening bars of Jocelyn Brown's "Somebody Else's Guy" began to play. My hand was in his, no shame, no guilt, a dream fulfilled. My every conceived notion intruding my mind for the last five years sped full force to reality. All I ever wanted reigned before me. Oz's seductive moves tantalized all that were in his presence. The way he gyrated his midsection in perfect harmony to the beat carried memories of our first night together. His slow and methodical dance of forbidden passion flashed in vivid color.

Once again, we teetered, chummier than ever before, on crossing the fine line of the forbidden. Jasmine's absence allowed us to delve deeper into our convoluted union. Inseparable, we continued pushing the boundaries, testing the limits of our friendship. Positioning myself closer, allowing his warmth to invade my space, my body grazed against his. Oz placed his arm around my waist while our bodies pranced in syncopated sequence. Raising

Vance N. Smith

my arms, fingers snapping to the tempo, my body rocked to the beat. We remained in that configuration the majority of our time on the floor. Seven musical cuts played before we became exhausted and needed a time-out. Holding Oz's hand in mine, I led him off the floor for a quiet place to chill. In the living room we found a spot in a dark corner, a few feet away from the bar.

"Are you ready for another drink?" Oz asked.

"You know I am!"

"Your usual?" Oz said, stepping for the bar. In the corner, waiting patiently for Oz to return, I noticed across the room Goodpussy watching our every move, holding his glass close to his lips. If looks could kill, I would be dead on the spot! *Damn, it was just a fuck!* I thought to myself. *I didn't force him to do something he didn't want to do.* I shook my head, returning my concentration on the one man who captured all my attention.

Oz returned holding two glasses in one hand, eyes fixed on mine. When he approached, he fashioned a seductive smile, signaling desires quietly bubbling to the surface.

I beamed a faint hint of a grin, straightening my posture and reaching for my Bacardi and Coke. "Thank you!" I spoke, taking a sip. "Are you having a good time?" I asked, removing the glass from my lips, resting my arm along the side of the chair.

"As a matter of fact I am! I wasn't sure I would, but you guys really know how to have a good time." Oz smiled.

"What made you change your mind? This is one thing I never expected you to do!"

"Why not?"

"You didn't strike me as the type."

Oz frowned. "That's a funny thing to say. I've always supported you."

"But you've never hung out with me before!"

"You never asked." Oz sat on the edge of his chair faced in my direction, leaning forward, resting on his elbows—taking a sip from his drink. Mischievously, Oz looked up and ran his index finger along the inside length of my thigh, sending uncontrolled chills in rapid-fire succession.

Battlefields

"What are you doing?" I questioned his intentions. "You have no clue what that does to me! So, don't start something you have no inclination on finishing!" I stated a bit annoyed, knowing his actions had no meaning behind them.

Oz lifted his glass, tilted his head back, and chugged, swallowing hard through clinched teeth, his face crunched with one eye closed. When he lowered his head, looking to the right of him, he noticed Goodpussy watching. "Who is this dude that keeps eye-ballin' you?"

"He's nobody, let it go!"

Oz reared back and swiveled in his chair, placing all attention in Goodpussy's path. "I don't like it! I don't like him staring you down!" Oz sat his glass down on the table, not once allowing his gaze to stray.

Hoisting myself from the chair, I reached for Oz's hand and said, "Let's go to another part of the house."

I waved to Isaiah and Bryce who entered the room, walking in our direction. "Help me get him out of here," I called out as they neared.

"What's wrong?" Bryce asked, once he noticed Oz's expression.

"He's buzzed and ready to get into some trouble," I remarked, pushing Oz away.

"I'm cool!" Oz stepped in, stating in his smooth, sensual voice, spliced with an edge. "I just want to know why that foo' keeps eyeballin' you!"

"What dude?" Isaiah asked with uncertainty.

Oz stood from his chair, pointing his finger at Goodpussy. In response, Goodpussy leered, lifting his glass in acknowledgement.

"Who's that?" Isaiah questioned, shielding Oz. "He's looking for a fight. What have you done to him?"

With my back to Oz, I mouthed, "His name is Aaron Whitfield. I met him a few months back, but never kept in touch."

"You fucked him then kicked him to the curb?" Isaiah remarked with disapproval.

"Damn, could you have said that any louder," I stated annoyed, not wanting to hear his viewpoint on the matter at hand. "Help me get Oz to another part of the house. I don't want him starting any shit! He's more prone to fight when he's buzzed, which wouldn't be good for Aaron."

"Why would you say that?" Bryce asked, puzzled.

"Oz enjoys fighting, a little flaw of his! So stop questioning shit and help get him out of here!" I demanded.

Oz fixed his viewpoint upon Aaron, with invisible steam spouting from his ears like a whistling teakettle. Aaron stood by his crew with a smirk, taunting Oz from afar, his body slowly rocking to the beats radiating throughout the house. Oz balled his fist next to his body in a combative stance like a general readying for battle, pledging a tactical, calculating move.

Pulling Oz's arm, I said, "Let's go, it's getting late." I turned toward Isaiah and said, "I'm taking him home. I can tell by his disposition, he's ready to beat some ass, and Oz is lethal with his hands; Aaron wouldn't stand a chance." Checking on Oz, I could tell his anger swelled wildly within. Alcohol and jealousy made for a dangerous fusion, and given the opportunity, he would welcome the battle, and for Aaron's sake, I could not allow that to happen. Although he was nothing to me but a brazen fuck one dark, lonely night, I could not allow harm to be placed upon him.

I managed to lure Oz outside, and the pending confrontation was averted. It was a quarter to two in the morning; Isaiah and Bryce decided they would end their night as well. On the way out, Bryce stopped, asking us to hold on a minute while he retrieved Rafael. Isaiah, Oz, and I remained along the sidewalk, waiting on Bryce's return.

Oz's agitation continued to propagate as shown by the scowl planted firmly on his face; his body stiff with anger. Over the years, I tried to squash his need to inflict bodily harm on anyone he felt disrespected him or someone he loved. While the need had subsided, he still relished physical altercations. I must admit, it frightened me how easily he became extremely angry, whether it was justified or not. He didn't look for trouble, but addressed any insinuation of combat, continually leaving the other individuals to reconsider their actions to pursue a war against him.

Grabbing Oz around the back of his neck with a firm grip, I asked, "Are you OK?"

"I'm cool!" he responded, bitterly.

Battlefields

"Are you sure?"

"I'm cool." His voice slightly lifted with jaw tight and lips tensed.

"Hey you, muthafucka," a voice called out.

The three of us turned to find Aaron and his boys heading straight for us. I reached for Oz's hand in an attempt to lead him away from combat.

"Yeah, take your bitch and run!"

"Go back to the house; no one is looking to fight with you," Isaiah stated, trying to defuse the situation.

Aaron walked up on Isaiah, and with one wide swing, he coldcocked Isaiah bull's-eye in his jaw, knocking him off his feet.

"Isaiah," I yelled in a haze of confusion, watching him fall to his knees. I ran to Isaiah's side while Oz bolted into action. The scuffle had begun, but as quickly as it commenced, it was over. One uppercut to the stomach, followed with a right-handed punch to the jaw, then a left hook to his temple, and that was all it took. Aaron found himself sprawled along the damp pavement of the sidewalk knocked out cold. Oz bounced back into a fighter's stance, shifting between his feet, positioned for another round of attack.

During the commotion, Aaron's boys ran back into the house screaming for help. Bryce and Rafael walked onto the porch when Oz's last punch knocked Aaron out.

"What the hell is going on?" Bryce called out.

"Oz, we have to go!" I reached out, pulling him away. "Let's get the fuck out of here! We can't be here when they call the police!"

By then, Isaiah had regained his composure. After Bryce helped him to his car, we all scattered like roaches frightened by the flick of a light switch.

Oz and I fled the scene like common criminals, with not a word spoken between us. High with adrenaline, Oz received a rush that reverberated throughout his jeep. My own heart caused my body to shake. Having witnessed him fight in my defense aroused my senses to a point I had not anticipated. I swooned in delight, loving him more now than I had in the past.

Vance N. Smith

Twenty minutes later, we arrived in front of my aunt's house. Oz pulled the car to the curb and parked.

"Are you coming up?" I said, hoping.

"Nah, I think I better head home."

"Thank you." I leaned in, planting a kiss to his cheek.

Oz turned his head, and for a split second, I sensed he wanted more; however, he backed away. He ran his hand down the side of my face. "You know I love you and would never allow anyone to hurt you. You don't have to thank me for doing what I needed to do." Oz paused for a moment then said. "I'll call you tomorrow. Get some sleep and forget about what happened tonight."

CHAPTER 41

THE FOLLOWING MORNING, I lay in bed contemplating the events of the night before, when Oz knocked Goodpussy on his ass! I did not condone that sort of behavior, though I guess he deserved what he received. I wondered what made people feel a disgraceful one-night stand meant more than it was—a coldhearted, callous fuck. However, I blamed myself for the continual situations I placed myself in, and the selfishness I possessed, thinking only of my needs and not considering the effects on others. The burden within, the unyielding requisite to wrap myself in intimacy, placed my life in danger on several occasions. Since the age of thirteen, I'd been on a never-ending search for the compassion of others. Twelve years later, I had yet to gain knowledge from the route I'd taken, including heartbreaks and disappointments, born into a world of seething torment, false hope, and unappreciative worth.

I awakened feeling disgust in the way Aaron, aka Goodpussy, conducted himself. What gave him the right to address me in such a foul manner? My mind raced in a million different directions. I was worried about the opinions Oz might have against me, having allowed my mischievous behavior to pull my dearest friends into a situation that could have resulted entirely different. I had not considered how I intended to deal with the unfortunate escapade of the night before. I knew all too well Isaiah would demand some sort of apology, followed by an incessant monologue on how I continued destroying my life. Clearly, I was not in the mood for that type of confrontation; so for the time being, I would simply avoid him. For a better part of an hour, I lay in bed, anticipating my next move. No TV, no soothing sounds emanating from the radio, just dead silence.

Around nine that morning, Aunt Raine called to say she was serving breakfast on the patio. Uncle Charles had not returned from attending some medical convention on the East Coast, and since I was not in the best of moods, it took all the strength within me to force myself out of bed, throw on some beaten-up sweats and tank, and join my aunt for one of her Sunday feasts.

I sat across from Aunt Raine, under a huge beige canvas umbrella attached to a wrought iron patio table. My aunt was forever elegant, a woman of considerable wealth who portrayed the true definition of Hancock Park society, dressed in one of her familiar frilly housecoats. She sat prim and proper, legs crossed, dangling her pastel-colored slipper. After each morsel placed into her mouth, she dabbed ever so slightly the corners of her tender lips. Resting her left forearm alongside the edge of the table, she positioned her right elbow on top with a firm grip around her fork.

I sat hunched over my plate, picking and shoveling scrambled eggs from side to side, barely taking a bit. The complete opposite of what a well-bred society child should present. However, let's not forget, I grew up on the lower south side of Baldwin Hills, a son of an establish dentist. I only lacked the highbrow upbringing afforded to those raised in one of the many mani-cured mansions lining the streets of this mid-city enclave.

"You're not hungry?" Aunt Raine asked with restrained tension in her voice.

I sensed trouble. Knowing she held ideas on her mind, I did not intend to give her any opportunity to lecture me so early in the morning. Aunt Raine reared back into her chair, waiting patiently for a response.

Nonchalantly, I lifted my glass of orange juice and guzzled before answering with a nondescript reply, "I guess I'm still full from last night."

Aunt Raine removed her napkin and gently placed it to her mouth, eliminating any particles of food that spoiled her dainty image. "Did you and Oz have another fight?" she asked, pushing the soiled plate away.

"Not at all, Oz and I are good!"

Battlefields

"What's going on with this charade the two of you are playing? Both of you need to wake up and realize you're meant to be together." Finishing her thought, she lifted her mug of coffee with eyes focused on mine, taking a careful sip.

"Aunt Raine, please! I don't want to talk about it," I stated, slightly raising my voice, startling her. Although I'd been completely honest with my aunt regarding my life, I never felt comfortable speaking with her regarding my relationships.

She placed her mug upon the tabletop. "You're not required to say anything if you do not feel the need!"

Fine with me, since I had nothing more to say.

After our hearty breakfast, we sat in silence. Aunt Raine, never one to mince words, appeared hurt and withdrawn. Ultimately she remarked the sun was a bit too much for her and retreated inside. I sat reclined on a patio lounger, reflecting on my life of reoccurring misfortunes. The warmth of the late-morning sun drenched my body, energizing me with the strength to muster the rest of the day. In my semi-comatose state with eyes closed, I stretched my lanky frame, with my arms resting along the edge of the chair's armrests. I sat shirtless, wearing only cut-off shorts. In this flaccid state, I found peace and not a care or concern except the remembrances of past indiscretions. In between the moments of idolized happiness and realized hurt, a smile bounced from my lips when the slightest hint of Oz came to mind. The one true thing I could count on was his undying friendship and devotion—of this I was certain. No matter how absurd our friendship may have been, there was no one, and I mean no one, who stood by me the way he had, at whatever the cost. Never had I experienced love as pure as his. Nevertheless, nothing in life was ever easy or simple. Everything in life came with conditions or consequences. Unfortunately, the same applied to Oz.

Subsequently, I remained outside on the patio an hour past noon before finally heading for my apartment to bathe and freshen up. Twenty minutes later, stepping out of the shower, the phone began to ring, echoing throughout the space. Hurriedly, I reached for a towel and ran with wet, bare feet for the receiver. "Hello?"

"Will!"

"Sedona! Where are you?" I answered eagerly. I dreadfully needed a conversation with a trusted friend who didn't have an ulterior motive in gaining my full attention. "Man, I have so much to tell you! You wouldn't believe the night I had!"

"What! You and Oz finally put all fears aside and—"

I didn't give Sedona the opportunity to form the words I so desperately wished were true. "Not even! You know his girlfriend Jasmine has been trying her best to steer him away. I know she's feeding him lies; I can tell by her tone whenever we speak, that condescending pitch in her voice fucks me up every time! She's up to something; I can feel it! Thank God she's been away on another modeling gig." Holding the receiver in one hand, I clumsily dried my body with the other hand. "Anyway, last night, we were having such a good time—"

"You and who? Oz?" she questioned.

"Oz, Isaiah, and Bryce, along with one of Bryce's new pieces. Some dude named Rafael."

"Oh yeah, I heard about him," Sedona remarked. I could hear her on the other end eating.

"What are you munching on?"

"Potato chips—go on with your story. Some dumb-ass drama must have happened!" I had not noticed the sound of annoyance in her voice.

"You know it, some downright ghetto shit!" I proceeded speaking of Goodpussy, filling her in on our history and what led to the events leaving him laid out cold on the hard concrete. "I didn't know what to do. First Isaiah was knocked on his ass, then Aaron!" I said, explaining the scene to Sedona, who uttered not a word—dead silence. "Are you still there?"

"I'm still here; I'm not sure what you expect me to say. I've told you before I'm clueless why you continue placing yourself in such ridiculous situations. You are the only person I know who seems to constantly have drama follow them, wherever they go!"

Battlefields

"Damn! Tell me how you really feel."

"I'm just sayin'…sometimes you need to hear it. Anyway, I have pressing news to share. Jackson and I—"

"How is Jackson?" I asked.

"He's fine, we're fine. He and I are having our second child. I'm six weeks pregnant!"

Damn! Now, I was speechless! I liked Jackson but wasn't too happy with Sedona having another child out of wedlock. Maybe I was a bit traditional with regards to babies outside of marriage, but then again, who was I to judge. Here I was, a man who had numerous sexual partners, some of whom I could not even remember their names. At least she could say her babies all had the same daddy and she was involved in a stable relationship, which was more than I could say.

"I'm happy for you, truly I am. I wish you the best!"

"But what? I know there is meaning behind it! You don't approve."

"I didn't say that."

"You didn't have to, Will. I've known you since we were kids, and I know when you mean more than what you actually say. It's cool, though. I know you'll support me in whatever I choose to do. I just wish you wouldn't judge so harshly when you never consider your own house and its many flaws," she stated matter-of-factly in a sullen tone.

It never mattered what Sedona and I said to one another; we never held a grudge. We stated our peace and moved on, next subject! Our friendship had always been that way. We got mad, and sometimes we said some awful things, storming off and reconciling the following day. That's what we did, and that Sunday was no different. She clocked my ass, I disapproved of her decisions, we voiced our concerns, and that was that. Three hours later, we were still on the phone. Damn, I missed my friend!

Later that evening with a complete spread of his favorite meal, Oz joined me for dinner. Afterward, we retired to the living room, playing a rambunctious game of spades. Ten games later I was spent with a body that was tensed, tired, and stressed by the altercation the night before, along

Vance N. Smith

with my uncomfortable gathering with my aunt, ending with the somewhat confrontational conversation with Sedona. Having Oz by my side, I finally began to unwind. I felt the weight of ten thousand pounds on my shoulders. Sympathetic to my needs, forever looking out for my welfare, Oz motioned to move closer. Politely I obliged, positioning in between his legs, where his large hands began massaging my stiff shoulders, which held me captive with each stroke. I succumbed to all the troubles of life's cruel games, tumbling faster than a plundering flashflood.

Half asleep, I faintly heard Oz say something regarding the bedroom. My eyes slightly closed. "What did you say?" I mumbled.

"Get up." Oz rose, lifting me by the arm. "Let's go to the bedroom."

Oz led me to my room, where he suggested I remove my shirt then lie flat on my stomach. On the nightstand to the right of the bed was a small table lamp that cast a warm glow throughout the room. Tenderly, Oz stirred about, setting the mood just right before retrieving a bottle of baby oil from the bathroom. Oz returned beside my bed, placing the bottle of oil on the nightstand. I lay frozen with eyes half-closed, watching his every move. In full view I noticed he had removed his shirt, leaving on his cut-off sweats.

"Relax and forget about the worries you've had the last few days, along with my lack of judgment last night," he stated, calmly and seductive. Oz reached over to turn on the radio, filtering the room with soothing sounds of classic R&B. In a precise rhythmic action, he straddled my buttocks. Oz ran the palm of his hand down the center of my back, forcing a charge of electricity to flow wildly from the nape of my neck down to my midsection. In a fluid, sequential movement, he returned his hand to the back of my neck, gently massaging. The force of his weight pinned my body helplessly against the mattress.

Oz mastered the fine art of seduction. Whether it was in the way he danced or the way he walked, it was everything about him—all of his many talents existing second nature. The slow, methodic strokes of his hands caressed and soothed my torso beyond indulgence. I became submissive to his strength, manipulating my muscles to an all-inclusive relaxation. He teased and taunted with a slip of the hand or a tempting, false brush across

Battlefields

the top of my ass, followed by subtle strokes around and under, barely escaping the area near my nipples, tormenting me to sublime capitulation.

On a wild rocket ride, I was hurled to the heavens above, left to descend slowly down to earth in reclusive, solitary internment. And once again, he fucked my shit up.

CHAPTER 42

THANKSGIVING HAD COME and gone, along with the freedom I enjoyed with Oz over the past few months. With the holiday season fast approaching, I was caught off guard with only three weeks left in the Christmas shopping season, unable to find Oz a sufficient gift. Jasmine was scheduled to return by the end of the week, meaning I would have to share the one true thing I treasured. Amid her impending arrival, Oz had become withdrawn, and making the situation worse was his custom-made furniture business had taken off after he built the handcrafted bookcases for Aunt Raine. Between his construction job and working late into the night, our quality time had become scarce.

On a chilly Thursday night, Oz suggested we meet at his newly opened workshop. It was a small storefront space on Washington Boulevard near Western Avenue, located amid other family-owned businesses and restaurant wholesale supply stores. Initiated by Uncle Charles, the arrangement was with one of his business partners, leasing the space for a small monthly fee. Believing strongly in his work, Aunt Raine used her influence to persuaded Uncle Charles to assist Oz with his venture. When it came to my aunt, Uncle Charles assumed what he was told; Aunt Raine had a way of getting what she wanted. Although, I'm sure there was something in it for Uncle Charles, but then again, Oz was considered a member of the family.

Arriving at the shop around seven that evening, I found Oz in the midst of carving a column to a four-poster bed made of dark mahogany. Pulling out a bar stool located in the far left corner of the shop, I took

Battlefields

a seat about eight feet from the workstation. My position provided a clear view of the door leading to the office, the main entrance, and the street. On a table situated to my left, a cassette tape player hummed the emotional sounds of Luther Vandross. Because of the noise of the milling machine and the blaring sound of the radio, not much was said. All I required was having him in my presence. Thinking back, I'm amazed how we lacked the physical intimacy, but our spiritual and mental connection fulfilled us, vacating the overwhelming inevitability to exploit sexual fantasies.

Seated quietly in the rear of the shop, I watched Oz's muscles ripple and flex, manipulating the wooden post. Every now and then he would look up, flashing one of his famous ice-melting, seductive smiles. Considering the soothing grooves of Luther and the sight of this definition of male masculinity, it proved too much to stomach. Many times I wanted to peer into his mind, combing the intricate corners of his psyche to understand how he felt regarding our friendship. I knew the thoughts were ridiculous, because what he didn't say he showed without hesitation. However, I needed the satisfaction of actually hearing the words I desperately wanted to receive, a true confession, a declaration of love. I was such a sentimental fool.

Rumbling emotions, smoldering hidden desires, and the call to love roared haphazardly along when Luther's "Because, It's Really Love" began to play. Closing my eyes, I savored the impassioned appeal, the fervent gesture of love, which reminded me of Sedona's evocative remake of Kenny Loggins's "Love Will Follow." The ultimate plea of love came with the final selection on Luther's *Give Me the Reason* album, "Anyone Who Had a Heart." He released a searing cry for the affections of another who couldn't see the love he held within. That solicitation of affection harbored all-consuming sentiments. Instantly, I thought of the continual mind game with Oz that I submitted to. Deeply inflicted, I knew anyone with a heart would realize my searing adoration.

Lost in a lovelorn wasteland, I was deadlocked in a subconsciously altered state. That's why I was startled when Oz ran his hand alongside my cheek in a tender gesture. Snapped back to reality, I watched Oz reposition with his right hand planted firmly against the wall. His large frame hovered, an expression marked with despondency, and his stance, rigid and penetrating. I reacted in kind to thwart the unknown. Our standoff lasted several seconds until he yielded asking, "Where's your mind tonight?" I responded with a simple hunch of my shoulders, conceding to submission.

Placing his hand to my chin, Oz peered deep into my eyes to say, "Look at me."

"What are we doing here?" I hastily asked, searching his eyes for truths.

Oz's demeanor collapsed when the words escaped my lips. I'd hit a nerve. Blindsided and slapped from behind, he was completely dazed and bewildered. No comeback came quick enough, and it was unmistakably written all over his face. He couldn't discharge it, no matter how much he tried; the obvious was finally out in the open. Oz placed both hands against the wall, cornering me. I abided my ground and didn't flinch; I did not intend to give him the opportunity to weasel his way around the subject.

Having Oz backed into a corner, I waited patiently for an answer. Befuddled, Oz placed all attentiveness in my direction, not noticing the opening of the door. I must admit, I wasn't giving it much thought either until I heard a gasp. Leaning to my right, I noticed a stylishly dressed young woman had entered the workshop.

"What the hell is going on here?" she spoke with a brazen voice. As luck would have it, another antagonist interfered, removing all hope of finally airing our dirty laundry.

Oz spun around, acknowledging the woman whom I speculated was Jasmine.

I stood from the stool to face my competitor. This whole debacle felt like a slow-motion clip, caught in a saccharin-sweet bad romance movie. Unfortunately, I hadn't placed much interest when I noticed the Mercedes two-seater sports coupe parked opposite the main entrance.

In full view, I sized her up. She was attractive, dressed in acid-washed jeans, a white blouse, and a leather jacket; her hair swept back into a French

Battlefields

braid. She had a slender face with striking features, a honey-bronzed complexion, and a slim build. She certainly wasn't some random black girl, for even I understood her beauty. She was easily capable of casting her seductive spell upon any individual who graced her presence. Nevertheless, I saw through that façade of hers, and deep down I witnessed a calculating individual.

Cautiously, I watched her ease farther into the room with apprehension, dropping her bag to the floor. Oz cut to his right with a quick glance checking my position, and then returned his attention to the young woman.

"What are you doing here?" he asked.

She smirked. "I think I should be the one asking that question." She came a foot or two closer. "I take it you must be Willie."

"Wilson!" I quickly corrected. "The name is Wilson and you are?"

"It's not important who I am." Stopping her stride, arms folded across her chest, the weight of her body leaned to one side with her right leg slightly outward. "It's a good thing I returned unannounced! What's going on here?" she calmly asked, peppered with suspicion.

I advanced a step, ready to confront my opponent; an approaching conflict I knew was sure to commence. With eyes locked ahead, Oz reached his right hand to his side, slowing my roll. "Let it go, this is Jasmine." He spoke in a low voice, barely moving his lips.

"Excuse me, did I hear you say something?" she asked.

"I don't know what you're alluding to, but you're way off base!" Oz then turned to me. "Let me handle this!"

"I know what I saw!" she responded.

"You saw nothing!" he quipped.

I'd had enough of the games and of the endless road I'd traveled leading nowhere. "I'm out of here!" I stated, reaching for my jacket. "Oz, we'll talk later."

In passing, Jasmine had one final word. "Yeah, I think you should go, but this isn't over, not by a mile. You and I have unfinished business to take care of!" Not once did she provide eye contact. Cold and collected, she made her point. She knew exactly what was going on, whether Oz knew it

Vance N. Smith

or not. She made her assumptions clear and wasn't about to let me get away without knowing them. That night she declared war on my ass, and from that point on, I knew I had to watch my back. My every move would have to be a deliberate one. I wasn't about to give her the upper hand, having dealt with far eviler rivals in my past. She would be no different.

Game on, bitch!

CHAPTER 43

STILL FLABBERGASTED BY my unfortunate encounter with Jasmine a few weeks back, and once again in classic Oz fashion, I had not heard from him since that calamitous night. Whenever a situation became too difficult, he would slip away, vanishing like some common street thug. Having suspected this would happen, I concluded I would not see him over the Christmas holidays. Therefore, I gathered my apologetic yesteryears, my dreams of grandeur, and went on my merry way. I loved Oz, but could not continue masquerading as if all was quiet on the home front. Year after year, I anticipated and prayed his love would justify and clothe me in love's luxury. Realizing I could not compete or win the sentiment of someone neglecting the courage to recognize what lay within, I had surmised it was time to secede and amass my daydreams.

Three nights before Christmas Eve, I received a call from Oz saying he wanted to discuss the incident with Jasmine. He refused to state the details, but suggested things were getting out of hand. Still reeling from the events, I initially rejected his request. But after a significant amount of persuasive discussion and pleading, I relented, agreeing to meet. As much as I loved Oz, he had my emotions so twisted I wasn't entirely sure how I felt. Maybe I should respectfully walk away, closing the final chapter to our book I had long finished reading. However, in order to turn the final page, this stand-off required a face-to-face confrontation to clear the plate, forcing all issues at hand.

I spent most of the day detailing how I planned to set the exchange in motion. *Do I simply go for the jugular, ending this senseless game of cards? On the other hand, should I give him a chance to speak his mind, allowing him to fill me up with more of his deceitful deception?* Throughout the remainder of the day, my subconscious sent my mind on a wild, turbulent journey of what-ifs, what could be, and what should I do. Hours passed and I still had not decided on any course of action.

Oz suggested we meet at his apartment around five that evening. I wanted to convene earlier, but he intended to work in his shop most of the afternoon, completing the four-poster bed he promised by the holidays. We would meet for dinner then discuss our unfortunate situation.

When I arrived, it was about fifteen minutes prior to our agreed time. Oz answered the door with a towel wrapped around his midsection. His appearance gave way to fatigued eyes and ruminating demeanor. "Come in," he remarked, speaking so low it was hardly audible enough to distinguish his statement.

I entered his apartment without uttering a word or making eye contact, sauntering straight for the recliner. Closing the door, Oz followed closely behind, stopping just short of the recliner where he stood motionless, helpless and regretful. Ignoring his silent plea for mercy with a deadpan expression, I refused to provide him an inkling of forgiveness. I wanted him to stew in his own self-pity. Oz was not ignorant to our delicate condition, and it was time he surrendered to our dilemma or sacrificed our friendship. No longer could we continue down this blind road of destruction.

Watching him simmer in clemency, I wondered how we acquired this disastrous place. I'd given him all I could possibly give another, walking that fine line of friend or lover nonsense far too long, and today this shit must end! I might have been the only fool who felt that way, having allowed my dreams and desires to get in the way, and being held hostage from visualizing a clear picture of what really mattered.

Oz sat slumped into the sofa with arms resting on his lap, twiddling his thumbs round and round with nervous behavior. His head hung low as the burden of our condition weighed heavily upon him, exposing a vulnerable side I had seldom seen. We spoke no words, as neither one of us wanted to

Battlefields

break the silence for fear of what we might say. I began to feel sympathy, and out of that compassion, my personal fortress crumbled. The hurt held hidden melted faster than ice placed upon a scorching sidewalk.

"Do you plan to get dressed? I would love to watch you in all your beauty, but that's not doing me any good. We need to get this show on the road!"

Oz stood; he gazed straight ahead and had yet to glance in my direction. Moments later with clinched jaw; he ambled away, returning about fifteen minutes later. Oz reentered the living room still not completely dressed, wearing nothing more than navy-blue sweats.

"What are you doing?" I questioned.

"Willie…"

"Yes, what's the matter?" I asked, worried by his demeanor.

"I don't know what's going on with me."

"What do you mean?" I said, positioning myself on the edge of the recliner.

"I'm sorry for the way Jasmine reacted the other day. She had no right accusing you or me the way she did." His thoughts appeared scrambled and unfocused, completely off track from where he started.

"OK!" Confused, wondering how she factored into the picture, I said, "Don't you think we should talk about it?"

"There's nothing to discuss! She walked in jumping to conclusions. I guess the way it looked, anyone would have the wrong idea." Oz wiped at his face then ran his hand through his hair. "I want to get past this and not make it more than we should. It was an unfortunate misunderstanding, and I want to move on, forget this even happened. Please—"

"Oh my god!" I fell back into the recliner in frustration. "Are you fucking kidding me?" I exclaimed.

"Willie, lower your voice!" he demanded.

"Fuck you!" I stated, sitting upright. "Don't tell me what to do! You caused this mess. You've been flirting with my ass for the last five years or so, sucking my ass in! Now, your so-called girlfriend busts you, and because of that, you tell me it was a huge misunderstanding! Fuck you!" At that very

Vance N. Smith

moment, all I could do was laugh, because the anger I held within left no other response to the stupidity of our situation.

"Willie, I've told you before, I'm not that way. I've never treated you any different from my other boys. It's not my fault you have misinterpreted my actions," Oz stated, looking down at the floor.

"You can't even look me in the eye with that garbage! You know you're full of shit!" Shifting my body weight from one side to the other, waving my finger at him, I shouted, "Muthafucka, you knew exactly what you were doing! You led me on, teasing and falsifying your intentions. What have we been doing all this time?"

"All you gay boys think the same! Someone gives you a bit of attention and you take it to heart and run with it!"

I heard it—I knew he said it—but couldn't believe the statement actually passed through his lips. How could he allow those words to filter from his mouth? Coming from a man I had known for years, where had this come from? I was in absolute shock, a monumental betrayal of our trust. I stood from the recliner shell-shocked. I'd rather he punched me in my gut than to hear him make such a statement. For a moment, I felt blinded by the anger swelling within me, trying to comprehend what had occurred. I shook from side to side, as if to shake the thought from my head. Mounting sentiments fueled to the surface.

Oz took a few steps in my direction. "Willie, I didn't mean to say that," he said, his expression mournful and filled with regret.

I raised my hand, motioning him to stop. "Don't," I said, shaking my head in defiance. "Don't take another step," I insisted. "The one thing I could always count on...was that you cared for me. You never treated me like the others, and I always knew you were there whenever I needed you, and for you to say that to me is unbelievable! I've never made any advances toward you. My actions only fed off what you gave me."

"I know that."

"Then how could you say such a horrible thing?" I paused. "What has she been telling you?"

"I don't know what you're talking about!" he insisted.

342

Battlefields

"You're a fuckin' liar!"

Oz reached to place his arm around my shoulders, but quickly I blocked his advance, pushing him away. "Get off me!"

"Willie, please don't do this!"

"Nah, muthafucka, you started this ill-fated pony show and the damage is done!"

"What do you mean by that?"

"I'm done! I cannot do this anymore," I said, looking around the room, "where's my jacket?"

The extreme hurt amplified within my soul, and the only thing I could think of was getting the fuck out! When I reached for my jacket, the doorbell rang. Oz hesitated before heading for the door. Not wanting to appear weak and show my tears, I hastily entered the bathroom. Once inside, I noticed the sound of a woman's voice coming from the living room. A few minutes later, I slowly opened the door just enough to see who entered. *Damn!* It was none other than Jasmine. And to add salt to the wound, I found them in a passionate embrace with Jasmine asking if everything was OK. She followed with a tongue-filled kiss.

I opened the door, revealing my presence. Jasmine caught my gaze then smiled victoriously. She had one-upped me, and the pleasure she received by her victory was etched across her face.

"Willie, so nice to see you again," Jasmine stated, releasing Oz's embrace. "I hope I didn't interrupt anything; it sounded heated. What were you two discussing?" Her voice was calm and steady with not a care in the world. She knew whatever lies she fed had worked.

Her incendiary remark stung to the core, but I refused to give Jasmine the satisfaction of knowing she got under my skin. I coolly walked into the living room, passing them both, and gathered my jacket, directing myself toward the door.

"Are you leaving so soon?" she remarked, when I placed my hand to the doorknob.

I stopped cold, deciding against stooping to her level. If he wasn't man enough to step in and take control of this fiasco, then why should I? She won—I gave in—I had thrown in the towel. I loved Oz with every fiber, but I wouldn't fight for anyone who tossed my love aside so freely. I could not sustain another disappointment in my life, and I didn't have any fight left. Therefore, I raised my white flag and surrendered.

I knew then that evil had left a Trojan horse at my door.

CHAPTER 44

The holiday season of 1986

With Christmas past, the holiday season ended with the start of a New Year and the hope of welcoming a fresh beginning. Oz's absence led to several inquiries to his whereabouts. Aunt Raine questioned repeatedly on what happened between Oz and me. Refusing to discuss the intimate details, I remained isolated in my apartment, keeping the outside world at bay. To anyone who had loved before, they understood the traumatic, spiral decline you undoubtedly yielded to, and it was no secret I fell victim to the complexities of life. Often times, we hung on to the perception or the optimism of what we wanted in our lives. I mourned for the love of my life but was compelled not to fall prey to its clutches.

On the morning of New Year's Eve, I awoke in a surprisingly serene state. I declined to dwell on not having Oz around, even though, I must admit, I desperately wanted to speak with my friend. However, when all hurt was expended, forcing you to the brink, there's no other choice but to go on with your life without looking back.

Since our last altercation, I had received numerous calls from Oz, with several messages left on my answering machine—all deleted without listening to them. In the end, I needed a clean break from the insanity. I speculated how I could live another day without his touch and his easy way of providing a safe haven. Honestly, that feeling never left.

So there I lay, alone on New Year's Eve, surrounded in my loneliness with no prospects for a brighter day. Life and love left me flat-out stone cold. Who was I to blame for this disastrous circumstance? Did I blame my parents for enlisting me in a society of faithless fools, or for leaving me to wade helpless in a sea of indirect dysfunction to navigate helplessly among the living? No matter what avenue I chose, torment and heartbreak waited recklessly around the corner. Ultimately, I was left with one provocative question: How do I relinquish the love and loyalty for Oz that I held deeply buried and entrenched in my heart?

After sulking all afternoon, I decided it was time to rejoin the land of the living. Propped along the edge of the bed, I stared blankly at the clock then lifted my head, watching two birds in some sort of strange mating dance. I smiled and thought, *even those damn birds found love!*

When I stood to slip on my slippers, my phone began to ring; I vacillated a spilt second then reached for the receiver. "Hello?"

"My nigga! I see you're finally answering your damn phone. What the fuck are you doing?" Bryce answered with a little too much enthusiasm.

"Not much, I'm just getting out of bed. What's going on with you?" I asked, scratching my head, yawning wide, and shaking away the drowsiness. "You're in a favorable mood!"

"Get yo' ass up and quit moping around like some love-struck schoolgirl! That nigga ain't thinking about you! His intentions were never meant to be anything more than a friend...you knew it...he knew it...hell...we all knew it! Get over it."

"I don't think it's that simple. It's easy for you to say get over it, because you have no clue how I feel or what his friendship meant! Maybe it's true he never intended it to be anything more than friends, but I cannot concede the fact that he led me into believing there was more to what we had."

"Are you certain that's how it actually was? From what you've told me, were you anything more than extremely close friends? I can't say for sure, unless you left out pertinent information. I've shown affection toward you on several occasions, does that mean it meant anything?"

"Well, it's a moot point now. I cannot continue this masquerade; it's weighing too heavily on my heart. If I'm ever going to allow anyone in, I have to resign him from invading my every thought. He's holding me

Battlefields

prisoner, and that imprisonment has confined me to a life sentence. I must break away or else I'm doomed."

"OK…well, let me flip the script. Have you ever considered that maybe he's in love with you, but unable to express how he feels? Have you even contemplated that? Not every man can accept this life and all the complications that go along with it. The shame and humiliation or the possible rejection from family and friends."

"I have…"

"But?" Bryce quickly added.

"It's just too much to deal with. I need someone who isn't ashamed of who he is."

"Will, it's not always about being ashamed of who you are. However, this has everything to do with how strong of a man you are to cope with the negativity that goes along with this life. You and I both know how difficult it can be."

"I don't know what to believe anymore."

"I'm going to take back what I said earlier and play devil's advocate. What if his intentions were real? Yet, as strong of an individual that you assumed him to be, maybe he's not the rock you imagined. Do you just give up on him?" Bryce pondered. "I know you don't believe that."

"I want to believe he is being truthful, but then again, I know I can't keep going on this way. It's just too much!"

"I could be wrong, but maybe you shouldn't give up so easy. I'm not here to change your mind, but to help you see through this shit!" Bryce inhaled, clearing his throat before finishing his thought. "I guess you have some serious soul searching to do! I will always support you in any decision you make. I can't tell you what to do. I can only provide guidance, which is why we have friends. In the end, you have to go with your gut."

"Thank you, I needed to hear that!"

"So, let's talk about what we plan on doing tonight."

"What do you have on your mind?"

"I've been invited to a New Year's Eve party, and you're coming with me. I've asked Isaiah and Rafael as well."

"Where's this party poppin' off?"

"It's some high-brow shindig in Century City, hosted by this brutha I know, Jordan Armstrong. He's this up-and-coming entertainment lawyer who represents a few new R&B music acts."

"Never heard of him," I responded casually.

"I think he's working with that dude Sedona toured with."

"Bulldawg? Really!"

"You know the rumor mill is working overtime that ole boy loves the dick!"

"They say that about every man in the industry, doesn't mean it's true! And Sedona hasn't mentioned anything about him being gay; she would have told me."

"Anyway…I'll do him!" Bryce stated candidly.

"Well…"

"Well, hell! You would, too, given the chance!"

Both of us laughed in agreement, because Bulldawg was phine and sexy as hell! There were no other words to describe him, other than he was a tall, dark Hersey's chocolate drop, succulent and mouthwatering, residing in the same hotness category as Oz.

Bryce and I talked on the phone for over an hour before ending the call, and finally I removed myself from the same spot I inhabited for most of the day. After speaking with Bryce, I felt far better than I had earlier that morning. I proceeded to climb into the shower, removing the grime collected from the previous day, and then reentered my bedroom just as the phone began to ring. I paused, allowing the answering machine to pick up, screening the call. After my message completed, I heard Oz's voice boom from the speaker. "When are you going to stop ignoring me?" Oz's voice sounded painfully anxious, filled with guilt and remorse. "I know you're home, so pick up!" If I didn't know better, I could have sworn I noticed his voice quivering. "I can see you in the window, so pick up!" *What the hell*, I thought. I quickly spun around and ducked, peering through the miniblind. Oz stood in the rear entrance doorway of my aunt's house. Anger swiftly raced through me

Battlefields

realizing Aunt Raine had entirely ignored my request to stay out of my affairs. I sat on the bed, contemplating my next move. My mind wanted to throw in the towel, but my heart was totally against it. "Come on, Willie, talk to me; I'm begging you!" His tone was filled with hopelessness.

Cautiously, I reached for the receiver. "Come up." Moments later, I lifted myself from the edge of the bed, grasping for some old blue-plaid flannel pajama bottoms I was unsure why I owned, since I had slept nude since high school. I slipped on a pair of fleece-lined leather slippers and casually strolled toward the door.

I paused shortly before reaching for the doorknob. Following my conversation with Bryce, I doubted how I truly felt. There was no question of the extreme hurt I suffered; however, I did not want to dissolve our friendship just yet. I exhaled, gathering all thoughts before I opened the door, and then without acknowledging Oz, I headed back upstairs. Oz cautiously entered. It wasn't until I reached the top of the stairs, making the right turn, before I heard the door close.

When Oz entered the living space, he appeared haggard, face unshaven, and his often neatly cornrowed hair unkept. Positioned next to the sofa and facing the landing at the top of the stairs, I watched Oz make his way around my left, with both hands stuffed in his pant pockets. I had not paid much attention to his appearance until now, and what I observed was a wounded man. Oz paced back and forth in front of the sliding glass door facing my Aunt's house and driveway below.

"I see you've been speaking with my aunt," I announced, displeased.

"And your point!" he snapped. "Besides you know I speak with Aunt Raine all the time."

"I'm not happy she's meddling in our business. That's my point!" I returned. "This is between you and me, not my aunt or Jasmine!" I stood in defiance, daring him to continue this farce our friendship had become.

Oz shook his head, signifying I was the one creating all our problems. "You feel like the whole world is against you." He stopped, focusing his attention. "Yeah, you had a hard life, the way your parents mistreated you. And you have every right to hate them the way you do. I get that! If I were in the same boat, I'm not sure I could love them either. However, to shun and cast away everyone in your life is unfair. There are times you have to find it in your heart to forgive and forget, realizing we as humans are not perfect, and we all are flawed."

My whole body trembled with discomfort and sadness. I forced my gaze toward the opposite side of the room with hopes of concealing the hushed afflictions I surrendered to. Resisting those camouflaged feelings, I stood strong, forcing my body and mind to maintain control of my outward appearance.

Oz stood opposite my direction with arms and hands extended. "Look at me!" he demanded. "Willie, look at me!" he shouted. I flinched by his elevated disposition. "See, you can't even look at me!" Oz massaged the nape of his neck with his massive hand then said, "Willie, I need you to look at me. I need to know you still love me. I know I messed up, and I want to fix it; tell me how to fix it!"

"You know what to do to make things right…" I turned to head for the kitchen, speaking over my shoulder. "And stop listening to people who want nothing more than to separate us!"

"What's that supposed to mean?"

"You know exactly what that means!" I stated, agitated, opening the door to the fridge, pulling out a can of Coke.

"What does she have to do with us?" Oz asked, following close behind, then stopped to lean against the side of the pantry cabinet.

Undoubtedly frustrated, I slammed the cold soda can down on the counter top, resting my palms on the edge with my backside facing him. Turning to my right and speaking over my shoulder, I said, "She has everything to do with this!"

"She's been nothing but kind to you!"

"How could you say something like that? You have kept us apart for months, and when I finally meet her, she catches us in a private moment. She has your nose so fuckin' wide open and your eyes closed that you can't see the truth standing before you!"

Battlefields

"I see exactly what's going on before me, and you're right! I didn't handle the situation correctly. I should have never kept you two apart, and I take full responsibility for that. Just so you know, Jasmine doesn't hate you!"

"Who are you kidding? If given the chance, she would slit my throat sure as my name is Wilson! I'm also sure she had plenty to say about our friendship and me, and that's exactly why you've been acting so fuckin' strange. You believed her lies, and you take that shit out on me!"

Out of nowhere, Oz charged with, "Why haven't you found a man to settle down with?" I was absolutely stunned by his clever, tactical-assault power move. The general was in rare form with his one-two sucker-punch mind fuck, which nearly knocked my ass out cold! Stupefied by his cross-examination, I wasn't about to reveal his target hit bull's-eye. I recovered quickly then played it cool, never leading on that he pierced my heart with an acid-spiked dagger.

My counterattack was swift and straight to the point, knowing he was not prepared or equipped to respond. "I have, and he's standing before me, too fuckin' ignorant to confess the love he has for me!" I cracked an insolent, satisfied smile.

Oz methodically walked upon me.

I gleamed; I had severely blasted his ass! "Say it! Say you love me and there is no one else that matters. Admit Jasmine is just a distraction keeping you away. So say it, muthafucka; I need to hear you say it!" Oz grabbed the back of my neck, his grip tight as a vise, pressing his forehead hard against mine. The strength of his clutch burned intensely with the energy of our standoff traveling from my body to his. Still, I didn't waver. "Say it, muthafucka! For once, stand proud and state what you sincerely feel. It's just you and me, *say* it!"

I sensed the sweat of Oz's forehead dribble down the side of my face. His profound, seated emotions were visible for the first time and poured from his glands, cascading free. I did not fight his advance; I simply held my ground and waited. Oz's push for dominance failed, forcing him to retreat, releasing his stronghold. "I'm not like you," he remarked then treaded back in defeat. "You have me all wrong, and I'm not sure how we can recapture the glow our friendship once had."

"That's all you have to say?"

"What do you want from me, Willie? You want me to stand here and confess my undying love for you, which is not going to happen. What I can say is, I do love you, but not the way you had hoped."

"I don't believe you!"

"I can't give you what you want from me."

"Then why even bother coming by?"

Oz huffed, pounding his fist into the wall, causing an indentation by the force of his punch. Again, I flinched, but this time out of a sheer act of fear. I had enraged him and his steadfast frustration with our condition had manifested. He paused for a moment, resting his hand alongside the wall. Soon after, he left without verbalizing another word.

CHAPTER 45

New Year's Eve, 1986

"I had hoped you wouldn't act like some love-sick bitch all night!" Bryce stated, returning with another Bacardi and Coke.

"Get off my back!" I countered, holding out my hand.

Handing over the mind-altering liquid, Bryce remarked. "Shit...you should have kept your ass home if you're going to act like this all night." Bobbing to the beat, he added, "Let's dance," completely changing the subject.

"I'm not in the mood."

"I told you to forget that nigga! What the fuck happened after we talked? I know this has something to do with Oz...stop thinkin' 'bout that nigga! Hell, it's New Year's Eve, snap out of it!" Bryce reached for my hand, rocking back and forth, pulling me toward him. "That's it, you know you want to!"

Eventually giving in, I placed my drink on the table before Bryce guided me toward the dance floor. Bryce, with all the moves, could best anyone foolish enough to challenge him to a dance-off. I believed I was as good with a few moves of my own, but nothing compared to his. On the floor, Bryce and I were a perfect match, and whenever I had a buzz, it was easy to discharge my inhibitions. Somehow I was able to forget my plights and release pent up frustrations.

After forty minutes of frenzied body gyrations, I was exhausted and drenched with sweat. Grabbing Bryce by his shirt, I said, "I must take a break!" Bryce and I stepped off the makeshift dance floor in one of the smaller banquet halls in the Century City Plaza Hotel. Once the effects of the alcohol had taken over, I felt liberated, along with the dissipating reflections of my altercation with Oz earlier in the day. In that moment, I knew I could no longer allow him to ruin another night of festive excitement and jubilation.

"Cool," he said, staring over my shoulder far into the distance. "I hate to leave you alone, but I see some eye candy. I'll talk with you in a bit, besides, Isaiah and Rafael just walked in," Bryce remarked.

"Figures! I'm resting here a minute, so send Isaiah over when you see him." Pulling out a chair, I plopped heavily onto the cushion. I had yet to catch my breath, and both knees felt like they were about to buckle.

I sat somewhat reclined; my left leg extended forward with my right bent, slightly cocked outward, and my left index finger was twirling the cubed ice floating within my firewater. The infectious activities of the night became apparent as I surveyed the boisterous crowd. What was it about New Year's Eve that brought out the best in people? Was it the idea of a better tomorrow or casting aside the misdeeds of the year before? Whatever it was, it ignited everyone into total fury.

Magically, out of thin air, a husky, velvety voice appeared. "Care if I sit with you a minute?"

Shifting my attention over my shoulder, I happened upon a rich dark chocolate of a man towering over me. I grinned, gesturing my hand toward the empty chair. "Have a seat!"

He smiled. "Thank you! How are you enjoying the festivities?" he asked, removing a chair from under the table.

"I'm enjoying myself, thank you for asking." Curiously, I watched as he sat, partially scooting under the table, positioning in my direction. I was temporarily distracted, having noticed Isaiah and Rafael in the distance heading in our direction then abruptly changing course when they noticed I was being entertained. Casually, I returned my attention to the handsome gentleman. "I'm Wilson James, and you are?"

"Jordan...Jordan Armstrong...pleased to meet you, Wilson," he said, leaning closer, flashing an enticing smile. "You had me captivated for the last thirty minutes while you were on the floor. I had considered bustin' a

Battlefields

move, bouncin' my way in." His eyes roamed up and down like a scanner of an X-ray machine, visually undressing me from head to toe.

"Is that right?" I conceded to be a bit fascinated. He was definitely my type—tall, dark, and handsome, not a pretty boy, but he exuded confidence, which was a major turn-on. For me, it was how people carried themselves. Unfortunately, gay men only viewed the outer attractiveness of men, and go from there, which is such a shallow way of perceiving people. Then again, I guess that was men in general; the visual was far more important than what was on the inside. The problem being, after you took away the muscles and the flawless face, what did you have left? Was it possible the inner being could match what was on the outside? In all fairness, Jordan's facial appearance was average, but his body told a different story. He wore his clothes well, dressed in a tight-fitted shirt, exposing every contour of his physique. He had chiseled features with a slightly large, wide nose and medium-sized lips; he was clean shaven with a high-cut fade; and he smelled good, radiating confidence. I reared seductively into my chair, savoring every bit of the chocolate morsel seated before me.

"What's on your mind?" Jordon asked, seductively.

"You!" I smirked.

"And what about me?" he asked with a half-sinister grin.

Reaching for my ice-melted, diluted drink, I secretly surveyed him, holding him in limbo, slowly replying, "Time will tell."

He beamed. "So, I'll get to see you again?"

I lightheartedly thought for a minute then said, "Did I say that?" Glaring hard and methodically, I nonchalantly remarked, "I don't believe that's what I said."

"Yeah, you did. I heard it plain and clear!" he replied, outlining my hand with his fingertip.

"I do believe I said time will tell." I removed my hand from his, and lifted my glass to my lips; my head held back, I emptied the contents into my mouth.

"Are you ready for another?" he offered.

Vance N. Smith

"Sure. I'm not driving tonight...Bacardi and Coke."

"Ah, you're here with someone," he stated.

"Friends. I'm with the dude you saw me dancing with."

"Bryce...I should have known! I have to give it to my boy, he knows all the handsome men in LA."

"Who are you trying to charm?"

"*You*...shit!"

"Please, I've heard it all before! You'll have to do better than that."

"Don't play hard to get, because I always get what I want," he smirked, rising from the table. "Now, chew on that until I return, and one more thing..."

"What's that?" I asked.

"Take a good look when I walk away; you know you been dying to!" He flaunted an ominous smile before strolling away.

I indeed caught a good glimpse. He definitely had the goods—a nice round rump, tall and nicely built—sustaining my attention until he reached the bar. Cocky fuck!

Jordan returned shortly with a glass of wine and my usual concoction.

"I've never seen you around before," he asked, sitting next to me once again.

"Are you someone I should know?"

He reared back and said, "Hell yeah, muthafucka, I'm your dream come true."

"Whatever," I remarked with a faint laugh "I think you need to take another look in the mirror!"

"You won't be saying that later tonight! Trust that statement as pure fact!"

Shifting in my seat, I said, "Please! You must think I'm one of those silly little boys you're used to playing with."

Jordan sat stumped, his mind clearly calculating his next move.

"What, you're not used to a real man standing up to you? Cat got your tongue?" I sat smirking, waiting on his next volley.

Jordan huffed, shaking his head, obviously smitten. "So, how do you know Bryce?" he relented, completely changing his course of action.

Battlefields

Silently, I chuckled. *Yeah, muthafucka, you met your match!* "Funny you should ask, I thought I knew all of Bryce's acquaintances."

"I guess you were wrong." He reached for my hand. "Are you new to the city?"

"Nope, born and raised. You simply never crossed my path, until now. Though, I speculate you feel the need to know every man in Southern California," I stated before taking a quick sip.

"Damn, you know how to hurt a brutha!"

"I only call it as I see it!"

"Boyfriend?" he wondered. "You must have some dude waiting patiently at home." He held his drink close to his lips, smiling childishly. "How many hearts have you broken tonight?"

"How many men have you said that line to?"

"Ouch, kick a brutha when he's down!"

A loud voice blared from the hall speakers, starting the countdown to midnight and the passing of a year. "Ten...nine...eight..."

"Take my hand," he said, extending his toward mine. "Help me welcome the New Year."

"Fine, but I'm not kissing you!" I stated flatly.

"Yes, you will, and you'll enjoy every minute of it!" he cockily stated.

The announcer continued, "Five...four...three..."

"Don't stand so far away, I won't bite!" Jordan reached around my waist, firmly drawing me to him.

"One...Happy New Year!"

The band played "Auld Lang Syne" while the large crowd broke into a raucous cheer. He whispered, "Happy New Year," then went for the kill. Our lips locked in feverish hunger, as my mind spun arbitrarily by our twisting tongues weaving unabatedly, remaining sheltered in our embrace longer than we should have.

The balance of the night continued with the usual lust-infused banter, along with a few important issues in our lives. He chatted in full detail about the virtue of his law practice and firm he worked for since graduating from law school. He was a man, I discovered, who was proud of his accomplishments and didn't hold back, providing a comprehensive rundown. Arrogant to say the least; however, he was mildly engaging nonetheless.

Bryce and my crew kept a close eye on us, keeping their distance at bay. When I decided it was time to head home, Jordan offered, providing a ride to my apartment, which initially I refused. It was no secret I enjoyed his company, but I was still reeling from the events emerging earlier in the day. Though I was attracted to Jordan, I was uncertain whether to seek the affections of another when the unfinished business between Oz and me hung perilously in the air.

In the end, Jordan's persistence paid off. I agreed to his offer, leaving the function around four that morning, arriving at my apartment shortly after four thirty. Jordan parked alongside the curb of my aunt's home with ideas written all over his face. "I guess you're expecting to join me for the night?" I asked frankly.

"Sounds like a good idea to me," he said, twisting his body in my direction. "How about it?" he asked.

"I'm not sure that is a good idea," I remarked

"I thought you said you didn't have a boyfriend."

"I don't and what does that have to do with anything. Just because I spent a few hours with you shouldn't mean you get to taste the goods."

"That's fair, but you can't beat a man for trying." He leaned forward, his right forearm rested on the center console, and his left hand held the steering wheel. He turned, searching the empty street. "Can I have a kiss goodnight?" he asked.

I accommodated his request, emitting a massive amount of high-voltage charge, recklessly igniting a tempestuous urge to forfeit my design to remain devoid of the act of intimacy. I had pledged not to answer the relentless ideas of required love, since my unfortunate squabble with Goodpussy. Nothing good had come from those blatant liaisons. Still, I remained alone, and none of them removed the overwhelming desires I had for Oz.

I should have known I was never going to keep that promise.

CHAPTER 46

A WEEK AND a half into the New Year, my budding relationship showed signs of blossoming from an emotionally turbulent one-night stand. Since that night, Jordan played every hand in his deck of cards. His plan of attack began with nightly calls, followed with a romantic dinner date, and presenting his most charming personality whenever possible. Sadly, the interest level on my part fell below the extent I received from Jordan. To his defense, I felt intrigued; he provided a pleasant diversion, whisking my thoughts away from the one who surrounded my heart with an indestructible barrier—a force field so strong it would take a clever soldier to disintegrate it. Jordan proved to be a man with an onslaught of calculated words, but the real question he left unanswered. Did he possess the discipline to follow through? To stampede a masterful general, he would need to gauge the strengths and weaknesses of his opponent. The problem being, Jordan had unwittingly ambled haphazardly into his rival's crossfire, in plain sight.

Far off into the skyline, the wraths of subdued emotions stewed and intensified. In that short week and a half, tempers escalated. The established general lay hidden, careful not to expose or give trace of his existence. Reluctantly caught in the barrage and privy to the order of each opponent, I knew all too well Jordan's position fell short in the hierarchy. Possessing that knowledge, I fought hard to protect the innocent. At any rate, it was my responsibility to shield the unknowing from a blitz soon to erupt.

Vance N. Smith

As luck would have it, my efforts were in vain. Not even I could predict the skirmish that would transform those involved. Making the situation even more attention grabbing, a well-mannered villain materialized beyond the horizon.

I knew I should have stayed home where I was safe on New Year's Eve!

CHAPTER 47

LIFE CAN BE a real bitch! That was the thought I recounted continuously all day. The ongoing disagreement with Oz had fucked with my head to the extent I could barely complete my work. It was as if someone with some sort of serum had locked my thoughts away in all the disparities of my life. Never one to feel sorry for myself—well, maybe that was not a true statement—I had risen from shattered remnants, resilient as a phoenix.

All day my life played in a perpetual loop, reliving the days of my youth, from growing up in a house filled with mayhem, to living with a man nearly twice my age straight out of high school. Lastly, now I was involved in this tortuous game of love me—love me not. My concentration was shot to hell!

I returned home from work, wasted, stressed, and in dire need of cleansing the guilt and shame oozing from every pore in my body. Sitting my briefcase and suit jacket on the wooden bench against the stairwell railing, I kicked off my shoes, loosened my necktie, and slumped into the sofa like a sack of potatoes. Exhausted, I nestled into the corner cushion with my head resting on the palm of my left hand. Before I could drift into aimless thought, the doorbell rang. I glanced at my watch and pondered who in the hell was at my door, uninvited!

I yelled out, irritably, "Who is it?"

"It's me, Oz! Open the door!"

Vance N. Smith

I expeditiously scooted my weakened body to the edge of the sofa. I had not heard from Oz since New Year's Eve, and again in his usual fashion, he reappeared to circumvent the inevitable—the disconnect building between us. Immediately, I reacted with the idea of urgency, giving him another opportunity to regain my trust. Then I wavered; I could not renege my pledge to halt the ongoing chaos that developed over the years.

"Willie, open the door! We need to talk!" Oz followed by several hard knocks. "Willie," he shouted, "Talk to me!"

"If you wanted to talk, why has it taken you all this time to come around? It's been three weeks; where have you been all this time? Now, I'm supposed to give in just because you're ready to have a discussion!"

"I'm sorry!" His voice trailed off. A loud thud radiated, rattling the door.

"Oz," I called out. No answer. Instinctively, I ran for the entrance without giving it a second thought. I opened the door only to find Oz with his large physique blocking the entrance.

"What's wrong with you?" I asked, viewing his distressed appearance. He did not respond. I reached for his arm, "get up and come inside."

Oz surrendered, rolling onto his side, then stood with clinched jaw, avoiding eye contact.

"Can I get you something to drink? How about a Belvedere and orange?" I asked, following him into the living room.

Oz mumbled incoherently, making his way toward the sofa.

"I take that as a yes?" I stared briefly at him before heading for the kitchen. "You said you wanted to talk, now talk," I stated sarcastically.

"You need to remove that tone!"

"I'm not going to argue with you; I don't have the patience tonight. I've had a hard enough day then to deal with your bullshit!"

"Why are you so angry with me?" he asked solemnly.

I shook my head in astonishment. "Are you for real? You actually have the balls to ask that question?"

"I can't have you mad at me; it hurts too much!" Oz thought for a moment to form his words. "I know it was a ridiculous question, and I know

Battlefields

why you're upset. I'm trying to make amends, but uncertain what I should do. It seems everything I do, it's not good enough. I hate it when we fight, and the idea of it tears my insides up. I can't eat, I can't sleep, and all I do is wonder what I can do to make it better."

Standing next to the counter, mixing his liquid mélange, I set the carton of orange juice on the counter top before grasping the bottle of Belvedere, and then it hit me. "You want me to back down on my position to make it easier on yourself. I'm not going to make this easy for you. You know exactly what I'm requesting. All I want from you is to be honest with our situation. Yet, you continue sidestepping the issue."

Oz entered the kitchen, positioning against my backside, wrapping his arms around my waist, and nuzzled his nose into the side of my neck. His clean, fresh citrus-infused cologne teased the senses. "I'm not trying to hurt you, Willie."

"I can't keep doing this."

"I'm going to make this right, I promise."

"Seems like I've heard a variation of that already," I remarked.

He placed a gentle kiss against my neck. "I mean it this time," he stated, faintly.

Turning to eye him, I needed to witness his truths. My gaze fell upon his in this paramount moment of honesties. I studied him intently without forming a resolute thought.

Oz pressed his forehead beside mine, with eyes closed—adrift in significant concentration.

Before I could open my mouth to speak, the phone began to ring. I withdrew my thought, remaining motionless, allowing the answering machine to pick up. After my recorded message played, he could not have picked the worst time to call.

"Wilson, this is Jordan; I'm just calling to see how your day went. You've been on my mind—well—you're always on my mind, and I cannot wait to see you again. Call me when you can, and I hope you have a restful sleep and think of me in your dreams. I know you're definitely in mine! Call me!"

Vance N. Smith

Instantaneously, Oz released his grip. "Who was that?" he asked cautiously.

Not wanting to answer, I thought, *Should I lie and make light of our involvement or—*

"Are you seeing someone?" he asked, interrupting my thought.

I guess my answer did not come quick enough because he instantly fired back.

"Who was that?"

"I…I…met someone."

Oz took a step back. "When?" His question filled with resentment.

"Why are you grillin' me so thick?" I responded.

Oz did not reply.

"Oh…so now you're dumb struck?"

"I have nothing to say!" he spoke, reaching for his drink. "See who you want to see!"

"Here we go again. This is the very thing I'm speaking of; commit to the feeling and stop wavering back and forth! This is too fucking exhausting!" Removing myself from the disagreement, I headed for the bathroom. I removed my clothing then proceeded to take my overdue shower.

Oz remained in the kitchen, finished his drink, and I assumed he promptly made another. Some forty minutes later, I exited the bathroom, pausing briefly when I found Oz sitting on the edge of the sofa slouched over, holding a half-emptied glass and then pouring the remaining contents down his throat. Reaching for the bottle of Belvedere, he had not even bothered to acknowledge my presence. Leisurely, I waltzed into the bedroom where I picked a few soiled garments off the floor, placing them in the laundry basket, and then folded the slacks I had worn to work, placed my loafers into a shoebox, and proceeded to slip into some old, worn sweats.

When I entered the living room, Oz fiddled mindlessly with his watchband in a dead stare. I wanted to do something, anything that would snap him back to reality. Ultimately, I decided to allow the events to play out on their own. In this defeated state, I knew there was nothing I could do to assist him in finding peace. Obviously, he was where he needed to be. All I

Battlefields

could do was not to agitate him further, hoping he would eventually come around. For the remainder of the night, we sat in silence. Oz was isolated and removed from the setting, until passing out from all the alcohol he consumed.

Eventually, our fears and apprehensions were laid to rest, while we stumbled securely into accustomed territory.

CHAPTER 48

WITH THE PASSING weeks, Oz and I quietly slipped into our comfortable old habits of nightly phone calls. Oz became far more attentive than he had in the past, causing friction between Jordan and me. Although they never met, tensions grew thick as an ash cloud spewed from a colossal volcano. And as time progressed, Jordan immediately became anxious by Oz's persistent presence, resulting in demeaning and inflammatory accusations.

Jordan's relentless interrogation regarding my association with Oz and how he equated in the scheme of things, weighed heavily on my mind. No matter how I tried to placate Jordan, his mistrust grew tenfold, becoming apparent that something had to give. Whether it meant relinquishing my ties to Oz or giving up my involvement with Jordan. Either way, I was in a bad situation. Severing ties with Oz was never in question, but leaving Jordan, an empty distraction, I could easily terminate.

For the past month, Jordan attested to be a noteworthy man in my life, doting to all my necessities. He was making a concerted effort, proving the level of interest he held in our commitment, or really, the lack thereof. Up to that point, I hadn't voiced any true feelings; I merely went with the flow. If he wanted to go to dinner, I obliged. If he wanted to spend the night—well, let's just say—I didn't turn him down. Again, Jordan was a vehicle to exhaust frustrated, bottled-up passions, proving no different from all the other men I had met over the years. He provided an extension to the unacknowledged relationship I maintained with Oz. Jordan morphed into a repeat of my involvement with Skyy. Oz provided all the emotional support; Jordan, on the other hand, provided the intimacy I lacked.

Battlefields

While the days progressed, I stumbled precariously on until the Friday before my twenty-fifth birthday. When fate indiscriminately opened the door to a mounting, head-on collision. What started out to be a satisfying, unobtrusive evening with a few close friends would end bitterly.

Bryce and I, along with Sedona (who returned from London a few days prior), were sitting around the dining room table, catching up on the events of our lives. Sedona explained in detail her faltering relationship with Jackson. Now, at five months pregnant, she was anticipating her next move after the realization that Jackson (in true soap opera fashion) had cheated with one of her backup singers.

I always suspected Jackson's intentions were not completely authentic. But whenever I chose to voice my opinion, Sedona quickly reminded me of my long, drawn-out relationship with Oz. Locked in a stalemate, neither of us cared or wanted to be reminded of the less-than-stellar relationships we were involved in. To keep the peace, we withheld our estimations even though the burden was evident. Then again, our friendship had gone through several occasions when we bickered, made up, moved on, and started the whole process all over again. It was who we were! It seemed the anxiety and pain forced us to reevaluate what we valued in one another. For the life of me, I could not replicate this with Oz. Our back and forth nature created unresolved bitterness. One month we were fine, the next we were feuding, followed by Oz's notorious disappearing acts. Each exploit diminished the balance of love I held.

Currently, we were reestablishing the commitment we once cherished in the infancy of our friendship. We reverted to expressing the legitimacy of our interactions, and as promised, Oz renewed the interest he held steadfastly.

An all-together different method, Jordan presented a more consistent approach. He never wavered; I knew precisely what I was getting. The problem with this scenario was that it was not exactly mutual on my part. However, Jordan entered my life at a time when I was vulnerable, but nonetheless, my gratitude was sincere. We always shared a good time, though nothing matched what I experienced with Oz. No other man has ever summoned the expectations set forth by the one who consumed my every thought. The destiny of this arrangement, unfortunately, was condemned from the start.

Sedona pushed her plate aside, picking her napkin from her lap and dabbing her lips. "Will, honey, that was a slammin' meal! I see you learned a thing or two while I was away."

Bryce interjected, "I agree with Sedona, that was one hell of a meal." He sat back into his chair. "I guess that new flame of yours has you busy in the kitchen, portraying the perfect housewife." Bryce flashed a sly smile.

Sedona raised an eyebrow. "Something you haven't told me, Will?"

Fetching Sedona's dinner plate, I said, "Nothing worth discussing. I met a man New Year's Eve, and we have spent a few evenings together, nothing serious." I maneuvered around Bryce, gathering his dish, then headed for the dishwasher.

"He's not being totally honest, Sedona! Homeboy is eager to displace a certain someone," Bryce smirked.

"Oh!" Sedona leaned forward, resting on her delicate elbows, not wanting to miss a single detail. "Tell me more!"

"I believe you know him," Bryce remarked.

"Bryce, mind your own business," I said, turning toward Sedona. "Do you care for anything more to drink?"

"I'll have another glass of water," Sedona responded. "Speaking of... how is Oz?"

"He's doing well, his furniture business has really taken off, along with his construction job. His dream is to someday start his own construction company and expand his custom furniture business. Uncle Charles helped him open a small shop on Washington Boulevard about six months ago," I said, placing the glass of water next to Sedona.

"I think that's wonderful, and Oz is a good man. Nevertheless..." she said, completely switching gears, "Will, honey...what about this guy you're seeing, and how do I know him? By the way, how would I know someone you're seeing?" Sedona retorted.

"He's Bulldawg's lawyer," I stated, taking a seat across from Sedona.

Battlefields

"You're kidding; you mean Jordan Armstrong—he's gay! I had no idea!" Sedona's reaction was priceless; the shock of the information sent her into a plunge. "I'm really taken aback."

"Why?"

"You should see how he gives the impression he's the consummate ladies' man, that's why! Hell, he even hit on me about a year back!" Sedona chuckled and said, "I have nothing against the guy, but he's a character for sure. Will, I would never have guessed he would be your type."

"Why would you make that assumption?" I innocently asked.

"Because, *honey*...I know you, and you never fall for the arrogant type!" Sedona rolled her eyes with indignation. "You forget, I've known you for most of your life, and I know what you like. Jordan is not your type!"

"I love it!" Bryce stated joyfully. "This couldn't get any better!"

Sedona reached to high-fived Bryce. "You and Jordan!" Sedona chuckled, "Lawd, help this fool!" Sedona placed her hand to her forearm and smiled. "You're not really into him are you?"

I shifted uncomfortably in my chair.

"Tell me the truth! I'll know if you lie to me!" Sedona stated.

"I'm intrigued," I offered. "Nothing other than that, although he's hoping for more than I could possibly give at this point."

"And what about Oz? Where do the two of you stand?" she asked.

"Oh, I'll answer that one!" Bryce responded, offering his two cents. "Because all he's going to do is dance around the subject."

"Fuck off, Bryce!" I snarled.

"Listen carefully, Sedona, the Oz saga has not changed, except for the constant bickering, leaving Will pouting and bitchy, and Oz withdrawn and in denial. Neither one willing to face what is so obvious to everyone else on the planet. They flirt and cuddle, cater to each other's needs, then the next day, they're not speaking. A few months back, we had such a good time hanging out, they appeared to be getting along just fine. Oz even stuck up for him when some dude tried to clown my boy—now where is he? Nowhere to be found."

Vance N. Smith

Sedona sat, fiddling with her dinner napkin, eyes fixed on mine. "I don't get it! Why is it so hard for you to reveal what is in your heart? This game you're playing isn't good for either of you." Sedona shook her head. "I just don't get it," she said, lifting her water glass to her lips.

"I've tried to get him to open up. I can't make him do something he's not willing to do," I replied,

"As much as I hate to say it, maybe you should move on with your life," Bryce stated.

"I agree," Sedona remarked. "I've said it before, I'm fond of Oz and believe he would be good for you, but if he's unwilling to give you what you desire, then maybe you should throw in the towel."

"He and I are on good terms; in fact, he's coming over this evening."

"And what about Jordan?" Sedona questioned.

"What about him?"

Sedona frowned. "See, that's what I mean! Is it fair to Jordan or Oz? You keep them in the dark, plus you place all your hope into the one who is causing you the most grief. Granted, I do not believe Jordan is right for you, but at least he's up front and honest with his feelings. Does Jordan know about Oz?"

"Yes," I answered. "But only that I consider Oz a close friend. They have yet to meet."

"What about Oz?" Sedona asked.

"He is aware of Jordan, but by accident," I admitted hesitantly.

"What does that mean?" Bryce asked.

"A little over a week ago, Oz and I were in a heated altercation, airing our differences. After we settled down, we were standing in the kitchen having a moment, when the phone rang. Not wanting to answer, I allowed the answering machine to pick up. It was Jordan, which allowed Oz to hear his message."

Sedona laughed aloud, waving her right hand in the air. "I would have loved to have seen his face…"

Knock, knock…knock.

"Hold on, I'm sure that's Oz."

Battlefields

I went downstairs and answered the door and surprise, surprise!

"Jordan!" *Damn*, I thought to myself.

Jordan smiled broadly. "Good, you're surprised to see me! How are you this evening?" Jordan reached over, placing his arms around me, holding me securely. "I've missed you!"

"I don't know what to say," I said, instinctively pushing him away. "You should have called first."

"I thought you would be happy to see me! We haven't spoken in a few days, and I wanted to see you."

"I've been busy, and you know I have that huge project I'm working on," I remarked, taking a few steps back.

"Will, is that Oz?" Sedona yelled from upstairs.

"Oz?" Jordan asked, suspiciously.

Looking past his shoulder, my mind drifted aimlessly, thinking...

"Will!"

"What!" I snapped.

Jordan paused then asked remorsefully, "Should I leave?"

I stammered with my words, "You should—I mean—no." Stepping away, I allowed Jordan to enter. "Come in."

Jordan dithered before entering. "Do you have company?"

"A few friends...we just finished dinner. Are you hungry?"

"No, I've eaten already," he answered.

Jordan and I casually walked into the dining area. "I believe you're familiar with everyone," I stated as we entered.

Sedona cracked an insidious smile. "Hello, Jordan, it's been a long time!"

With a false, quizzical expression, he said, "Have we met before?" However, his manner revealed he remembered more than he led everyone to believe.

"You don't recollect?" Sedona scowled before turning to Bryce. "Funny how people have selective memories."

Bryce smiled, extending his hand toward Jordan, and said, "Good seeing you again."

"Have a seat, Jordan, make yourself comfortable. What would you like to drink?"

"I'll have a beer." Jordan fixed his gaze upon Sedona. "You do look familiar."

"I should—we've met before, backstage after Bulldawg's concert last year in Saint Louis," she stated snappishly.

"I'm sorry," Jordan paused briefly. "Wait a minute, you're that singer!"

The expression drawn upon her face, you knew she was ready to knock some common sense into him. Sedona immediately opened her mouth to reply. Hastily, I diverted her attention. "Sedona, can you help me in the bedroom?"

Sedona glared harshly before responding to my request. "Sure."

"We'll return shortly. Bryce, keep Jordan busy."

Together we walked toward my bedroom.

"What are you doing?" I asked, closing the door behind us.

"Nothing! He's acting like he never met my ass before, and I'm calling him on it!" she replied angrily.

"Let it go! It's not important."

"Yes, it is, Will, and you know it! He's coming into your crib, playing this game? I'm not having it. That muthafucka knows who the fuck I am!"

"So! What if he does?"

"And you don't see a problem with that?"

Bryce's muffled voice pierced through the door. "Will! Your bell is ringing!"

I returned my attention on Sedona. "Let it go!" I demanded.

"Will!" Bryce shouted.

I maneuvered, cracking the bedroom door slightly ajar. "Can you get that please?" I yelled. "What's with everyone tonight?" I stated, closing the door.

Sedona leaned against the side of my dresser, sulking.

"Do we need to discuss this further?" I asked.

"Whatever!" Sedona replied, moving for the door. I regrettably grabbed Sedona's arm, sending her gaze toward my hand. "Have you lost your mind?"

I quickly rethought my action, releasing her arm.

Sedona and I reemerged, finding Oz standing awkwardly in the entrance-way to the dining area, his expression stiff and unnatural, unsuccessfully

Battlefields

masking his hidden anger. He slowly forced his attention to acknowledge our presence.

"What's up, Oz, have you met Jordan?" I timidly asked.

Oz completely ignored my question. "Good seeing you again, Sedona," Oz stated respectfully, placing his solid arms around her waist in a gentle squeeze. Sedona rested her head against his chest, as Oz gazed ahead with uncertain eyes securely locked onto mine. His thoughts read loud and clear.

Sedona fell limp in his arms. "Nice! I love strong-armed men, and you smell good, too!" Turning toward Bryce, she jokingly stated, "This is a real man here!"

Bryce opened his mouth to speak.

"If a large mass of muscle makes you a man then that he is!" Jordan commented, lifting his bottle for a sip.

The room fell silent.

Searching around, Jordan said, "What! It was a joke! No one has a sense of humor?" He lurched back in a sarcastic gesture.

Oz shot a stern countenance with narrow eyes in my direction. Bryce sat wide-eyed, withholding any form of communication. Jordan relished in the uncomfortable atmosphere in which he placed all involved.

"Who is this foo' talking to?" Oz questioned, releasing Sedona from his grasp, repositioning himself.

"Oz, why don't you tell me about the furniture you've been making? Will said your business has really taken off." Sedona pulled at his hand, directing him from the escalating exchange. Oz's initial reaction was to resist, holding his ground, calculating his position. Sedona's persistence tempered a hellish storm swelling from the depths of jealousy.

Crisis adverted!

Two hours later, our friendly conversation replaced a once-mounting campaign of hardened, opposing opinions. Oz completely removed himself from the social activities, planting himself on the sofa within perfect eye-shot of Jordan. An unspoken standoff ensued, smoldering under a cloud of disguised formalities. I could not explain the strained relations with Jordan, particularly since there was never a formal introduction. Jordan welcomed the veiled invitation to battle, a high that fed his already enormous ego.

Eventually Oz entered the kitchen, positioning himself against the side of the pantry with crossed arms.

"Looka here, he finally decided to join the rest of us," Jordan remarked with a malicious grin.

"Oz, you cool?" Bryce asked.

"Yeah, I'm cool." His eyes followed when I reached into the fridge. "Babe, can you get me another beer?"

"Sure." I stood from the fridge, catching Jordan's perplexed observation when I handed Oz the ice-cold bottle. Leaning against the side of the counter, avoiding Jordan's gawk, I nervously asked, "Anyone want some apple pie or something to drink?"

"I'm good," Bryce responded.

Sedona shook her head no, while Jordan continued with his incriminating perspective.

"Yeah, I'll have a piece of that apple pie," Oz stated.

"Can you hand me a plate from the cabinet behind you?"

"I know where they are," Oz quickly reminded me, handing over a small dessert plate, flirtatiously pressing his body along my backside, whispering into my ear, "When is this foo' leaving?"

Speaking under my breath, I said, "Oz, what are you doing?"

Flashing his heartbreaking, making-you-weak-at-the-knees smile, Oz seductively slid away with plate in hand, removing the fork from his mouth. "Babe, it's perfect as always!"

Strike! A clearly missed opportunity, Jordan recoiled, retreating to his corner. Volley—your serve mofo—another game point in Oz's favor.

After witnessing such a prudent power play, the disinclined spectators left the battlefield dumbfounded by the unfortunate chain of events enacted in their presence.

Life and love is a muthafuck!

CHAPTER 49

Please do not shut me out! That was all I remember hearing Jordan stating the day after that unfortunate night. With each passing day, he pleaded his case, fast and steady, never allowing me to forget how good he'd been the last month—far better than any man in my past. He said this since I'd made the fundamental mistake of revealing the true nature of my relations with Oz and all the poor choices I had made. Assuming he would be the one to come to the rescue, he could not for the life of him understand how I placed so much interest in someone who refused to commit.

It was now five weeks past my twenty-fifth birthday, which proved to be an unhappy affair. Having found myself in a disastrous, misguided triangle, the escalating feuding, fighting for my affections had reached a boiling point. Oz's conflicting behavior forged a path leading him to the brink of revealing his true feelings, yet stopping a hair short of fully committing. For the first time, I sensed there was more he wanted to express but for whatever reason could not bring himself to do so.

On the other side of the fence, Jordan's relentless cross-examinations and plea to sever all ties with Oz became an arduous commentary whenever we were together. Slowly, I began to distance myself to have a moment's peace. Determined, Jordan continued his crusade to oust Oz, regardless of whether he won the fight or not. I firmly believed his campaign was no longer about me, but to destroy Oz at all cost.

Since my birthday, Oz had spent every Saturday morning with my Aunt Raine and me for breakfast, or just he and I alone. It was the second Saturday of March, the morning air clean, fresh and crisp—unusual, given

Vance N. Smith

the pollution from all the industries spewing dangerous emissions, along with the millions of cars roaming the streets of LA. Thankfully, the rains came a few days prior, cleansing the wounded sky above.

This renewed energy Oz exhibited forced the speculation where all this might go. I could not help but wonder if *once* again, he was setting me up for failure—could his wobbling behavior prove to be a recipe for disaster. I never sensed his intentions were malicious, though the repressed anger sweeping my mind stemmed from that notion, but I wasn't resilient enough to stand my ground and demand answers. As much as I wanted to be sympathetic to his concealed, twisted thoughts, I found it difficult to comprehend. A life placed upon me left no other option but to embrace and accept the consequences. It didn't define me, only a small portion of whom I had become; I merely made the best of it, good or bad. Someone or something far greater felt this was a better choice. I did not question it—I dealt with it.

Upon finishing our meal, Oz and my aunt engaged in a friendly political debate regarding LA city politics. I sat, admiring the man I loved to the core of my soul; I wished I could diminish the anguish rendering him a slave to his forbidden demons. Unyielding anxieties left a man crushed and afraid to disclose his innermost convictions, evident to all except to himself. I speculated if he truly realized the magnitude of guilt he carried upon his shoulders.

For a better part of an hour, their sparring generated animated hand gestures, followed by distorted facial expressions. I held my ceramic coffee mug close to my mouth, entertained by their comical behavior. Both believing their opinions signified the ideas of the general population.

Finally, Oz removed himself from the conversation stating, "You *will* see it my way eventually," before leaning and placing a tender kiss to her cheek. Pretending to resist his charm, however, secretly Aunt Raine melted whenever he displayed any form of affection toward her. Her reaction was undeniable, though she would never admit it. Her love for him was unbreakable, and because of that formidable admiration, I sensed she blamed me for the circus act our friendship had become. Oz held my aunt's tiny hand upon

Battlefields

his and said, "I love you," lifting his duffel bag from the patio chair. Facing my direction, he asked if I would walk him to his vehicle. I nodded OK, extending down for my sandals.

We reached Oz's jeep where he threw his duffel bag in the back before sliding into the driver's seat. "What do you have planned for today?" he asked.

Placing my hands along the driver's side door, examining the street ahead, I stated, "I'm not sure, I have some work to catch up on." I delayed for a split second, obviously hiding something, as exhibited by my nervous behavior. The information I withheld was Jordan wanting to spend the remainder of the day together. With forearms planted firmly against the upper most portion of the doorframe, I rested my forehead, avoiding his scrutinizing gaze.

Oz grabbed my chin, forcing my attention toward him. "What are you not telling me? Is that mofo coming around? I guess that blows the idea I wanted to suggest!" Oz placed his key in the ignition, starting the engine. "I guess I'll speak with you when I see you, whenever that will be!"

"Oz, that is not fair. I have enjoyed every moment we spent together for the past week or so! What are you trying to do?" I asked, struggling to keep my emotions in check. "Sometimes I feel you don't want me to be happy!" Rearing back from the jeep with both hands planted on the frame of the window, I said, "I so desperately want to be happy! I need love in my life. I need to know someone is thinking of me day and night." I took a step back, standing away from the jeep. "Remember, you have someone—I don't. All I have is a dream…"

"You have more than that!" he remarked.

"Do I?"

"You know you do—don't even front!"

"Prove it," I said, placing the palm of my hand to his shoulder. "Tell me what I know to be true. Prove to me that what we have is real. You know you're in love with me, why won't you admit it!"

Unlike before, I finally pierced that brick wall built around his heart. The rumblings of mortar gave way, crumbling with a resounding thud. It exposed a vulnerable man who hid behind a manufactured façade at all cost, refusing to reveal his truths. "I need to get out of here before Jasmine is all over my ass, again!" Oz's eyes locked on mine. "If I could be all that you want me to be, I would do it, believe that! The situation we're in—I know it's *fucked up*! I wish I could change it. What more do you want me to say, I'm hurting too—this thing..." With eyes closed tight, Oz shook his head in defiance. "This thing has my mind so fuckin' twisted. You have no idea the turmoil consuming me each and every day!" Biting down on the corner of his lip, Oz placed his hand on the gearshift. "I need to go," he said, staring off down the street before returning his attention. "See me tonight, so we can talk about this."

"I have plans!"

"Cancel them!" he stipulated. "I'll see you later tonight." He placed his jeep in drive, speeding down the street.

I remained by the side of the parkway, watching him drive into the distance. All thoughts I had converged into one convoluted mess. What explanation could I possibly give Jordan for cancelling our plans? One thing was for sure, I did not intend to disappoint Oz.

Leaning against one of the brick light posts flanking either side of the walkway, I fixated on what lie I could possibly say that would not cause alarm, followed by a gazillion questions.

Oz's jeep was far into the distance before making a right turn out of sight. When suddenly a familiar Mercedes two-seater pulled up alongside the curb and parked. Without much of a warning, franticly the driver's side door opened, revealing the last person I wanted to confront. I regained my posture, standing straight, poised to take on any confrontation heading my way. I opened my mouth to speak, but all words stunted before I could free them from my lips. In an agitated fashion, Jasmine leapt from her vehicle, scurried around the front end, and before I knew it, spat vile expletives accusing me of taking her man away.

"Leave him alone, stay the fuck away! I'm only going to warn you once," she expressed with flared nostrils and veins a poppin'. If it were not for the seriousness of her actions, it would have been downright farcical. How

Battlefields

many more ridiculous circumstances could I possibly be subjected to? Now I had to contend with some deranged, scorned female.

"Maybe you should direct your anger to the one you suspect has hurt you. I'm not the one you should blame," I stated as calmly as I could without agitating her more.

"It's because of you he's distant! You're the one he secretly longs for, and with you around, there's no future for us!"

"You should have thought about that when you left him back in New York following your dream. You should have suspected that would forge a wedge between the two of you."

Her eyes widened. "You know nothing about why I left New York. How dare you stand in judgment?" she stated with authority, clearly pain reined deep.

"Why should I give him up? If he wanted to be with you, that's where he would be; you wouldn't have to come here and demean yourself, begging me to step away."

"Fuck you! You poisoned his mind with all your fag ideas! You deliberately turned him against me!"

"I knew nothing about you until you returned last summer. I didn't even know you were around, so if anyone should feel rejected, that certain someone would be me!"

"He's mine, stay away; I'm warning you!" she screamed.

"And what if I don't? What could you possibly do to me?" I threw my hands up in desperation. "You know—whatever; do what you feel you need to do. I'm not going to stand here and listen to some whack-ass female." I retreated, walking toward the driveway.

"Don't fuckin' test me!"

Slowly I turned, confronting the lunatic. "Are you threating me? Because if you are, that is not a wise move!"

"He's in love with you!" she blurted out.

"You don't know what the fuck you're talking about!" I quickly returned.

"It's you he thinks of…"

"How do you know that? What has he mentioned to you?" My heart raced.

Vance N. Smith

"It's not what he specified, it's the way he speaks about you; the sparkle in his eyes when he mentions your name. It's written all over his face the same as when he would speak of..." she informed, her babbling fueled by a jumbled mix of disjointed thoughts. At that moment, for the first time, I felt compassion.

"Speak of who? What were you going to say, finish your thought?"

"It's not important." She gathered her misgivings, picked up her pride, and surrendered.

"Will, what the hell is going on out here? What is all the commotion about?" my aunt shouted, standing in the doorway.

Jasmine yelled toward my aunt, "Did you know your son is fuckin' my man!"

"Who is this woman?" Aunt Raine asked infuriated.

Positioning myself in front of Jasmine, blocking her eyesight of my aunt, I said, "Have you lost your fuckin' mind?" I turned, speaking over my shoulder, not wanting to remove an eye off Jasmine. "Go back into the house, Aunt Raine. I got it under control. It's nothing I can't handle!" Aunt Raine reluctantly closed the door. I stepped toward Jasmine.

"Don't!" She held her hand motioning me away. "I don't need your pity. That is not why I came here!" With her hand still extended, her head held low, an errant tear publicized her fractured agony. "Please, don't!" Her voice cracked. "All I need is for you to back off. Leave me with something. That's all I'm asking." Tears flowed steadily as she spoke. "I've been watching the two of you at his jeep. I parked down the street, so he would not notice my car; I had suspected he left me to see you, leaving my arms last night with some lame-ass excuse why he couldn't stay. I followed him, and to my dismay, he rushed right over here! Early this morning I called him repeatedly. I knew he had not returned home, so I drove back only to find he'd stayed the night with you...*you*, of all people!" Her expression filled with wayward emotions. "How do I compete with that?"

"For what it's worth, nothing happened." I tried to appease her feelings.

Jasmine snidely chuckled. "Fuckin' faggots, I can't stand you muthafuckas. All you muthafuckas feel the need to brainwash our men to your sick deviant life."

Battlefields

That was it; I had enough of her ranting. "Get the fuck out of here! I was beginning to feel sorry for you, but you crossed the line." In an impulsive reaction, I reached for her arm to force her toward her car.

"Let go of my fuckin' arm!" Jasmine snatched her arm from my grasp.

I released my grip. "I need you to leave—*now*—and never return here again!"

"Yeah, I'll leave, but if you refuse to heed my warning, you'll discover that your decision was the poor choice to make!"

"Bitch, don't fuckin' threaten me!"

"Fuck you, faggot!" she screamed, reaching for the driver's door handle.

"You're pathetic!"

"Stay the fuck away!" Jasmine hopped into her car, careening dangerously down the street.

Approaching the rear of the driveway, Aunt Raine met me with crossed arms, disgusted. "Who in the hell was that, and how dare she—*you*—bring that ghetto shit around my house!"

"Aunt Raine..."

Aunt Raine moved closer. "Boy—don't you ever interrupt me again! You hear me?" she stated matter-of-factly.

I nodded yes.

"Answer me!" she coolly bellowed under bated breath.

"Yes!"

"I have lived in this neighborhood, peacefully and quietly. Never have I had any unnecessary attention directed toward this house, and I will not stand for it now! Whatever is going on with you—it ends now! Do I make myself clear?"

"Yes—*very!*"

"Don't get smart with me!" She stated her peace, marched back into her comfortable Hancock Park home, and slammed the door.

She definitely made her point, loud and clear.

CHAPTER 50

THERE I SAT, waiting patiently for an all-out brawl, round two of a conflict I was unwilling to fight. Round one of this calamitous clash occurred unexpectedly, leaving me exposed without the proper ammunition on the fields of love. Jasmine's untimely visitation without a doubt initiated a time bomb's fuse dangling precariously close to a flickering flame.

Therefore, I waited—I waited diligently, contemplating my next course of action. Should I confront this beast head on speaking frankly, or shirk the issue altogether, postponing the inevitable? Laying all suspicion aside, I would bet my last dollar Jasmine conceitedly believed her actions had given her the upper hand, with the idea her tactical move drove a wedge, splintering our friendship into pieces. Her display of espionage gave credence to my theories of having him in my back pocket, along with his unspoken truths that rallied in my favor. She erroneously divulged valuable intelligence to her competitor, which I undoubtedly would use to my advantage. I'd been embroiled in this onslaught of war with several individuals far too long to allow an amateur to best me. I read her veiled, poised disposition, disguising evil from the very beginning. There was no way she could have known I once resided with the malevolent personified, which provided me the ability to smell and sniff any fiend or its henchmen from a hundred yards away, like flies to shit! *Yeah*, I knew her type, but sadly and far too often, less-adept victims had surrendered to their charms, eventually swept into their traps. This conflict of rivalries proved a dangerous affair; one false move would be my undoing.

The métier I possessed to thwart the uninvited proved ineffective with my inability to persevere against Oz. Whatever conviction I summoned,

Battlefields

it fell to the wayside whenever he graced my company. Loving him consequently substantiated the concept he was my poison. The potency of his toxin flowed unrestrained throughout my veins, for which I could not expel. The preceding years permitted it to seep further, removing all hope of freeing oneself from the dramatic contamination.

The hands of the wall clock read 6:32 p.m. when the doorbell buzzed, broadcasting Oz's arrival. In expectancy of our gathering, I had cleaned house, top to bottom, and prepared a hearty feast to pacify the grumbling gremlins sure to surface. I attended to loose ends requiring gentle treatment, specifically to breach my engagement planned before Oz instructed me to cancel, leaving a secondary player out in the cold. Immediately after I dealt with the drudgery of hostilities, I took a soothing shower to cleanse away the grime of these preemptive strategies, followed with a shave and a splash of a light flagrance.

Moving for the door, I stopped, catching my reflection in a floor-length mirror, taking one final inspection before proceeding down toward the entrance of my apartment. All day I had contemplated, reflecting on the realities of my life. The never-ending conflicts placed upon me, relegating me to reevaluate my sole purpose in everyone's lives.

Often, I was left wondering what I had done to incite such harsh attacks from my critics, and what I could possibly do to turn this tide around for the better. Although I was forever a supporter of Oz, my involvement with him had steered into territory of mass-misperceptions. With the passing of time, those misunderstandings led to animosities, extreme hurt, and crumbling fractures of trust. Amid all the unfortunate instances, Oz was, and would always be, my best friend.

With all that in mind, I decided my plan of attack would be simple: I would remain calm, would not provoke, and would listen openly and honestly. An optimistic approach, if I stood any chance to regain the levels of trust once enjoyed in the beginning.

Vance N. Smith

I stood briefly, tormented at the base of the stairs, collecting my angsts with the hope of reining them in check. "Oz?" I called out.

"Yes, Willie…it's me, open up!"

When the door opened, I found Oz on the other side, holding a box of popcorn and a rented VHS movie, his right hand concealed behind his back. He was dressed to impress, wearing Guess jeans and a crisp white dress shirt, with black leather loafers and jacket. The first thought that came to mind was, *damn, he looked good!* "What's all this?" I stood to the side, clutching the doorknob, providing Oz access. "You're looking mighty spiffy tonight!"

Instead of answering, he revealed a large mixed bouquet of flowers hidden behind his back. "I come in peace," he said, flashing his trademark toothy smile.

"Wow—what could I possibly say, besides thank you?"

"You don't have to say anything; your reaction was all I needed." Oz lifted his head, savoring the aromas filling my apartment. "What's for dinner?" he asked, removing his stylish black leather jacket, laying it across the banister. "How was the rest of your day?"

I lingered a split second, wondering, *did he just present a trick question?* Reaching for the bundled flowers, I said, "To your first question, I grilled some porterhouse steaks with sautéed onions and mushrooms. To your second question, eventful, productive, but let's not talk about my day. I'd rather enjoy a magical evening with you and the possibilities of what's to come. How about that?" Placing my hand in his, I led Oz up the flight of stairs into the living room. "I'll place these in a vase—make yourself comfortable," I commented once we reached the top of the stairs.

Oz proceeded toward the sofa where he kicked off his shoes before reclining, resting his head on a set of propped pillows. "How much longer before dinner is ready?" Oz yelled with his voice resonating throughout the room, before turning on the boob tube, flipping through channels.

"We can eat in about fifteen minutes. I gather you're hungry?"

"You have no idea; I have not been able to eat since I left you this morning!" Oz stated, sprawled across the sofa.

384

Battlefields

Once we completed dinner and dessert, we situated in the living room, and it was just before eleven when we finished watching a classic Hollywood movie. Shortly thereafter, the atmosphere of the evening changed to a more somber note. Since he and I evaded our tribulations all evening, the time had come to place the pleasantries aside, diving into the meat of our dispute. Neither one wanted to be the first to set forth a course sure to lead to hostilities. Thick as a dense ocean fog, our temperaments shifted dramatically, as silence clung to every molecule of miffed relations.

For most of the evening watching the movie, Oz's head rested upon my lap, his left hand partially placed beneath the seam of his underwear, whereas the other hand lay across his chest. Casually he shifted his attention in my direction, his expression muted, displaying the weight of loitering displeasures. When our eyes met, locking into place, I inhaled steadily before I spoke. "I know the purpose of us meeting was to discuss the mounting issues we have been plagued with the past year or so."

Oz repositioned himself, sitting up. "I wish the solution to our problem could be an easy fix, but I'm not so sure it is." He followed his statement by carefully squeezing my right thigh.

"How did this become so difficult?" I questioned.

Oz leaned forward, his right hand placed against his forehead, attempting to dislodge his growing, throbbing pain. "I don't know…" He solemnly chuckled. "I want to be everything you require of me; I'm just not sure I can become that man." With his jaw seized tight, his head faintly moved from side to side. "Sometimes, I feel you're forcing me to become someone I'm not." The focus of his attention was directed straight ahead, hypnotized by the luminous, flickering flame radiating from the fireplace.

"My intentions were never meant to make you feel coerced. I know my own insecurities, and lack of familiarity has played a major factor in my actions."

"I know and I should have been extra sensitive to that," Oz stated.

"You've been good for me. You've always been sympathetic, my benefactor; I should not expect you to be my emancipator as well. Your strength is what I should have fed from, that should have been enough for me to flourish into a stronger individual."

"Never forget you're stronger than you give yourself credit—"

"Oz, I'm not like you!"

"No, you're not like me, and that's what draws me to you. I have become a better man because of you. You gave me direction, a reason to be here—here with you. I'm the one…" His thought suddenly stopped, replaced with a loud, rumbling growl with balled fist. "I hate what I'm feeling…"

My eyebrow raised in suspicious surprise. "What did you mean by that?" Oz shuddered in defiance. In response, I placed my hand upon his shoulder, attempting to force him to confront me. "Tell me what you meant by that!"

Oz restrained his position firm, and not once would he make eye contact. "It meant nothing!" he answered.

"Don't lie to me!"

"Drop it; I'm not in the mood to discuss the matter with you!"

I withheld my immediate reaction, since I promised myself to remain calm, steadfast on an intelligent path. "I'm not going to allow you to throw out a statement of that magnitude and simply allow you to drop it!" I sat up and said, "It's not gonna happen! You're going to tell me what you meant by that!"

"Willie, I take back what I said. It meant nothing!"

"Oz, you have to talk to me. We will never be able to pass the roadblock standing in our way. This thing…it's eating us alive."

Oz rocked unintentionally. "I'm not going to argue with you."

"Neither am I! OK, let me take a step back." I lifted myself from the sofa. "Can I get you something?"

"I need something hard!"

"Do you want a vodka and orange?" I asked.

"Do you have Belvedere?"

"You know I do; I only have it because that's what you drink."

Emerging from the kitchen, I thought how appropriate the heavens above opened the floodgates with a tremendous force, pummeling the earth

Battlefields

with thick pellets of rainwater. I entered the living room accompanied by a resounding, crackling flash of white lightning illuminating the entire space. Oz remained unphased by the enthusiastic spectacle Mother Nature descended upon the environment around us. As I sat, I heard a second display of decisive energy echo and reverberate through and through.

In one quick swoop, Oz lifted the flavored firewater and devoured it with one gulp, producing a distorted facial expression. He proceeded to lean forward, placing the glass upon the coffee table with a hard thud, causing it to wobble as it slid a few inches across the smooth surface. I knew then that clandestine quandaries consumed and entrapped a proud and defenseless man. Unspoken perceptions plagued his intellect, holding him captive and isolated from the world around him. I felt helpless, and my only inclination was to conciliate and support, instead of oppose.

We remained in the stated position for a better part of thirty minutes, during which time, the music from the CD player broke the silence. A calm stillness supplanted once escalating resentments. In an effort to turn this madness around, I repositioned closer to Oz, placing my hand to the nape of his neck, kneading gently. Each stroke sluggishly began to dissolve his pent-up tensions, causing his body to respond in kind. A slight tilt of his head downward signaled the acceptance to explore the invitation further.

"You know I love you more than you could possibly imagine." His voice trailed off to a point where it was barely audible. Oz placed his hand to my thigh with a gentle caress, and his eyes narrowed seductively.

"I never doubted where we stood, but because of that understanding, it makes the situation even more confusing."

"I need you to be patient with me," Oz explained.

"For the last six years I have been more than patient, bordering on being foolish. Our entire friendship has been based on riddles and unspoken truths. I think it's time we set aside our misgivings, our fears, and express the obvious. You know where I stand; I believe I know where you do, too." Shifting myself to counter his position, I faced him head on, leaning forward, placing my forehead against his. "We can get past this," I stated in a whisper.

Vance N. Smith

Oz marginally rolled his forehead along mine before he lifted himself millimeters away, the warmth of his body pierced through my core. Oz nervously chewed at his lower lip with his eyesight fixed downward, avoiding contact. He clasped his left hand into mine, his palm sweaty and moist. "Someday we'll look back at this and laugh," he stated.

"I wish I could believe that. As it stands now, I'm not sure it's even possible. In light of what happened earlier today after you left," I conceded.

"What happened?"

"Before I tell you, promise me you will not get all crazy and shit!"

Oz did not speak.

The palm of my hand was still planted firmly around his neck—I tightened my grip, shaking him mildly. "Promise me!"

"All right," he responded hastily.

"When you left, Jasmine pulled up shortly thereafter. She had been waiting and watching down the street..." Oz swiftly released my hand, and his entire body stiffened. "She confronted me, accusing me of taking you away from her."

"She did what!" His voice rose as he tried to maneuver himself from my grasp.

"No! You're not going to run from this!"

"Willie, let me go!" he stated, placing his hand to my chest, attempting to push away.

I locked my arms in a death grip around his upper torso. "I will not allow you to run from this, so you might as well give in!"

"What did you say to her?" he angrily accused.

"What was I supposed to say—what could I say? I'm not even sure I know what is going on between us!"

Oz's eyes furrowed. "There's nothing going on, and I hope you didn't insinuate otherwise!"

Instantly, I released my grip, shoving the crown of his head, and said, "Fuck you, muthafucka, I didn't insinuate anything, but she sure had plenty to say!" Angrily, I reclined, resting on my forearms. "Go ahead and run like you always do, you fuckin' coward—but to be clear, Homegirl said a

Battlefields

mouthful, even incoherently, mentioning why she moved to LA in the first place."

"She's crazy, don't believe a word she said!" Oz remained seated.

"I can handle her, she's not my problem—that problem is yours, but you need to get your house in order—and let me say this, make sure she doesn't show her ass around here, ever!"

Oz mumbled his response

"I did not hear you!"

"Yes!" he shouted.

"Fine, now that we have that out of the way, back to our main issue." I repositioned my left leg around his midsection, my other bent at the knee with my right foot tucked under my thigh. "Come here!" I yanked the sleeve of his shirt, pulling him into me where he landed on my chest. "Ouch— wait—I have to move my leg!" Straightening my right leg, I stationed Oz's body between my thighs, where he lay snuggled like an infant wrapped in his mother's arms. "OK, that's better—comfortable?"

"I am," he sheepishly answered.

Enveloping Oz's torso within my arms, I secured my standpoint neatly inside my grasp. "We can get past this—I'm sure of it!"

"Do you think it's possible?" Oz questioned.

"I know we can!" Leaning forward, I placed a kiss to his forehead.

In a shocking show of affection, Oz raised his head and repaid with a kiss just below my chin. I rapidly followed with another to the side of his cheek. A game of reciprocation commenced until the flirty exchange ended when our lips met. I hastily retreated; Oz held his position before tenderly kissing my chest. My mind raced as Oz rearranged, facing me square on. His gaze was mired in hesitation, afraid of the plunge into uncharted territory. My breathing became heavy, heightened to a level of uncertainty.

Oz's large hand grazed the side of my cheek; his unspoken words heard loud and clear. His eyes investigated as his gentle touch traced the contours of my jaw, beckoning the invitation to continue his quest to conquer. My scrutiny was summoned, welcoming the solicitation to resume his advance. A hush fell upon us, removing the detrimental chatter that usually consumed and devoured, stifling a once-promising love affair.

In a monumental show of communication, Oz inched closer with hesitation before placing his lips to mine. A soft swift touch, he then withdrew; I collapsed limp by his tender kiss. A suggestion of a smile graced the corners of his mouth; his body shuddered with delight, when I traced the outline of his left eyebrow. No time to waste, he plunged with his mouth parted, slightly open; he filled me up unlike anything I had experienced until now. Our tongues fought for dominance, twisting and coiling, dazed by the unrelenting, bombastic fireworks exploding, one right after the other. His sweet warmth tasted the way I imagined. Never had I surrendered to another so enthusiastically, wrapping my long slender legs around him, holding him captive, and refusing his release. His lethal toxin overwhelmed and devoured my subconscious, transporting my soul to the stratosphere. I was gone, and it all made sense; this was where I was meant to be, here in his arms. Smothered by the ravenous emotions that desolated my entire thought process, I lay whipped. These heated revelations revealed hidden truths, exposing his stiffening love against mine, strong as steel. His summation was unavoidable, and his inner thoughts were revealed; no longer could he escape from what was real. He knew it, as well as I. The mission of his toxin was complete.

Our bewildering appetites initiated unabated lust, wild and raw. Our bodies twisted, held within the clutches of repressed cravings. Oz released his grip then rose, hovering in an attempt to catch his breath. His hard gaze fired off, penetrating and full of intense power, consuming all my idolized fantasies. I slipped my hand between to unfasten the first button of his shirt. I paused for a moment then continued with the second, and then with the third, exposing solid flesh. With eyes fixed on his, I slid my hand under, across his right pectoral muscle, tenderly grazing his nipple. Oz released a slow grunt, holding his head back with eyes closed, his body quivering under my touch.

Battlefields

Continuing my journey, I gently pinched his nipple, which quietly sent him to another realm of awareness. His left arm wobbled by the electric charge permeating throughout his body, grinding his midsection against mine. A slow drag of his tongue along this bottom lip signaled awakened desires.

My exploration continued until I found the last button above his jeans. With his chest fully exposed, Oz was muscled and covered in coarse semi-curled hair that lay perfectly against his skin. Extending to unfasten his jeans, Oz grabbed my wrist, shaking his head no. "I'm sorry, I...I can't do this!" He rose, kneeling.

"What happened, you were feeling so good?"

"Willie, I don't want to do this." Oz stood from the sofa, stepping back. "I'm not trying to hurt you!"

"Then what are you doing? You started this; you opened the door and walked through. Now you've changed your mind!"

"I'm not gay; I've told you before!"

"Then what was that? It felt like you wanted it just as much as I did!"

"It was a mistake; I don't know what you're doing to me! It's like, you're filling my mind with these philosophies." Oz fastened the buttons of his shirt.

"Have you lost your muthafuckin' mind, *me*...filling your head with these ideas, this didn't just start today! This started the very first day I met you, our whole problem is with you! You're the reason we cannot get our shit together! I didn't do this to you; I can't make you into something you're not!"

"I have to go!" Oz proceeded for the door.

"Get back here!" I shouted.

"I'm sorry, but I can't do this. I don't want to be gay!" Oz stopped at the top of the stairs, turning in my direction. "I don't want to be like you!"

"Get the fuck out of here!" I screamed. "You're a fuckin' pussy! You fuckin' coward!"

Oz took a few step down before he stopped, with his head turned slightly, uncovering the grief concealing his face. I slumped deeper into the sofa, burying my shame.

Vance N. Smith

"Get the fuck out!" I mumbled.

Once again, I experienced false hope. Where there was happiness, heartbreak cleverly waited around the corner. Filled to capacity, I blindly treaded tremulous waters, unaware I would sink head first into an empty well.

CHAPTER 51

My suspicions were spot on point! One month passed with no sign of Oz, no phone calls, nothing—typical! He had opened the door and walked through without indecision, only to back away when the heat became too much. I would not deny the pain I'd experienced since that unfortunate night, which bore through, piercing my heart with a white-hot iron rod. But with the help of friends, I pulled through a winner. I'd been able to set aside the lingering sentiments I held with distinct gallantry. However, now and again, I reminisced, reflecting on that fateful night, when we kissed for the first time, and how it made me feel alive, full of courage. I would close my eyes to imagine his sweet taste and the softness of his lips, expressing our love. Even now, I perceived the crushing weight of his massive torso smothering mine in pleasure. The mere thought of it sent unrelenting shockwaves rampaging throughout. How I craved his warmth against my flesh, when in the end, I was denied the opportunity to articulate what I felt for the last several years.

Another month later, I still remembered and would never forget that night when we crossed that fine line of hurt—to love, to hate. I presumed hate was a rather zealous word, since I could never hate my one true love. However, when a special someone was consistently coming in and out of your life, the conflicting behavior, and the uncertainty of your future eventually took its toll. I suspected his love surmounted far above what he led everyone to believe. The unfortunate realization was having that revelation reveal a far more complex individual. Along with that was the disclosure that the battlefield I stepped upon was one he initiated. All the while, I fought a war predetermined to lose.

After the bloodshed subsided, a persistent adversary loomed, waiting unwearyingly in the remote fields of war, beaten but nonetheless eager to crusade the ongoing campaign. He stood fortified with hand extended, as he summoned. Left to rot among the weak, I grudgingly aligned with enemy factions. On the horizon, a presumed enthusiastic rebel was adeptly qualified in forging a valiant course to victory.

Yes, I was a winner indeed!

CHAPTER 52

Maybe I was not a winner after all; my ricochet alliance was not all I had hoped it would be. Sometimes you could not make sentiments appear that were not there, along with how I had not been able to escape the clutch of Oz's grasp. The thought of him consumed every living moment of every living day. I hated to sound melodramatic, but sometimes the truth hurts! Even after all the turmoil and the anguish, I subconsciously believed somehow there was a possibility we could reconcile our differences.

So the story goes...

Spring of 1987

I've always believed springtime was a rebirth, a renewal, a time of changed behaviors, and most certainly, a time to heal. On the second Saturday of May, a rather pleasant morning, two months after Oz and I slipped into forbidden territory, I sat alone, sprawled along one of several patio lounge chairs in the rear yard of my aunt's home. I was leisurely dressed in cut-off shorts, a white tank, and rubber beach thongs, and holding a tall glass of sweet tea. I was lost in the music of one of my favorite singers, other than Sedona. My ideas and worries floated above, mindlessly bewildering, allowing my indiscreet thoughts to fester out of control. Just when I thought I had packed away all sentiments and designs, a chapter of my existence crept back to reality, suffocating and strangling the life from a once healthy body. It was unfortunate I was unable to shake Oz's infiltrating virus. Relegated to solitary confinement, I played out the ill-fated lessons of love and life. Lost in my self-imposed quarantine, I felt the slight touch of a delicate hand snap my ass back to reality. Startled, I opened my eyes, finding Sedona and Sahara standing before me. I smiled broadly and said, "Hey," reaching to remove my headphones. "When did you return from New York?"

"Last night..." Sedona smiled, taking a seat on a lounge chair next to mine. "You better be listening to my music!" she stated, half jokingly.

"Of course, who else would I listen to?" I lied.

Sedona flashed her famous black girl hood expression. "Let me see— any one of my competition—like, Stephanie Mills, Phyllis Hyman..."

"OK, I get it, but there's no other like yourself!"

"And never forget it!"

We both fell into laughter.

"Sahara, you're becoming a lovely little lady! How old are you now?" I asked, winking toward Sedona.

"I'm five," she giggled.

"Five! You're almost grown, a little young lady, you are!" I remarked.

Sedona straightened her lemon-yellow sundress. "Now, like a good little girl, go play with your dolls while Uncle Will and I talk."

"Uncle Will said I was a lady!" she frowned.

Sedona sighed. "Do what Mommy asked you to do."

"All right," Sahara reluctantly agreed. Sedona and I watched Sahara saunter off, pouting, dragging her doll behind her with a firm grasp of the doll's hair.

"She's getting so big. It seems like she was just a toddler, and now you're about to have a second child. Have you ever imagined how your life would turn out?" I asked, witnessing Sahara in all her glorious innocence.

Sedona paused. "For the most part, yes." Brushing a fallen leaf from her dress, she admitted, "I wish I didn't have Sahara so soon." Sedona was blunt, forcing a smile. "I do love her with every fiber of my body, but I wish I had done things differently. Now, here I am making the same mistake once again."

"I never heard you state regret before. What brought this on?" I asked.

Battlefields

"It's everything, this shit I'm going through with Jackson, having Sahara so young, my career...everything!"

"It's normal to have doubts, and I'm not saying you don't love Sahara, because I know you do."

"I know what you're asking." Sedona reached to gently squeeze my hand. "I would change things if I could. I realize now I had her too young, but I have made the best of it. Except, there are times when my guilt suppresses the happiness she deserves." Sedona shifted uncomfortably in her chair. "Being away so much, the focus I've placed on my career, I hope she doesn't resent me someday."

"You're a good mother, never forget that! You're doing the best you can. You have a promising career ahead of you, you're making a name for yourself, and the world is finally recognizing your talent, along with the beauty that lies within, not just the outside."

"Well, you didn't feel that way six years ago. If I remember correctly, you weren't too kind initially," Sedona chuckled.

I laughed. "I was a bit mean, but I would not have been a true friend if I didn't speak the truth. At least I can say we built our friendship on trust and honesty. Over the years, we have said some awful things, but stated with love. Unlike others I know, who will remain nameless!" I turned facing Sedona, finding her glaring with that black girl smirk.

"What did I say now?"

Sedona calmly straightened her dress over her knee. "Do you want the long or short version?"

"Neither!" I remarked.

Sedona rolled her eyes. "When will you allow the past to remain the past? What's going on now; I know this has something to do with Oz."

"What do you mean by that?"

Sedona snickered. "You know exactly what I mean!"

"Are we going to have one of those conversations?"

"What do you think?" she asked, snidely.

"I think I need something stronger than this tea, if we are," I stated, leaning for my glass.

"You need to let go of the idea of Oz in your life. He obviously has issues neither you nor anyone else can understand or cure. Until you accept that reality, you'll remain in this constant state of confusion. I mean, *really*— what more do you need to get over him? You give me grief regarding Jackson *all the time*, and it's true—maybe he wasn't the best choice I could have made, but at least he initially gave me the love and affection I required. I never had suspicion on how or what he felt about me. However, I will give Oz points for being a faithful friend, who always had your back, but at what cost? He led you on with the possibilities of your friendship turning into something more, then pulled back leaving you with nothing. Yet after all that, you still hang on to this silly dream. The two of you continually teeter back and forth, which way should I go—which way should I go, like some fuckin' cartoon. It's ridiculous—"

"We kissed!" I said, interrupting Sedona's outsider commentary.

Sedona snapped forward from her chair. "What the fuck did you say?" she expressed in utter shock.

Removing the moisture-covered glass of tea from my lips, I said, "We kissed the last time we were together. Not just any kiss, but a real tongue tussle, spit swapping, full-on wide-open-mouth kind." I reared back into the patio lounge chair, waiting on Sedona's response.

Sedona leaned forward shaking her head in disbelief. "Just when I thought I had it all figured out, you tossed in one hell of a wrench!" She placed her dainty hand to her lips, "I'm not even sure how I'm supposed to comment on that. When did this bit of news transpire?"

"A few months back." I regretfully answered.

A momentary silence fell upon the two of us.

"Where do you guys stand now?" she asked.

"I'm with Jordan now. I've moved on," I stated with no emotions.

Sedona's reaction was harsh. "What!"

I placed my hand to her knee. "Let me rephrase that statement. I'm concentrating my attention away from Oz, and focusing on Jordan, where I vaguely foresee a future."

"I'm confused. What happened, and where is Oz now?"

Battlefields

"I have no idea. We haven't spoken since the night we kissed."

"Wait…" Sedona closed her eyes, shaking her head swiftly, holding her hand up, trying to process the information received. "Go back to that night, explain what happened."

"Oz stopped by to discuss the issues we've been having, along with I needed to inform him that Jasmine confronted me earlier that day, accusing me of taking him away from her."

"Stop! Stop—stop it right there! Jasmine did what!" Sedona yelled out a quick laugh, slumping back into the lounge chair.

"Yeah, well, that's a whole other story! She followed Oz to my place, then when he left she bum-rushed my ass on the sidewalk, threatened and accused me of stealing her man." Reaching for my glass of iced tea, I said, "She's unimportant. Anyway, Oz and I had a pleasant evening and talked without accusations, expressing our feelings. Oz opened up a little, revealing some of his insecurities. We were lying on the couch, when one thing led to another, and that's when we crossed the line. It became heated, the energy flowed unrelenting, and the moment was insatiable. I felt myself drowning in the emotions; all the while an explosion of sparks ignited in full succession. He was just as enraptured, but suddenly stopped, running away as he is so famous of doing. No explanation, just mouthing he's sorry, and I haven't heard from him since. It's been two months now.

"I cannot make heads or tails of what's going through Oz's mind. He's obviously struggling with deep-seated demons, identity issues, whatever you want to call it. He's conflicted and isn't sure how to discuss it with you or anyone else," Sedona commented.

"He should understand he could talk to me about anything. I've always made myself available."

"Have you?" Sedona asked.

"What is that supposed to mean?"

"Will, honey…you've been just as guilty. You withheld how you felt for years, and you're going to sit here and fault someone for not being open? I'm surprised at you!"

I refused to comment, holding the ice-cold glass to my lips.

Sedona's harsh glare pierced straight through me. "You have nothing to say, no comment?"

"Nothing to say, he knew how I felt."

"As well as yourself...hell, we all knew, but the two of you played this game for years, and it's come to a critical juncture with neither of you prepared to deal with the consequences."

"I'm dealing with it!"

"No, you're not; that's why you're sitting here sulking like some foolish kid, fleeing to the arms of another."

"I don't know what to do, and my dilemma is...what to do when you know someone is fundamentally perfect for you? That's my battle. Oz never treated me poorly, besides his conflicting behavior." Leaning, placing the glass on the table, I settled comfortably into the lounge chair, raising my focus toward the sky. "I like Jordan, but we constantly fight about you know who."

"About Oz? Ha, I wonder why! You obviously have not let go, and he knows it."

"I never gave him that impression," I foolishly stated.

"Sure, you haven't!" Sedona remarked.

"Anyway, I'm torn with what I should do."

"Only you can figure it out. I cannot tell you what to do, but I will say this, you should rethink your actions and this Jordan thing. All I can say is, why?" Sedona glanced toward Sahara. "Take that out of your mouth! Now!" she stated sternly. "Changing the subject. How's Vivian?"

"I guess she's doing OK, but we haven't talked in over seven months," I painfully stated.

"What's going on with the two of you?"

"I'm not sure, but I believe it has something to do with her resenting me for leaving her alone with our mother. I believe she feels that I abandoned her."

"That's unfortunate, you guys were so close!"

"It is what it is...and I've tried to reach out, but it hasn't worked," I stated, staring out into the distance. "She started a new life in DC, leaving

Battlefields

all the drama with our family behind. I guess this is the fall-out from our dysfunctional years, but I always felt she was much stronger than that."

"Isn't it funny how we are at the brink of doing something great, yet our lives appear to be crumbling from the inside out," Sedona theorized.

Sentenced to a life of confusion, that pretty much summarized all I had been through. One huge letdown!

CHAPTER 53

MY HEART-TO-HEART CONVERSATION with Sedona placed me in a state of profound reflection. Coincidentally, a week later I remained absorbed by it, steeping on her insight into my many faltering relationships. I concluded now was the time to take a serious stance with my life, including giving up the dream of a blissful future with Oz. For years, I had placed all energy into one man who continually eluded my every prayer of someone to love. On the other side of this ominous storm, I wondered had I seen the same qualities in Jordan. The alarming thought materialized, threatening to shatter all I had dreamt of the last six years.

The beginning of the Memorial Day holiday weekend found Aunt Raine and Uncle Charles, along with my mother, out of town visiting relatives on the East Coast. Surprisingly, my mother and I were on better terms as of late, but nowhere near reconciliation, if that were ever to happen. I had come to the realization it no longer mattered whether we discharged the unfortunate memories or not. My only driving force was to someday discover peace and happiness.

Wishing to bring a celebratory atmosphere to the big holiday weekend, I planned a small gathering of a few close friends. All the usual suspects were invited, my motley crew and a few others, for drinks, food, and one hell of a good time. The festivities were in full swing until well after four in the morning, until I had enough, and kicked the last guest out.

I awakened late Saturday morning, shuffling hazily for the kitchen to brew a much-needed caffeine fix. I was feeling groggy, along with the mind-crippling effects from the seven-too-many glasses of Bacardi and Coke I

Battlefields

had consumed the night before. Once the coffee began to drip, I entered the bathroom to shower, hoping the fresh, warm water would remove the alcohol stench oozing from my pores.

Dressed in green plaid pajama bottoms and a white tank, I reentered the kitchen, propping myself against the counter top for support, while the intense aroma of brewed coffee consumed my nostrils.

Moments later, Jordan stumbled into the kitchen, nursing a pulsating hangover. "How much did I drink last night?" Jordan asked, grabbing my waist, pulling my body into his.

I smiled. "Well…good morning to you, too. I'm not sure how much you had, but I can still taste the Bacardi I was drinking!"

"*Fuck!* My head is killing me," he remarked, as he rested his temple against the nape of my neck. "Baby, never allow me to drink like that again." I'm not sure why I rolled my eyes, but there was something about the way he called me baby that irked me every time. Could it be, I felt he was trying too hard to move in on my space? Regardless, he was too comfortable for my taste. Jordan nestled into my neck. "When are we going to make this official?"

Before I would allow Jordan to finish his rant, I partially twisted to my right, slightly looking over my shoulder. "Make what official?" I asked, pretending I was thunderstruck, but really I was irritated by his endless nagging on the subject of relationship.

"You know what I meant, you and me—us!" He teasingly placed a kiss on my neck. "Don't play me boo, you know you want this! We have been hangin' strong for a while now, and I finally got your boy out of the picture. Now it's just you and I."

It amazed me how people could make something out of nothing! I had yet to give him any inclination I wanted more than what we had. In addition, I found it comical he believed he was the reason Oz had not been around—if he only knew. It was all I could do to keep from laughing. "I've told you, I'm not interested in anything serious. I have too much on my plate with work and unfinished personal business I must attend to before I could consider moving forward."

"You're still in love with him!" Jordan blurted out.

I stepped back, pushing away from his grasp. "Do we have to go through this all over again?"

"Why not, you constantly trashin' my heart, stomping all over it like a pile of shit!"

"I've never portrayed anything more than what it is. I told you I wasn't ready for a committed relationship!" Another boldface lie I told. I knew exactly what I entered into when I pledged that devil's agreement, emerging from the war torn skirmish, waving my white flag—stumbling for safety. Without hesitation, I ran to the arms of the nearest, willing participant, namely Jordan. Once the deal was sealed, I tried in earnest to retract a pact I foolishly entered. The more I fought against our concord, the harder he strong-armed my end of the agreement.

"I don't get it, you have all of this..." Jordan motioned at his body, "right here, right now, and you'd rather throw all *this* away for some confused clown who isn't even here! He will never be here or provide you with the love you deserve!"

"Why are you making this about Oz? It has nothing to do with him!" *An added lie, damn I'm going to hell!* "This is all about you and how you refuse to relax and enjoy the moment. You forget how I've made myself available to you. I'm not seeing anyone else!"

"You're still seeing that nigga behind my back; that's what this is really about!"

"Have you lost your fuckin' mind? I have not seen Oz in months and you know it!"

"Doesn't matter whether you have or not, it's who you'd rather be with!"

Tensions escalated with each statement made, and neither of us relented or called a truce. The volume of Jordan's voice rose in a vain attempt to win his point. Never one to easily accept defeat, I stood my ground, refusing to bend or break under pressure. "Why are we arguing about him; he's out of the picture? But do you really want to know what's the real problem? Do you! Fine, the problem is you believing everything is all about you. That you're God's gift to humanity and we should worship the fuckin' ground

Battlefields

you walk on." I backed up a few steps to provide space between Jordan and I—waving my arms in the air. "Newsflash! You're not the one!" I was hot as hell, having allowed this muthafucka to get the best of me, forgetting my place and blowing my top. Nonetheless, my outburst continued unfiltered. "Why do you have to spoil everything? Why don't you fuckin' get a grip, and maybe we could move past this!"

Jordan reached for my arm. "Baby!"

Pushing back, I shoved his hand away. "Take your hand off me and stop calling me baby! I got your fuckin' baby." At that point I knew I had snapped, knowing enough was enough.

"I'm sorry, baby!" Jordan lowered his head. "I mean…I'm sorry." His voice cracked under the pressure. Wanting to rein control of the situation, Jordan proceeded to console me, struggling to pull me into an embrace.

"Stop," I said, pushing him off, "I'm done with this conversation!" I left Jordan hanging in the balance before grabbing my ceramic Disney mug of hot coffee, heading for the balcony, where I stewed for well over an hour, fretting over the constant barrage between Jordan and me.

When I ultimately reentered my apartment, it was eight past two in the afternoon. Walking into the kitchen, I overheard Jordan turning on the water to shower, and minutes later, the shower door closed. I placed my mug upon the counter top in front of the coffee maker to prepare myself another serving. Turning for the jar of sugar, I was interrupted when I heard the doorbell ring. "Who in the fuck is that?" I yelled out the kitchen window to the individual below, aggravated.

"Come down and open the door, Willie!"

Immediately, my heart sank. The one who haunted me for years, the ghost from my past, materialized out of thin air the same way he disappeared two months prior. "Oz?" I answered, cautiously.

"Willie, open the door! We need to talk!"

"Talk about what? There is nothing left to talk about!"

"Willie, open the damn door!" Oz uncharacteristically insisted. "Don't make me kick this muthafucka down!"

Vance N. Smith

Pausing to collect my thoughts, I answered with uncertainty, "Hold on a minute." I listened to be certain Jordan was still showering before I headed downstairs.

"What do you want?" I blatantly asked, opening the door.

"You need to change that tone; I'm not in the mood for your shit today! I came here to talk and work this out—no arguing, no fighting—just shed some light on where we stand."

"Where we stand?" I snidely chuckled. "Exactly, where do we stand, Oz? Seems to me you made your stand loud and clear when you ran out of here two months ago! Besides, now is not the right time, I have company."

"Tell him to leave," Oz demanded.

"You can't come here barking demands; you don't fuckin' own me!"

"I can and I did! Are you going to let me in?" Oz reiterated.

"Oz, I told you now is not the time. I don't need you causing another scene. What are you trying to do, get me in trouble with my aunt?" Without warning, Oz pushed me aside, entering the bottom entryway of my home, standing his ground with desperation on his face. "What the fuck do you think you're doing?" I stated, reaching to remove Oz from the premises. "You cannot be here!"

"Willie, please. I'm begging you, get rid of ole boy."

I must admit I was on the verge of breaking. In light of the current situation with Jordan and myself, I knew there was no way this would turn out well. "Oz, you can't keep leading me on, get angry, then run off, only to return demanding my full attention. Do you have any idea what you're doing to me? Every little hurt you give takes away all I have felt for you, but I promise we'll talk, just not right now. You could not have picked a worse time to drop by unannounced."

Oz leaned against the banister, defeated. "Willie, I'm so lost! All I'm asking is a chance to redeem myself." Oz grasped the back of my neck with a firm hand, pressing his forehead next to mine.

My whole body crumbled beneath his touch. "Why are you doing this to me?" I asked with a heavy voice.

"Why are you with ole boy?" Oz asked with paralyzing guilt.

Battlefields

"How could you ask me that? If I recall, you clearly stated you didn't want to be gay, or to be like me. How could you say that…why would you say such a thing? That shit hurt like a muthafuck! You left me no choice."

Oz placed his hands against my skin, cradling my face. "I'll make it up to you!"

"Oz, *stop* with promises you can't keep!" I replied, eventually conceding, wrapping my arms around his waist.

"Willie, I shouldn't have to tell you how I feel. You should never have to question my intentions," Oz stated, increasing his grip.

At the worst possible moment, and caught in a passionate embrace, Jordan stumbled upon what he feared most. "What the hell? I knew it!" Jordan yelled from the top of the stairs before descending then abruptly halting halfway.

"Jordan!" I called out, releasing my embrace, taking a step back, wiping at my tear-swollen eyes.

"I knew it! You lied to me, you promised you hadn't seen him!"

"Jordan, I haven't!" I responded.

"Then what is he doing here?"

"Look man, I didn't mean to disrespect either of you," Oz offered.

"Muthafucka, I'm not talking to you! It's because of you that he and I are in this shit! So go back to wherever the hell you came from and leave us the fuck alone! If I have to, I will help show you the door."

"Jordan, all that was uncalled for," I stated.

"Man, my intentions were not to cause a scene, so I'll leave," Oz remarked.

"And do not let me find you around here again!"

Oz quickly terminated his actions. "What?"

"Nigga, you heard me!" Jordan yelled.

Oz backed up his step, turning to face Jordan. "I don't think it's your decision to make," he said, working his way toward the staircase.

"Oz…let it go!" I spoke, followed by a futile attempt to restrain him. In an enraged, unconscious motion, Oz blindly pushed me into the side table positioned against the stairs.

"I'm gonna kick your fuckin' ass!" Jordan yelled down at Oz.

"Come on with your punk-ass!" Oz, never one to sustain from a fight, welcomed the challenge, immediately charging up the stairs toward Jordan.

Realizing he would have to battle for what he claimed to be his, Jordan returned to the top of the stairs, forging a stronghold, and stood his ground. Oz trailed Jordan by a few feet, reaching him as he entered the living room. Jordan stopped, standing strong as a fortress. Oz stepped to Jordan, invading his personal space. "What you got to say now, you punk-ass bitch," Oz coolly confronted Jordan, his face distorted in anger with speckles of spit flying free as he spoke.

"Back the fuck off me! I don't want to hurt you!" Jordan countered.

"Hurt *me*!" Oz let out a sadistic laugh. "Go for it, and I guarantee it will be the last time you raise a hand to anyone else."

"Is that a threat?"

Approaching the top of the stairs, I said, "Jordan, you have no idea what you're setting yourself up for." However, it was a failed endeavor to thwart the inevitable.

Oz yanked Jordan by the collar of his shirt, and in one quick successive move, he planted a one-two punch directly into his left rib cage. The altercation erupted into an all-out brawl. Oz quickstepped into a fighter's stance, shielding any blow thrown his way and swiftly responding with either an uppercut or full-on punch landing squarely into his intended target. The heated fisticuff found Jordan thrown into an end table, breaking all items I had neatly arranged; the table lamp, picture frames, knickknacks, everything shattered finding its final resting place on the floor. The violent tussle continued unabated with Oz locked in some sort of crazed, deranged state. Although fighting back, Jordan was no match against Oz's unabashed beating. The one-sided assault Jordan sustained petrified me to the core.

Interjecting, I struggled to subdue Oz's unrelenting battering, as each swing of his fists made firm contact. The scuffle continued with the three of us wrestling along the floor until I was finally able to remove Oz from Jordan. Once Jordan stood, he wildly swung his foot making contact with Oz's stomach.

Battlefields

In a mad-dash scramble, I positioned in between Oz and Jordan, temporarily halting the ruckus. "What the fuck is wrong with the two of you!" I held my hand against Oz's torso, holding him back; his chest palpitated by the adrenaline rush he received whenever he found himself caught up in a fight. Surprisingly, he obliged my inaudible demand. "Look at my place!" Returning my attention on Jordan, I said, "Are you happy now?" Heavy handed, I pushed Oz toward the opposite side of the room. "Move over there and keep your mouth shut, and don't say another word!" Oz reluctantly obeyed, repositioning next to the sliding glass door leading to the balcony, wiping blood from the corner of his mouth. I guess Jordan actually landed a solid punch after all.

"Will, let me explain myself!" Jordan insisted.

"And you, get the fuck out!" I demanded.

"Are you taking his side?" Jordan asked with restrained shock.

"I need you to gather your shit and leave my apartment, now. I have nothing left to say to you. I'm so fuckin' angry!"

"Make *him* leave!" Jordan contested.

"Get out," I screamed.

Defrocked by my pending assessment, Jordan gathered his spent estimations, his disintegrating pride, and neatly packed them away. Leaving the fields of war, a fallen hero, while his nemeses flashed a flicker of condescension. I astutely watched Jordan hastily pack his shit, fueled by his self-indulgent behavior exhibited moments earlier.

Once I knew Jordan was satisfactorily removed from the scene, I unconscientiously pounced into Oz, which totally caught him off guard. With both hands, I shoved Oz, knocking him into the corner wall, following with a right-handed punch into the side of his chest. "What the fuck did you think you were doing?" I chastised. Oz remained stoic, clinching his jaw, his stare locked point-blank. Not once did he speak, though his body language rung apathetic. "Say something, anything…look what you've done to me, to my place!" With all my strength, I pushed against Oz's immense torso, then again, leading him toward the stairs. Oz's massive body lumbered sullenly without wavering. He did not resist and granted my wish without debate, leaving my apartment.

Vance N. Smith

I walked toward the sliding glass door, watching him meander in defeat down the driveway. When Oz reached the end of the carport, he stopped with hands stuffed into his pockets, shoulders hunched, collapsing along the side of my aunt's house. Oz stayed propped limply against the wall for several minutes before he straightened himself upright, twisting slightly to his right. Stepping back, I hid in the shadows of the drapes, not wanting to be noticed. Oz glanced up toward the balcony of my apartment then slipped into the darkness of the covered carport.

I stepped back into view once Oz disappeared down the driveway. When I was sure Oz left the premises, I returned my attention to my disheveled unit. Slowly I moved, avoiding broken glass from pictures knocked from the wall, and reaching down, I picked up a framed photo of Sedona and myself. Nearly an hour and a half passed before I was able to restore order to my apartment.

Once I was done with the cleanup, I called my crew, cancelling the barbeque I had planned for the following day. When ask why I changed my mind, I simply answered, "It's my prerogative, leave it at that!" After I placed all appropriate calls, I hopped into the shower once again to refresh and cleanse the ordeal of the afternoon away. Then I fixed myself a much-needed cocktail and plopped on my bed, exposed, where I lay until around six that evening.

Half asleep, I heard a sudden pounding at my front door, startling me awake. "Willie!" I heard Oz yell, followed by more pounding against the door. "Willie, please!" *What the hell*, I thought. Grabbing some old sweats and a tank laid across the arm of a chair, I slipped them on, proceeding for the door. Oz's thud became more frantic. "Willie, open the door!"

"I'm coming, hold on, but I told you I didn't want you around here. So why are you here?"

"I need you! I need you to talk to me!" Oz's pitch tapered off. "I really need you to talk to me!" The despondency in his voice sent chills throughout my body. And as soon as I opened the door, Oz swooped in, cradling my face in his hands. "I need you," he said, planting his lips to mine. Although

Battlefields

he tasted as sweet as our last intimate entanglement, this was not the appropriate occasion to rekindle lost memories. I struggled, freeing myself from his clutch. Oz held on tighter, his kisses more aggressive than before, as we danced a soldier's lament.

Ultimately, I gathered enough strength, freeing myself from his grasp. "Oz, what the fuck is wrong with you?"

"I'm begging you to forgive me. I need you to remove me from this dark place I've fallen victim to."

"Oz, what are you talking about?"

"You, me—everything we stood for. I'm so absent of what is reality, what I stand for? Who I am as a person? I cannot control it, and it's consuming me!" Oz reached for my hand leading me up the stairs.

Entering the living area, I ceased my step. "Hold up!"

"Trust me, Willie."

"I don't know what to feel or trust with regards to you or us—too much has happened. How do you expect me to remove all those instances of heartache?" I pensively looked into Oz's eyes, searching for any resemblance of the truth.

"Knowing me all these years, no matter what happened, should be all you need. Forget about the past, think only of the present," Oz stated, nervously biting his lower lip.

"What are you saying?" I asked, drowning in angst. "I don't have the strength to deal with you delivering the slightest bit of hope, only to renege your offer, removing it from the table."

"All I know is when I'm with you, I'm happy—you make me happy. I feel I can do anything, face the troubling ideas flooding, invading, and swallowing me whole." Oz ran his hand through his loose curly locks. "When I feel I can't go on, it's you I see in the distance providing hope, a future. No one else is there, but it's you who stands strong, lifting me when despair is consuming the world around me." Oz moved in closer, laying his cheek next to mine, gently caressing and nuzzling his nose into the side of my neck. "Take a chance on me for once in your life, and forget about the hurt and open your mind to the possibilities," Oz whispered, nibbling my earlobe.

"I don't want to be hurt again; I don't think I can take it!" I pleaded.

"I'm not trying to hurt you; I never meant to hurt you! I could never hurt you intentionally, that is why this pains me so. I know I have destroyed the faith you had in me."

Leaning forward, I rested my head beside his shoulder. "I love you so much! I have always loved you," I confessed.

Oz smiled, placing a kiss to the crown of my head. Tilting my head back, Oz slid the back of his hand down the side of my cheek. His slight, cracked smile warmed me throughout, pressing his body hard against mine, revealing the swelling truths he held within. Eventually his lips found mine, kissing me deeply and intensely, igniting a concentrated outburst of tantalizing emotions. My entire body wept under his touch. "Take my hand," Oz commanded. His lips grazed mine when he spoke; his hot breath weighed heavily against my skin. I followed without hesitation, placing my hand in his leading me slowly toward the bedroom.

Oz sat alongside the edge of my bed, where he preceded to lift my tank over my head. "I want you to show me how to love you. I'm willing to be everything you require of me."

"Simply take your time, do what comes naturally. There is nothing you could do that I would not like. I'm your vessel to explore," I smiled.

Oz ran his hand down the length of my chest and stomach. "You have always been a beauty to me." Oz pulled me into him, kissing the center of my stomach, just above my navel.

I placed my finger under Oz's chin, raising his eyes into view. "Are you sure you're ready for this?"

"More than ever!" Oz replied. "I've been wanting to feel you openly, without second guessing my own actions for some time now."

"You're shaking," I said, sensing Oz trembling with each touch I placed upon him. "Nervous?"

"Yes," Oz answered.

"There's no need to be nervous; there really isn't much of a difference being here with me," I remarked.

"Yeah, it is," Oz paused, "because it's you!"

Battlefields

"What do you mean, because I'm a man?"

"No, not because you're a man, because it's you," Oz answered shyly, completely out of character.

I smiled. "Are you blushing?"

Oz withheld his nervous laughter, forcing his shoulders to bob.

"Stand up," I said, lifting Oz to a standing position, unbuttoning his usual flannel shirt. One by one, I methodically unfastened each button, seductively revealing his beefy, hairy chest. Oz stood withholding a childish grin, reveling in the moment, unashamed, as I completely undid the buttons of his shirt. I smiled, admiring the man before me, sliding my hands over his broad shoulders, removing the garment, and allowing it to plummet freely to the floor. Oz's body was remarkably rock solid, pure beefsteak, mouthwatering and full of flavor with kisses sweet and sensuous and full of passion. The shockwave bolting throughout my body catapulted me to heights I had never experienced. Far beyond anything I felt with Elijah or Jordan, Oz was my *everythang*!

Taking a seat on my queen-size bed, I proceeded with Oz's jeans, first unbuckling his belt then the top button of his faded 501 Levi's, until I reached the last one, revealing gray Calvin Klein men's bikini briefs and a mound of happiness. Oz rested his hand upon my shoulder for balance, helping remove one pant leg at a time. I muttered under my breath, *Goddamn!* Carefully, I scooted further back along the mattress.

"Roll on your stomach," Oz directed, and I eagerly obliged. "Where's your baby oil?"

"In the bathroom." I spoke low and drawn out, soaking in the moment I had patiently waited for.

"Don't move, I'll return shortly."

I nodded OK.

Oz returned with a clear plastic bottle of oil and a towel. Images flashed in my mind of the first time Oz massaged my body, knowing this time he would deliver much more. Oz laid the towel down at the foot of the bed then positioned himself on top, straddling across my thighs. With oil in hand, Oz flipped up the cap and drizzled the oil along the full length of my back. After which, he rubbed his hands together, creating friction to warm them up before he applied light pressure, spreading the oil evenly throughout my back. Light rhythmic strokes radiated from top to bottom, and the pressure increased with each swirling motion. I was enraptured, lost in escalating sexual tension. The kneading and the gentleness of his strokes, followed with increasing intensity, led me to float to a space and time I only dreamt of until now. Once Oz finished manipulating my muscles, he followed with rapid strokes of his fingertips, light and soft as a feather, rocketing me to near convulsions. Holding my face in the palms of my hands, I suppressed the innate need to wail in deep-rooted elation. First he worked my backside, and then he directed me to turn over where he finished my front.

Talented to say the least, he did things with his hands that were incredible! He paid close attention to every nuance, of which each touch sent me escalating toward a surreal ecstasy. Whenever he knew he hit a spot, Oz concentrated solely until it was evident I would explode, then he retreated, navigating an invisible roadmap to another erogenous zone marked for his exploration.

Never had I experienced such an erotic explosion of intimate relations. I had no idea the sexual tension an individual could place upon another just by the touch of his hands. Oz had me so wound up, my body and soul wept in pleasure, begging for relief. It was a sexual awakening one can only experience once in a lifetime, not by any lover, but only by the one who fatefully held the key.

By the end of the massage, we lay side by side, flesh to flesh, our bodies melting into one. More than two hours had passed, during which he tantalized and erotized, tormenting me into a lustful frenzy.

"Who knew you possessed the ability to pleasure someone like that," I whispered.

Oz smiled. "I saved all that for you!"

"Liar!" I stated, running my fingers through his loose curls. "You have me so fuckin' hard!"

"You feel mine don't you?" Oz remarked.

Battlefields

"How could I not," I responded. "You mean to tell me I've missed out on that all this time?"

"I've given you a massage before!"

"Yeah, but not like that! If I remember correctly, you teased and gave the illusion then stopped."

Oz repositioned on top, weighing his massive body down. "Am I too heavy?"

"Not at all, I love the feel of weight on top of me."

"All two hundred and fifty-six pounds of rock-solid meat?" Oz jokingly asked.

"Especially that! Now, shut the fuck up!" Cradling the back of his neck, I pulled him forward until his lips met mine. Once we touched, we embraced in a passionate kiss. There I drowned in the realized dream I wished for since the day we met. Our bodies twisted and contorted, wrestling in love's supremacy.

"Damn, you're like a wild animal!" Oz professed.

"You haven't seen anything yet, now turn your big ass over!" I ordered.

Slowly Oz flipped his large physique, lying on his stomach, "What are you going to do to me?" Oz jokingly asked, cracking a smile.

Resting on my knees between Oz's legs, I said, "Wait and see, just relax and enjoy." For a moment, I admired the mound of flesh lying before me. Deliberately I ran my right hand down the length of his right thigh, feeling the hairs of his leg part within my fingers. Oz's lower body parts were simply beautiful, thick and massive with a large, round rump. His legs and ass were covered in thick, silky hair. *Just what the doctor ordered!* First his right leg then his left, I traced every inch from the bottom of his buttocks down to his feet. I followed with the tip of my tongue, gliding up then down the other then back up again, where I stopped at the base of his ass. There I hovered, mesmerized by his rather large, firm rump encouraging me on. I gently stroked my swollen flesh before I proceeded, leaning in with a tender kiss between his woolen sack and pleasure dot, followed with a subtle flick of my tongue of his tasty treat.

Oz quickly reacted as his body flinched. "What are you doing?"

Vance N. Smith

Not once did I remove my face, parting the furry sea with my hands. "Do you trust me?" I asked.

"I do…"

"You'll enjoy it, I promise!"

Oz hesitantly answered, "OK."

Inhaling deeply, I blew a steady stream of warm air into his deep-sea eye, while it winked and contracted. Oz's midsection twisted in delight with his moans of pleasure increasing and growing to a higher pitch. While I worked the fuzzy gulf, I found his throbbing, pulsating flesh, freeing it from its trapped confinement and pulling it down into the light. All the while, I circled with my tongue around his darkened abyss, teasing and taunting, skyrocketing Oz into a hurried slow groan.

Oz reached back, grabbing a handful of my hair. "What the fuck are you doing to me?" he growled.

Ignoring his plea, I continued my exploration, dragging the tip of my tongue down the center of his ass and back to his woolly sacks where I paused, tussling them in and out of my mouth, leaving every bit of my being. Eventually I released, slithering down the shaft of his swollen flesh until I reached the tip, finding the eye of his storm. There I darted the eye, filling it before I swallowed it whole, consuming it to the base.

Oz rose, arching his back, succumbing to the warmth that surrounded his hardened flesh. Repositioning and reaching to subdue Oz from breaking rank, I held him firmly against the mattress, choking on the meat occupying my throat. There I remained, swallowing his tool then retreating for air. With each stroke and rhythmic motion of my tongue and throat, Oz convulsed, twitching back and forth until he could no longer take the sensation. I recoiled, tracing the outline of his back with my mouth, sliding my sweat-soaked body along the length of his. Once I reached the nape of his neck, I wrapped my arm around him, pulling his mouth to mine, kissing him aggressively, pumping my midsection and parting the crack of his ass with my stiffened flesh.

Overcome with unbridled desires, Oz suddenly reversed the entire script with one complete swoop. Lost in the immense power of his strength,

Battlefields

I reluctantly found myself lying flat on my back. From the top of my head down to the tips of my toes, Oz licked, nibbled, sucked, and kissed my entire body. Overwhelmed by raw male dominance and forced to submit to the demands of his prowess, I surrendered, giving in wholeheartedly to his requests. Back and forth, we fought for control with wild abandon; a singing bedframe filled the room full of creaks of rattling sounds.

Mounting strong as a lion of the wild, Oz pressed his body firmly against mine with one arm locked around my throat and the other turning my mouth into his, kissing me deeply. His strokes began slow and steady, filling me up. My hand held tightly against the headboard, holding on for the ride of my life, exploding into a fiery passionate collision.

Our marathon lovemaking lasted late into the night, and the aggression and the necessity to please carried us into an unabridged level of fulfillment. Never had I experienced unrestrained passion of this magnitude with all the unanswered pieces of the puzzle complete.

There was no turning back!

CHAPTER 54

It wasn't until the morning of Memorial Day holiday when Oz and I finally decided to come up for air. Since Saturday night, we remained in bed, watching TV, making passionate love, rekindling the past, and bridging a road to our future. All I could say was, it was just fine by me! Oz had roused something deep within that spun my world into a frantic frenzy, and *yes*, it was just fine by me.

I awakened to the soft rumbling sound of Oz sleeping in a state of bliss. A slightly blinding light streamed through the cracks between the thin slats of the miniblinds, forcing me to squint. I gently stretched then rolled to my side, making sure not to disturb the one who held my heart for the majority of my young adult life. Sliding his shoulder length hair away from his face, I viewed a man lost in a state of serenity. How easily we forgot the past when the slightest bit of hope entered our lives. When I traced the outline of his prominent nose with the tip of my index finger, Oz twitched then unconsciously swatted. A faint smile graced my lips, settling back into a set of propped pillows, drifting off to sleep.

Around eleven that morning, I was startled awake, not sure why or what had jolted me, but the sheer thought of it sent a surreal chill throughout my body, leaving me panting for air. Gathering my thoughts, I realized Oz was absent and nowhere in sight. "Oz," I cried in panic—no answer received in return. Frantically, I scurried out of bed, slipping into a pair of pajama bottoms.

Entering the living room, I heard the entrance door at the bottom of the stairs open then close.

Battlefields

"Oz," I called out, my heart raced fast and furious.

"Yes, Willie—what's the matter?" Oz responded. "Were you expecting someone else to walk in unannounced?"

Hastily, I regained my composure before giving the impression I was on the verge of a complete state of alarm. "No, not at all, I woke up and you weren't there. I wondered where you had gone, that's all."

Oz spoke, approaching the top of the stairs, "I left you a note on the nightstand."

"You did—I didn't see it!"

"Where did you think I had gone?" Oz flashed a heavy frown. "I went to the store to pick up a few things. You were out of milk and a few other items I wanted for breakfast."

"What do you want?" I asked.

"Relax, I got this," Oz stated, walking past me, entering the kitchen and placing the grocery bags down on the counter top. "I'm making *mangu con tres golpes.*"

Following Oz into the kitchen, I propped myself against the archway leading into the dining area. "I love it when you make that, and it's been a while since I had it!"

Oz chuckled. "All right, go into the other room and allow me to work my magic."

After breakfast, Oz and I settled on the living room sofa, cuddled together, listening to the radio, drifting in and out of a dreamlike state. Sprawled along the entire length of the sofa, I lay on my back with Oz's cheek resting on my chest. His right leg intertwined within mine, his right arm wrapped around my waist. While he slept, I innocently ran my fingers through his loose curls, gently massaging his scalp. I knew I had found my heaven the moment we renewed our commitment. The miffed relations we encountered, along with the pain placed on one another, had finally drifted to some other obscure place. I felt secured, and for once all the scattered pieces had finally fallen into place. I knew then I was in a far better state than I had been in before now. All the heartache, all the pain I suffered, seemed to drift to some faraway place.

Vance N. Smith

Oz and I lounged lazily the remainder of the day, and it wasn't until well after nine that Monday evening when he gathered his belongings, leaving for his side of town.

A new chapter was beginning, and no longer would the past haunt and confuse me. For now, I was whole.

CHAPTER 55

THE WEEK FOLLOWING the Memorial weekend provided the opportunity to reignite the fire we once had. To my surprise, Oz became the man he formerly was, and I loved every minute of it. Among this newfound energy, we connected on a whole other level. Our marathon lovemaking proved this revelation true. The stamina he possessed was purely unimaginable. He would not stop until it was clear all my needs were thoroughly satisfied. Oz made love to every inch of my being and my subconscious, erasing all misguided fears. I *swear* he should bottle that shit and sell it for some obscene price! The way I felt about him was above anything I had craved in the past. He completed me, made me his equal, his partner, and although this was nothing new, this time around was certainly an eye-opener. More than ever before his love potion invaded my body and firmly planted itself deep into the fibers of my existence. The infiltration process was complete with no means of ever expelling it. No antibiotic, no exorcism, not even hocus-pocus would purge his captive nature, and even if I could, there was no reason I would. I had found my heaven; however, I was still consumed with caution.

The end of the weekend also signaled the end of my week-long vacation. As Saturday turned to Sunday morning, Oz returned from his intense early morning gym regime, which included fortifying his boxing prowess. Something I righteously encouraged because it appeared to fulfill his inclination to fight at the drop of a hat. Once Oz showered and dressed, he ate the hearty breakfast that awaited him on the dining room table. Afterward we lounged around the balcony of my apartment, chugging mug after mug of coffee. Once we finished our morning cup of Joe, Oz stated there was unfinished business to attend to and would speak with me later in the evening. It wasn't until noon when he finally packed his gear and headed for his side of town. Upon leaving, Oz kissed me passionately to the point I thought my knees buckled.

I watched from my balcony as Oz strolled down the driveway, disappearing under the shelter of the carport. After his departure, I remained on the balcony soaking up rays from the sun for another thirty minutes.

When I was about to enter the sliding glass door, Aunt Raine, Sedona, and Bryce appeared from the covered driveway—a visit I was not expecting.

"Bring yo' ass down," Sedona yelled toward the balcony. "We'll wait for you on the patio."

"I'll be there shortly!" I begrudgingly answered.

"Do either of you want something to drink?" I overheard Aunt Raine say in the background, when I exited the balcony.

"So where have you been all week and weekend?" Sedona nonchalantly asked, concealing a smirk. "Several times I've called and you haven't returned any of them." Sedona casually swatted a fly from her face. "Something's up! You blew all of us off Memorial weekend, cancelling our barbeque with no explanation, not even a go fuck off. All week not a peep from you, and I'm not happy." Sedona turned to Bryce, and said, "What about you, what is your take on the situation?"

Bryce reared deep into the patio chair. "I think he blew us off for some man."

"My sentiments exactly, so who was it, and I hope to God you didn't choose Jordan over us!" Sedona stated.

"Jordan and I aren't speaking at the moment," I offered.

Sedona leaned in close, totally ignoring my last comment. "There's a radiance about you!" Sniffing fictitiously, she said, "I detect—wait—hold on. I can smell it, but I—I smell a man, but it's not Jordan!"

Battlefields

I sat rolling my eyes. "You don't know what you're talking about."

"Hot damn, I knew it! Who is he? Who did you meet?" Sedona cheered.

Aunt Raine approached with a tray of glasses and a pitcher of iced lemonade, setting them on the table.

"Damn girl, you're good!" Bryce joked. "I didn't pick up on that bit of information!"

"It's Oz," my Aunt casually remarked, stepping back from the table.

Sedona let out a ruckus scream, waving her hand in the air. "I knew it!

"What the fuck?" Bryce shouted.

"Spill the dirt, Auntie!" Sedona shifted in her seat, giving Aunt Raine her full attention. "What do you know about this evolving headline? Spill it!"

Silently, I sat motionless, not at all amused, flashing my aunt the stink eye.

My aunt waved her hand, dismissing my stance. "I'm not sure what happened, but when I returned from Virginia last night, Oz was here and hadn't left his side until this afternoon! You just missed him." Aunt Raine pulled a chair from under the table, taking a seat. "It's about time…you two played that game of chance far too long."

"I agree," Sedona stated freely.

Reaching for one of the iced drinks, I said, "There's still a cloud of mystique; we've advanced our friendship."

"What do you mean by advanced? Are you saying the two of you finally fucked?" Bryce placed his hand to his mouth. "Sorry Aunt Raine, I didn't mean to be so forward."

Aunt Raine just smiled and nodded.

"Yes, we have taken that final step, but nothing concrete on where we officially stand." I answered.

"But it's a start, at least it appears you're moving forward, something you should have done years ago. How you allowed it to go on for such a long time is beyond me," Bryce offered his opinion.

"Well, we'll see how it plays out. I'm not placing my hopes too high just yet," I stated before taking a long sip of my iced tea. I was not about to give

Vance N. Smith

them more than they needed to know. As happy as I appeared, a cloud of suspicion still hung low over our heads.

Previous hopes and dreams left me high and dry with nothing more than whimsical ideas. I guess time would tell.

CHAPTER 56

HAVING SPENT THE better part of the afternoon entertaining uninvited guests, finally I was able to boot them from the property. I loved my friends dearly, but today I simply wanted to relax, enjoying the time alone and my last day of a much-needed vacation. I had hoped to recoup entirely prior to the pending hectic workday I was sure to have the following morning. Once alone, I let the remainder of the day drift leisurely along like a billowy cloud, lost in the possibilities of what was to come. Round and round, my mind played continuous vignettes of past pleasures—markers of my life, his life—our life. To the general public, I guess these fanciful notions played out like an adolescent fantasy, rather than something any true-blooded man would ever imagine. Nonetheless, I never considered myself an ordinary man, not because of my lifestyle, but because of my sensitive nature and lone-wolf mentality. However, the one thing that controlled every aspect of my life, whether good or bad, was the never-ending desire to feel loved.

With the passing of the week, my angst of self-imposed doom lifted, vanishing with time itself. A calming spirit revealed the truths I long summoned, releasing the inner beauty I had long forgot. What a difference a few fantastic days could make!

As the day pressed on, I waited patiently for a call from the man I idolized since the beginning. Six o'clock, then seven o'clock turned to ten o'clock, and still no word from Oz. Butterflies fluttered haphazardly within the confines of my stomach, souring the abundant, fanciful memories of days past. The last time I glanced at the time it was ten forty-seven, Sunday night. Hoping to push all fears aside, I placed a call to Oz to wish him a goodnight before I settled in. I got his answering machine.

For whatever reason I was unable to fall asleep, staring aimlessly out the window, watching the leaves of the tree rustle in the damp night air. Every worst scenario floated in and out of my mind, egging once enchanted remembrances to disseminate deep into the extended depth of despair.

None of it made sense; I knew it had to be deep-seated self-destruction ruminating to the surface, destroying any happiness that appeared on my doorstep. I hated what my life had become, never affording the opportunity to experience absolute happiness without some indiscriminate, concealed antagonist blocking the chance to respire. I was forever faced with unabridged intuitions circulating, clouding my judgment. In vain, I tried to fight the concept that heartbreak had crept into my room—an ominous oppressor dictating every avenue of my existence. Broken and beaten, I was unable to break free from the warden who held the key to my cell for far too long.

I tossed and turned for hours into the night, while a vengeful, imperceptible tyrant swept through, asphyxiating the life from a jubilant soul. Purposely, I pleaded for a reprieve, and mentally I pushed the withering contemplations away, locking them into entrenched sections of my imagination. I slipped profoundly into slumber, finally experiencing sweet dreams that replaced ill-advised reservations returning the exultant pleasantries of days past.

That night, in my dreams, I pledged for a savior as I laid a weary head to my pillow.

CHAPTER 57

CONTEMPLATING DOWN UPON the sea below, I scrutinized the ebb and flow of its misty-foamed waves crashing against the jagged, broken boulders laid askew. I watched while my storied life played in visual notes; it was a constant reminder of the highs and lows I'd endured over the years. Resting, leaning against the edge of an expansive picture window, I witnessed a naked reflection appear with strong hands reaching, gently caressing around my waist—secured in place. His embrace was forever the touch of a savior; I had succumbed to his affections. Closing my eyes, I spoke his name: Oz. Where have you been? Yet, no answer I received in return. I opened my eyes, faced with an empty silhouette. Panicked, I swung around, finding only hollow space. I cried, come back to me.

Awakened in a haze of confusion, I felt my heart palpitating and my forehead drenched with sweat. *Damn dreams*, I thought. Dreams, which had been a recurring phenomenon for the past year, albeit, currently beginning to wane. I was haunted by a reality that never materialized—a life with the one who detained every conceived opinion of what I pledged. And every time I laid my head to rest, the perception fled from view in an instant. A week of bliss was now marred by the inconceivable; Oz had once again shattered all I prayed for.

How did I get here? I thought. Well, to make a long story short, there were times when you wanted something so bad, you found yourself making choices you normally would not choose. Oz was my untouchable dream, and once he walked, vanishing from my life, I stumbled into a dreary, deep funk. Adding insult to injury, I was haunted by these harrowing dreams. Six months after our friendship danced to the other side of adult relations,

I remained alone, locking all from existence. Jordan had relinquished his fight for my affections after his disastrous altercation with Oz. And as far as my crew was concerned, I certainly didn't want to hear from Isaiah, with his "I told you so's," and "you never listen to me" preaches. Fortunately, Sedona and Bryce remained neutral, whereas my aunt stayed mummed, but her disapproving silence rang loud and clear.

During the summer of 1988, a year after Oz's disappearance and departure, Uncle Charles informed me that he spoke with his acquaintance that had rented Oz the storefront. Uncle Charles discovered Oz had closed shop some nine months prior, and moved back to New York. To say I was shocked by the news was an understatement, which somewhat explained Oz's absence and why I could not get in touch with him. As luck would have it, the very same day I learned about Oz, Sedona invited me to an intimate gathering held at Bulldawg's house, her collaborative singing partner. It was during that invite that I blindly reunited and reaffirmed my relationship with Jordan against my crew's wishes. I should have listened because the union has not been a particularly pleasurable one. I did love Jordan, but the salacious triangle between him, Oz, and me had taken its toll. The lack of trust and fermenting insecurities caused a fractured bond with Jordan, along with my inability of releasing Oz from my heart. I truly gave Jordan my best, and for all appearances sake, the exterior revealed a loving and caring relationship. Even among my inner circle of friends, my life appeared to be smooth sailing, except with Sedona and Bryce, who saw straight through my fake smokescreen.

Fast-forward to the summer of 1991, which marked four years since that fateful weekend ripped my world apart. And after all this time, I still had no explanation as to why or what happened. No phone calls, not even a fuck

Battlefields

you and your life. Once again, Oz flew me to the edge of heaven before selfishly snapping my ass back to reality! I was so close I could see it, touch it, and then in an instant, it all crumbled away. It didn't make sense, but why should I have expected anything more than what I had.

Funny, when in love, we grieve, we hurt, we cry, and no matter how much we think our lives can't go on—we do. We never seem to notice time, yet with every moment, every second, and every thought, whether we are conscious of it or not, time marches on. It leaves many of us unable to march in step before we awaken, realizing the years have passed us by, feeling cheated and consumed with regret. All that is left are faded memories, shattered dreams, lost loves, and misguided ideas and choices. I wondered, *where have I been the last four years, and how am I back in the arms of Jordan?*

Shortly after the birth of her second child, Savannah, Sedona and Jackson crossed a point where there was no longer happiness to be found. A year later, there was definitely trouble in paradise. Faced with the realization of losing her first true love, Sedona was forced to reevaluate her life. During this period of self-evaluation, she met Dawson Meeks, an aspiring actor who happened to be a close friend of Bulldawg's. She met Dawson the summer I reunited with Jordan, but it wasn't until this past year that they moved to something more than friends. Dawson became a close confidant who was there for support during trying times. Dawson, a man three years her senior, was handsome, athletic, and confident, but a polar opposite of what she believed she would learn to love—a Caucasian man from the deep south, blond haired and blue eyed no less. Sometimes God has designs for us we simply can't explain. You never know where your heart might find comfort. A fate Sedona easily welcomed.

Ultimately with that same blind faith, I considered my situation with Jordan to be God's plan all along. The trials and tribulations I endured were set forth to appreciate the value in what I had, which I failed to see in the past. I must admit my life with Jordan had evolved to one of some stability. Then again, jaded by failures in love, I found it hard committing.

Thankfully, in recent months, just as the sea ebbed and flowed, life evolved to a happier place. I had come to terms with my many tragedies and had warmed to the ideas of a life with Jordan, though reservations dogged my ability to fully accept. Our fighting had slightly subsided, replaced with Jordan's constant begging we should seek cohabitation. I anticipated the suggestion and avoided giving a firm answer. You see, emptiness held my hands bound behind my back, holding me hostage.

I guess you wonder how a man with a life filled with seeming happiness, moderate wealth, and a loving man could feel so empty. I contemplated that very question several times throughout the years. In fact, today, I was consumed by the thought from the moment I opened my eyes. Melancholy, at best, described my feelings. When in reality, I was well aware of where these positions originated. Yes, I had a man who loved me, and I loved him as well. Did I yearn for him? No. Was he good to me and for me? Yes. Would I be a fool to give him up? Yes. But my heart burned quietly for a man I could not summon, and although it had been over four years since I last laid eyes on him, he consumed my every thought, each and every day. Silently I pined for his touch, to hear the sound of his voice—I would forever desire the love of Oz.

Yes, time passes us by, and far too often we're unable to stay in step. It appeared as though you go to bed, wake up, and its years later. No matter what you do, time continues to march forward.

CHAPTER 58

A MOMENTOUS OCCASION emerged when the summer of 1991 bowed to autumn with the purchase of my first home in the Crenshaw district of Los Angeles. Living in my aunt's garage apartment for the last ten years had afforded me the ability to save my money, achieving the American dream. I was forever grateful at a time when I needed stability and a roof over my head. Aunt Raine provided a safe haven without question, proving to be my rock, a force no other could crumble. I innocently smiled in thought as I wandered the aisles of Bullock's department store in Century City.

Three hours into shopping for necessities, I settled into an outdoor cafe corner table a few feet from the movie theaters. I sat with a sub sandwich and large cup of Coke, thumbing through a home improvement magazine picked up from Brentano's bookstore. Breaking my concentration, I faintly overheard a deep, rumbling voice. "I know you heard me the first time, but I'll say it again. You can't sit here all day taking up space when there are others who would like to sit and enjoy their meals." A cold shiver crept throughout my body; I held my composure taunt, slowly shifting in the direction of a ghostly reminder of years past. "You have always been a cocky fuck!" The stranger spoke with a sly chuckle.

My heart sank. "Elijah?"

"Yeah, don't act like you don't know who I am!"

"What the fuck!" I responded.

"I bet I'm the last muthafucka you thought you would ever see again," he stated, pulling out a chair to take a seat.

Vance N. Smith

Holding the chair in place with my foot, I said, "I don't believe I asked you to join me!" Laying the magazine down next to my sandwich, I reared back into the hard metal chair. "What are you doing here?"

"Still a hard-ass," Elijah smirked. "You know how that shit turns me the fuck on!" He smiled seductively, licking his lower lip, trying his best to entice me once again.

Withholding any form of a smile, I was indecisive if I was elated to see him or still harbored ill feelings. All the negative experiences of the past, I had locked in an ironclad box, tossing the key, never looking back. I had not thought of him much besides considering the huge mistake it was involving him in my life, but I guess he served some purpose. I held my scrutinizing observation long and hard before I spoke. "What have you been up to?" I casually asked, not particularly interested in actually knowing.

His insistence paid off as he sat into the chair. "You look good! In fact, the past ten years have been good to you. You've grown into a handsome man."

"Life has been good...I can't complain." I hesitated before I paid him a compliment in return. "You, too, as well. How are Belinda and the kids? How old are they now?"

"Teenagers now," he stated as any proud papa would, all smiles and teeth. "My kids are doing well!" Elijah pulled his wallet out, removing two photos of his children, grinning from ear to ear.

"They have grown into beautiful young adults, and your son looks just like you." But better looking, I thought.

"Yes, they have!" Elijah paused for a moment. "You never left my mind," he said, biting down hard on his jaw. "I've thought of you often with the hope I would have the opportunity to meet with you again."

"Why?" I asked bluntly.

"Why do you hate me so much?"

"Do you really need me to answer that?" I remarked.

"I gave you everything you ever wanted!"

"No, you didn't. How dare you make such a statement?" I could not believe this mutha would come at me with some lame-ass shit! Angrily, I

432

Battlefields

held my voice behind clenched teeth, seething with anger, leaning closer with a pointed finger. "I was the one who gave you everything you could ever want!"

"Will, chill for a minute."

"I played by your rules, I stayed locked in that house away from my friends, waiting, craving for your affections."

"Will—Will! Shut the fuck up, damn! It's not always about you. I gave you all I was capable of giving. I could not give any more than that."

"Then you should have stayed away."

"I couldn't stay away, I loved you too much. I'm still in love with you."

"That's convenient, Elijah, but I grew up. I no longer fall for the bullshit. All you dead-weighted muthafuckas have hardened a once-carefree heart."

"So what we had meant nothing to you?" Elijah asked. "I took you in when you had no other place to go. I saved you from that crazy-ass momma of yours, and you're telling me I meant nothing to you? That's fucked up."

"You took advantage of a situation, swoopin' in when I was vulnerable, using that to your advantage, but I'm not going to sit here and say I didn't play my part. I knew exactly what I was doing, and I take ownership of it. However, in the end, you turned out no better than my mother. You held me prisoner, same as she did, just in a different way! That is what I'm angry about; I was so in love with you, wanting nothing more than to be whole with you."

He bowed his head. "I know..." Elijah sat motionless before turning to his right, his gaze focused far into the distance. "Sometimes we find ourselves mixed up in shit we can't see ourselves out of. I was not trying to fall in love with you, but I did. I knew I had an obligation to my wife...my kids. I knew you were my responsibility, and I let you down. If I could do it over again, I would. I would turn back the hands of time to prove to you the man I could be."

"Elijah, I don't believe a word you're saying."

"I want to make love to you again, hold you in my arms, caressing your back. Be all that I can be..."

Vance N. Smith

"Stop! This is such bullshit! I will not allow you to fill my head with any more of your lies, your empty promises. All this means nothing; you still have your wife, your children. I'm the one left struggling to find a means of normalcy, commitment, and security. You have that—have always had that! You would not give it up back then and you're certainly not about to give it all up for me now!"

"Why wouldn't I?"

"You couldn't—wouldn't—do it then, so why would you now?" I asked.

"Time and maturity can change a man."

"Yes, it can, and time has taught me not to be moved by bullshit you and everyone else in the world want to lay on my shoulders."

"You have grown bitter and that's not good!"

"Fuck you! What the fuck do you know about me?"

Elijah removed himself from the table, taking a step back. "At some point you have to learn to forgive. Not everyone is out to hurt you, Will. I was not out to hurt you. I cannot speak for your mother; maybe she was simply incapable of loving you and your sister."

"So you're saying I was the one who imagined all the horrible things she's done to my sister and me."

"No! That's not what I'm saying. What I am saying is, at some point, you have to let go of the past, forgive, and forget. Hell! Do I have to mention, you had some muthafucka coming to my crib looking for you?"

"We will not speak on Oz. You jumped to some crazy-ass conclusion without even considering you may be wrong."

"Was I?" Elijah placed his hand on the table, leaning forward. "Did I jump to conclusions? Where is that muthafucka now? I bet he's still stiffing around yo' ass?" Elijah snidely chuckled. "You don't even have to answer that, your expression told me all I needed to know. Yeah, I bet that nigga couldn't wait for me to get out of the picture—or have you kicked him to the curb and moved on to some bigger fish?"

"I think it's time for you to leave," I suggested.

He completely ignored my request.

Battlefields

"Come with me to the house on De Longpre," he stated, retaking his seat at the table. "Let's relive old memories."

Immediately my mind flashed to happier times when love felt untroubled and uncomplicated. Wait, did I just suggest uncomplicated? Let me retract—complicated, but oh, so good! "Nah, I'll pass."

When I removed myself from the conversation, Elijah sat speechless by his inability of conquering his reminiscent prized toy once more. I would bet my last dollar he suspected I would lose all self-respect, relapsing into a meaningless afternoon rendezvous. Nevertheless, you see, the years had taught me not to fall prey to such callous individuals who only thought of themselves and not the welfare of others. Maybe, I had grown; the vacant years without Oz had placed me in a position where I no longer pined for a love I knew would not be mine.

I found the fortress built around my heart slowly crumbling away to an idea that maybe I would concede to the one who had shown the stability I needed. Just maybe the battlefield I fought upon would finally see a rebirth of sorts, a testament to trying times once pledged against me. Could it be, I was warming to the idea of cohabitation, the one thing I vehemently fought against?

Now, there was a thought I must gestate on a bit!

CHAPTER 59

FACING ELIJAH A few months back had forced a reevaluation of decisions I'd made throughout the years. I reflected on my existence to date, envisioning a continuous series of imposed misery. Had it been fair placing all the blame on the people I felt had done me wrong? Maybe the battlefield I stepped upon was a civil war of sorts, causing anyone in my path to fall victim to my wrath. And dare I say, it was one hell of a revelation!

The preceding months sped haphazardly along, first Thanksgiving then Christmas followed by New Year's Day, and I found myself entering 1992 bewildered and confused. Well, at least I had one bright spot, and that was settling into my first home on Sunlight Place. Despite recent events and the anguish over long-held resentment, I heralded toward a happier place. I was even coming to terms and ultimately beginning to relinquish some of the hatred I held toward my parents. Were we on speaking terms? I would have to say the answer was no. Let's just say I was taking baby steps toward learning to forgive. Unfortunately, forgetting the past was proving to be a difficult endeavor.

I was rediscovering my independence and breaking free from the bondage of required love. I realized I'd been in a better place living alone, being my own man, my own person—an ideology far from the opinions of Jordan. His interpretations were taking our relationship to a higher level, the one sore spot forcing the glue of our union apart. Happy with the way things were, I saw no need to further complicate our lives more than we should. I may have been in a better place living alone; however, there were unresolved issues I had to contend with, namely dealing with my bitterness.

Battlefields

The weekend before my thirtieth birthday, Jordan found himself in the midst of planning an extravagant birthday bash. Swept into the moment, my heart slowly eased to the possibilities of building a life with him and without Oz. Even though I deeply cared for Oz, the pain of his untimely exit caused unsentimental emotions I could not escape. I could say, in the past five years, I had learned to move forward, letting go of the passions holding me hostage all these years. Thinking back, I should have known Oz's love was too damn good to last! For now, what was most important was my renewed focus on Jordan, repairing and mending hurt feelings. My only issue with Jordan was his constant nagging to cohabitate, which was not an easy feat when the pressure he mounted proved undeniable.

"Will, the telephone is for you; it's Vivian," Jordan yelled, causing my loss of concentration.

Setting my notepad aside, I rolled over and reached for the receiver. "Vivian, how are you? Long time, no hear…what have you been up to?"

"Everything, life is good! Listen, I'm calling because I have good news!" Vivian responded with jubilance.

"You're coming home for my birthday!" I secretly prayed. It had been forever since we'd seen one another.

"No, I'm sorry, I can't. I wish I could, but I can't. Well, if I had not been offered a staffing position at the Supreme Court, I would have," Vivian stated, filled with excitement.

"That's great news, when do you start?"

"Next Monday," Vivian paused with dramatic fashion, "also, I'm getting married!" she squealed.

"DeWayne finally popped the question?"

"Yes, he did! After four long years, he's finally committing to marriage."

"Cool, I like DeWayne. He's a good man. Have you set a date?"

"Yes, next summer. We're thinking of possibly June. That should give me time to settle into my job and allow us time to save more money for the wedding."

"Have you told Mom and Dad?"

"I haven't had a conversation with Mom in over six months, and with Dad, it's more like three years! I've told you, he and I have not spoken since our last altercation, and I have no interest in hearing any negativity Mother might say. They're both dead to me! Anyway, moving on to better things, how's Jordan?"

"Jordan is good, we're good..."

"I hear a 'but' coming," Vivian remarked.

I withheld a smile. "Why would you say that?"

"Because I know you! You're happy, but not completely. I'm cool with Jordan and would love him much more if he wasn't so damn arrogant!"

"I know and that's the same thing that bugs Sedona."

"Speaking of Sedona, we met for lunch last week in New York, did she tell you?"

"She mentioned something about it. What were you doing in the city?"

"A girlfriend of mine and I were there for the weekend. She could not believe Sedona is a close friend. I love having that bit of information in my back pocket to pull out on occasion, just to floor people." Vivian laughed. "OK, big brother, this was just a quick call to share my good news. Again, please forgive me for not being able to attend your birthday celebration. You know if I could, I would be there without a doubt."

"I know you would. I'm not mad, just disappointed."

"I'll make it up to you, I promise!"

"I'll hold you to it!" Hanging up the receiver, I thought back on Vivian's comment against our parents, *they're dead to me*. It was deep, to say the least, even for her, the one who did not receive the full wrath of my mother. After graduating from high school, Vivian left to attend Howard University and never looked back, only returning twice to visit. I never guessed Vivian would be consumed by just as much anger. The lost years had forged a distance between us that neither had been able to bridge. I definitely placed blame on myself. Obsessed in finding my own happiness, I had lost sight of the one who needed me most.

CHAPTER 60

Friday, February 7, 1992

The evening festivities commenced with a crisp, cloudless sky piercing the night. My thirtieth birthday celebration launched full swing with music bumpin', pumping urban sounds throughout the entire house; hands swayed in the air and bodies gyrated to the energetic beats. Guests danced with drinks in hand, while wallflowers stood with heads a bobbin', everyone experiencing the time of their life! In a corner of the dining room, an elaborate buffet featured an enormous spread of food, complete with the required staple of unlimited alcohol. The festivities were in full swing for the last few hours, and my sincere gratitude went to Jordan, Bryce, and Isaiah for throwing one hell of a party!

"I hope you're enjoying yourself," Bryce stated excitedly, gently rockin' to the music.

"I am! You guys really outdid yourselves…I couldn't be happier," I stated gleefully.

"That's what we want to hear, and you look hella good tonight. I'm lovin' the jeans and wool sweater," Isaiah commented.

Innocently, I smiled. "Thank you, Isaiah!"

Inspecting my sweater, Bryce commented, "You are fly as hell tonight, my nigga!"

"Well, you knew I had to make an impression on my thirtieth birthday!"

"Yeah, you do, and the party is turning out to be a huge success!" Bryce remarked.

Vance N. Smith

"It has, hasn't it?" I said, surveying the room. "I want to thank you for your hard work in putting this together! I just wish Sedona and Vivian could have made it," I observed, swaying to one of my favorite jams.

"How's Sedona doing with the tour?" Isaiah asked.

"The tour is coming along well; the shows have all been sold-out and her current CD is selling extremely well. I believe this will be her biggest project yet."

Lifting his drink and taking a quick sip, Bryce asked, "You think this will push her mainstream?"

"I believe so. Her CD has already turned platinum!"

"Good for her! Where is she performing?" Isaiah asked.

"I believe she's in New Your City…I think."

"How long has it been since the last time you spoke with her?"

Distracted for minute, I observed around the room then said, "Earlier today she called, sending her regrets." Still distracted, I continued scanning my surroundings. "Have you seen Rafael?"

Bryce was quick to answer. "Yeah, that hoe is in the family room all up in some man's face!"

I thought how typical, with his man-hungry antics. "That's our boy, always on the prowl."

"I keep telling that slut to slow it down!" Isaiah added, laughing at his comment.

In the animated moment of laughter, Rafael entered the living room. Bryce's swift gaze spoke volumes, rolling his eyes with a smirk. Rafael stopped at the bar and mixed a cocktail before joining the group. "What are you children talkin' 'bout?"

"You, bitch!" Bryce answered.

"What have you been up to, or should I say—who you been in to?" I asked.

"Well, you know I do what I do!" Rafael remarked.

"Do you ever stop?" Bryce retorted.

Rafael responded with a devilish smile. "Hell yeah, when I go to sleep!"

"Damn, boy!" I stated. We all continued laughing hysterically.

440

Battlefields

"Will, I believe he's taken your place in the hoe department," Bryce remarked.

"Yeah, I left that life a long time ago."

"Isaiah, can you find Jordan so we may wish Will happy birthday and cut his cake?" Bryce stated before heading for the kitchen.

The electric atmosphere frenzied the entire room, music blasting with everyone rocking to the beats. It took Bryce several tries to settle the unruly diverse crowd. "Listen up, everyone—listen up!" Bryce observed around the room. "Everyone quiet, please. Quiet!" he yelled. "All you muthafuckas shut the fuck up! It's time to sing happy birthday and cut the cake. Everyone, please gather around—come on, we don't have all night. We still have some serious partying to do!" Bryce pumped his fist high above, singing, "Let's get this party started!" In that moment, a jubilant chorus of "Happy Birthday" filled the space. Hands clapping, bodies bouncin', smiles that enveloped my soul; I was thankful for having such close friends surrounding me when other important members of my circle were nowhere to be found, namely Aunt Raine, Uncle Charles, Vivian, and Sedona.

After all the cheering, the singing, the congratulatory handshakes and kisses, Jordan presented a small box with a gold key inside, a symbol of his affection and constant nagging to live together. Jordan stated, "What do you say?"

I mean really, did I need this right now in front of the whole world? Things had been going well between us with our relationship moving toward a better place. But I should have known Jordan would somehow make this evening all about him. This was supposed to be about my birthday. Anyway, I looked to Jordan, taking his hand in mine. I thought before addressing the crowd. "I want to thank everyone for sharing this special moment between Jordan and me. He and I have traveled a long road, and though it hasn't been easy, I now understand where I belong." I stated the words, however, did I actually believe the meaning behind them? I wondered if anyone else was able to see through the fantasy I created. While I spoke, I surveyed the room filled with friends who wished the best for the both of us. "I love this man and want nothing more than to spend the rest of my life with him." I continued speaking, wondering if my words flowing from my mouth sounded sincere. I considered the many faces, the joy showered upon us—the smiles, the tears, and the adoration—but if only I could explain the heaviness of my heart. I turned to Jordan. "I salute you, Jordan, for the love you give me each and every day. You stood by when you could have easily walked away, and for that, I love you with all my heart." Honestly, I did love Jordan, but was it in the way he wanted? It was a question I had yet to answer completely.

Jordan leaned closer, kissing me gently on the lips. "Are you happy?" he asked barely above a whisper.

Glancing toward Bryce, I saw that look on his face. I hated that look! You know the one people have when they disapproved. Bryce knew my love for Jordan was of convenience, a messy necessity filling a void I could not seem to fulfill. "Yes, I'm happy," I answered.

Jordan analyzed me with a look of doubt. "Just checking. What's your answer to the key?"

Holding my hand, I sensed him trembling. Fleetingly, I changed the subject. "You're shaking! Are you OK?" I asked.

"Just nerves, I guess." Jordan placed his arm around my waist, pulling me closer. "I don't want to lose you!"

"You're not gonna lose me," I stated, forcing a smile.

Jordan returned his attention to our guests. "Listen up, everyone! I have a special treat for all of you." Jordan repositioned. "And especially for you, Will. I have a huge surprise,"

Oh god, the surprises just kept coming, when would it stop!

The room suddenly filled with the sound of a familiar voice, singing, resonating from the hallway. Through the crowd, I noticed people allowing an unknown figure to advance forward. Rumblings from the guests gave way to a thunderous cheer.

"Ms. Sedona Jacobs has flown in just for this special occasion," Jordan stated, smiling like a child lost in a candy store.

"Sedona," I yelled. I was excited, since I had not seen her in over six months. "Thank you, Jordan!"

Battlefields

Sedona entered, singing a heartfelt version of Stevie Wonder's "Happy Birthday," and hidden beneath the melody, the doorbell rang. Bryce tapped my shoulder, stating he would answer; however, before he reached the door, it opened. Everyone in the room was clapping and chanting, which hastily changed when a gasp echoed near the main entrance. Sedona turned and in midsong stopped, placing her hand to her mouth, as more gasps and looks of sheer shock appeared among the faces of the many guests.

Jordan quickly changed his position, attempting to gain a better view. The crowded room of revelers turned in my direction with the frightful look of, "Oh shit!" Sedona peered in my path, stunned. I noticed Bryce giving someone a hug with a kiss to the cheek. Because of the crowd, along with the stranger having his backside facing me, I was unable to distinguish the individual. So I mouthed to Sedona, "Who is that?" Sedona impulsively ignored my inquiry, turning toward the guest causing an uproar.

Isaiah and Rafael strained to intervene, walking in my direction. I asked once again, "Who is that?"

"You don't want to know," Isaiah replied.

"What?" I asserted.

"It's Oz!" Rafael stood, blocking my view of the room and the man who caused everyone to become so uptight.

Oblivious to all others, Jordan looked to Isaiah, asking angrily. "Is that Oz?"

I gazed beyond Rafael, and sure enough, the one person I did not want to see appeared out of thin air! As swiftly as the mood changed, so did all the emotions I held bottled up. "What is he doing here, and how did he even know how to find me?"

"I have no idea," Isaiah remarked.

Irritably, Jordan asked, "What the fuck is he doing here?"

"Jordan, do not cause a scene, please!" Isaiah stated, resting his hand to Jordan's chest, attempting to hold him back.

"Muthafucka, get your hand off me," Jordan declared, pushing past Isaiah.

Immediately, I grabbed Jordan's arm, "Please, don't do this!"

Vance N. Smith

Unconsciously, Jordan jerked his arm away. "This muthafucka has the nerve to show his face around here!"

"Jordan, please be the bigger man and let it go!" Isaiah pleaded.

Jordan stood, glaring toward Oz, then turned to confront me. The look upon his face, the pain and history among the three of us, crashed to the surface, and once again proved more than he could stand. Unsure of what to do, I instinctively wanted to leave—turn the fuck around and bail the hell out, unwilling to deal with the drama of Oz and Jordan, not tonight! Right when I finally began to surrender my heart, giving in to the feelings I forfeited to Jordan, Oz literally walked through the door after all these years of not knowing what in the hell happened. I felt petrified, feet nailed to the floor with everyone else frozen in panic.

I had been prejudicial, secretly holding on to my feelings for Oz, not allowing the ability to explore the opportunities available with Jordan. For the last five years or so, Jordan and I were involved in some form of a relationship, maybe not totally committed, but together. Certainly, we were something more than friends, fuck-buddies if you will, but not a couple until maybe two years ago.

When Jordan thought of us as a couple, in my mind, I was unsure of such a simple complication. I speculated I was over Oz, but seeing him tonight, his love virus resurrected within my veins, slowly burning to the surface. I knew I couldn't possibly give Oz any consideration, because three times he played my emotions, reeling me in only to run and hide. How could I ever trust him again?

I remained at a loss for words, staring at the only man who flipped my whole existence upside down. The thought of having another encounter, rehashing old wounds of the past, was not what I intended on my birthday. Damn, life could be a muthafuck!

Bryce continued speaking with Oz, listening intently to his every word with Sedona positioned slightly behind. Bryce occasionally glanced in my direction, to which I provided a stern twist of my head, "No." Bryce returned with a solemn nod, "OK."

"Will, what do you want us to do?" Rafael asked.

Battlefields

"Throw his fuckin' ass out!" Jordan shouted.

"Stop—just stop! Yelling isn't going to make it better! What I need you to do is keep your mouth shut and not get in the middle," I demanded. "The last thing I need is you causing a scene!"

Staring Oz down, Jordan asserted, "If he gets in my face, it's on!"

"And what do you plan on doing, Jordan, huh? I thought you figured that out the last time, and besides, what do you need to prove?" Pushing Jordan back away from the crowd, I said, "I'm telling you, don't you say or do a fuckin' thing, and I mean it!"

"Will is right, stay calm. I don't believe Oz is here to start trouble," Rafael stated.

Agreeing, I said, "I don't believe he is either, but he is here with some sort of motive."

Gazing over my shoulder, I found Sedona holding Oz's hand, directing her eyes in my direction, and then she leaned toward Oz to whisper into his ear. Bryce remained beside Sedona. Oz responded with a quick nod of his head. Sedona gave him a tender kiss to the cheek before walking in my direction. When Sedona approached, I asked. "What does he want?"

"He wants to speak with you," she answered.

"Why?"

"He didn't say, except he is afraid you will not give him the time of day. He understands he messed up, but would like the opportunity to explain."

"Explain what?" I stated, annoyed.

"Will...honey, you need to let go of the anger. I know he hurt you, which we all are well aware of, but the two of you were the best of friends at one point, inseparable in fact." Sedona placed both hands to my shoulder, taking a deep gaze into my eyes. "Both of you allowed the friendship to become clouded, skewed. He knows he fucked up! Now, give the man a chance to say what's on his mind. You need this as much as he does, so you can move on with your life and have something real with Jordan, if that's really what you want." Sedona gently placed her soft hand to my chin. "Will, I know you still love him and always will, but sometimes who or what we love isn't always the best for us. Maybe he has changed, I mean..."

Sedona looked toward Oz, "he seems different, like…" turning back to me, "so sure of who he is."

Refocusing my attention back to Oz, I found his eyes fixed dead on mine with the intensity of a royal lion.

"What do you want us to do?" Isaiah repeated.

"Tell him he needs to leave! There is nothing left to say, plain and simple! Whatever we once had, and whatever reason why he left, I no longer care!" Yet, the truth was, I did care. The very sight of Oz conjured feelings I never had for any other man—the weak knees and butterflies in the stomach, the cascading warmth flushing over. However, crossing that fine line of friend to lover, followed by the disappearing acts and betrayal, I had refused to accept. How did one forgive when duplicity replaced loyalty and faith?

Sedona asked, "Are you sure that is what you want?"

"Yes, I'm sure."

Sedona searched my eyes. "OK, if that's what you want, we'll tell him to leave, but it's a choice you should reconsider…"

"I don't believe I asked your opinion," I said, cutting Sedona off midsentence, not wanting to hear her preach.

"You know what, I'm only trying to help! I don't need your shit tonight! I don't give a fuck what you do, but I'll give you a pass tonight." Sedona shook her head, as she sauntered toward Oz.

"You owe her an apology, because she didn't deserve that," Isaiah offered his opinion before joining Sedona.

Slowly, I backed away from my guests, watching Sedona, Isaiah, and Bryce speak with Oz. I grabbed my drink from the table, as I observed the dialogue unfold. Oz shook his head no with his attention firmly locked in my direction, his defeated expression stinging profoundly. He seemed crushed with Sedona appearing to console him, though he kept resisting, shaking his head no. By that time, the other guests had forgotten about the unfortunate events of the evening. Rafael somehow forced Jordan to one of the secondary bedrooms, hoping to calm him down. The sound of music returned blasting from the speakers; bodies gyrated to the beats with glasses in hand, unknowing the walls had collapsed

Battlefields

around them. *Why now, why here—why did he have to pick this day to return to my life?* I couldn't breathe; I felt as if I were suffocating—I needed air and quick! I sat my drink down on the table then headed for the back door.

Once the cool night air covered my face, I sensed relief. Taking a seat on a patio lounger, I leaned forward, resting my forearms upon my thighs, the fingers of my right hand played with a ring on my left. Shortly thereafter, a creak from the back door radiated throughout the rear yard. Raising my head, there Oz stood at the base of the porch, our eyes locked. A cool breeze brushed against my face, and I shivered. Turning my head with intent to break the lingering trance between us, I noticed out of the corner of my left eye that he moved closer to the edge of the porch, placing his massive hand around a wooden post.

"What do you want, Oz?" I asked, waiting for an answer he would not provide. So I asked again, "I *said*, what do you want?" Unable to displace the anger from my voice, I turned to face him—still he did not answer. He remained bolted in place, staring and tightening his jaw, as revealed by the porch light. Nervously, shifting my body, I stated, "What are you doing here? Where in the fuck have you been? What the fuck…"

"You still have that nasty-ass mouth!"

Completely blindsided, I said, "What did you just say?"

"You heard me!" Oz stepped from the porch. "You're angry—I get it!"

"What the fuck did you expect?"

"This is exactly what I expected, and you have every right to be angry with me."

"Why now, Oz?" I asked the question again. By now, Oz had repositioned to a few feet away. Looking fly as ever! The last four and a half years had been kind, except now he was more muscular, more refined, more matured, more everything…and damn, he smelled good!

"Why not now? We're friends—at least we used to be. Time should not have changed what we are."

"People change, Oz. I've changed."

"Have you?" Oz stated with implied sarcasm.

Vance N. Smith

"Yeah, muthafucka, I have! I've moved on. I no longer think of us as friends, or whatever our fucked-up friendship was!"

"Damn—could you actually hate me that much?"

"Good, now you know how the fuck I feel!"

"What? You think I'm not hurting? You think this is easy for me—to walk back after all these years knowing the reaction I would get!"

"Then why did you?" I yelled.

Oz looked to the house. "I see you still with ole boy."

"Don't change the fuckin' subject," I demanded.

Annoyed, Oz returned his attention to me, keeping his cool. "Look, I didn't come here to fight. I had hoped you would find it in your heart to forgive me." Oz placed his hands into his front pant pockets. "I had to see you. You're always on my mind, and I missed you."

"Is that right, you sure have a funny way of showing it!"

"You think I would forget what we had, or didn't want to see you? My life hasn't been easy, and I've tried to move on, but it's hard when you love someone so much. I could never forget what we had. I wanted more from you, I wanted to build a life with you, but it was me who couldn't get his shit together!" His voice was tense.

"Look, Oz, you don't owe me a goddamn explanation! My life has been just fine without you," I said, gesturing toward the house. "I have a man who loves the shit out of me. Who would do anything for me. He wouldn't walk out on me like you did!"

"Willie—"

Cutting him off as I moved closer, pressing my finger into his chest, I said, "You wanna know what the fucked-up thing is...we fucked...we fucked like animals! I was so fuckin' happy I couldn't see straight! Never had I been so happy, and then you were gone like some thief in the night!" Pent up emotions flooded to the surface uncontrollably, causing my voice to quiver. "How fucked up is that?" Pausing for a moment, I said, "Almost five fuckin' years passed without a fuckin' word from you!"

"I know..."

Battlefields

"Yeah, you knew! You knew all those years how I felt, but I see now it was just a game! I was no different than all those women you fucked around with."

Oz tightened his mouth before he spoke. "You think it was easy for me?" Oz's voice methodically began rise.

"Hell yeah, it was too damn easy for you! Do you even know how many women I watched you play...huh...do you? You couldn't commit to any of them!"

While I yelled, looking into Oz's eyes, I saw a well of tears swell to the surface, and his jaw tightened, attempting to resist them from falling. Oz wiped at them before he spoke. "Willie, you don't understand!"

I was bowled over, since I'd never witnessed Oz cry before, believing he was incapable of such an emotional display. But his demeanor did not sway me; he was only trying to sucker me in once again, and I refused to give in. "I understand you play games, that's what you do, plain and simple."

"Willie, you have meant more to me than anyone I've known. I'm a better man because of you, and because of you, I wanted to change my life. You may not be able to see it, but you have."

"I didn't teach you to run away when it became too tough, that's not what I taught you. So, how dare you say that to me?" I stated with complete authority.

"I left because I had no choice. I couldn't give you what you needed then..."

"But you can now, is that what you're saying? What the fuck is that? What can you possibly give me now that you couldn't back then?"

"All of my love completely, the love you deserve."

"Man, that's priceless! That is fuckin' priceless! Do you know how fucked up that is? I would have given my right arm to have you love me!"

"Willie, I knew exactly how you felt."

"Yet, you walked away! That's some fucked-up shit! How could you say that to me? What was I to you? The weak fag lusting over the straight dude? Maybe in some sick way you got pleasure from that. I guess you thought you would play with the gay boy's mind, flip his ass out, and then simply walk away! How sick is that? And the sickest thing is, you actually took it to the point where we fucked!"

"Where are you coming up with this shit? Willie, you're talking crazy. Besides, we didn't fuck, we made love...there's a difference!"

"You sick muthafucka, get the fuck out of my face! I can't believe I ever had feelings for you." Struggling to step away, I said, "Move out of my fuckin' way, I'm not listening to anymore of your shit, not tonight, not on my birthday! It ain't happenin'!" I tried to push past, but with forceful arms, Oz stopped me in my tracks. I had to admit, his touch sent me into a spiral. No touch from any man had the effect that Oz had, no matter how hard I tried to deny it! I would forever be his captive. Oz owned my heart, no doubt about it.

"Have you lost your mind? Where are you going?" Oz commanded.

"I have guests, remember!"

"Come back here, we're not finished!" Oz kept me immobile, holding my arm firm.

I stood with my backside against his chest. "I want to leave! I cannot do this with you anymore, I can't!" I turned, searching his eyes, looking for some kind of explanation. "It's too painful, and the truth is, I lied! I love you so much it has orchestrated every aspect of my life! Do you have any idea how intense that is? What we had was unlike anything I experienced before or since. I never loved anyone the way I love you. None of those muthafuckas I've known could compare to you!"

"I do understand, Willie." Oz struggled, pulling me closer. Instinctively, I placed my forearms against his chest to push away.

Oz held me tightly as I spoke. "Nah, I don't think you do! All the times we would just sit and talk about whatever, the most inconspicuous, minute aspects of life. You were the one person I never had to hide who I was. I felt free to be myself, never ashamed. You accepted me with all my faults, my insecurities, and losses I endured over the years. You were the one person I could always count on!" Held steadfastly in his arms, I sensed my heart would give way. When the floodgates opened, I could not stop the heated anger that swelled. "You couldn't let me be! You had to play with my state

Battlefields

of mind as well? You teased, lured me in, all the while knowing this wasn't where you wanted to be!"

Oz held a death grip around my waist. "How fucked up do you think I am? Do you honestly believe I would do that? My love for you is just as strong, and you know it!"

"Let me go, Oz!" I wrestled, trying to break free.

"Willie, stop!"

We scrambled.

"Oz, you fucked up!" I shouted.

Our scuffle grew aggressive.

"Listen! Willie, *stop*!" Oz demanded.

Finally, unable to turn myself around, my back held against his chest, Oz pressed his cheek next to mine. His touch, the warm of his breath, softened me. I relented.

His breathing became heavy, and he whispered into my ear. "I'm not saying I didn't fuck this up, because I did. I won't contradict that."

"I love you so much!" I surrendered.

"I know, baby, I know!" Oz loosened his death grip.

I stepped away from Oz then turned around. "The thing that's so fucked up," I said, wiping tears from my eyes, "I'm so in love with you, I can't see my way out! You have my head so wound up; I'm powerless to loving anyone else. What am I supposed to do with that, huh? You tell me what am I supposed to do! I want to trust you, but there is no trust left. You have come in and out of my life so many times with only concerns for your own feelings. All the while, I became increasingly fucked up in the head! Now you return after being gone for almost five years, and I'm supposed to give into you once again?" A massive flood of blood rushed my head, as all the emotions I held within, the hurt, the abandonment, boiled to the surface. "Oz, I can't—I don't think I'm strong enough!"

Exhausted with defeat in my heart, I knew this must end. How do I walk away from the one thing keeping me going all these years? From the one who enslaved my heart, incarcerated my mind, body, and soul since the first day I laid eyes on him. How do I walk away a free man returning to a life of the living? I wondered as our eyes penetrated for the truth.

Oz licked his full, red lips moving forward, placing his huge hand around my neck—pulling me close. Shifting, Oz pressed his lips to mine, and without a doubt, I gave in. Our tongues connected, intertwined, and he firmly pushed his chest to mine, and I conceded helplessly. There was no denying he sent bolts of lightning through me whenever we kissed! It was the same reaction as our first kiss. I knew now, as I knew then, no other man could ever bestow the sensations as Oz.

"You have every right to hate me," Oz spoke softly. "I hate myself for hurting you the way I did. Somehow, I have to make it up to you. I promise," he revealed, holding me close.

"I want to believe you, Oz."

"Just say you'll at least think about it."

"Oz, I don't know." Shaking my head in confusion, I said, "I—"

"Don't say it. Don't say you can't. Don't!"

Disturbed by Sedona's sudden burst out the back door, hysterically she shouted, "Will, come quick! Jordan has lost his damn mind!"

I turned toward Sedona, not quite sure what was stated. "What?"

"Jordan has lost his damn mind, he's tearing up the place, throwing everyone out!" Sedona franticly waved her hand, motioning toward her.

"What the fuck!" I spun away from Oz, darting for the house. Oz followed close behind. What else could go wrong!

"Where's Jordan?" I asked, entering the living room. Isaiah was helping Bryce off the floor. One of the bookcases was knocked over; photos and books tossed everywhere, broken glass lay across the floor. "What the hell happened?" I shouted.

Bryce brushed debris from his clothes. "I don't know what he was trippin' on! I think it may have something to do with you and Oz, because Jordan had walked to the back door looking for you. Moments later, he returned enraged, cursing, picking up glasses and throwing them across the

Battlefields

room, and then he kicked over the table! After which, he ordered everyone out of the house, pushing people toward the door."

I stood in disbelief.

Sedona returned from the kitchen. "Here, place this over your forehead," she stated, handing Bryce a towel. "You have a cut; hold this against your forehead to stop the bleeding." Sedona looked to me. "I don't know what you two were doing, but his ass flipped the fuck out! He was yelling, screaming he was going to kill you both! I've never seen anything like it!"

"Everyone was trying to get the hell out!" Isaiah stated.

"I tried to calm him down, getting him to realize what he was doing, then he lunged at me, knockin' my ass into the bookcase!" Bryce recounted, holding the towel next to his forehead.

The front door opened, and in complete panic, everyone quickly turned toward the door.

"Rafael! Man, you scared the shit out us!" Isaiah stated nervously.

"I went after Jordan, but he jumped into his car and sped down the street before I could reach him." Rafael began picking some of the items off the floor. "There were people milling around the front of the house, but I made them leave."

"Thanks, Rafael!" I looked around the room. "This mutha fucked my shit up," I stated, shaking my head. "Damn," I said, looking at Oz, "This is your fault! You knew he was jealous, but you came here anyway!"

"You're not gonna blame this on me! Ole boy always had a problem with our friendship and me. That's why I kicked his ass the last time, and it's obvious he needs another beat down!" Oz moved to help Isaiah replace the bookcase. "I know for a fact he better not come up in my face! Besides, how was I to know you were still with ole boy?"

"Oh, so you think you gonna be around to give him another ass kickin'? I think you're being a little arrogant that I'll let your ass back in, especially after what just happened," I stated, heading for the kitchen to retrieve a trash bag.

"So, we're going down that road again?" Oz remarked.

I stopped dead in my tracks. "Hell yeah…you got that shit right!"

Sedona approached Oz. "Maybe you should go. This may not be the best time for the two of you to work out your problems."

"Yeah, get the fuck out!" I shouted.

"Will, stop before you say something you might regret!" Sedona stated.

Oz maneuvered around Sedona. "I had the best intentions when I came here!" In a failed attempt, Sedona tried restraining Oz but to no avail. "I didn't come here to have this huge confrontation and definitely not with ole boy. Sometimes people make mistakes; I made a huge mistake, and I came here to make amends. I had hoped you would be able to forgive, but I forgot you have no clue of the concept. I see some things never change!"

"Muthafucka, get the fuck out of my house!" I screamed. "I don't want to see your ass around here again!"

"Will, you really don't mean that," Bryce stepped in.

"Don't tell me what the fuck I meant! I know what the *fuck* I'm saying, and if you don't like it, you can get the fuck out too!"

"Bitch, don't fuckin' speak to me like that! What the fuck is wrong with you?" Bryce snapped back.

"Bryce, you don't have to stick up for me. I'll leave if that's what he wants!" Oz stood mere millimeters away with eyes focused on mine. "Is that what you want?" Tension filled the air, heavy as two tons of bricks hanging tethered above our heads. A quiet hush swept the room. Oz spoke in a soft, deep, deliberate voice. "Is that what you want?"

Tears engulfed my eyes, and I was unable speak. I did not want him to leave, and he was right, I could not forgive. Locked in fear, I could not find the words to say, don't go. So I stood there; his face was so close I could see the tiny veins in his forehead pulsating. His eyes searched mine, hoping for answers within my blank stare.

Oz stepped back. "Fine, I'll take that as a yes." He stood for a moment.

"Will, say something!" Sedona spoke franticly in Oz's defense.

"It's cool, Sedona, his silence said it all," Oz walked toward the door.

Sedona pleaded, "Will, what are you doing?"

"Will, you're making a huge mistake!" Bryce offered. "Sedona, go after Oz and talk to him."

Battlefields

"No," I finally spoke. "Let him go." I had resigned the fight.

"Will," Isaiah jumped in, "you don't know what you're saying."

As Sedona hurried after Oz, she stopped, approaching the door, and turned to face me. "Will, you are wrong," then she scurried into the darkness of the evening.

CHAPTER 61

I AWAKENED EARLY Sunday morning with an earth-crushing headache, accompanied by memories of last Friday night's event replaying repeatedly in a perpetual loop. Since my birthday extravaganza, Jordan remained missing in action, and the several messages I left—all were unanswered. I was worried, yet relieved, because I wasn't in the position to relive or recall my exchange with Oz, or having to explain our conversation. All along, my main issue with Jordan was his jealous nature toward Oz, and certainly I was smart enough not to divulge or express my true feelings. Along with the fact that Oz and I had slept together the night after their fight. The confrontation five years ago could have been avoided if Jordan had stayed out of my affairs with Oz.

Regarding Oz, on the other hand, it remained unclear why or how our situation had become so twisted. My friendship with Oz was the one true thing in my life I knew was pure. Our unbreakable bond appeared stronger than what I had with my own family. So why did it go so wrong? I guess straddling that fragile line between friends and lovers caused our involvement to spiral uncontrollably into a pummeling tailspin.

Having loved Oz since the first day I laid eyes on him, I couldn't get enough of his mannish scruffy beauty, his big, toothy wide smile, and his kind, warm heart concealed by his rugged exterior and intimidating demeanor—a total bad ass.

Oz loved his motorcycles, his trucks, the outdoors, and his lust for adventure. Of all my friends, Oz was the one who enjoyed the same zest for fun as I did. We enjoyed the beauty this planet had to offer, and he was the brother I never had and the lover I desired. I loved the human being he was,

Battlefields

though he had his faults. He supported me in anything I wanted to pursue or obtain. His support was unquestionable even when our bond began to show signs of breaking. It was not until the end when I allowed my love to obscure what our friendship meant.

The majority of Saturday and this morning, I lay in bed, contemplating what my life had become and what I should do with Jordan. Our relationship could not move forward with the constant notion of envy. If he missed a day without hearing from me, I must be fuckin' some other man. I had never given him any reason to doubt my love. Well, in essence, I guess I had, which took me back to my convoluted relationship with Oz, including his mysterious disappearances only to return with no explanation as to why he left. Lost in self-reflection, I was shaken by the ringing of the telephone. "Hello?"

"Hey Will—it's me, Sedona."

"Hey, Sedona," I said, responding in a sullen voice.

"How are you? I called yesterday, left you several messages on your machine with none returned. I'm worried about you."

"I'm good…just didn't want to speak with anyone."

"What are you doing?"

"Nothing, in bed…just lying here."

"Hmm, you don't sound good; I'll be over shortly." Sedona paused then said, "Tonight, I return to New York, and I want to see you before I leave."

"I would like that."

"What time is it?" Sedona asked.

Rolling on my side, checking the clock on the nightstand, I answered, "It's ten forty-two."

"OK, give me about an hour."

"I'll be here." I hung up the phone.

Yesterday it rained on and off throughout the day, at times quite hard. Now today, staring out the window, I surmised it to be a repeat event. The weather echoed the murkiness and gloom I felt in my heart. I gazed across the yard. The wind blew violently as leaves swept transversely throughout the neighborhood—a perfect accompaniment to the distressed, emotional condition drowning my spirit. Suddenly, a brisk blast of wind snapped me out of the trance I succumbed to. Glancing at my watch, I saw the time was 11:55 a.m. A little over an hour had passed, and Sedona still hadn't arrived. Patiently awaiting her arrival, I finally comprehended how much I needed to speak to someone, hoping to digest the incident that transpired Friday night. Contemplating what my future might hold, I knew that during this past weekend I had reached a crossroads: should I go left or should I go right?

After gathering a quick bite to eat, I sat at the breakfast table lost in meditation when a distant knock broke my concentration. "Hold on," I yelled.

Opening the door, Isaiah, Bryce, and Rafael stood on the other side. "Hey, I wasn't expecting you guys!" I stated, greeting them with a notation of surprise.

Isaiah spoke, entering the doorway. "Sedona called stating you needed an intervention. So we're here."

"Where's Sedona?" I annoyingly asked.

"She'll be here shortly," Bryce answered.

"Hey, Will!" Rafael greeted, tagging along. "How are you doing?" He stopped to give me a hug.

I needed company, but not a congregation! Besides, Rafael can be meddlesome, which was why I gave him few details regarding my life. I loved him dearly, but he talked too fuckin' much, I thought. "Hey, Rafael," I responded.

"Sedona said she was going to pick up some pizzas when I spoke with her about thirty-five minutes ago. She was about to head for Mario's Pizza," Bryce stated.

"Good, I'm hungry," Rafael remarked.

Not allowing myself to become annoyed, I said, "I have iced tea in the fridge."

Bryce followed close behind. "What have you been doing?"

"Nothing—in bed, trying not to let this shit get next to me!"

Battlefields

"Have you spoken with Jordan?" Bryce asked

"I haven't seen or heard from him." Upon entering the kitchen, the doorbell rang. "Rafael, can you get that for me," I asked.

"Sure," Rafael responded.

"Why is he here," I asked irritably, reaching for the pitcher of iced tea and a six-pack of beer. "I don't want to discuss the details of Oz with him. You and Sedona are the only ones who knew the full extent of our relationship."

"I know," Bryce answered in an apologetic tone. "But have you wondered how Oz knew where to find you?"

"Yes, I have, although I wasn't hiding. I didn't have a problem with him getting in contact."

"Are you sure about that?" Bryce questioned. "You haven't shown Oz much love since the last time you had that little encounter. If anyone mentioned his name, you got all crazy and shit!"

I smiled. "True, true...I was angry, I won't lie about that, and I'm still—"

"Hey, honey, I'm home!" Sedona joked, walking into the kitchen, with Isaiah and Rafael following behind. "I brought some goodies, something I knew would cheer you up!"

"Smells good," Bryce said, opening one of the pizza boxes and taking a quick look. "Ooh, with mushrooms, my favorite," he remarked.

"Hold on, I have paper plates we can use," I said.

"So, Will, tell me what's up! What's the deal with you and Oz?" Sedona commented, reaching for a slice of pizza. "What do you plan to do?"

"What do you mean?" I asked, aggravated.

"Can we at least start with some small talk before you blast his ass?" Bryce asserted.

"Look..." Sedona said with her famous black girl smirk, "I have a plane to catch; I don't have all day to be pussyfootin' around the issue. We might as well get down to the dirty business! Besides...Will knew the reason why I was coming over!" Wiping tomato sauce from her mouth, she continued, "Anyway, Will, honey, you know I love Oz, and truth be told, I had hoped you two would have worked out your issues years ago. I get that you're upset. He walked out on you after your few days of bliss, but this anger you hold toward him—baby, you need to let it go!"

"I agree!" Bryce jumped in.

Placing my hands on the island counter top, I leaned forward, looking out the window. "I have let go!"

"No, you haven't, that's why you're so angry!" Bryce remarked.

"And that's why your relationship with Jordan is strained," Sedona added. "You wonder why Jordan is so jealous of Oz. It's because you created that monster. Jordan is no fool, he's well aware there's more than what you have told him, which is what? What details have you given him?" Sedona stared intensely. "Did you ever tell him you two fucked?"

"What!" Rafael responded, shocked by the statement. "I thought he was straight?"

"He is," I answered.

"Please," Bryce rolled his eyes.

"Confused you mean!" Sedona looked to Bryce and winked.

"When did you and Oz—you know?" Isaiah asked, generally shocked.

"That's not important!"

"The hell it isn't!" Sedona took another bite of her slice of pizza. "What do you think this is all about? Why do you think there is so much tension against Oz?"

"I always thought your friendship was strange, but I had no idea it had gone that far!" Isaiah remarked.

"Will, baby, we're not trying to get all up in your business, but you need some help with this," Sedona commented.

"I love Jordan, and I love Oz. I love them both, but differently," I stated.

"Who do you love more?" Isaiah asked.

Bryce quickly answered for me. "Oz, who else!"

Rafael looked puzzled. "Now I understand what he meant!"

"What who meant?" Now, I was puzzled. *Why is everyone all in my shit!*

"Rafael, baby, what did you mean by that?" Sedona wondered. Rafael stood quietly for a moment; obviously he knew something but was refusing to tell. "Rafael, is there something you need to tell us?"

Battlefields

"If there is something you know, you need to tell me, right now!" I was not about to allow him to back out of it. "Tell me, now," I demanded.

"I ran into him the day before your party," Rafael blurted out.

"What…and you didn't tell me?" I said, angered by his comment. I was at a loss why he would withhold such valuable information.

Shaking his head, his voice barely audible, he said nervously, "He asked me not to."

"How could you keep that from me?" I commanded.

"He said he needed to speak with you, but he wouldn't go into details. He only stated he had to speak with you and knew it wasn't going to be easy. I asked where had he been all these years. He said it was complicated and wouldn't go into details. I asked what he meant by that. At the time, he believed leaving was the best for both of you, and that was all he would say. So I let it go." Rafael shrugged his shoulders. "You know, he scares me," he said, picking up a slice of pizza and taking a bite. "I'm sorry, Will, I didn't know you didn't want to see him. I thought it would have been a nice surprise on your birthday."

"You know, you're a dumb bitch!" I snapped. "I mean, really! You had no clue of—"

"You know, when people try to help, you always have some smart-ass comment," Sedona said. "You brought this on yourself. Don't dump your shit on Rafael!"

"How do you figure that? I didn't tell his ass to run away. He ran out on me!" I stated, making an effort to defend myself, annoyed that everyone was blaming me for the drama surrounding my life.

"First of all, you don't know why he left!" Sedona stated with sarcasm. "To me, it's plain as day, but anyway, that's neither here nor there. You have a right to be angry and you should be, but because of the friendship, you owe him the opportunity to explain his side of the story. I'm sure a big part of it was the feelings he had for you. He probably didn't know how to handle those emotions, and up to that point, lived his life as a straight man, only to discover he was in love with you. Once he came to terms with this revelation, Jordan was in the picture. What do you think that fight was about? It wasn't just Jordan who was jealous. Oz had his demons, too. Hell, he didn't like it when we took you away from him!"

"Preach," Bryce stated sarcastically, "and you know it's true! Anytime we wanted to spend time with you, he made sure you were occupied."

"She has a point, Will! You would only see us if you wanted to go out. During the day you were with him, all damn day! You were in a relationship and didn't even know it. Neither one of you knew it!" Isaiah declared. "I've asked you several times, what's the deal, and you blew me off! It was none of my business, and besides, you never listened to me anyway. If you wanted to be delusional, then so be it! That's what this is all about!"

"I'm with Isaiah, y'all's friendship was not normal, and you admitted that yourself. You even said he made the comment *too bad you weren't a woman because you would be perfect for him*…that's what you said!" Bryce took a swig from a bottle of beer. "Theoretically, you were in a relation-ship—you just wasn't fuckin'!" Bryce laughed, and everyone else followed.

"Nah, he was fuckin'. It just wasn't with Oz!" Isaiah declared.

Laughing, Bryce could hardly contain himself. "He was doing a whole lot of fuckin', but not with Oz!"

"You're sick!" I stated, but had to laugh myself.

Sedona held her hand to her mouth, trying to keep food from falling out, holding back her scream. "Now, Bryce, you spoke the truth!"

"Well…" I stopped midthought unable to find the words to finish my sentence.

"Well, my ass! You know it's true—poor Jordan walked into some shit he didn't see comin' and couldn't handle!" Sedona commented.

"Shit, no one could compete with that," Bryce countered.

"So, what are you going to do?" Sedona asked.

"I don't know," I replied.

"You have to come to terms with your feelings for Oz. You have to for-give him then move on," Bryce expressed his feelings. "You have to either allow Jordan to love you or set him free, because fuck-buddies ain't workin'! That's what you two are."

"Bryce, you just said a mouthful," Isaiah stated.

Battlefields

"We are more than fuck-buddies, and that was not a fair statement! We have our issues, but we are more than mere fuck-buddies. I will admit, I have not truly opened my heart, which he did not deserve. He deserved more than that, and I should have been honest with Jordan and not allow it to go as far as it did, but seriously, I didn't believe I would ever see Oz again!"

"But Will, five years have passed; how long had you planned on holding on to a dream with no future?" Isaiah questioned.

Sedona shook her head when she spoke. "What are you waiting for? Were you hoping Oz would return?" Sedona sat back into her chair. "Your actions explained the anger you held. You were secretly wishing Oz would come back."

"You guys make it sound so simple."

"Will, it is that simple; if it wasn't, you wouldn't hold that much hatred toward him. Have you ever thought about that? Have you sat back to dissect the cause of your pain?" Sedona quizzed.

"I'm not gonna lie and say I don't have feelings for Oz, because I do. I don't hate Oz, but I hold extreme hurt in my heart. I want to forgive and say, let's be friends, but how do you turn back time to rekindle the innocence we lost?"

"The two of you have to sit down and talk it out. It's that simple. Whether you scream and shout or remain calm and collected, as two civilized individuals should. It must be done or that monster inside will fester forever." Sedona thought for a moment. "What did Oz say to you the night of the party?"

"He said he had hoped I would find it in my heart to forgive him. He stated I was always on his mind, that he never stopped caring or loving me. He claimed he missed me."

"That's all he said?" Sedona asked puzzled.

"Well, maybe I didn't give him a chance to say much." Clearly, I was unwilling to admit the truth.

Sedona started laughing. "I wonder why; could it be you were acting a bit crazy?"

Again, Bryce could not contain himself. "Bitch, I can hear you now! 'You hurt my heart! You left me all alone!' On and on…" Bryce let out a roar of laughter.

"I bet he did!" Sedona added.

I was not amused. "I hate you two!"

"We speak the truth, boo! We've read that novel several times before," Sedona stated.

"We know you," Bryce remarked.

"Where do I go from here?"

"You must move forward, and someone is going to be hurt, no doubt about it. You have set the stage where the three of you cannot coexist. Someone is gonna be left on the sideline."

"But I don't want to hurt anyone."

"Do you think Jordan is gonna allow Oz to stay in your life?" Bryce asked.

"It's not up to Jordan. He must put aside his misgivings and man up. Rafael made sure the tension will remain," I remarked.

Rafael slammed his glass down on the counter. "Stop placing the blame on me! This is your fuck-up, not mine! I'm not the one stringing folks along when all the while you're longing for another!"

"Wilson, baby…what do you say to that!" Sedona replied.

There was nothing more I could say. They were right—all of them!

CHAPTER 62

THE WEEKEND FOLLOWING my birthday disaster, I found myself sitting across from the one person I was not quite ready to face. The two of us sat locked in a stalemate, waiting patiently for a battle in which neither wanted to partake. It was another cold Saturday morning; a cloud-filled sky, dark and moody, befitting the intensity of the surrounding space. Holding my stoneware mug filled with hot coffee, I cocked my head to the right, staring out the breakfast nook window, delaying the inevitable. We spoke few words. Maybe a flat-lined statement here, a nicety there, but neither would look the other directly in the eyes. Life can be so strange when two individuals who knew each other so well were now at a loss for words. Twenty minutes had passed since he arrived, fortified with an armful of regrets. His disposition was written all over his face, and I knew entirely too well this meeting would not be an easy one. The empty years had broken a once mighty general—he was beaten, but not down. He still maintained a fighting spirit, and because of that, my skirmish had to be on point. Because of this new revelation, I decided I would relent and recoil my rifle, resisting a rampage I had planned from the start. A much more subdued approach would benefit me more in the end; so let the games begin!

After the so-called intervention, I earnestly sought to repair the damage I inflicted toward Jordan, yet his unavailability baffled even me. It appeared Jordan had dropped off the face of the earth. He returned none of my telephone calls; to knocks on his condominium door—nothing—and it didn't matter the time of day. He completely vanished, an inconceivable disappearing act by Jordan. A damaging ploy used by Oz, but never by anyone else.

Vance N. Smith

Now, here I sat, mulling over the possibilities, regurgitating old wounds—asking myself the question, *did he still love me?* Would this be the day I finally found the right lane to travel, leading to a road of happiness? Whether it meant we should move on and never revisit our past, or finally commit to rebuilding our fractured friendship, setting aside the pain treading so deeply in our hearts.

Inhaling deeply, attempting to conjure the strength to proceed, he leaned forward, speaking in a sorrowful tone. "So…are we going to sit and stare at one another all day?"

Rearing deep into the high-back dining chair, I answered, "No, I guess my mind wandered somewhere else. How we got here? When did this all start and why?" I stated my point, clear and simple.

I could not help but succumb to his charming, easy ways, and the longer he remained in my presence, I realize how much I missed him. He was still just as handsome as the day we met, back in '81. Only now refined, matured, and humbled; the passing years had been kind. And that body! He returned thicker, sculpted, chiseled, and bangin' to the point I found it hard to concentrate.

"I didn't come here to argue all over again."

"I've stated my point. I felt, and still do, that you do not have a right to be upset. I'm the one you hurt, and you have no right coming into my home dictating what I should feel."

"I'm hurting, too, and you have no idea what I've been through. You have yet to ask what I was going through! It was all about Willie and his feelings, or who had done *Willie* wrong. It's not all about you. So wake the fuck up! There are other people involved, and until you understand that, we will never make it out the gate. Since day one, you have blamed me for everything. I can sit here and admit I fucked up, but can you? That's the real question."

"*Wow.* If I'm so screwed up, then why even bother?" I retorted.

"Go ahead and play the victim, it serves you so well."

"Fuck you!" I yelled, standing from the table. "You know nothing about me! So, fuck you!"

Battlefields

"Sit yo' ass down! I'm tired of going down that road with you! I came here to make amends, and you're gonna to face me like a man and hear what I have to say."

Listening to the words forged from his lips, I felt my mind race from the impact. Slowly I stepped away, involuntarily removing myself from the onslaught.

"I said, sit down! Don't you even think of backing away from this."

"What do you want from me, Oz? I can't keep doing this with you! It hurts too fuckin' much, and I will not allow you to game me anymore! I fell for your shit in the past, but not anymore. I have finally found the strength and courage to remove you from my life and my system. Now, here you come again, demanding I drop everything around me. Why are you here? I need you to set me free and go back to wherever you came from!" Standing my ground, I was trying my best to inflict as much pain as he had on me. It was a dirty psychological move, but in times of war, you made use of your best weapon.

"I'm going to forget you made that statement." Oz pounded his fist into his chest, making his point, speaking through clinched teeth—his breathing elevated, "Because I know in my heart that's not how you feel. Play hard all you want, but you're still in love with me; same as the day we first met. The very day I fell in love with you!"

Tears swelled, flooding the corners of my eyes. This profound hurt had burned, buried in every fiber of my soul. Years of rejection hardened into everything that made me who I was today. Where does one go after such torment? No matter how I tried, I could not break the masonry wall built around my exterior. I could not shake it; I could not break it—clearly fortified with iron rebar.

There I stood, listening to a howling wind ripping me to shreds, peeling back each layer, one by one, exposing all my concealed honesties. Oz found my weak spot and pounced. Yeah, the general was back in true form with his tactical assault, reigning terror upon his prey.

"Now sit yo' ass down and face me like a man!"

Without even flinching, I eased back into my chair, giving him my full attention.

Vance N. Smith

"You haven't heard a word I said, have you?" Oz asked.

"Yes, I have! I've heard every word."

"And you have nothing to say? All these years you had plenty to call my ass on."

Wiping tears from my eyes, I said, "I'm not going to say a word; I want you to speak your mind, and I won't butt in, or call you a liar, or anything of that nature. You have my full attention."

Oz repositioned himself into a chair next to mine and placed my hand in his, speaking barely above a whisper. "I have been crazy in love with you since we met at Monica's party. When I spotted you that evening, immediately I was intrigued and knew I had to get to know the dude sitting alone on the other side of the pool, under the cool night sky. I watched you from the moment you walked onto the patio, to the time homeboy made his play, and until our eyes initially locked onto one another."

"Why didn't you say something?" I confusingly quizzed.

"Willie, not everyone is comfortable with what they're feeling. At that time, I had no clue what was going on inside my body. All I knew—I had to get to know you."

Scratching my forehead, utterly confused, I said, "Was that the first time you felt that?"

"Do you mean about you?" Oz asked.

"No, about any man...was that the first time?"

"Honestly, no. Back in New York I had a mad crush on a good friend of mine, Eddie, who I had known since middle school. We were thick as thieves," Oz recollected, forcing a smile from gracing his face. "We were extremely close, same as you and me, and I loved him more than I loved my own brothers. I would have given him my life. Then I met Jasmine and that was the end of that."

"What do you mean?"

"She hated that he and I were so close...mind you, nothing was going on between us. However, I was madly in love. The problem being, Jasmine sensed it, and insinuated to all that we were fucking. Nothing I did or say would convince her otherwise. The summer after we graduated from high

Battlefields

school, her tirades continued, escalating until the winter before my twenty-second birthday. Shortly thereafter, she moved to LA pursuing her modeling career. By the time she left New York, my friendship with Eddie was ruined, and everyone in town assumed we were lovers. Foolishly, I followed her to LA, unable to deal with the humiliation."

"Was the feeling mutual? Did Eddie feel the same way?"

"No, at the time I wasn't entirely sure what I was feeling; it wasn't solely sexual."

I frowned. "It wasn't?"

"Well, I guess it may have been a little," he remarked.

"Either it was or it wasn't. If it were just an extremely close friendship, why should you care what other people think? You should have said, fuck you, get a life, and dropped her dumb ass, but you knew it was more than that."

"It's not that simple. Eddie and I had a bond that went beyond the physical, but you may be right; I just never wanted to admit it."

"She still feels that way, doesn't she?" I asked before reflecting on a memory. "It all makes sense; that's what she was referring to."

"Referring to what?" Oz questioned.

"The day she came by the house, all crazy and shit! She slipped, mentioning something happened, and then retracted the comment. She wanted me to know, but then thought against it." Leaning forward before I asked my next question, I said, "I'm at a loss, why would you follow her after what she had done? It doesn't make sense."

"Why, I'm not sure. I loved Jasmine, but not the way I loved Eddie. I guess with Jasmine, a lot of it had to do with lying to myself, honoring my family and everyone that believed the lies she told. I had to prove them wrong. The choices we make," shaking his head in defiance, "we live our lives in a fool's paradise."

A brief silence fell between Oz and myself.

"Oz…the thing that puzzles me was that you knew how I felt, so why would you fight me every step of the way? It would have been so easy to give in."

Vance N. Smith

"Willie, not everyone is strong enough not to care what people think. I didn't want to disappoint my dad, my family, humiliate the people who surrounded me. Hell, I couldn't even be honest with myself. I admired you for your courage and wanted that same strength. Willie, you had the balls to leave your family and start a new life with a man who was twice your age, living in his house! I could have never done that!"

"Believe me when I say this…it was not easy, but at the time I had no other choice."

"Yes, you did; you had your aunt who would have gladly come to your defense."

"Maybe, maybe not. I have no ill feelings toward Aunt Raine, but she knew what was going on in our house and not once did she step in to save us. Even after I moved into her apartment above the garage!"

"Willie, she felt trapped in the middle. You have to understand that was her sister, and she didn't want to believe the horrible claims stated against her," Oz offered.

"So she didn't believe a word I told her?"

"She believed you, Willie, but you have to remember you held onto that secret until you moved into the apartment. What you did not realize was that your aunt harbored so much guilt because she felt she should have known and done more to rectify the situation. Again, the choices we make aren't always the best decision. By the way, how is Aunt Lorraine? I have not been able to contact her. Is she OK?"

"Aunt Raine is doing just fine. She and Uncle Charles moved to the East Coast three years ago. Uncle Charles was offered a position with a hospital in Baltimore he could not pass up."

"Good for them, I'm happy to hear that! When I couldn't contact you, I tried contacting Aunt Raine, but discovered her phone was disconnected. How long ago did you move?"

"I purchased my home last fall, and the reason you couldn't contact me was because I changed my number about six months after you and I last saw one another."

Oz hesitated. "Willie, you hated me that much?"

Battlefields

"At the time—yes!"

"What about now?"

"I'm not gonna lie and say I'm no longer angry, because I am. I'm so fuckin' angry with you it pains me. I want to forgive you but find it hard to do so! I will say, having this conversation helps, but it's not enough. If you had only been honest with me from the start."

"You could have been honest as well," Oz stated. "You were so strong with everyone, stating what you wanted and went for it, but with me you held back."

"I held back because I couldn't figure out what the fuck you wanted, what we were, or how to get you to open up. That's why."

Oz slumped into his chair, his head held in defeat. "You never asked me up front what I was feeling," Oz remarked.

"Are you kidding me?" I commented, shifting my weight within the chair. "What do you think all our arguments were about? Now, you sit here stating I should have just asked? You have got to be fuckin' kidding me!"

"You should have known how I felt after I danced for you."

"Then, why didn't you make a move?"

"I was too scared to place myself in that position."

"And if I had made the first move, would that have made a difference?" I countered.

"Maybe, I'm not sure how I would have reacted."

"You're speaking in riddles, and that's exactly why I didn't go there with you. I wanted you to make the first move." Stepping away from the table, entering the kitchen, I said, "First off, I didn't know who the fuck you were, and if I were wrong, there was no question you could have easily kicked my ass. There was no way in hell I would have made a play on you."

Oz laughed. "I guess you have a point, knowing my state of mind at the time I probably would have, just to make a point." Oz wiped at his mouth. "But seriously I would never have done that. I felt something special for you. I cared too much to ever want to harm you, and that's real, trust me when I say that!"

"Then why did you allow it to go so far? You knew you were killing our friendship and you continued anyway," I commented, pouring water into two glasses.

"I had to protect my standing. I didn't want to give in to those emotions, thinking it would have made me weak or less of a man."

Returning to the table and placing one glass in front of Oz, I sat holding the other next to my lips. "And what does that make me?"

"I never said you weren't a man, "Oz quickly remarked.

"In a way you just did!"

"I was referring to myself. It is what *I* felt. You have always been a man to me. You don't get it, I wanted to be strong like you and not give a fuck what people thought, but I couldn't. I was too ashamed, too scared, too much of everything!"

I was swallowed within a mounting tidal wave, swept by guilt, regretting the concealed emotions of hate and bitterness I clutched in the arms of pain. I neatly swept away the happiness and the reasons why I had fallen so madly in love. In an odd twist of fate, his virus, which had infected me fastidiously, could not penetrate the antidote given by his opponent. A sudden wave of repentance disbursed any notion of reconciliation. An abundance of thoughts swirled haphazardly in my mind, fighting for a chance of acquittal. My judgments were guided by confusion and chaos, leaving my mind a garbled mess.

"Oz, I have one question to ask. Where have you been the last four and a half years, because I'm confused? I thought that night we had settled our differences, placing the past behind us. Then, in your usual fashion, you were gone, and not for a few months, but years! How do you expect me to rebound from that?"

Oz clinched his jaw, wiping the beads of sweat from his forehead. "After that weekend, I *was* ready. I had found my happiness and that happiness was with you. I felt free and alive, and everything I said that weekend, I meant."

"Then what happened?"

Oz shifted uncomfortably in his chair. "Jasmine…that's what happened!" he said reluctantly.

Battlefields

Angrily, I stated, "I should have guessed. She couldn't stand to see you happy."

"Well, something like that," he remarked.

"This isn't helping your case knowing she has that kind of hold over you."

"She doesn't; she didn't then and she doesn't now! All of this is because of my own head trip."

"So how does she figure into the equation?"

"When I returned home that Sunday night, she was waiting in my apartment and laid a bombshell that changed everything."

I braced myself for a detonation I certainly was not prepared to take. "I'm afraid to ask."

"I knew she would be waiting, and my plan was to end our relationship. Willie, you must believe me, I wanted to spend the rest of my life with you, but before I could gather my words, she calmly announced she was four weeks pregnant."

Hearing that statement caused my entire world to collide in an instant. I could not believe what I was hearing.

Oz held his head in shame. "Willie, I wanted to tell you. In fact, I came by the house to beg for forgiveness, but never made it past the carport. Foolishly, I decided it would be better if you forgot about me and moved on with your life. I had fucked up, and there was no way I could leave Jasmine knowing she carried my child. I left LA returning to New York and married her."

Once I heard pregnancy, my mind heard nothing else. "You have a child!" My heart sank, plummeting to the pit of my stomach.

Oz cleared his throat. "Yes, I had a beautiful son named Jacob." Oz reared back into his chair,"

"Wait a minute, did you say you married her!"

"Yes, we were married. Willie, I'm so sorry. I really made a mess of everything."

"Yes, you did, and now you want me to just forgive everything and pretend nothing happened? It's not that easy! And where is Jasmine now? How do I know she's not going to interfere once again? What about your son?"

"Jacob died in a car accident two years ago. Jasmine was returning home from a visit with her parents on Long Island when an eighteen-wheeler rear-ended them, killing my little boy instantly; however, Jasmine was spared."

Stung by the information he presented, I sat immobile, listening, refusing to allow his words to register. "Oz, I am so sorry!" I stated, remorsefully. "How long have you been in LA?"

Oz reached for my hand. "I moved back to LA last November when our divorce was finalized. I came back looking for you. Please don't get upset, I never loved her the way I love you."

"Sincerely, I'm sorry to hear of your loss, and I can't imagine the pain you must have gone through. I never would have wished anything horrible like that on you or her. Please forgive me for what I'm about to say, but the idea you married her knowing she would have done anything to destroy what we had is too much to process."

"Willie, I was so lost, losing myself in the pain was what I needed to come to terms with in my life. I was not the man you needed me to be. If we had gotten together then, we would not have made it. We were doomed from the start."

"We are still doomed. Oz, I'm in a relationship. You cannot expect me to forgive and forget all the years you wasted trying to figure out what you really wanted. Besides, Jasmine is still in the picture. How do I know you're actually done with her?"

"Because I'm comfortable with who I am. It has taken me some time, but here with you is where I want to be. I knew it all along but was too stupid to allow myself to give in. You never have to worry about Jasmine being an issue again."

"It's too late, Oz. You waited too long and caused too much pain. I belong here with Jordan."

"Willie, you're making the same mistake I made with Jasmine. Your heart belongs to me—here with me is where you belong. I was a fool and now I'm paying the price, but you also played a part in this menagerie. I'm not taking all the blame."

Battlefields

"I understand I played my part, but this anger has me in such a dark place. I'm lost without a light to find my way out. My only saving grace is I found some stability in Jordan. At least he understands where his heart lies."

Stepping away from the table, Oz reached for my arm, holding it firm, stopping me in my tracks. "Come away we me, right now. I will give you whatever you want. You can count on that."

"Oz, let me go, I'm begging you! It's too late for us now. You left me praying, pleading for you to love me. When I was optimistic, you simply walked, no good-bye, not a word, just leaving my existence empty."

Standing, wrapping his thick arms around my waist, he locked me in a bear hug. "Say you'll forget all the shit in our past."

"Our time has passed; we lost that chance almost five years ago. Why should I believe you now, and besides, my love belongs to Jordan," I remarked, struggling to break free from Oz's vice grip.

"Because I'm everything you'll ever want. I've grown and am able to give you what you deserve, that's why. I'm not giving you up so easy; we can start fresh as friends. I just need you in my life." Oz nuzzled into my neck, speaking as his lips grazed my skin. "I wanted to mention, you look damn good! Willie, I want you more than ever. I have been such a fool. Don't leave me." Oz franticly spoke with mish-mashed statements.

"Stop making this so hard!" I could feel the effects of his love potion infiltrating once again, and my artificial bond with Jordan was weakening. I struggled to resist his counterattack. "I'm with Jordan now." A hidden rumbling emerged, weakening the very foundation I built, fortifying the love I surrendered to Jordan. "Both of us have been fools; I played my part as well, but the pain is too great. I'm not sure I can get past it!"

"Please, don't say you can't! Give me the chance to renew our friendship. I promise I will respect your commitment with Jordan," Oz stated, pleading his case righteously.

However, was that enough?

Epilogue

ONCE OZ LEFT, my energy level landed on zero, following six hours of banter and rehashing old wounds. My mind was clearly spent. Oz removed himself around eight that evening, but nevertheless, as fate would have it, shortly thereafter, I received a call from Jordan. I swear they must have planned that shit, plotting…let's sucker-punch this bitch dead in his gut! I was too exhausted to entertain another debate, besides Jordan had been missing in action for a week. Certainly he could wait one more day to highjack my ass!

I was armed with an arsenal of artillery, staking my claim, equipped for the bombastic assault he assuredly would pledge against me, and without a doubt, this would somehow become my fault. Even though Jordan was the one who ran and hid like some little bitch, as if I did not get enough of that with Oz. Now, here this fool came displaying the very same behavior. I should drop both of their dumb asses!

Sunday Afternoon

At about half past two in the afternoon, my doorbell rang. I gathered my thoughts and composure, heading for the door. When the door opened, there he stood, holding a large bouquet of mixed roses and an assortment of other flowers, displaying a pitiful disposition. I frowned, not impressed with this seemingly inadequate peace treaty. After a nonstop onslaught of forevers, I would not have expected him to up and walk, as he did. I guess I believed our relationship had been based on sincerity, along with the ability of conversing our disagreements, certainly, above the typical. I suspect his legal pedigree played a major factor in persuading his captive audience,

Vance N. Smith

namely me. He stood silently with a faint, empty smile filled with fake forgiveness. Our standoff had begun.

Jordan entered, leaning for a kiss; I cautiously turned my cheek—no, not that easy! Surprised by my reaction, Jordan maneuvered around, making his way toward the kitchen, where he found a seat at the very table Oz and I had our confrontation the day before. Following close behind, I asked, "What would you like, something to eat or drink?" He snidely replied, "I want you!" My response was simple; I was not on the menu. Knowing this interchange would progress into an all-out war, I determined that hard liquor was a fitting choice for the occasion. From the fridge I pulled a couple of beers, surely one would not be sufficient, and definitely I required a tall Bacardi and Coke. Hell, I would need four or five of them!

I went straight to the point. "Where have you been, Jordan?"

"Work," he coolly replied.

"You just gonna up and leave without giving me a heads up?"

"I don't owe you any explanation to my whereabouts…seems to me I'm not privy to your comings and goings. You have niggas showing up unannounced that you felt I didn't need firsthand knowledge of. So, what's fair is fair…"

"I didn't know Oz was coming, and besides, why are you still obsessed with him? I've told you several times, he's just a friend, always was just a friend."

"Bullshit! He means more to you than you lead me to believe, and I am tired of your fuckin' games! I saw the two of you in the backyard." Jordan stood from the table, snarling, pointing his finger into my chest. "You were kissing him, and not like a friend, but someone in love. Therefore, I will not allow you to feed me your shit you know I'm not going to eat. Be a fucking man and be honest for once! He is the reason you have kept your heart under lock and key." Jordan finished his exposé into my life, panting like some ravaged dog; his heated breath stung, piercing every pore on my face.

"Get the fuck off me," I said, pushing the palm of my hand into his chest. "Oz kissed me, I tried to resist, but his grip was too strong," I selfishly replied.

Battlefields

Jordan raised his hands in defense. "Will, we cannot move forward with lies. You are the one I want, but not like this, not with him around blocking your ability to love me the way I want you to!"

"Jordan, believe me when I say there is nothing going on between us. You're the one I chose…have chosen…here with you is where my heart lies."

"Well then, we have a problem, because I do not accept it as truth. This was not second-hand information; I witnessed the transgression with my own eyes. Your body did not resist his advance; you wanted it, and with that, how do I compete? You and Oz have years of history, and I have tried to break that bond, and unfortunately, I now comprehend I will never be able to. Watching you with him, I knew there was nothing more I could do."

"Jordan, I swear we're just friends. It's no secret we have history, but that doesn't mean what you and I have isn't real."

"Then why won't you fully commit to me?" Jordan painfully inquired.

"I'm here, and I'm ready to be all that you require of me. As your partner, your lover, I will accept the key you proposed on my birthday. We can rent my house and find our own little slice of heaven. I promise, I have left all that behind, and my focus is totally laid upon you."

"How do I know I can trust you?" he asked.

"You have my word on it. Oz and I are just friends and that's all!"

"Friends…you plan to stay in touch?"

"He's a friend, always has been a good friend, and is extremely close with my family."

"Then there's nothing left for us, Will," Jordan flat-out stated.

"You don't mean that!" I stated in a panic.

Tapping frantically on the computer keyboard at a dedicated pace, I filled hundreds of pages of history with my storied life. I paused to stretch and refresh, gazing toward the clock, realizing it was now past six thirty in the evening. Rearing back from my huge custom-made mahogany desk, I smiled. Life had been good in spite of all the foolishness I yielded to. Becoming the honored architect I had hoped for and settling down with a man who, regardless of my faults, loved me unconditionally was all I ever wanted. At fifty, I could appreciate what it meant loving another, the union that eluded me for a better part of my young adult life. I could not have fathomed the possibilities of what loving this man would bring.

Returning to the keyboard, I typed out another three pages before a knock on the door interrupted my flow. "Come in." I stopped to concentrate on ideas before they were lost. The door opened with heavy footsteps approaching, a comforting hand laid upon my right shoulder.

"How's the book coming along?" His thumb caressed my cheek.

I reached, holding his hand to my lips, kissing it gently. "It's coming along and close to being finished. I must say, I'm satisfied with the outcome. If I never do anything with this, it has been therapeutic," I stated, swiveling my chair around. "Thank you."

With a confused expression, he stated, "Thank you for what?"

"Thank you for never letting up, never giving up on me...on us."

"From the moment I laid eyes on you, I knew you were the one for me. As cliché as that may sound, I knew! I knew you were worth fighting for, and in a few months, we will celebrate our seventeenth anniversary as a committed couple. We had a few rocky years, but we pulled through."

I smiled. "We have, haven't we?" Holding his hand, I said, "Writing this book allowed me to reconcile feelings I didn't want to face. Something about actually having them on paper made it more real than ever before."

"I told you that was all you needed to do to let go! Give in to those emotions and have faith in knowing who you are, and never waver from that. I know it hasn't been easy, dealing with the hurt, the loss, and the trust, but you pulled through."

"Sadly, I have hurt others as well, and I had to take responsibility for my actions." Standing from the large leather chair, I placed my arms around his waist, holding him tightly. We embraced, kissing passionately. I loved this man and always will!

Battlefields

The choices of my young life led me down a road of misguided behaviors, followed by several instances of heartache. Stinging desires too disinclined to address or control drove my young-adult existence, and I was never willing to fully understand the reasons behind my wild inhibitions. All the one-night stands were a meager, synthetic bandage to repair wounds of years past. I had an unwavering aspiration to obtain what I had not received from meaningless individuals claiming their love. Bogged down by defeat, lost within my own self-pity, I blindly searched the darkest recesses of night for affections that were a temporary fix, not a long-term solution. Throughout the years, my compulsion to submit to individuals who showed any form of affection became apparent. The void left by my parents fueled emptiness within me, making it easy for unsavory entities to walk in and take over. My lack of self-control and self-worth made for a dangerous mix, charting a course I could not control. Early childhood emotional starvation set the stage for years of confusion, despair, and introverted self-isolation. Damned from day one, how could anyone survive such an impossible destruction?

Many have stated that I unfairly judged my parents, and even they believed my deep-rooted hatred was unsupported. It was easy for others to make assumptions about how I should feel when the seed of hate came in many forms, emanating within subtle nuances of neglect to outright abuse. I blamed my parents; it was their job to instill life's values of real love and commitment. The lack of love burned slowly, hidden beneath false support, leading to strained relations with all those I encountered. However, I am learning to forgive, releasing the entrenched pain and anger with the sight of reconciliation on the horizon.

Years of self-reflection have led me to a life closer to the edge of a dream I've always envisioned. I am finally able to move forward, unyielding to the past disappointments I've endured. Now I can safely say I have conquered those fears and can proudly state my feelings.

Yes, I am Wilson James, and I can safely say—I am truly happy at last.

About the Author

VANCE N. SMITH was born and raised in Southern California. He attended the University of California in Santa Barbara for two years, but began working during a leave of absence and never returned. He currently works for a public utility company where he's been employed for the past thirty-one years. Though he'd written a few poems over the years, Smith didn't tackle fiction until 2011, when he started on his first novel, *Battlefields*

Made in the USA
Charleston, SC
20 August 2015